DEATH AT HOME

Tom Walsingham Mysteries
Book Eight

C. P. Giuliani

SAPERE BOOKS

Also in the Tom Walsingham Series

The Road to Murder

A Treasonous Path

Death In Rheims

A Deadly Complot

A Snare of Deceit

A Matter of Blood

The Man From Morocco

DEATH
AT HOME

Published by Sapere Books.

24 Trafalgar Road, Ilkley, LS29 8HH,
United Kingdom

saperebooks.com

ISBN: 978-0-85495-858-0

DEATH AT HOME

Published by Sapere Books.

24 Trafalgar Road, Ilkley, LS29 8HH,
United Kingdom

saperebooks.com

ISBN: 978-0-85495-858-0

To Paola, my dear Godmother — who is always there, always on my side.

ACKNOWLEDGEMENTS

Heartfelt thanks to Michael Meekums and Steve Simmonds, of the Orpington and District Archaeological Society, who were so generous with their help and suggestions about Scadbury Manor. While I tried my best to stay true to archaeological evidence, there were things I had to make up or tried to guess at. All mistakes, blunders and imprecisions are, of course, mine.

Thanks also go to Mark Ballard, Archives Service Officer at the Kent History and Library Centre in Maidstone, for his help in navigating the archives from afar, and his suggestions.

Jean Fox's online Index of Wills in West Kent was a truly invaluable resource, together with her vast *History of Sevenoaks up to 1650.*

And, of course, there are always the usual suspects — without whom the journey would be a good deal less fun and pleasant: Rosie, Milla, Pip, the ladies at Baratta and everyone at Sapere Books.

PROLOGUE

16th of November 1589, Scadbury Manor, Kent

The window banged again — the cursed window in the hall downstairs.

Above the howling wind, the roar of the blood in Edmund Walsingham's ears, his own painful gasps — above it all, the window banged and banged. How long since he'd sent that good-for-naught lad downstairs to secure the shutter?

Gripping the bedpost, he hauled himself up, pain biting harder inside his chest and down his arm. He thrust the covers aside and slipped out of the bed.

"Foal!" he called hoarsely, just as the wind redoubled its noise, cackling around the chimneys, flinging the rain against the glass panes. "Foal, curse you!"

No answer came, no hurried steps. Would the dolt even hear him amid the din? The chaos of the elements, Rector Harvey had called it — one long-winded sermon among many.

But then, Edmund didn't want to wake Susan, who'd been ill all day…

Breathlessly, he waited for his heart to stop pounding in his temples — not that it did — for the pain to curl back inside his ribs, and still the infernal shutter rattled and banged.

Curse the storm, curse the lad, curse Foal!

He dragged himself to his feet, and pain flared again. The candle on the sideboard — they left it burning in his room all night now, a bad sign if ever there was one — dipped and hissed: laughing at him, like the wind outside, like Foal in his bed, like his brother Tom in London — or wherever the devil he was — counting his inheritance before time… And that hellish banging downstairs: did soulless things do Satan's work to torment a man in his illness? He'd have Wollans nail it shut in the morning.

Step by shuffling step, he staggered in the dim light: one bedpost, another, the sideboard, where he grabbed the candle, and then the high-backed chair by the hearth. Dragging a breath through his teeth, he tottered across to the door. With cold, slow fingers, he worked the latch, and a tail of wind whistled through the gap. Bracing himself against the jamb, he shielded the flame, nearly dropping the candle. Wouldn't Tom have a good laugh! *My brother set fire to his own shirt, burnt himself to death…* Or perhaps not. Tom was never a Puritan — not with his gambling, fine clothes, and Latin poets — but he was the long-faced sort who would never gloat over a man's death, much less that of his own brother. What was inside his heart, though? He was up to his ears in debt… Not that inheriting Scadbury would change much, for their father had enmired them all until doomsday.

A hand curled around the flame, he shuffled along the passage, gasping for breath after painful breath, wishing he'd never left his bed, but for the cursed window.

The noise was as insistent as Tom himself — come to demand his annuity… The annuity! Another of Father's misguided notions, for the favourite son. Well, there was no money for the annuity, and that was that. Edmund's lips curled at the memory of his brother's white-faced fury and his own words: *And who knows? There may be some worse surprise awaiting…* His chuckle became a hiss as pain sank its teeth into his arm again. It had been worth it, if only to see Tom in a dudgeon.

Edmund stopped at the head of the Great Stairs — cursedly draughty and, if his candle were snuffed out, he'd have to feel his way through the dark parlour. But there was another way down, past the narrow L of the passage, with its closed doors like upright coffins. It seemed very long before Edmund could sag against the newel post atop the Old Stairs that the servants used, and run a sleeve across his forehead. Lord — that Longe was a quacksalver, with his purges that left one weak-kneed, and not a whit of relief. It was cursedly cold, too — and the stairwell yawned black and steep, beyond the light's reach.

All the way down now, and then he'd have to climb up again… Edmund shook his arm, hissing when the pain only gnawed harder — and then froze.

Had he heard a step? A creak of the old oak floor?

"Who's there?" he called, his voice quavering like no man's should in his own house. When he raised the candle, the shadows writhed on the ceiling. "Don't hide, damn you!"

A pale-faced shape advanced out of the darkness. A well-known face — no ghost, after all.

"Haven't you plagued me enough?" Through the wild beating of his heart, past his aching jaw, Edmund made his voice as hard as he could — and the shadow glided closer, closer until it filled the gloom.

Closer, closer, and the grip on Edmund's arm tightened like iron. He stepped back, his spine grinding against the post. *Go away!* he wanted to cry, as the candle twitched out of his fingers. He gasped for breath that wouldn't come. *Go away!* The wind roared in his temples. The window banged in his chest. He clawed for the banister as the world tilted — and then there was nothing but pain and swirling darkness.

CHAPTER 1

17th of November, Accession Day, London

Sometimes Tom Walsingham truly loathed London. Especially on a festive day.

For the dozenth time he reined in his horse before yet another knot of cup-shot Londoners bellowing in song. Just by a whisker he kept his mount from treading on a thin old fellow, red-faced with far too much ale — and didn't the churl curse at him, shaking his fist for good measure!

After two wet days in the saddle and two sleepless nights, one spent all but in the rain, Tom wasn't averse to flattening all the merry-makers in London. Cursing back, he nudged his horse ahead — and let those who cared step out of his way. The old man and his cronies did — in some haste — their jeers soon drowned out by yet another jangle of bells. Saint Dunstan's bell-ringers rehearsing, no doubt — unless they thought this din a fitting peal for celebrating the Queen's Accession Day.

Close to the corner of Tower Street, he had to slow down again. Men, women and children rushed to amass fuel for a bonfire, in the middle of the crossing, of all places! Armfuls of half-rotten straw, faggots, scraps of wood — everything, it seemed, would do. The merry-makers hailed every new addition, and an apprentice was trying to set fire to the pile. The day was grey enough for it, Lord knew — but what would they do by night, pillage the houses? And of course, of the Watch there was neither hide nor hair to be seen.

All Hallows' bells started to clang right above, and the crowd broke into cheers for the Queen as Tom turned into narrow, muddy Seething Lane — where the celebrations were just as noisy but a tad less wild — and reached home: the house of his great cousin, mentor and master, Sir Francis Walsingham, principal Secretary to the Queen.

He found wooden planks thrown over the ruts by the gate, and the family carriage ready in the yard. Was Mr. Secretary going to Whitehall for the day's festivities? He had been unwell when Tom had left two days earlier and, reckoning by the servants who scurried to and fro with furs and pans of embers, he hadn't improved.

Leaving his horse to a groom, Tom entered the house and, in the dark back passage, all but walked into Fisher, his cousin's butler. This personage clapped his hands together at the sight of him. "Bless you, Mr. Thomas — here you are!" And why his face must fall, Tom wondered very much. Had Sir Francis taken a turn for the worse? But then the ready carriage…

There was little reassurance in the way Fisher leant close to whisper, "Master is getting ready to go to Court with Her Ladyship and Mistress Frances — Lady Sidney, that is. They worried that you were late." The man's gaze travelled over Tom's mud-stained person, down to his wet boots and back.

"I was caught in the storm the other night," Tom said, sighing. "My horse was lamed, and I spent the night in a collier's hut. Well, no matter. I'll change and follow to Whitehall."

As he turned to go, Fisher stopped him with a hand on his arm. "Master would see you before he leaves — but, Mr. Thomas —"

That was as far as he got, because then Tom's own servant thundered into the passage, quiet as a trained band with drums.

"Oy, Master!" Nick Skeres bellowed. "'Is 'Onour wants to see you —"

"Yes, Skeres — I was just telling Mr. Thomas." Fisher was a tall man of formidable mien, known to have daunted servants of all standing and the occasional guest, but Skeres, who possessed both the build and spirit of a scantling Minotaur, was utterly undauntable.

As a rule, Tom would have chastised the lad; that morning, tired and wrong-footed, he couldn't find it in his heart to do more than glare when Skeres sniffed.

"Ay, Mr. Fisher — and while you tell 'im, 'Is 'Onour's waitin' in the 'all. Davies says to send the carriage round."

And, having dismissed a man who was his elder by ten years, and his better by several degrees, the Minotaur grabbed Tom by the elbow and steered him along the dark passage.

"'Tis your brother," the lad muttered out of the corner of his mouth.

Well, now… Tom frowned. Hadn't he seen Edmund the other day? Had the fool thought to complain to Mr. Secretary? "What of him?" he asked — and, for all answer, he found himself steered through the door and into the tall, grey hall, with its chequerboard floor and the oaken staircase.

Across the room, three cloaked people stood huddled together, caught between the dull light from the oriel window above the stairs, and the glow of an unseen candle: Sir Francis's big Welshman Davies, and Sir Francis's women — Lady Ursula, his wife, and his widowed daughter, Tom's cousin Frances.

It was Frances who turned around and saw him. "Tom, dear!" she called, and broke away from the little group, revealing her father, equally cloaked, and hunched almost double in a chair.

She hastened towards Tom, a hand held out, her triangular face a picture of uncertainty. Three years a widow, she was well out of mourning now, and yet she'd never quite resumed the warm colours she'd once liked to wear. Clad in grey velvet trimmed with grey furs and a ruff of silver lace, she seemed made of November light. Only her dark eyes glowed as they searched him from head to foot, and the cold, slender hand that caught his was strong.

She tugged him gently ahead, leading him to her parents. "We all so hoped to see you before we left," she murmured.

Why, what happened? Tom swallowed the question, his eyes straying to Sir Francis, and then back to Frances's eyes, glowing under a frown.

Both Sir Francis and Lady Ursula were frowning too, as Tom bowed to them. What could Edmund have written?

"Madam, Sir…" he murmured. "I'm sorry it took me longer than —"

He stopped short when Sir Francis waved a thin, liver-spotted hand, and Lady Ursula reached out to pat his arm with a small click of her tongue.

"Thomas…" Sir Francis's voice was little more than a rasp. "I am sorry. A messenger came from Scadbury yesterday afternoon. He carried a letter from your Uncle Guildford…" He turned to the Welshman. "Fetch it for Mr. Thomas, will you, Davies?" Even the small movement had shortened his wind, and the hand he laid on Tom's wrist was hot with fever. "I am very sorry, child: your brother is dead."

Dead… For a few heartbeats, Tom blinked stupidly. Dead. Sour, spiteful Ned — the last of his brothers…

"But I saw him the other day," he blurted out. "He was ill, yes — but…" And here he stopped, because Ned hadn't looked half as ill as Sir Francis did, gaunt and sallow, his mouth pressed into a line of constant pain. Ned had been sullen, bloated, pugnacious, gloating that Tom would not like his will.

"The messenger said it was sudden," Sir Francis said. "As the Lord willed it in his mercy. Now you must go to Scadbury at once."

He began to brace himself for rising, as Davies reappeared with the letter and handed it hastily to Tom.

Shoving it in his sleeve, Tom rushed to assist his great cousin, supporting him at one elbow with Davies on the other side, and Frances hovering.

Over Mr. Secretary's head, bent in the effort, he exchanged a glance with Lady Ursula.

"Scadbury can wait, Sir," he said. "I'll ride with you at Whitehall, be at hand —"

"Absolutely not, Thomas." Sir Francis's mouth twitched upwards, and his sunken eyes crinkled at the corners. "You are the head of the family now. It's not to be taken lightly. Now, be so kind as to assist me to the carriage."

Lightly! Lightness was the last thing on Tom's mind as he bowed his head and moved slowly on — he and Davies carrying much of his cousin's weight between them. Once Sir Francis almost stumbled on the steps, a grunt escaping him as Tom held him upright, and Lady Ursula glowered — most likely calling the Queen traitorous names in her head for forcing this ordeal on her husband.

Not that anyone could ever force Mr. Secretary Walsingham into anything he didn't want to do, was the thought that rose to Tom's mind — and yet, as he and Davies all but lifted the great man into the carriage, it felt like heaving a bundle of sticks wrapped in velvet. Tom prayed he'd kept the sudden fear from his eyes as he'd again met Lady Ursula's magpielike gaze.

The poor lady's round face sank into a smile. "You've always been a dear boy, Tom," she said. "But we must not call you that now — nor a child. Not the head of the family." Her smile was warm as she let him hand her, a little laboriously, into the carriage — and it struck Tom that she wasn't overly grieved over Edmund's death. It must be dreadfully unchristian that this warmed him a little, and so did the brisk little way Lady Ursula asked him to go and hasten Frances — bless the girl! — just as she had when they were children.

He hurried inside, knowing that his cousin had been waiting for him — and, indeed, there she was, rushing to take his hands the moment he stepped into the hall.

And, of all the things in the world, he blurted out, "I'm the head of the family now, Poppet. Scadbury belongs to me." Because there was nothing in God's creation that he loved more than Frances, and after her came Scadbury, the dear old moated house... Oh, Jove! He hadn't known himself to be smiling until the smile fell, and shame flooded him. "Lord, I've no heart. My brother's dead, and all I can think of —"

"No." Frances was a tiny woman. Even in her high-heeled Court shoes she still had to reach up to cradle Tom's face, and make him look straight into her serious eyes. "If you had no heart, you wouldn't be ashamed of it — but you must not. Edmund was never kind to you, and you've always wanted Scadbury."

Taking her hands, Tom kissed one narrow palm, and then the other. "So had Ned, Poppet. Poor Ned — churl that he was. The other day he was still well enough to shout at me. Well, I shouted at him first, but... Oh, Lord!" He stepped away from Frances and ran a hand through his hair. That had been the last time he'd seen his brother — and they'd quarrelled over money.

Frances was at his side again, slipping a hand under his arm. "I wish we didn't have to go to Whitehall," she said, sighing.

"Then don't!" Tom replied, like the fool he was. "I'm sorry — I shouldn't..."

"Dear love, you've seen Father. And even if he didn't need me, he wants me to go..." She broke away, not looking at him as she recovered her gloves from the sideboard. "Lord Essex is tilting."

Oh, Tartarus take Lord Essex! The Queen's new favourite — handsome, rich, scrambling to be powerful, to tread in Sir Francis's steps with the subtlety of an ox, and succeeding at least in that Sir Francis would give him his daughter in marriage. Tom's heart sank very low. But then, what had he expected? Essex had an earldom, the Queen's favour, every prospect of gaining power and influence. What could the master of Scadbury offer, compared to that?

Only a great love running both ways, whispered a bitter little voice inside Tom's mind — and, as though she'd heard it, Frances turned to him, her eyes huge, the candle limning golden streaks on the coils of her dark hair.

"Why, Mr. Thomas!" called a cheery voice — and both cousins turned.

A small young fellow — pinch him! — stood in the doorway from the scriveners' room, with a narrow moustache and sleeves of the gaudiest oxblood colour. For Tom he had an easy grin, and he bowed low to Frances. Kit Marley bowed surprisingly well for a cobbler's son.

"Your Ladyship's pardon," he murmured, and Frances nodded at him.

"You are Master Marley. The poet." She had her father's manner of not quite asking questions. "My cousin will be leaving very soon — but until he leaves, I'm sure the company of a friend would do him good."

And see the warm, sad, yearning smile on Marley's face as he bowed again. "He'll have it, my lady." Was the fool besotted with Mr. Secretary's daughter now?

It drew, if nothing else, a smile from Frances — a rare thing these days. She thanked the poet gravely, rose onto her toes to kiss Tom on the cheek, and with a whisper of "God be with you, cousin," she was gone.

Try as he might, Tom couldn't shake the chilling impression, as the door closed behind her, that she was gone from him forever.

Marley came to stand at his elbow. "I'm sorry about your brother," he said — and then stopped, tilting his head. "Or am I?"

Tom was startled into a huff of laughter. "So not only the whole household knows, but also passersby! What are you doing here, Marley? Have you gathered more rumours for Phelippes?"

"One hears all sorts of things…" A shrug — then he seemed to catch what he'd said and grimaced a little. "Not about your brother, though. Your Cyclops told me."

"Minotaur," Tom corrected half-thinkingly — and trust Nick Skeres to babble…

"Ah, yes — I'd noticed 'Cyclops' annoys him. Does he know the difference, that he should prefer two eyes in a bull's head?"

"I don't call him either to his face, as a rule, though I might, now — for wagging his tongue."

Marley chuckled. "Well, it will hardly stay a secret for long. And besides, the creature was eager that I shouldn't pester you." He raised an eyebrow at Tom — and, when he was repaid in kind, added, "Now you're your own man, Mr. Thomas. Lord of the manor. Wealthy…"

Wealthy! If only the lad knew! Landed, yes; as for wealthy… Tom snorted under his breath. "Are you hoping that I'll turn patron to poets, Kit?" he asked, and started up the stairs for his garret and his trunk, half his mind already reckoning black clothes — for all that he'd have to leave the packet from Chatham with Cardenas, Sir Francis's secretary.

Marley followed. "Patron to poets now…" he said, airy as you please. "It would suit you — and besides, you've always wanted to be."

"Aren't you shameless?" Shameless and quite right, if truth be told.

Tom hadn't climbed four steps before Skeres emerged from the shadows on the upper landing.

"The mourning gloves from your mam's funeral are all a-ruined, Mr. Tom," the Minotaur announced — and even as he spoke, he glowered down at Marley, fit to set a fire. *Didn't I tell you…?*

In one thing Marley was like Skeres: impervious to many things. Or not quite, perhaps. Had he been impervious, he wouldn't have smiled brilliantly and raised a rhetorician's hand. "Yes, you warned me, O Mighty Cyclops — but Lady Sidney's slightest wish supersedes your warning, and Her Ladyship commands that I should never leave Mr. Thomas's side."

Which wasn't what Frances had said, and was couched in words calculated to make Skeres scowl even harder.

"Enough — both of you!" snapped Tom, before the lad found words dire enough. "My black velvet will do, and something black for yourself." He looked down at his mud-stained riding clothes and boots. "And something for me to change into. And hot water — and the new boots —"

"Ay, ay, and some bread and ale while I'm at it — like I don't know!" the Minotaur grumbled. "What of the gloves? They's a disgrace, what with the mould…"

Which they wouldn't be, if you'd paid mind to your work. Tom bit down the flare of annoyance. There would be plenty of time to scold Skeres when Marley wasn't around with that amused and scornful manner. "Then you run to the Exchange, and…" And then a thought occurred to him, like a small clap of thunder: he was the lord of the manor now. He was *the* Walsingham. "No — wait. I'll buy a pair in Bromley."

"What for?" protested Skeres, stopping with a foot raised. "You've no need to scrape now…"

Oh, where to begin? Nowhere, it seemed, for Marley beat him to the answer.

"Because, O Cyclops, simple country minds find it God's own justice that their betters should spend in their pockets!"

Face reddening in splotches, Nick Skeres descended two menacing steps towards the poet. Oh, Lord give patience!

"I said, enough! My hot water, Nick — at once." Tom watched severely as the lad lumbered downstairs, glowering askance at Marley as he went, and only then did he turn his glare on the poet. "A pest, that's what you are! A pest and a nuisance. Go away, go and do whatever it is that you must do with Phelippes."

Quite unperturbed, Marley grinned and shrugged. "I've done all I must — except obey Lady Sidney. I think she'd want me to ride to Scadbury with you."

As though Tom needed Skeres and Marley bickering, on top of all the rest. "Not on your soul!" he said, earning a shrug.

"But you'll need some sort of retinue now — and the Cyclops alone will never do —"

"A retinue!" A laugh escaped Tom, louder and harsher than he'd meant. "What do you think I've inherited, a duchy?"

And he stalked upstairs, slipping the letter from his sleeve as he went, with the glum sense of long, hard days ahead.

Marley, of course, followed him like a shadow.

By the time Chislehurst came into sight — the small steeple of St. Nicholas poking at the late morning sky — Skeres was still grousing in the manner he thought of as being under his breath. To the fulminations about that upstart Marley, he had added of late a show of wondering why they hadn't stopped in Bromley for the gloves — since Tom was so bent on having Kentish gloves — and for a bit of dinner while they were at it.

For the most part, Tom ignored him. Twice over the dozen miles or so he had commanded silence — to variable success — but now he was too taken with his thoughts to care much. Black thoughts they were: only two days ago he'd come the same way, rehearsing in his head how he'd talk his annuity out of Edmund. Much good it had done him! They'd had a row of rows — Ned sitting in bed, short-winded and feverish, mocking Tom's debts, his logic, what he called his airs, laughing breathlessly as he repeated that there was no money. *Bring me to court, Tomkin, for breach of Father's will. Do, and we lose Scadbury for good!* They'd shouted at each other — and now... He shook his head with a sigh, coming back to his surroundings just in time to swerve his horse into the hedged lane to Scadbury. And that was when he caught three words out of Skeres's grumbling.

"'Is Lordship says..."

And because, ever since a short stint of couriering in the summer, Essex had become *His Lordship* to Skeres, that was also when Tom had enough. Halting his horse abruptly, he turned in the saddle.

"Cuds-me, Mr. Tom — a bit of warning —"

"You want a warning?" Tom snapped. "Well, then, be warned: not another word out of you! Let it be at least a day or two before my brother's people judge you a blathering halfwit, and…" And he wasn't going to mention Essex. "And don't let them hear my servant name Lord Essex like an oracle all the time."

There! So he'd made a fool of himself — for Skeres, say what you will, was not slow in catching slips.

It was in a heavier humour that Tom resumed his way for the last mile or so, and with an earnest wish that he could turn around and go back to London.

Rags of rust-coloured leaves hung from the hazels that fringed the lane, with a bare elm here and there, and a gnarled old oak tree when they reached the corner of the garden wall. The other day, old Wollans had come from the gatehouse at the sound of an approaching horse; now, nobody showed. Even when Skeres bellowed, "Oy!" with all his considerable might, for all answer a pair of crows were startled into flight, cackling.

Lord, had the place grown this forlorn in two days? But surely the archway — Grandfather Walsingham's pride, by all accounts — hadn't been overgrown with limp, grey ivy the other day?

Past the arch, the outer courtyard and the stables looked just as deserted. The house itself sat squat on its moated island — a tall, jettied, timbered storey over bricks, a yellowish grey against the overcast sky.

Scadbury — Tom's own place now — didn't offer much of a welcome.

An untended cart sat in the yard, half-blocking the way to the bridge — the only access on this side of the island — and why it should be there at all, Tom wondered very much, until a boy came running out of the gatehouse.

Nudging his horse ahead, Tom hailed him and asked what cart was that.

Stopping in the act of climbing into the bed, the lad squinted at the newcomers. "Master Burten's," he said. "The joiner. From Bromley, y'know." And, when it was plain that Tom didn't, he added, "We're putting up a trestle…"

"And who told you to come in this way?"

The boy shrugged. "Housekeeper, she did." And with that, he snatched up a wooden mallet, jumped off the cart, ran away across the bridge, and disappeared into the gatehouse, leaving the door to swing ajar.

"An' welcome you 'ome, Mr. Thomas!" grumbled Skeres.

Tom dismounted and threw the reins to the Minotaur. And then, unannounced and un-greeted, he crossed the bridge and entered his house.

Past the gatehouse, past the passage room that looked upon his mother's herb garden, the old-fashioned, nail-studded door creaked on its hinges to open into the cavernous hall. Never light during the lightest summer day, it was bathed in a grey gloom now, the chill, damp air smelling of new rushes and, faintly, of cold smoke. How empty it seemed, with no fire on the hearth, and the great table removed — for all that it was not deserted…

And surely there should be some particular solemnity when a man first stepped under the roof that was his own? He should not be met with hammer blows and squabbling voices?

But so it was: at the hall's far end, old black brocade hung in heavy folds over the wainscoting, down to the flagstoned floor.

There, under the Walsingham standard of black and white stripes and a red band, a dais had been erected, where the boy from the cart was hammering at a sturdy trestle, under the acrimonious supervision of a pair of women. A tall, stooping man in a gentleman's attire of drab brown stood a little apart, and it was he — a lanky, tawny-headed fellow — who turned around and caught sight of Tom advancing.

"Why, Tom!" he called. "You've arrived!"

It was with every appearance of relief that George Guildford, after calling over his shoulder for the women to be quiet, strode to meet his nephew by the empty fireplace.

"Ah, but it's good to see you here, lad!" An uncertain smile flickered over his long, red-flecked face as George took Tom by both shoulders. "I sent for you and the girls as soon as I could, but that young fool came back saying that you were away on Mr. Secretary's business. Ah well, no matter. You're here, now, Mr. Walsingham." Again that fledgling smile wavered and fell, and George lowered his voice to a church-whisper. "Poor Ned — poor Ned…"

"Yes, poor Ned." Tom extricated himself from his uncle. "But how did it happen? He didn't look that ill the other day."

George Guildford sighed and pulled at his thin whiskers. "Only two days, yes — who thought we'd see each other again so soon, eh, Tom? And in this manner."

"Not I, for one. Had he worsened so much? What did the physician say?"

A shake of the head. "He had a surgeon, out of Greenwich. He came yesterday morning, said —"

"For shame, Mr. Guildford!"

Tom turned to see one of the women bustling his way — tall and strong, in a snow-white coif and apron, her wide face creased in a rueful smile. She stopped a few steps away to curtsey, as though she hadn't many times caught the child Tom with his finger in the buttermilk — and boxed his ears for it sometimes.

"At last I see ye, Master Tom," she said, Kent broad in her speech. "Not like the other day, gallop in and gallop out — and we keep ye standing like a beggar in yer own hall." That last to George, with a click of the tongue.

She, too, spoke under her breath, and Tom did the same as he took her hand. "Your husband said you were unwell the other day, Kathryn … or I should say Mrs. Wollans, now that you're housekeeper?"

Oh, how Kathryn Wollans's face darkened, and how she jutted out her bottom lip!

"I thought…" Tom floundered, and Old Kathryn reached out to pat his arm.

"Never ye mind, Master Tom," she said, with a portentous nod that meant, *Oh, mind very much.* "Cut my tongue before I speak ill of the dead — but … yer mam's dead too, poor lady, and she always called ye the one child of hers as had wits. Where have ye left the horse?"

Pushing aside faint surprise at his mother's posthumous praise, Tom told her of Skeres and the horses, and, with another brisk curtsey, Kathryn bustled away. On the doorstep, she stopped to call to the joiner's boy that the trestle wouldn't make itself, and then turned to the other woman, who stood by the dais with her arms full of black cloth. "And ye could come and greet the Master, *Mrs. Foal.*" Such sourness she put into the words, that it hung in the air like a fog after she'd gone.

Well, now… Tom raised both brows at George, who shifted his weight from foot to foot.

"You haven't been much at home of late, have you?" his uncle asked.

"You saw how things were the other day. I barely spoke a word to anyone but Ned — and before that, I don't think I'd been here twice in five years." Tom shrugged. "But I thought Kathryn must have taken Mrs. Turley's place."

There was no mirth at all to George's crooked smile. "Ay, and so did she, and her husband — but…" He stopped and nodded at the approaching woman, raising his voice to introduce her. "This is your housekeeper, nephew: Mrs. Susan Foal."

And there came a dumpling of a woman: small, round, and young — no more than three or four-and-twenty — with jet-black hair and a small red mouth pursed tight. She never unpursed it, nor did she lower her black eyes as she curtsied. Tom remembered her from the other day, when she'd opened the door for him — and even then, in his angry haste, he had noticed in passing her embroidered coif, far too fine for one he'd taken for a maid. Now, as he took a better look at her, he also observed the fine lawn partlet that covered her abundant bosom.

"Mrs. Foal," he greeted coldly. "I'm sure you've work to attend to. I'll speak to you later."

And see if this shrew didn't glare at him, and raise her chin as high as it would go while she curtsied again. What else she might have done to signify her displeasure Tom was left to wonder, because then the door to the stairs swung open, and old Wollans backed into the hall, keeping the heavy leaf open.

With a squeal, Susan Foal ran away. "Wait!" she called in a harsh, rasping voice. "Wait, you lackwits! Don't ye see it isn't ready? Who told ye to come down? Where be the joiner's man?" And much more scolding like that, while she gathered from the table a folded length of black cloth.

"If ever a woman had pretensions..." George twisted his mouth, watching as two men struggled backwards through the door, carrying each a corner of a black-swathed board, and tangling themselves with Wollans. "Though I'll say she didn't grow them all by herself."

Having had enough of the ado, Tom strode to the door and pushed it open wider. "Hold fast, Wollans," he ordered, earning from the old man a soldierly, tight-lipped nod. He glanced over his shoulder at the joiner's boy. "Are you done?"

"Ay, Yer Honour." The boy nodded with the zeal of one who feared he'd been dismissive to the master of the house.

"Then, Mrs. Foal, do what you must with that drapery of yours."

Susan Foal had to raise her chin and protest. "Kathryn —"

"Goodwife Wollans is doing my bidding." And, because the woman still hesitated, Tom ordered, "Have the boy help you. The sooner it's done, the sooner my brother can lie decently."

In a trice Susan Foal was shaking the black cloth into place with a noise of sails, and the bearers were stepping through with the shrouded body of Edmund Walsingham. One was the young, sullen groom Tom remembered from two days earlier, while the older man with white hair and an angelically fresh face was Barker, the cook. The other two he didn't know. They all nodded silently at Tom and walked in a fair approximation of solemnity to lay their dead master on the trestle. As soon as it was done, and Susan Foal began fussing with the black folds, Barker came to bow to Tom.

"It's a sad day to welcome you home, Master." A demure frown creased his pink face. "But things must be as God wills them." Very frank and placid he sounded. Then, promising dinner, he disappeared with unhurried purpose, without a

glance for the body on the trestle or his fellow servants still busy around it.

"Not overcome with grief, is he?" George asked a little sourly.

Neither are you, Tom didn't say. "Mother hired him. From what little I've seen of him, he's always going on about the way Her Ladyship wanted things done. I don't think that he much endeared himself to Ned."

"Or that Ned much endeared himself to him?"

"Ned never much cared to endear himself to anyone." Tom was surprised at the pang of sadness this gave him. "Or else Barker is just sounding out the new master."

Because these were his servants now — Lord help him. After years of struggling to pay even Skeres's wages, he looked with misgivings to a household of … how many? "These are not all my people, are they?"

There was some consolation when George shook his head. "Not the boy and not the one with the yellow hair —"

And just then the one with the yellow hair jumped clumsily off the dais, bumping into the Foal woman. When she shoved him away, he made a great show of staggering back.

"Not this skittish once, were ye, Sukie?" he laughed — and it was not the laugh of a sober man. "Grown mighty fine ye have, girl."

On a moment's acquaintance, Tom was ready to swear that few things could have sent Susan Foal into a greater passion than that name of girl — and, indeed, she hissed like a cat, and the fourth bearer jumped into the fray, both calling the tow-headed joiner names. It would have been comical at another time — because this, who must be Susan's husband, was just as small and round as she was, with a squealing voice that did him no favours as he cringed away from the much bigger, mallet wielding foe — but here and now…

Shoving aside old Wollans, who was trying to separate the contenders, Tom grabbed the small one by the scruff of his neck. "Enough!" he snapped. "What sort of household is this? Have you no respect? Who are you?"

The small man squirmed and wheezed, and pulled at his badly cut round beard, until the housekeeper answered in his place.

"Robert Foal, Master. My husband, if ye please." And, to hear her, it pleased *her* not at all. She scowled at the fellow when he yapped:

"Mr. Edmund's man, I am. I was. His *valet* —"

Valet — Lord help them all! "Then you should be twice ashamed." Tom turned his glower on the joiner's man. "And you?"

"Frank Burten's man," he said. "The joiner…" He took a step back then one forward, turning the mallet in his hands. "'Tis that the bier needs mending, so we brought the trestle…"

"Well, be gone, now, if you're done."

The fellow nodded, shoulders up to his ears, turning and turning the mallet — and all the time Tom had a sense that he'd seen him before. The big frame, the wild flaxen hair, the sullen twist of his face…

"Ay, Master," he muttered. "The bier we'll bring tomorrow, or the day after." He made for the door, his gait not so much clumsy as uneven.

At once, Tom knew the crabwise, half-hopping limp. "Jack Fuller!" he called. "That's never you?"

Fuller stopped, shoulders hunching. He handed the mallet to the round-eyed boy, sent him running, and then turned and squared himself. "Ay, Mr. Tom — Jack Fuller."

Or the ruin of him, judging by looks. This unkempt fellow with the sagging face resembled little the stable-groom Tom remembered, who'd grown up at Scadbury, where he'd acquired the limp under a trampling horse. Across the hall, Wollans and the Foals were lighting candles for the dais — Susan scolding her husband — while George fingered the candlesticks on the French sideboard. All were most carefully pretending not to listen.

With a nod at Fuller, Tom led the way into the passage room, where the man stopped, scuffing at the rushes with a worn shoe.

"Well?" Tom asked, crossing his arms. Not that he thought the loss of this roistering braggart a great harm to Scadbury, but Father had always made a point of keeping him in service after the accident. "What have you done at last?"

Fuller shrugged one shoulder. "Yer brother kicked me out, he did. For a drunkard — but…" He looked up, eyes pouchy and reddened. "I never was no drunkard while I was here!"

The way Tom remembered it, Fuller had been a rough bully even when sober, and often whipped by Wollans for it. In fairness, whatever Father's wishes, there was no blaming Edmund for getting rid of him.

"Well, you've found yourself another place. See that you keep it, by not making rows where you work."

Another might have taken this for the dismissal it was, but Jack Fuller snorted. "Ay, another place, with Mr. Edmund, Wollans and his wife — every soul here — speaking ill! If it hadn't been for Mr. Wood as had Frank Burten hire me… Mr. Wood's a good man, he is!" *Unlike all you Walsinghams*, hung unsaid but plain as day — and then, with a careless bow and a "Mr. Tom," Fuller was gone.

And why John Wood — wasn't that Ned's steward? — must have gone to the trouble for this tearaway, Tom didn't know. He waited until he heard the gatehouse door close, then went back to the hall. No one was left there, except the body laid on the black-draped trestle, and the candles burning in silver sticks at the dais' four corners made the hall gloomier still. Even just past noon, the shadows gathered thick in the corners and above, among the age-dark trussed beams of the ceiling. For a heartbeat Tom had a strange sense of being back at his mother's death, and that of his father, and Guil, his middle brother … as though all the deaths were one, and in this old, dusk-filled hall no time had passed between one and the next.

Fanciful — that was what he was becoming! Shaking away the cobwebs, he walked up to his brother's body, swathed in linen and more lustreless brocade, strewn with rosemary sprigs. Ned had been a burly man in life, and now there was so little left of him. The waxy face wore a frown even in repose.

"Ah, Ned," Tom whispered. "I'll never feel but that you must dislike to see me in your place…" And he felt a sting behind his eyes.

"Mr. Thomas?"

Whispered as it was, the call echoed in the empty hall and startled Tom. He blinked at the sight of Kathryn peeking out of the passage door — and the old woman would never know how grateful he was to be called to dinner.

CHAPTER 2

Old Kathryn had laid out the second-best plate in the parlour, and George was there already, looking out of the window. Only at the last moment Tom remembered his new station and veered for the high-backed chair at the head of the table.

George sat on his right with a strained smile.

"You'll have to get used to it all, eh, Tom?" the old man said, with painful cheer.

"So I will," Tom tried to smile back. "Until last night, I slept in a garret in Mr. Secretary's house…" And he let it trail. Until last night he'd been a landless, penniless, unmarried younger son, just like George. Until last night, at this table, the two of them would have sat side by side, exchanging glances when the landed ones grew pompous.

Bless Kathryn for stepping in squarely. She was serving them with her own hands, while her husband hovered by the fireplace. They'd lost no time in taking possession, as it were, of the new master.

"That lad of yers — and has he an appetite!" she said, as she served them roast beef with a sauce of vinegar and pepper. "Well, he asked where he must put yer things — not as that ye've brought much with ye. Will the yellow room do for tonight?"

Thrown yet again, Tom chewed on a bit of beef. He had his choice of half a dozen rooms, now, and clothes-presses, and chests to fill. The garret, with its timbered walls and gable, flitted through his mind again — empty of his things, or given to someone else. Did owning Scadbury mean he'd never live in

Seething Lane again? Did landed men still work for Mr. Secretary?

"Well, there's Mr. Edmund's room," Kathryn said doubtfully, "but for tonight —"

"No." Tom was made brusque by the memory of his row with Edmund, the harsh words, the stench of sweat, piss, and illness in the close air. Let them think him superstitious, if they liked. "I'm not sleeping in the bed where my brother died."

Old Kathryn and George stared, and Wollans, blinking in that odd manner that came of him having one eye filmed almost white with cataract, said, "But, Master, he didn't die in no bed at all!"

Tom set down his knife, looking from the servant to George, who had written that placidly plain letter. "So he didn't die *peacefully in the night* after all?"

Wincing, George raised a hand and let it fall. "It's not the sort of thing you put in letters."

Commendably prudent, surely — if something was amiss... Tom pushed away his plate, queasy of a sudden with misgivings. "Well, I'm here now. How did Ned die?"

Did the Wollanses think Tom wouldn't catch them trading glances behind George's back? When he made to dismiss them, his uncle waved his hand.

"Oh, let them stay," he said, sighing. "There's nothing I have to say that they don't know already." A thin smile. "Some of it better than I do, I'll wager."

And see how Wollans shifted his weight, and Kathryn looked away — as though Tom must rend his garments that his uncle had been in his cups.

"Let's hear it, then," he prompted, and George began.

"The surgeon called it an inflammation of the heart. He said he had his humours discomposed..."

"Ned told me the other day," Tom cut in. "And called the surgeon an ass."

"Ay, well, you know the way Ned was." George shrugged. "Call it what you like; he took a turn for the worse after you'd gone away. I was all set to leave, too — but he was so ill…" George shook his head again. "And then, very late at night… Such a storm there was that night!"

And this, too, Tom knew only too well, having spent it with a lame horse on Dartford Heath. But this dilly-dallying… "So what of it?"

"Perhaps it was the storm that made Ned restless, I don't know. He rose and wandered off, and…" George swallowed. "And he fell down the stairs."

Jove… Tom gaped, questions battling for precedence on his tongue. "And nobody heard?"

"Such wind and rain, there was…" Wollans said. "It broke the chimney over at the gatehouse."

And he meant the one past the moat, by the walled garden — because that was where he and his wife slept. But…

"What of the Foals? They sleep here, don't they? Foal calls himself my brother's valet. Why wasn't he with Ned?"

There was a snort from Wollans, and Kathryn clicked her tongue.

"That one!" she scoffed. "Mr. Edmund never wanted him around at night, for he wheezes like a hog."

"Then why…?" *Why not seek another manservant?* Tom shook his head at his own simplicity: another servant would not have Fair Susan for a wife. "But still, to leave him alone if he was that ill!"

They all spoke at the same time.

"Will should have been with him," said Old Kathryn.

"You know the way he was…" said Uncle George.

"Mr. Edmund kicked young Will out of the room," said Wollans.

Will Everest, it turned out, was the youngest, last-hired of the servants. Not a bad lad, but heedless. Young folks didn't know what it was to work, these days. Half scullion and half groom now, since the last one was sacked.

"But Mr. Wood says as we don't need no other boy," Wollans grumbled. "For all that, what with the grounds and the stables… I don't grow no younger, Master."

Before they talked him into hiring another groom, Tom thanked the two servants and dismissed them.

George didn't even wait for the door to close behind them to smirk. "They see the planet of the Foals setting already. Make the old crone housekeeper, Tom, and you'll have the most faithful of friends."

As though Tom could have missed the manoeuvring… "But Ned, Uncle: if he'd taken a turn for the worse, why was he alone with a scullion?"

"Poor Ned…" Sobered at once, George poured himself a good measure of claret. "You heard, he didn't want Foal — and faith, I wouldn't want that fellow around, either. Kathryn had a pain in her back, Wollans is clumsy as an ox, and Barker — not that I see *him* watching the sick. Beneath the dignity of a cook, I'll wager."

"What of Mrs. Foal?" asked Tom.

A snort. "She'd have cheered up Ned, I'm sure — but she'd been unwell all day, eaten something that didn't agree with her. And that only left that young churl, Will Everest. Fair Susan has been at the boy's throat for letting Ned chase him away — but truly, Tom: a scullion! What was he to do?"

"Go and wake the valet or Fair Susan?" Tom suggested a little testily.

"The Foals treat him worse than the stable dog. Perhaps he'd no taste for more shouting." Twisting his mouth, George peered into the depths of his wine. "Be that as it may, he found himself some place to sleep, and…"

"Where, that he never heard Ned fall?"

"A fox awake under the stairs wouldn't have heard. What with the wind and rain, every door and every window rattling… Fit to tear down the house, it was."

It surely had seemed fit to tear down the collier's hut and the whole copse around it. Tom very much doubted he would have heard a trained band passing him by, that night. "Who found him, then?"

"Susan Foal, at first light. She screamed her head off, roused the whole house. Stupid woman!" George threw down his wine in one gulp. "We moved him to his bed, cold and stiff as he was…" A shudder. "Wood sent young Will to Greenwich for the surgeon — but it was plain as day that he was dead. Lord rest him." He seemed aged of a sudden, poor George — his eyes sunk deep in his bony sockets, his little veins a purple web on his pasty cheeks.

And then something occurred to Tom, a name he'd heard more than once today. "Is Wood the steward? Why haven't I seen him?"

"John Wood!" George sneered, leaning half across the table to pour himself more claret. As an afterthought, he also splashed a little in Tom's glass. "Marvellous proper fellow, is Wood! Knows his place and everybody else's. Ned, rest his heart, leant on him a good deal, from what I saw. Why, he made honest, faithful Wood his executor — him and that other paragon, Foal."

"What?" Tom half choked on his wine. "Not you?"

"Not me, not you, not your Uncle Buffkin, not your sisters' husbands — no: his faithful servants Wood and Foal!" He laughed harshly. "Never look so disbelieving, lad. I should know: who do you think witnessed the will?"

Tom sat back. Two uncles as witnesses, and two servants as executors… "Had he lost his mind?"

The way Uncle George sniffed was far from reassuring. "And where's Wood, you ask? In London, that's where. Up at cock-crow this morning, off to the Prerogative Court. 'Wait for the heir,' say I — and he looks down that long, thin nose he has. 'No, Mr. Guildford,' he says — the gall of him! — for he's executor, don't I know, and it behoves him, ay: *it behoves him* to get the will to the court with all dispatch and diligence! And all the time Foal nods at every word, keen as a spaniel!"

"Not that he's wrong." Tom morosely studied his uneaten dinner. When his father had died, Sir Francis had been one of the executors — a cousin and a gentleman being a most sensible choice — and had explained the law of the matter. "It does fall to the executors to take the will to the probate court."

"Well, then." George rose to his unsteady feet and raised his cup. "Here's to zealous executors." And, having thrown down the claret in one gulp, he fled, leaving Tom alone with his uneasy thoughts.

"A fine 'ornet's nest this 'ouse is, Mr. Tom!" Nick Skeres pronounced, busy taking noisy possession of the room Tom had once shared with his brothers. "There ain't one of them that wouldn't dunk half the others in the moat. And for sure they'd all dunk *me*."

This dragged Tom out of his half-hearted contemplation of the fire in the hearth. "We haven't been here three hours, Dolius. What have you done?"

Behold the Minotaur indignant: "What 'ave *I* done?" He flung Tom's black velvet doublet on the four-poster bed, and went to rummage inside his own saddlebag. "'Tis what you'll do that 'as 'em all in a tiff. They reckon you'll get rid of your brother's servants, and bring in your own."

"Of which you make the sum total, have you told them?" Tom turned back to the fireplace: the flames were hissing to an early death. "Besides, do they think that dunking you would make a good impression? You *must* have done something."

It was always wasted breath to call out Skeres on his logic — not that it ever stopped Tom from trying. This particular attempt only earned a huff.

"They's just a sour-hearted lot." The lad yanked a brush out of the bag. "Not Goody Wollans, though: she gave me 'alf of an 'umble pie for dinner."

"Are you sure she hasn't just chosen poison over dunking?"

With a sudden frown, Skeres tilted his head, a hand splayed over his drum-like belly, as though feeling for signs of agony — then huffed again. "'Tis all this 'unting murtherers for 'Is 'Onour, Mr. Tom. Un'ealthy, I call it!" And with that, he started to brush the poor doublet as though it had done him injury.

"You'll wear through it!" Tom scolded. "Didn't you brush it this morning in London?"

A shrug. Skeres did that a good deal. "There wasn't time this morning — an' besides, you can afford a new one now."

And here was another one who thought that Scadbury was made of gold… He'd find out soon enough. Meanwhile, he resumed his brushing a little less truculently, and Tom turned back to the moribund fire. On the mantelpiece still sat the same old boxwood figure of a hound, its nose chipped where

Ned had once dropped it. Tom tried to sink himself more comfortably into the yellow padded chair — and failed.

"I've never liked this room," he said — and Lord, how peevish he sounded!

Skeres hummed. "'Tis only a night or two — but the row they 'ad about it! That chit of an 'ousekeeper wanted to put us somewhere else while they get the big one ready, and Goody Wollans bit 'er 'ead off. A right 'ornet's nest, I say. Shrews, dullards, thieves, and all of them a plague."

"Thieves?" Tom sat up.

"Ay, a groom that was kicked out."

That was not what Fuller had said. "Not for a drunkard?"

"Don't know about no drunkard," Skeres said. "But there was a silver spoon went missing, and this lad Kickly, a bit of a sneaksby anyway, was sacked on Martinmas, and now there's only Everest, who plays scullion and groom, and is all amort for it. Say what you will, Mr. Tom, I'll sing you a song when we go back 'ome."

Home being London, to the Minotaur's mind… If only! Tom was spared the need to answer when there came a knock on the door, and Skeres went to open it.

Susan Foal stood on the threshold, and whatever Edmund had found in her, it couldn't have been a sweet temper: only by an effort of generosity could the stiff dip she gave be called a curtsey, accompanied by a scowl to make milk curdle.

"Yes, Mrs. Foal?" Tom called. Lord — but this woman set his teeth on edge!

Surely it couldn't have been her comeliness that had bewitched Ned. Dark of complexion and round of face and body, she had abundant hair and a long-lashed gaze, but both black as soot, and her red mouth was pursed in sourness. Even her voice was grating. "Mr. Guildford says as Mr. Wood be here."

Surely she must feel it beneath her dignity to run Uncle George's errands? Had George sent her just for that purpose? There was no saying with him, for sometimes he had a childish malice.

Ah, well. Tom said that he would see Mr. Wood at once, and it should have been dismissal enough, shouldn't it? But Susan Foal stood her ground.

"Would ye see me after, Master?" she asked — and for a heartbeat, Tom stared at her. Did she mistake him for his brother, that she should…? But no: he had said he'd talk to her, hadn't he? Fates send she hadn't guessed his thoughts!

"I'll send for you, Mrs. Foal," he said, and again meant it as a dismissal.

Again, the confounded woman made no move to go. "And my husband, Master?" she asked. "Will ye want him for a valet?"

Heaven forfend! Tom motioned towards the glowering Skeres. "I have an attendant already," he said — to a satisfied grunt from the Minotaur.

It was comical the way Fair Susan ran her gaze up and down Skeres's person, and sniffed. "Then what's Foal to do, that he be a valet?"

Where had Ned found this mannerless shrew? "I'm sure he wasn't born one, Mrs. Foal. Was he a groom before? Stables or house?"

So an added measure of sternness worked on Susan Foal. Cheeks colouring dark, she lowered her gaze at last.

"The house, Master."

"Then he can go back to do just that — for now. You may go, Mrs. Foal."

Very stiffly — and no doubt cursing her new master in her heart — Susan Foal curtsied herself out.

The moment the door closed behind her, Skeres let out a low whistle. "The cheek of 'er! But you've given 'er what for, Master!"

Had he? Tom wasn't sure at all. He had a sense he should have told her that such decisions should be taken without bothering the master of the house. Ah well, it was too late. Ordering Skeres to do something with the fire, he straightened his doublet and went to meet the steward he wasn't sure he'd like any better than he did the housekeeper.

The same childhood tutor who had taught Tom to count in Latin before speaking in anger, had also warned him against hyperboles. So often and so strongly had he warned, that, as he descended the Old Stairs, Tom's mind shied away from the notion that no two men could have been more different than George Guildford and John Wood.

All else apart, it wasn't true, but still the notion made itself felt as he stopped on the lower landing of the stairs, a hand on the baluster of carved oak, and observed the two.

Where George was lanky, with his drab suit hanging untidily about him, Wood was compact, and so straight-backed and trim that one felt to be slouching only to look at him. Nothing could have been graver than his bow.

"Mr. Walsingham, I am most sorry for your loss," he said, with a plain, even frankness that should have made it hard to dislike him.

"Thank you, Mr. Wood." Tom descended the last of the stairs, studying the man and judging him to be three or four and thirty. "I hear you rode to London?"

Before the steward could answer, Uncle George cut in. "Before it was quite light — like one with the devil at his heels!" he griped, sounding childish beside Wood's quiet, deliberate manner.

"Like one with duty on his mind, Mr. Guildford." The man turned to Tom. "Mr. Walsingham, your brother — Lord rest him — made me his executor. It was only the thought of being equal to Mr. Edmund's trust that spurred me —"

And again George interrupted him. "Spurred you to seize the will and run with it! Cursed quick, weren't you, without a by-your-leave, without a word for the heir!"

"But you saw to that at once, didn't you, Mr. Guildford?" Wood had the manner of a grown man dealing with a fractious child.

"And a good thing I did! Had it been for you, my nephew would still be in London, not even knowing that his brother had died!"

Something flickered in Wood's hazel eyes as he drew even straighter. "As the executor, I would have sent for Mr. Walsingham and his lady sisters, but I was preceded!" he retorted — and that was when Tom, judging that these two had bickered across him more than enough, stepped in the middle.

"Surely a member of the family takes precedence in such a matter," he said firmly, to George's approving grunt. "You knew where the will was kept, I take it, Mr. Wood?"

And see how he raised his chin. "I wrote it under Mr. Edmund's dictation, and then he made me place it with other papers in his chest upstairs — as Mr. Guildford knows." He turned a very stern look on George. "And if Mr. Guildford suggests that I have tampered with the will, then he must think me a fool, for he and Mr. Buffkin were both present as Mr.

Edmund dictated it, and they read what I wrote before signing it."

Wood and George mustn't have made themselves pleasant to each other these past days. "Mr. Guildford suggests nothing of the sort," Tom said. "I'm surprised that you should think so. And I'm sure you have much work to do. I'll want to see the accounts and the papers — but it can all wait until after my brother's funeral."

Surely Wood had never expected the new master to side with the steward against a kinsman? Still, it was with a marked stiffness that he bowed, declared himself at Mr. Walsingham's disposal, and walked away, very straight.

"Upstart jackanapes!" George griped before the man was out of earshot. "A yeoman's son, and you'd think him the Lord Chamberlain himself!"

On second thoughts, Tom wondered, was he truly surprised at the steward's outburst? "You're *not* suggesting it, though, are you, Uncle?" he asked. "That Wood tampered with the will?"

At first George hitched up one thin shoulder and sniffed; then he hummed, and last of all, exclaimed, "Wait 'til you read it, lad! Hadn't I been there to hear Ned dictate it — to hear him with my own ears…!" A shake of the tawny head. "But mark me: that Wood is a scoundrel — blind me if he isn't!"

After that, he made a great show of not wanting to say more — which was very much like George and, knowing from long experience that the surest way to draw out his uncle was through a show of indifference, Tom said, "I'll wait, then." He began to slowly climb back up the stairs. "Where is it that you found him?"

And indeed Uncle George must have been expecting more insistence: there was no answer at first, and when Tom turned around, there he stood, at the foot of the stairs, staring up with his brow furrowed.

"Ned. Did he tumble all the way down?"

"No … no. He…" George pointed to the lower landing, just above the place where Tom stood. "He was lying up there."

"Poor devil!" Tom shook his head. A spell of dizziness, a step missed in the darkness… It all seemed so cruelly puny. "Perhaps, if he hadn't sent away the boy…"

At the foot of the stairs, Uncle George still stared up without a word.

Tom jolted awake to raised voices and the stamping of feet. Where on earth…? Finding himself in a padded chair, he clumsily caught the book that was sliding from his lap.

Ah, yes: Mother's drawing room.

"Let me fetch that nephew of mine," called a gravelly voice — and at once the door to the parlour was thrown open. Tom blinked against the yellow candlelight as Leven Buffkin, Esquire, blustered into the drawing room with the grace of a Spanish invasion.

"Uncle!" Tom called, still hoarse with sleep as he scrambled to his feet. He might as well have called to the door-jamb.

"Thomas! What the devil…?" the old man boomed, stopping to throw over his shoulder a careless, "Pardon, Sir," before he caught sight of his quarry. "There! Playing the gentleman of leisure already, eh?"

There were relatives Tom wouldn't have minded catching him asleep in the middle of the day; Uncle Buffkin wasn't one of them. The widower of a Guildford aunt, he was stout, loud, and gruff, with a moustache like iron bristles, big teeth, and a constant need to show his Walsingham in-laws that he was not cowed by Mr. Secretary's cousins. Of all the kinsmen Edmund could have chosen to witness his will…

"Don't just stand there all addled, Thomas!" The old man slapped a soft hat to his thigh. "What are you doing, hiding there when you have visitors?"

Tom swallowed a yawn: he wasn't going to admit that he'd been catching an hour's sleep. "I didn't know that I had any," he said instead. "I think I'll make this my writing room —" And then he stopped short, his sleepy mind catching up with the callousness of making plans for the house with his brother still unburied.

Not that his uncle minded. "Ay, sink more money into this place!" he groused instead. "Besides, what's the use? You're the last of the litter, Tomkin — you'll need a wife, and she'll want a drawing room. Now come, don't keep Rector Harvey waiting."

Oh Lord, yes — the rector. It wasn't in the most welcoming spirit that he stepped into the parlour to greet Richard Harvey, whose drooping eyes and corn-coloured curls he remembered from his sister Mary's wedding.

Just that once, before, he'd met this sour, bearded cherub — and he hadn't liked him much. Back then, the reverend rector had had no time for a younger son; now things were different, and the effort at being courteous to the lord of the manor was plain — if not overly effective.

"Mr. Walsingham, I offer you my condolences," he said, whitish voice pointed. "I would have offered them earlier, but you weren't here yesterday."

As though it had been Tom's fault! "Thank you, Mr. Harvey. I only arrived this morning —"

"In no great haste!" Uncle Buffkin muttered.

"*I arrived this morning* — as soon as I was advised."

"As soon as you could, I'm sure." A nod that was, perhaps, meant to be benign. "I only wish I could have spoken to you earlier — about the bonfires tonight, and the pealings —"

"The pealings!" Tom exclaimed, inwardly cursing Accession Day in a most traitorous manner. "You would have pealings while Scadbury mourns?"

If plums could ripen all at once — that was how Harvey reddened. "Never!" he replied, flustered. "I could not — would not allow it. It's just that not all in the village…" He swallowed the rest, cleared his throat, and seemed to step on an invisible pulpit. "The Queen herself would not wish Her Majesty celebrated so to offend Death and Grief."

Of this, when he thought of the glittering, capricious, formidable lady he'd once met and heard described countless times, Tom wasn't so sure — but, thinking of the years ahead, he met the sentiment with a grave nod, and an assurance that all he expected was that no noise, no games, no marks of celebration should reach Scadbury in any way. "As I'm sure has always been your intention, Mr. Harvey."

This restored the rector's humour. Restored it even a tad too well: he was full of his own opinions as they discussed the funerals — as though Dignity, having retreated in good order enough, were back, reclaiming the honours of war from Caution. They settled for a solemn burial to be held on Saturday, to allow Tom's sisters the time to arrive, and a smaller service in the great hall on the eve. In the end, Richard Harvey announced that he would read a psalm before going, and made for the hall without a by-your-leave, the tails of his coat billowing after him.

What a tiresome fellow!

"Well, you tamed him!" Uncle Buffkin chortled as they lingered in the parlour. "Though I'll say, I'd have been less easy on him. Pealing!"

"You won't have to live with him as a rector for Lord knows how many years," Tom replied glumly.

The old man snorted in a manner that said, *I'd know how to deal with the fellow!*

"That he should even think to come here and ask you!"

"You heard him: *not all in the village…* Not all in the village were so fond of Edmund to give up their good cheer for him."

Another snort. "And you're on a fair way to being just as well-loved, by leaving them without their sport — and their coin. Bell-ringers are paid, aren't they? Mark you, Thomas — I'll turn Turk if we make tomorrow without a jangle."

That he was half-minded to pay the ringers' fee himself, Tom didn't say. "Oh, I doubt it: the Reverend Harvey will redouble his efforts now, if only to show that he can manage the parish."

Having started to scoff, Uncle Buffkin stopped short, frowning, and then the frown became a broad grin. He guffawed loudly. "Why!" he exclaimed, slapping Tom's shoulder with a heavy hand. "Is it your Sir Francis who taught you this trickery? Never think to try it on me, eh, boy?" And so pleased he was with his wit, that he kept chuckling to himself, even when they followed the rector to the hall.

Dinner with one uncle had been a cheerless affair; supper with two was twice as unpleasant — the one consolation being that Mr. Harvey had declined Tom's half-hearted invitation to join them. Still, Tom soon tired of Uncle Buffkin's boisterous ways, and also of George's glumness in the presence of his brother-in-law — which only ever succeeded in greatly amusing the other, and an amused Leven Buffkin always grew all the more irksome for it.

It hardly helped that the night had closed in early, dark and windy, so that every draught in Kent found its way inside the parlour whenever a door was opened, buffeting the flames of the beeswax candles and making the fire hiss. The silver candlesticks, the fine plate with the tiger's head, even Barker's wine-roasted capon, served little in cheering the company.

Uncle Buffkin ate and complained with equal will. "Lukewarm," he grumbled for the third time in a row. "Never you eat a mouthful in this house that is proper warm. Told Edmund just on Martinmas, didn't I, Guildford?" A sigh and a sip of wine. "Less than a week ago, and now see: dragged out of my own home again, to eat lukewarm capon!"

The first two times Tom had bitten his tongue; the third he couldn't help himself. "Inconsiderate of Ned to die so soon," he groused. "Never a thought for the convenience of his elders!"

There was a strangled sound from Uncle George, and a glare from Uncle Buffkin. "Just like his brother, eh?" he grumbled around a mouthful of capon. Then he swallowed and wagged his knife at Tom. "Not that you thought to inconvenience me, mind. My nephew dies, and I must hear of it from the steward!"

Oh, that again… "He summoned you before I even knew, Uncle," Tom ground out — and indeed, why he must…

When George, as he poured himself more wine, muttered of Wood taking liberties, Uncle Buffkin slapped his napkin on the table.

"Am I not a kinsman?" he griped. "And a witness just like Guildford? Nothing more than that, mind — and if you tell me that Ned must have been addled, to make executors two servants over his own kin, on that I won't gainsay you. Why, over his own heir!" His small eyes glinted with malice — and, when Tom only shrugged, he turned on George. "You've told him, you jackdaw?"

Having drunk more than he'd eaten, George was in no mellow mood. "Was I to leave the pleasure to you?" he bit back. "To me, at least, it was no pleasure at all."

Oh, Lord give patience! *Unus … duo … tres…* Tom took a good deep sip of wine and counted in Latin — lest he end up scolding his uncles at the table.

It wasn't long before Uncle Buffkin found his biting merriness again: "You must have done something to miff your brother well and truly, Thomas!"

"Everything I did miffed Ned." Tom frowned at the carved tiger's head as he sopped the wine sauce with a bit of bread.

"You like this plate very much, Thomas?" asked Buffkin.

"Never have. Why?" Tom looked up to find his uncle sneering, all malice again.

"Just as well —"

"Buffkin!" George hit a palm on the table. "And you call *me* a jackdaw?"

Before Tom could ask, the door was thrown open and Skeres entered, carrying a plate of custard tarts with a demure manner that made Tom stare. Even more he stared as the lad began to gather empty plates. Such lip-chewing absorption he put into the task, that there was no catching his gaze. Well now, behold a minor prodigy: the Minotaur waiting at table! They all watched the clumsy work in silence, until Skeres had disappeared with arms so laden that he had no way to close the door after himself.

George huffed with laughter, and Uncle Buffkin exclaimed, "Even that niddicock Foal knows better! What would your mother say, Thomas, that you hire stable-grooms to serve at table?"

Nothing good, no doubt. "That's my man, not a stable-groom. He's never served at table before." Tom wished he'd kept the protestation to himself when the old man burst into an ill-humoured chortle.

"His man!" He turned to George with a manner of surprise to make milk sour. "Edmund was right, eh? The boy's a scattergood: not a penny to his name until yesterday, and yet he has *his man*!" Bracing himself with both hands on the table, he rose heavily, making the chair scrape on the floorboards. "Better men than you go about without *their man*, Thomas. God knows there's no help from your brother. Keep on like this, and you'll sink Scadbury in the moat before a year's gone!"

And, snatching up a tart, Leven Buffkin removed himself from the company of his nephew and glowering brother-in-law.

"Ah, well!" With a sigh Tom sat back in his chair and watched George, who, for all comment, raised both brows without so much as looking up from his cup. How did one explain the Minotaur at all, outside of that world where men went against foreign spies and murderers for a living? Did Tom himself still belong to that world now? And, if he didn't anymore, was he truly going to sink Scadbury in the moat? Not that he lacked his own misgivings on the matter. And this brought back another thought: "What did he mean, about the plate?" he asked.

George's fascination with his claret only increased. "Buffkin's a prattler and a viper," he muttered. "Always has been…"

"Amen. But what of the plate?" Tom found himself short of patience for George's wincing and humming. "Uncle…"

With a portentous huff, George pushed away his tart and glowered at his nephew. "If you must know, Ned has left all his household stuff to Wood and Foal!"

For a few heartbeats Tom gaped down at his plate. No, not his plate: Wood's, or Foal's. How were they going to split it between them? Where would they keep it? Wood had a house, surely, but would the Foals hide away their half of the plate, while Tom and the funeral guests ate out of wood trenchers? Or were the trenchers willed away, too? And what of the pewter? *My most abject apologies that there's no dinner, but I have not a spoon I can call mine.* Propping both elbows on the table, he took his head in his hands and laughed — and let George think he'd gone mad, if he liked!

It was late when Tom entered the hall — dark but for the branch of candles burning on the black-draped dais.

Someone sat huddled on a stool close to the body's head. *Watching* was a superstition for country wives — but, as Tom's old nurse Cicely had used to say, what was the ill of it? It had been done for Tom's grandmother, for the children who had died small, for Guil, for Father, for Cicely herself. When Mother's turn had come, Ned had tried to forbid it, and their sisters had rebelled, backed, more or less quietly, by the servants. Much to Ned's outrage, Tom had sided with the women: a superstition, yes — but what was the ill of it?

Surely it was an irony that now Ned had his own watcher? And that Tom's eyes stung to see that his brother wasn't alone. Calling himself half-hearted names for it, he approached quietly. He was half a dozen steps away when the watcher startled and turned around: Susan Foal. No great surprise, considering — but must the stupid woman stumble to her feet and come to bar Tom's way?

"My brother called watching the dead a Papist mummery," he said in a stern whisper.

Standing to her full height, Susan Foal barely reached Tom's shoulder, and she had to scowl up at him.

"Wasn't he left alone enough?" she seethed, eyes glistening with unshed tears. "If that fool Will had stayed with him…!"

"Not that you were there, either." She flinched so badly at this that Tom felt a twinge of guilt. "But look, Mrs Foal: if his heart was so inflamed, there's nothing you could have done — or young Will, for that matter."

Like Skeres, Susan belonged to the sort that can't whisper. "Soothe him, mayhap!" she growled. "Not shout at him, not let him work himself into a passion!"

There she stood, bristling, hands fisted in her apron — and addled in her head, thinking the scullion would shout back. But no — it was not the scullion she blamed.

"I was sick, Master!" She cupped a hand over her round belly. "Else, you wouldn't have gone near him enough as to make a row!"

This now … this! Tom took a step forward. "What makes you think that I ever needed your leave, Mrs. Foal? Now go back to your watching — and mind a servant's place, while you still are one!"

But, as he strode away, leaving her with the fiercest scowl and both hands splayed across her belly, he had a pretty shrewd idea of just what power this brazen hussy thought she held.

CHAPTER 3

18th of November

Having fallen asleep at first light, Tom awoke later than he'd meant and in an ill temper, with a heavy head full of restless thoughts.

The first, as he washed, was that he'd give the sack at once to that Foal minx and her cuckold husband. The second, right on the tail of it, was that he'd have a house full of guests, come Saturday, and too few servants for it as it was. Retribution would have to wait until after the funeral.

It didn't improve his temper in the least to find the household in a sort of whispering disorder that bode ill for the preparations.

The kitchen at Scadbury was large and inconvenient, built across the yard after the old fashion. At some point it had spread into a low-ceilinged room in the house proper, with its own table, its own fireplace and many cupboards, so there had long been an old kitchen, with the scullery and the bakery, and a small kitchen that served as dining place for the servants.

It was there that Tom broke his fast, with Skeres grumbling at his elbow.

"All wanting to know what's to be done," the Minotaur complained. "Like I should know about funerals!"

Not that Tom knew, either. His sisters would — but they wouldn't arrive for another day or two. For a heartbeat Tom let himself long for Frances and Lady Ursula: they would know what to do; they would take charge, gentle and firm.

"Well, then." Tom shook himself out of his megrims and attacked another manchet, spread with Old Kathryn's honey. Stewards knew about these things, didn't they? And executors. "Where's Wood?"

"Don't live at the 'ouse, says Goody Wollans. 'Asn't come in yet. And *Mrs.* Foal 'as told Goody Wollans to mind 'er dairy, and she's sent Wollans off to the stables. And Mr. Barker's in the pantry, and Mr. Buffkin's off for a walk, and Mr. Guildford's still abed. Oh — and there's folks wanting to see you."

"Folks?" Good Lord, visitors already! Somehow Tom hadn't thought they'd swarm to Scadbury the way they had for Father. Had he been wronging his brother? He swallowed a mouthful of bread and honey and rose, with a sudden sense of being besieged. "What were you waiting to tell me? What have you done with them?"

"Nothing!" protested Skeres. "*Mrs.* Foal put them in that mouldy roomlet just inside. There's a glover — just as well — and some old bumpkin… What's the 'urry? Like as not, they'll be owed money: they've 'eard the new master's 'ere, and they run like flies!"

Tom sighed and went to see the folks that were most likely owed money.

Skeres's *roomlet just inside* wasn't mouldy at all — just rather damp than not. It led from the old guardhouse to the hall and had always resisted all attempts to make it stately. Pressed between a part of the long south porch and the herb garden, it had a door on each side, a chest and two benches. From one of those a man leapt to his feet as soon as Tom entered. He bowed low and rose to reveal himself as a neat fellow with a narrow face and a wooden box pressed to his stomach. The glover, then.

"Mr. Walsingham, Sir — my respects. My condolences," he gasped, clutching the box tighter to his bosom — so tight that one would have thought him struck with grief. "I'm Henry Wood, Sir, from St. Mary. The late Mr. Walsingham's glover. May his soul rest."

And the late Mr. Walsingham owed you… But, even as he braced for the inevitable, Tom's mind laced on a detail. "Thank you, Master. You said your name is *Wood*?"

Tilting his head, the glover gave a guarded smile. "Henry Wood, Sir — your steward's germane cousin. 'Tis through John Wood's good offices that I came to serve your brother, Sir."

Tom eyed the box. "And through your cousin's zeal you've heard already of my brother's death?"

As though someone had touched a string, the man rearranged himself, shaking his head most dolefully. "Ah, Mr. Walsingham — the news has spread." Not that he denied his cousin's hand in it. Instead, he held forward the box, unclasping the lid to show several pairs of leather gloves — all of them black. "And being the glover of the house, and knowing the necessities of a funeral…"

Just as well, as Skeres had said. Though not of great elegance, the gloves were decently made. Tom chose a pair — and, if he thought himself done with Wood's oily cousin, he found himself much mistaken.

"Now, Sir, for the mourners…" the man said, eyes wide in the sort of expectation one saw in children at a fair.

Oh yes: this was one thing to provide — black gloves for the mourners. Tom quickly counted in his head. Uncles, brothers-in-law, cousins, a few friends…

"Don't forget the pall-bearers, Sir," the glover suggested — just as well again, for Tom had not even begun to think of the pall-bearers. In the end, he found himself ordering a dozen pairs, to the glover's moderate satisfaction. And this was only the beginning, for the gloves had put him in mind of the black gowns. Perhaps the steward would prove to also have a tailor cousin? Or perhaps that was the other visitor — the one who was nowhere to be seen?

When questioned, the glover tightened his mouth in prim disapproval: it made him look very much like his cousin.

"He went inside, Sir — to pay his respects, he said. Which I would also do, please you, Sir — but never without your consent."

This consent given, Tom went to the hall to find Skeres's old bumpkin standing by the dais, head bowed and cap between the hands he kept clasped before him.

He turned around at the sound of footsteps and limped to meet Tom, revealing himself for a gnarled fellow, grey of hair and clad in what must be his Sunday best of brown kersey. As he came close, the grey light from the windows of leaded glass showed that man and suit had seen better days: the doublet was worn to a sheen at the elbows, and the keen-eyed, lined face had the sallowness that illness brought to sun-browned skin. Most definitely not a tailor.

"You be Mr. Walsingham?" he asked in a deep rumble, studying Tom from head to foot. "The new one?"

"I'm Thomas Walsingham, yes," said Tom.

The old fellow gave a small sigh. "Ye be much like yer brother."

It was something that few said. Edmund had been taller and a good deal softer, not having spent half his life on horseback

— though they both had their mother's Guildford colouring of light hair and blue eyes.

To see him, this man didn't find much consolation in the likeness. With another, deeper sigh, he squared himself. "My name's Robert Mace." He paused and braced for recognition — and not of the best sort. When Tom only raised his brows, he forged ahead. "Mace from North Cray, Yer Honour, as owed four-and-thirty pounds to yer brother … to ye now, come Lady Day."

Not a procession of creditors then, was Tom's first relieved thought. The second was less pleasant: all the time he'd withheld his annuity, Edmund had been loaning out money? "I see," he said — but the old man shook his head.

"'Twas forty-four pounds, Yer Honour."

Better and better! "Yes — but —"

"I repaid what I could — five pounds at Midsummer, and five more at Michaelmas, for all that the harvest was bad, but then my wife sickened and died, Yer Honour, and the rains have rotted my stored grain…"

So this was where Old Mace was heading. Tom held up a hand.

"I'm sorry about your wife, Goodman —"

"Yer Honour!" One gnarled hand grabbed Tom's sleeve. "I ha'an't four-and-thirty pounds, and won't have 'em by Lady Day. Yer brother wouldn't listen, wouldn't see me…"

The same brother that lay in his shroud, not a dozen steps away.

"Come with me," Tom ordered.

There was a room, looking over the north arm of the moat, just by the Great Stairs — a chapel once, it had long been the steward's counting-room. With its big writing table, and all the chests and cupboards where the papers were held, it seemed a better place to conduct this sort of talk. Judging by how he halted just inside the door with red-rimmed eyes afire and mouth working, Mace must not have had good memories of the place.

"Not even see me, he would," he repeated with a shake of his grey head. "But there's not a soul as won't say Mr. Edmund's brother is made different."

And didn't all these helpful souls also say that Mr. Edmund's brother could likely do with four-and-thirty pounds, come Lady Day? How many more of these loans had Ned made? How many more debtors would flock to Scadbury now, with their woes of sick wives and bad harvests? Tom leant back against the table.

"Goodman Mace, truly, I know nothing of my brother's ways and means — and I won't know until I've read the will and seen the books. This will have to wait."

Mace set his mouth into a hard line. "All I ask for is a word, Yer Honour. A word as I won't be out of house and land by Lady Day."

Had this been Edmund's game — waiting to seize the insolvent Mace's land? *Lord, Ned…* "All I can promise —" Tom stopped short as he pictured Uncle Buffkin at dinner, bright-eyed with malice. *God knows there's no help from your brother…* It had not been about the plate, had it? So sudden, so ominous was the revelation, and such a fool he was that he blurted out, "I don't even know that I'll inherit your debt!"

Small wonder that the old man should gape, face darkening. "Just like yer brother!" he rumbled. "'Tis only a bit of land to ye — but I've worked it all my life, and my dad before me, and my granddad. I ha'an't nowhere to go if —"

Oh, Jove! "Goodman Mace!" Tom straightened. "I'm not after taking your land — but you must come to me again after I've seen the will. More than that, I can't say for now."

And perhaps, in this worn yeoman's place, he, too, would have narrowed his eyes in bitter distrust, and muttered, "Ay, Mr. Walsingham," through gritted teeth, and squashed his cap on his head, and limped away.

In his own place, Tom very much wished he could see both the ledgers and the will.

He considered the room, the shelves, the chests and cupboards. Surely the books would be kept there, but well locked. Unlikely as it was that the key were there, Tom inspected the table. The top only showed an old inkwell and three pens in a copper pot. The single drawer had no lock, and was filled with odds and ends: a penknife, tally-sticks, balls of string, bits of wax, a broken piece of wooden moulding, all a-jumble in a way Tom wouldn't have expected of Wood. Half a dozen bills had been pushed to the back of the drawer: a saddler from Dartford, the local blacksmith, a tailor three times — all of them from the last couple of months. The oldest ones were pinned together, the more recent just thrust there. If this was any hint of the general state of the Scadbury accounts…

Tom closed the drawer and quelled a fleeting thought of Skeres's lock-picking skills. He was the master here, by God — entitled to see everything he wanted. Everything but the will, for now — but there were those who knew what the will said. He needed George or, even better, Uncle Buffkin — who had no qualms about dispensing ill tidings. And he needed Wood, for the keys and the books.

He set off at once on this quest for knowledge, only to pause in the passage that ran along the hall when, through a window, he caught sight of… Was that Mace's brown-clad figure in the kitchen yard? Tom squinted through the uneven glass: who was arguing with the old man? By the time he reached the door to the yard, Mace was limping away angrily towards the causeway across the moat, and Susan Foal stood by the kitchen door, fists on hips like a pudgy Victory. She turned around when he called to her.

"Was that Old Mace?" he asked. "What did he want?"

The housekeeper shrugged. "To pester ye, but I sent him a-running, I did! And, Master…" Had nobody ever taught this churless not to shout across yards? "There be ladies as wait for ye in the parlour!"

Lord — but Tom's mother would have thrown this one in the moat! "Thank you for advising me so promptly, Mrs. Foal!" he groused, and off he hurried.

One lady turned away from the fireplace as Tom entered the parlour. She was tall and handsome-faced, and wore a very fine riding costume of sage-green velvet. Tom wasn't sure he knew her. She swept forward with a manner that spoke of life at Court.

"You won't remember me, Mr. Walsingham," she said. "I'm sure I don't remember you at all — though I know we've met. I'm Lady Grace Wildgoose, Sir Brian Annesley's daughter."

"Lady Wildgoose," Tom greeted, as they exchanged a bow and a curtsey. The Annesleys were good acquaintances, if not quite friends. Beside a few hunts, Tom had crossed paths with Sir Brian at Court. He must have met the daughters, too — for there was more than one, wasn't there? The other visitor, attired in a darker green, must be another. She had fair hair under a small beaver hat, a pointed chin, and measuring grey eyes. Eyes that Tom had seen before — but that could never be…?

"And I believe you know my god-sister, Mistress Etheldreda Shelton?" said Lady Wildgoose.

Well, now! "Mistress Shelton and I have met, yes." Tom bowed to the woman who had once been the unmoved object of Edmund's courtship. What on earth was she doing here?

As though she'd read his thoughts, her lips curled in a half smile. "I'm visiting with Lady Wildgoose at Annesley house, Mr. Walsingham, and we heard of your brother's death. I hope you don't find me importunate to have joined my friend in her visit of condolences?"

"Of course he doesn't, Audrey!" Lady Wildgoose said with placid amusement, before Tom could find a word to say. "And, Mr. Walsingham, I bring my father's condolences as well. He's in London, and…" She spread her gloved hands. "Here I am in his stead."

Tom bowed again and thanked both ladies, and had them sit at the table, where someone — Kathryn, most likely — had had the wit to bring sweetmeats and wine. Tom asked about Sir Brian's health, and answered Grace Wildgoose's enquiries about Barbara — and all the time he wondered. It was … what? Near on three years since Ned had briefly sought the hand of Sir Ralph Shelton's daughter. Nothing had come of it, and the young lady herself had never troubled to hide her dislike of the match. So what brought her here now? Surely not regret. Why, the arch-browed way she studied Tom and the whole parlour was that of one thanking the Fates that she wasn't now the widowed Mrs. Etheldreda Walsingham.

Well, Tom too was thankful — that she hadn't married Ned and given him a son. Etheldreda — what a name for a girl! But then they called her something else, didn't they? Lady Wildgoose had just said it: Audrey. *Audrey Walsingham*, now, would have sounded rather better —

"…can be expected?"

Blinking out of his absorption, Tom found that he'd been staring at Audrey, and had no idea what Grace Wildgoose had asked.

"Er…" he said — such eloquence — and amusement gleamed again in Lady Wildgoose's dark eyes.

It was Audrey herself who came to the rescue. "How can he have a date for the funeral, Grace?" she chided — just a little too demure, a little too sweet. "He must wait until his sisters are here, at least, and you know how the roads are at this time of the year."

In fact Tom did have a date, thanks to Rector Harvey, and for a while they conversed of funerals, and of the roads, and of the weather, and of how sorry the ladies were not to meet Barbara and Mary, and of the excellence of Barker's sweetmeats — until, for a blessing, Lady Wildgoose decided that the visit had lasted long enough. They spent a dutiful while before the dais in the hall — and it was with considerable relief that Tom escorted the two visitors across the bridge and to the stable yard.

If nothing else, all the chatter about funerals had put Tom in mind of something else to worry about. So, when he ran into Foal a-wander in the kitchen passage, it was him whom he asked: had a plumber been summoned?

Round-eyed and gawping, Foal looked one way and the other, as though a plumber might have been stashed in some dark corner. "A … plumber?" he stuttered.

Lord — but how had Ned put up with such a dullard? "Yes, Foal, the plumber. The sort that makes lead coffins. Has Mr. Wood sent for him?"

Not that lead coffins were an everyday thing — but surely a house servant must know about them? Not Foal, apparently, who only shrugged his shoulders. "Mr. Wood has yet to arrive, Master."

And just where the steward spent his days, instead of being there to take care of things, Tom would have liked to know. Still, it was hardly Foal's fault. Swallowing his irritation, Tom said he'd speak to Mrs. Foal, then — and that caused more offence: Foal led the way, all the time quivering, all the time wheezing, and now and then peeking at Tom over a fat shoulder. Did he expect the new master to look on Fair Susan as another piece of his inheritance?

Try as Tom might, it was hard to be fair to the fellow — or to the fellow's wife. From a distance he could hear Susan Foal berating someone, most likely the scullion, about the water being just out o' the cold. They came upon her in the small kitchen, fussing with the plate in the cupboard — no doubt regarding it as her own already.

"Not even good at heating water!" she griped, as young Will slunk away carrying a full pail, and then, observing that her husband wasn't alone, she dropped one of those scowling curtsies Tom was already heartily tired of.

Just as her husband had, she grew flustered when asked about the plumber, as though she'd never heard of such a thing before.

"He was called for my mother," Tom insisted, "and for my father before her."

"'Tis that back then…" Foal tried, only to whither in silence under his wife's scowl. Back then, neither of them had been at Scadbury, in fair truth — but never let it be said that Susan Foal sought easy excuses.

She sniffed instead, and tried for an air that said, *Why do you bother me with these things?* "Mr. Wood will know, Master —"

"But Mr. Wood isn't here," Tom cut in. "There must be a record in the accounts — if you'll show me where the books are."

Something passed across Susan Foal's face that Tom couldn't quite read, and she pulled her mouth tight. Had the books been kept from her — by Wood? By Ned himself? And then Old Kathryn bustled in from the yard, red-faced and short-winded.

"'Tis the plumber as you want, Master?" she asked, drying her hands on a rag. "There's one as came out of Greenwich for your mam. Wollans knows, for he was sent to fetch him back then — and for old Sir Thomas, too."

Good Old Kathryn. Behind her, it was worth noting, Barker stood placidly on the threshold. Tom swallowed a smile.

"I should have known to ask you, Kathryn," he said. "Fetch Wollans, will you? He'll have to give directions to Skeres." He turned to the Foals to order that Skeres be fetched. Robert Foal scurried out, worrying at his beard with thick fingers; Susan, thin-lipped with fury, only dithered long enough to glower at Barker before flouncing away on her husband's heels.

A hornets' nest indeed…

When the cook retreated to the old kitchen, Tom followed him. The old kitchen was larger, smokier, darker with soot, with small windows, copper hanging off the walls, and the scullery tucked in the far corner, past the immense fireplace. Strings of onions, dried apples, garlic and mushrooms hung from the rafters, together with a bacon and a net full of walnuts — and for a while, Barker busied himself detaching three plaited strings of last summer's onions from there. He brought them to the huge table and began to sort them into two piles. He didn't even try to pretend reluctance before he began his tale.

"When poor Mrs. Turley took ill, we all thought Goody Wollans would become housekeeper — what with all the years she and her husband had been here." He held up one small onion and turned it this way and that.

"All but my brother, I take it?" Tom prodded.

With a hum, Barker laid the onion in one of the piles — by no difference that Tom could tell. "Susan Foal was a maid, and not a good one at that. Her Ladyship would never have put up with her. Ah, well, things changed afterwards and, what with the girl's husband being Mr. Edmund's *valet*…" Another onion was picked up and scrutinised.

"Or the other way around."

Barker chuckled low in his throat, more seraphical than ever. "The Wollanses didn't like it, not a bit, and they weren't always prudent in their speech. Not that I blame them, and work would be easier with a housekeeper knowing her way. But Mr. Edmund was a young man, and Susan Foal… If not much else, she knows how to blow on the fire." A click of the tongue, and the onion followed its fellow.

Did the cook think he was being prudent in his speech with the new master? He was still humming at the onions when Will came in carrying two large buckets, and all but dropped them by the fireplace. He looked around like a startled hare and, at no worse than a rumble from Barker, scuttled away. Tom waited for the lad to be gone and then picked up an onion of his own — smallish and hard through the layers of yellowed, translucent skin, just like all the others.

"So she got the keys, and my brother's bed — though not in that order," he not quite asked. "What of Foal, though?"

"Ah, Foal..." Barker took the onion from Tom and unhesitatingly put it on top of the largest pile. "Foal fancies himself a butler, some day — another notion the Wollanses don't like."

And, since there was no butler at Scadbury, and Barker himself was the closest thing to one, Tom rather thought that the Wollanses weren't alone in their dislike. Before he could voice the thought, there came a sound of whistling, the door was thrown open, and a cheerful Skeres barged in, bellowing, "Where's it that you send me, Master?"

"Where you won't be whistling within feet of my brother lying in state," Tom groused without much heat. One full day, and Skeres was already raring to be gone from Scadbury. "Anything to avoid serving at table again, eh?"

If there was one thing Skeres was quick at, it was seeing when he wasn't truly in trouble; he did quieten and listened demurely enough to his instructions, and yet nobody would have called him chastened. What Barker would make of the Minotaur, Tom decided not to wonder.

To see his sprightly step, one would have thought Skeres on a quest for the Golden Fleece. He was already out in the yard when he called back, "Oh — and Master: Goody Wollans says there's folks to see you, and one of the ladies ain't gone away."

"What do you mean, one of the ladies...?" Tom gave chase, but Skeres was gone. Ah, well: he'd find out — and he had half a suspicion already.

As Skeres had put it, there were folks waiting in the hall — three or four well-dressed men Tom knew for local gentlemen, and two ladies. One of them was simpering, unmarried Bess Poyntell, there with her lackwit of a brother; the other was Mistress Shelton. She waited while Tom waded through the commonplace of mourning with the visitors, but slipped into the parlour as soon as Bess Poyntell began to drone about insipid childhood memories of Edmund.

By the time Tom had extricated himself and followed, she had installed herself on the seat under the great window, gloves and horsewhip discarded on the table in the manner of one in no hurry to depart.

"I sent Grace home with her groom," she announced. "You'll lend me someone to escort me back to Lee later, I'm sure?"

As though he had people to spare, with even most of the farmhands away, carrying messages to kinsfolk! "Mistress…"

"It is most kind of you." She settled more comfortably, spreading her skirts on the settle. "Grace has a husband, and children, and a house. She says she envies me the freedom of waiting for your dear sister — not that I believe her very much."

Then again, Tom didn't much believe Mistress Shelton. "I didn't know that you and Mary are such good friends," he said, and wasn't half surprised when she shook her head.

"I never met her," she said — the gall of her! — and leant forward with a little frown. "But, even to Grace, I could hardly say that I must speak to you alone."

"To me — alone?" Tom very much wished he'd found something cleverer to say.

He couldn't have blamed Audrey if she'd shown impatience, but she only knit her brows tighter — she had dark brows, in spite of her fair colouring — and nodded. "It's quite a serious matter. I hope I'm not wrong in telling you." Her light, keen eyes studied a speechless Tom for a long moment. "This morning, a constable came to Annesley, asking for Sir Brian."

Of all the things Tom could have expected from such an outlandish beginning, this had to be the very last. "A constable," he repeated, and there went a little flare of impatience.

"Yes, Mr. Walsingham — a constable," Audrey explained, with the forceful slowness one used for the half-witted. "The Chislehurst constable, seeking the Justice of the Peace."

Because Annesley had become magistrate after the death of Tom's father, hadn't he, in spite of spending most of his time in London. "And he didn't find him."

"Indeed. Grace and her husband were busy, so I spoke to the man. He was very put out that Sir Brian was not there, for he truly had need of a magistrate. I asked him what of Mr. Walsingham at Scadbury, and he said that he was no justice, and was dead, anyway. I was much surprised. The day before yesterday, the constable explained. *In fact…*" She held up a forefinger, and slowed her speech. "That's what he said: *in fact* — and then he went crimson and bit his tongue. 'In fact, that's why you need a magistrate?' I asked, and he looked down, and shuffled his feet, and would say nothing."

Tom shook his head. "What has he taken into his head?"

And, as though it were the plainest thing in the world, Audrey said, "That your brother was murdered."

A sudden chill ran down Tom's spine. Edmund — murdered. But then… "Baggage!" he exclaimed. "He was ill, he had some sort of seizure — and fell down the stairs. Why would the constable think…"

"Someone must have whispered to him. More than whispered." Audrey lowered her voice. "He had a piece of paper that he turned and turned in his hands. The moment he heard that Sir Brian was in London, he thrust it into his sleeve and never mentioned it."

"And this made you think that someone made away with my brother?"

"No, just that something made the constable think it." She rose impatiently. "Your brother dies, and two days later the man is seeking a justice about it… Also, he has a paper — *and*, you will observe, he didn't run to you with this."

Surely there should be something shrewd to say to this, rather than gaping and protesting, "To *me*?" Because surely, if there were doubts…

Mistress Shelton's whisper took a more pointed edge. "I asked him, wasn't Mr. Edmund's brother at Scadbury? And all I had was more looking away, and a hasty retreat." She tilted her head, brows raised in question, as if to ask, *What must one think?*

What indeed! A laugh bubbled in Tom's throat. This was past ridiculous. Walsingham's wolfhound, chasing murderers these past ten years — and now…

"You think that *I* made away with Edmund?" he exclaimed, sounding a little wild to his own ears.

"Hush!" She slapped his wrist, glaring most severely. "Would I be here telling you, if I did?"

A consolation, in its own unexpected way — and yet… "This begs the question, though, of why you *are* telling me." When the grey eyes widened in disbelief, Tom hastened on: "Forgive me, Mistress Shelton, I have no wish to appear ungrateful — but…"

Up to this moment, she had appeared very collected, but the tiniest toss of her head made her younger of a sudden. How old was she? Younger than Frances — not much more than twenty.

"You do appear ungrateful," she retorted. "And if you must know, it was that note — the one the constable had. He was so furtive about it, it *had* to be an anonymous note."

"You can't know that," Tom protested — and the illogical creature raised her chin.

"Had you been there, you'd agree with me," she said. "And there is little in this world that I despise more than sycophants and tale-bearers."

"Very upright of you, I'm sure. But because you didn't like the way a man handled a piece of paper, you have decided that my brother was murdered and I'm under suspicion — and a slandered innocent at that?"

It was quite possible that Audrey was reconsidering her decision. "Of course not," she said, with a sigh of exaggerated patience. "Well, I couldn't know at that moment. I didn't know that your brother was much ill — but your constable seemed so dim-witted and uneasy. Still, I had to make sure before committing to a course of action."

"Make sure of what?"

"Of you, Mr. Walsingham!" she said, as though nothing could be more obvious. "It was hard to tell, after only exchanging a dozen words with you three years ago, so I let Grace persuade herself that we should pay your sisters a visit."

"And what does Lady Wildgoose think of it?"

"I haven't told her yet. Her father is a Justice of the Peace; she would be bound to tell him — and fond as I am of Sir Brian…" She pursed her mouth delicately. "He does leap to conclusions."

It was more than Tom could help: he laughed, earning a very displeased frown — but truly… "And now you let your friend ride home still unenlightened. I take it you've reasoned I'm no fratricide?"

"I have — and let me tell you, I'm an excellent judge of character."

"Why then, I thank you, Mistress."

"But —" she held up a forefinger — "this will be no help to you when your constable goes to another magistrate with his worries — and his letter."

Because he would, of course. Tom shook his head and leant against the wainscoting, arms crossed. "It still seems very fantastical to me. My brother died of an inflamed heart." Or did he? A man could suffer from an inflamed heart *and* be pushed down the stairs. "And even if he didn't, I don't see why I should be suspected in particular: I wasn't even here that night!"

"Well, this is very good!" Audrey leapt to her feet, clapping her hands together. "Why didn't you say so at once?" Not that she left him time to answer. "And where were you instead?"

Again Tom laughed in disbelief. "This is ridiculous —"

"In London with friends, I hope," she cut in severely. "Friends who will vouch for you."

Oh, Jove — this woman! "If you must know, I was on the road, on my way to Chatham."

"In some inn, then. Well, it's good enough. Someone must remember you there, surely?"

"You should be a justice, Mistress!" And yet, for the first time since the beginning of this silly conversation, unease curled a small tendril inside Tom's mind. "In truth… There was a very bad storm that night. I got myself caught in it, lamed my horse on Dartford Heath, and spent the better part of the night in a collier's hut…"

"And no collier around!" Audrey threw up a hand. "So nobody can vouch that you were anywhere else but here?"

"But why would I be here, for God's sake? I'd just visited my brother —"

"And argued with him."

Good Lord — had the constable known that too? Small wonder, then, that he should think… And look at him: a seasoned Service man, gaping in stunned silence for this little shrew to read like a book! See how she watched him, one black eyebrow raised.

"Your Goodwife Wollans," she said, "seems to think, as you do, that you having just been here must mean you didn't come back."

Having taken breath to protest, Tom snapped his mouth shut at the absurdity of the notion — but on the heels of this thought came annoyance at Audrey gossiping with Old Kathryn, and that shook him out of his bewilderment.

"And you haven't been here two hours, Mistress!" he groused. "But, let me be blunt, aren't you being a tad fanciful?" He held up a restraining hand before she protested. "What have you seen, after all? The local constable seeking Sir Brian, and fiddling with a piece of paper — and on that you've built a castle-come-down… Why, no: you've built a scaffold for me!"

For a minor marvel, Audrey coloured a little — but recovered at once. With a little sniff, she lifted her chin and straightened her shoulders. "Very well, then, Mr. Walsingham," she said, voice clipped in its sudden coldness. "I'm sure that you are right, and I am wrong and fanciful — and no one is trying to throw any blame on you. Or at least I hope so. For your sake, more than for mine. I gave you what warning I had to give, so my conscience must be at ease."

She went to the table and gathered her gloves and horsewhip with such an air of unappreciated virtue, that Tom felt like the worst, most thankless cad in Christendom.

"Mistress," he pleaded, "I'm grateful —" He stopped short when she turned to him, in the act of slipping on a glove.

"I'm sure you are," she said, in purse-mouthed stiffness. "Now, if you could spare a groom to escort me back to Lee..."

The most thankless cad, indeed.

As it happened, there were no grooms to spare. There were no grooms at all, in truth — but this Tom wasn't going to admit — and Skeres was on his way to Greenwich, while Everest had been sent to the village on an errand, and Wollans himself was in the stables, seeing to the coming and going of visitors.

There was, on the other hand, a small, long-faced man waiting in the courtyard. He hopped up to Tom and Audrey.

"Percival Eliot, Your Honour." He bowed twitchily, uncovering long fore-teeth in a grimace that might have been either a smile or pained sympathy. A rabbit if ever there was one. "From Orpington. Mr. Walsingham's tailor — Mr. Edmund, that is. That was."

Jove, what tailor named his son Percival? At least, he didn't seem to be another cousin of Wood's.

He blinked up in the most mournful manner. "Your Honour's brother, God keep his soul, I've served him these past three years. And, in fact..." He started to rummage in the satchel he carried, and Tom's heart sank. Oh yes — the bills in the steward's drawer.

"I would have expected, Master Eliot," he said, trying for severity, "that you'd wait at least until after the funeral before running to claim your dues — whatever they may be."

By the long-suffering glance the tailor darted up from his bag, one wouldn't think the man had much trust to spare for the Walsinghams.

"Ay, Your Honour — and I'm right ashamed of myself," he said, not looking ashamed at all as he kept rummaging. "It's just... Lord bless me, where have I put them, now?"

And that was when Audrey, having observed the proceedings with some amusement, swept in with the assuredness of a woman twice her age.

"But no, Mr. Walsingham," she said. "I think that you mistake poor Master Eliot's intent. I'm sure he has come about the mourning gowns — haven't you, Master?"

Poor Master Eliot's chin — what little he had of it — dropped, and the man stared, hand gone still inside the bag. And, having silenced the tailor to perfection, Audrey turned on Tom. Sir Francis himself would have applauded the way she couched an order in the shape of a question: "You do need to order the mourning gowns, surely?"

"I've ordered black gloves enough for a regiment of pike," Tom tried feebly — and the brisk tilt of Audrey's head (it made the feather on her hat dance) had his mind conjure up black-clad processions: his father's, with half a dozen pall-bearers, his mother's, his brother Guil's… He was the head of the family now. He couldn't send Ned to his eternal rest with the mourners in no better than black gloves. Besides, even had he been minded that way, there were surely provisions in the will. "Yes — yes, I do need gowns, Mistress." And bless her meddling ways! In fact, if there were provisions… "I'd think an order must have been made already, Master Eliot?"

Poor rabbit, half-poised for flight — and caught again! He shook his head. "Oh no, Your Honour, no — not at all. No order, no. In fact, that's why…" He cleared his throat and fell silent.

That was why he'd rushed to collect his money, and small blame to him — but what of the provisions in the will, then?

Leading Audrey and the tailor inside, Tom would have left them in the passage room, had she not stopped him. "Where are you running?" she hissed.

"I need more gowns than I could ever wish — but you'll forgive me if I won't have them made twice." And, leaving her to discuss cloth and cuts with the rabbit, he went hunting.

CHAPTER 4

A returned Uncle Buffkin had joined the very persistent Poyntells by the hall fireplace, and only heeded Tom's beckoning with a great deal of winking and chortling.

"That Poyntell's minded to foist his sister on you, Thomas," he said as soon as they were ensconced in the passage — loud enough for all the hundred to hear. "You're a good catch now, boy! Or so they think, eh?"

Ignoring the malicious needling, Tom shushed the old man and asked about Edmund's provisions for the mourning gowns.

"Provisions?" Uncle Buffkin mused, pulling at his earlobe and chewing his moustache. "Why, he made none. I laughed about it with Guildford. Ned's either more tight-fisted or less ill than I thought, I said, that he shouldn't leave an eel of cloth for mourning blacks."

Very unusual, yes — though it seemed that quite a few things were unusual in Edmund's will. Unless… "Perhaps he left separate dispositions with his executors?" mused Tom — and earned a harrumph from his uncle.

"With all they'll get, they might well go to the trouble!" he grumbled — and that was the other side of enough.

The thought of the visitors in the hall alone kept Tom from snapping. "We haven't been here a day, Uncle, and you've shot half a dozen of these arrows. There's worse than the plate, isn't there?"

And didn't the man have the cheek to bristle? "Guildford told you, didn't he? Blathering fool!"

"He told me about the plate, after you'd thrown a hint like a church door in my face. And now you're at it again, so I ask: what's with Wood and Foal in the will?"

See how Leven Buffkin huffed, looked away, and sucked his teeth, like a man forced into some dishonourable act against his will.

"I shouldn't say, Thomas — you know I shouldn't," he muttered.

Crossing his arms, Tom waited. Didn't venomous hints count as saying? Perhaps they didn't to Uncle Buffkin's conscience: when at last he spoke, he had an air almost of guilt.

"Did you know that Ned had made some loans?"

There — there! All of Tom's misgivings flared up. "I met one of his debtors just this morning, come to beg for more time."

It wasn't even much of a surprise when the old man hummed and said, "He's come to the wrong man, then. All in all, there's some hundred and fifty pounds, next Lady Day. Most of it goes to Wood and some to Foal, and the rest to pay Ned's debts."

A hundred and fifty… Tom's mouth went dry of a sudden. A hundred and fifty pounds out on loan, and he wouldn't see a farthing of it! There was a narrow bench in the passage; Tom sank onto it, took his head in his hands, and laughed bitterly. A hundred and fifty pounds — enough to pay his own debts twice over! Well, not truly — but still…

Uncle Buffkin had inched closer. "See? I shouldn't have said. Are you that down at the heel, Thomas?"

At once Tom regretted his outburst: even in childhood, showing weakness to this particular kinsman had never been wise.

"Down at the heel!" He huffed, with all the unconcern he could manage. "It's just, to see a hundred and fifty pounds go like this..." He pushed to his feet. "And still I don't know about the mourning blacks. Has Wood come in, do you know?" The old man's hesitation brought up another cheerless laugh. "Never fear, Uncle — I won't throttle the man. It's Ned I should have done in before he made that cursed will —" His voice died in his throat. Ned murdered — and he himself under suspicion... Oh, baggage! "Where do I find him?"

John Wood was to be found in the counting-room, sorting through some papers with all the appearance of a model steward. He rose at the sight of Tom, in unhurried respectfulness.

"You've been asking for me, Mr. Walsingham? I've been seeing the tenants; I told them that the heir has arrived..."

The too-patient manner would have set Tom's teeth on edge even in the best of humours. As it was, he studied for a heartbeat the man his brother had gifted with a hundred pounds — the chiselled features, the gleaming chestnut hair, the straight-backed carriage — and then questioned him about the mourning blacks.

Wood thought carefully, eyes moving as though he were re-reading the will in his head. "Mr. Edmund made no provisions," he said at the end.

"You are his executor, Mr. Wood. Didn't he leave dispositions with you?"

"He never mentioned the matter to me. It seemed somewhat strange, I'll own — but it wasn't my place to make suggestions."

No, just to make him leave you a fat little fortune. "Could he have left word with Foal?"

"With Foal?" Wood raised a brow. "I very much doubt it," he said — and, when he thought of the wheezing, squeaking fellow, so did Tom.

"Go on, then, Mr. Wood," he said — and when the steward bowed and sat back down to his work, it was with a most irksome manner, that of a man returning to grave occupations after some childish interruption.

Well, Tom gloomily considered, he could as well put the tailor to work, if he hadn't run. With any luck, what remained after Wood and Foal got their part on Lady Day would be enough for the mourning gowns … as long as Mace found his four-and-thirty pounds. It was with the bleakest thoughts of unpaid tailors and ruined old farmers that he made his way back to the passage room.

About one thing he shouldn't have worried: cornered by two women, Percival Eliot hadn't managed to bolt, poor rabbit. Two — because Old Kathryn had joined the congress with a will and was counting on her fingers the black gowns in the clothes-presses upstairs — one of Guil's, Ned's own, two of Father's — all of them fine broadcloth.

Audrey clapped her hands. "Excellent! Those you'll have to alter and no more, Master Eliot. A new lining, perhaps…"

"If there be no moths…" the tailor hazarded, only to be silenced by an offended Kathryn.

"Moths!" she exclaimed. "I've minded the woodworm myself these past two years, seeing as others didn't know to do it."

"Would you fetch the gowns then, Goodwife Wollans? So Master Eliot can begin his work at once…" Audrey smiled at Kathryn, who beamed back as though she'd known her since a child.

When she caught sight of the returned Tom, her gap-toothed smile grew larger. "Why, Mr. Thomas! Mistress Shelton has it all sorted!" She stopped by him as she went, nudging an elbow in his ribs and lowering her voice to whisper, "Now, there's a girl with a head on her shoulders!"

And look at her, the girl with a head on her shoulders, giving orders to the overwhelmed tailor, as though she'd haunted Scadbury her whole life. Who would have said, to see her, that she'd arrived that very morning, with warnings of murder most foul and dire suspicion?

Because the Poyntells showed no inclination to depart, and because, even though Everest and one of the farmhands had reappeared, Audrey pronounced herself minded to see Eliot set to work, they had a dismal dinner that, if nothing else, proved it took more than three unexpected guests to discompose Barker.

It also proved that Uncle Buffkin wasn't wrong in his reckoning of the Poyntells and their intents, judging by how Bess kept chirruping about the many happy times she'd spent at Scadbury, and reaching out now and then to pat Tom's arm. Audrey, it was worth noting, ate with excellent appetite and kept her gaze carefully lowered to her plate, mouth quivering at the corners, while Bess's brother pretended to discuss the newish law on the building of cottages with Uncle Buffkin. George sat sideways, despondent and heavy-eyed, eating little and talking even less.

Lord — but if this was a taste of the entertainment of guests at Scadbury…!

At least, having no good excuse left to linger, the Poyntells took their leave soon afterwards. Audrey Shelton, having fetched the tailor from the kitchen, had him fit the gown for

Uncle Buffkin. When he heard her whisper to Eliot that there was no need to tell Mr. Buffkin that the gown had belonged to old Sir Thomas, Tom could have kissed her brow.

As for himself, he caught Uncle George in the act of slinking away, poor George, and suggested they take some air.

The walled garden, just off the island, was the pleasantest place in spring, and a plentiful Eden in summer, and it was made to cling long to its autumn graces of medlars, late roses and hollyhocks. Late in November, however, it was as bleak a spot as one could imagine.

Bare were the trees of peaches and apricots that lined the walls, and the creeping roses dangled a few withered leaves in the breeze. Cabbages, leeks, and the rosemary bush in the corner alone still proclaimed themselves alive. The paths, their gravel so white once, were overgrown with grass and choked with dead leaves. "Mother would have a fit to see…" Tom looked up to find that George had wandered to the south wall, where he stood by the pear tree.

"There used to be half a dozen of these," he said without turning, voice raised just enough for Tom to hear from a dozen steps away. "You'd climb up them, and drop down the pears for Mary to catch."

"Too green, more often than not!" Tom shook his head at the small boy he'd been. "The canings I got for it — and the pears ruined anyway! Still, let high summer come, and I would do it again." Once, a visiting Sir Francis had assisted to one of those punishments. How the boy Tom had striven not to cry!

George turned around, bloodshot eyes gleaming like glass in the grey light. "I never gave you away, you know, Tom. Not even once."

And I was caught all the same. "Uncle, I've been thinking…" Tom hesitated. He didn't believe Audrey Shelton's fanciful notions, surely? But still… "The surgeon was here the other day, was he?"

George went back to contemplating the pear tree. "Wood sent for him at once." He hitched up a shoulder. "By the time he arrived, I'd had Ned carried to his bed — not that it made any odds."

To hear him, one would think the ten miles or so to Greenwich were the surgeon's fault. "And what did he have to say?"

"Say?"

"*Say*, Uncle." There were times when Tom understood his late mother's lack of patience with her brother. "What did he say had killed Ned?"

Had he been asked for the Hesperides's golden apples, George's face couldn't have creased in greater perplexity. "Why, what was there to say? He blathered of the heart, of the humours — you know his sort."

"And the fall?"

"He'd cracked his skull. It took no surgeon to tell that. Why?"

Because a certain lady I've met twice in my life has all sorts of conceits. Skeres was right: spend too much time 'unting murtherers, and a few words were enough to make one see what wasn't there. Tom shivered in the stiffening wind. "For no great reason, truly. Come, Uncle, let's go back. That rabbit of a tailor will be waiting for you."

And see how George's faded eyes lit up at the prospect, pleased at having a new mourning gown — that wasn't even new.

They left the sad garden side by side, crossing the outer yard towards the bridge, under the swelling, darkening clouds. Percival Eliot wasn't going to have much more daylight to work by. When the rain began all at once, harsh and cold, Tom broke into a run, making for the bridge, George windless and cursing at his elbow. Every crackle of gravel under their steps sounded like mocking laughter — at Audrey Shelton's fancies and at Tom's own.

Not long after the rain had started, Skeres made his reappearance, drenched to the marrow, huffing and dripping water all over the passage room, to Susan Foal's noisy dismay. Tom swallowed a smile when Old Kathryn serenely took charge, by sending Skeres to the small kitchen and explaining to Fair Susan that God had made floors to get wet and be dried.

"Cheery as an adder, is Mrs. Foal," the Minotaur announced, when Tom found him sitting by the fire, bootless and wreathed in vapours from his own drying clothes. "Fit to do murther over naught, she is. 'Is Lordship, 'e sent away 'is 'ead-groom for being like that, back when —" He stopped short, wincing, and slumped lower on the stool — Dejection itself. "Ay, ay — don't scowl, Mr. Tom, I know. No talk of 'Is Lordship…"

He could have spared himself the trouble, for Tom was less scowling than wondering: was Susan Foal truly fit to do murther over naught? Jupiter — but talk of murder seemed to crop up everywhere, whether he wanted it to or not. It was with some brusqueness that he questioned Skeres about his errand. The plumber, it seemed, would arrive on the morrow, with his cart and apprentice, and all.

"Even if it rains?" Tom went to peer at the downpour outside through the half-open window. "You took your time, didn't you?" he groused. "I wanted Mistress Shelton escorted back to Lee — but now…"

Skeres harrumphed: the Minotaur wounded in his pride! "'Tis ten miles there and ten back!" he protested. "An' I 'ad to seek the plumber 'igh and low, for Wollans misremembered the place, pinch 'im, and it rained in me face like the Flood all the way back..."

Which Tom rather doubted, for it hadn't been pouring half an hour. "And a leisurely dinner, I'll wager."

"Ay, next time I'll go empty-bellied," muttered the lad. "It will be of a piece with all the rest! 'Is —" He snapped his mouth shut — but not to bite down yet another mention of Essex's perfections. He sprang to his feet instead, and bounded to the door, throwing it open. "Do I trounce 'im, Master?" he bellowed into the dark passage — and, beyond the lad's shoulder, Tom caught a fleeting vision of Foal's retreating back.

"No, you don't trounce him," Tom said wearily — not that Foal didn't deserve it.

"Ear-pricked weasel..." Rumbling like distant thunder, Skeres went to throw himself back onto the stool, and gave a great, gusty sigh. "Cuds-me, Mr. Tom — what an 'ouse! When is it that we go back 'ome?"

Never again — but Tom had no heart to say so aloud, to Skeres or himself. "Well, one who isn't going home now is Mistress Shelton," he griped instead — and went in search of Old Kathryn, to have a room arranged for the guest.

He found Susan Foal instead — or at least he heard her, still cawing crossly in the passage room. Lord — could Ned have found no better than this pie-voiced shrew to warm his bed? She had gone by the time Tom entered the room, and the scullion was there, down on his hands and knees, brushing Skeres's rainwater and mud from the flagstones. The lad scrambled to his feet, all but backing into a corner. What on earth had they told him of the new Mr. Walsingham?

"You're Everest?" Tom asked.

"Ay, Master. Will Everest..."

No more than seventeen, thin as a rake, all knees and elbows and ears, with a pocked face, the lad was as unprepossessing as they came — and forlorn. See how he stood hunched, turning the brush between rough hands.

"Well, go ahead." Tom nodded at the floor. "Where do I find Goody Wollans?"

A sullen shake of the head. "'Tis Mrs. Foal as sent me."

"And where is Mrs. Foal, then?"

With a nod to the hall door, the boy took a great gulp of air and asked in a great rush, "You be sacking me, Master?"

"Sacking you? Why on earth?"

"Mrs. Foal says..." Everest looked up, his Adam's apple bobbing up and down. "But it was Master as sent me away!"

So this was what they'd told him: that, first thing, the new Mr. Walsingham would kick out the scullion who had left his sick brother alone.

"I expect a scullion to obey his master." And besides, this scarecrow was the last person he'd have left to watch an invalid — but this Tom would keep for the Foals. On the other hand, here was a chance to find out more about Ned's last hours. "So Mr. Edmund sent you away?"

Why wasn't young Will more grateful, more eager to leap at the chance to explain himself? Instead, he nodded warily, and all he said was, "Ay, Master."

"And...?"

Another of those swift glances. "And he threw a candlestick at me head, he did. Said as he didn't want the likes of me around."

"What had you done?"

The boy swallowed and fidgeted with the brush. "I ha'an't done naught, Master — 'tis just… He was ever so fretful, he was. There was naught as pleased him. The storm, the fire as smoked, every time as I shifted, the…" He looked away again, with a forlorn gesture. "Then he shouted and threw the stick, and I…"

"Why didn't you raise the Foals? Where do they sleep?"

"Just by the Master's room — so they be close." Whether there was malice in the boy's mumbling, Tom couldn't tell.

"And you didn't think to raise them."

A shake of the lowered head — and little wonder. A scullery boy, having had his share of abuse already, having failed in his task… There were mumbled words that Tom had trouble catching: "Mr. Foal said as he'd whip me dead if…"

"And they never heard when Mr. Edmund shouted at you?"

The scullion shrugged. "The gale was ever so howling…"

Just as Uncle George had said. So the Foals wouldn't have heard when Edmund rose and wandered away, and fell down the stairs. Nor would have Barker, who also slept upstairs in the attic. As for George himself, two rooms away from Edmund… Tom very much suspected his uncle wouldn't have heard a cannon firing.

"So, what did you do?"

"Went to the small kitchen to sleep by the fire, until Mrs. Foal screamed."

All of it plain and plausible — and truly, why he questioned it, Tom didn't know. The more he heard, the plainer it seemed to him: nothing had caused Edmund's death beyond a bad heart, a bad storm, and a disordered household.

*

Supper began less awkwardly than Tom had feared. The persistence of the rain had discouraged Mr. Harvey from paying another pious visit, the leek soup was quite fine, and, for a wonder, both uncles found Audrey Shelton to be congenial company. Or at least, Uncle George paid her amiable attention between one glass of Rhenish and the next, and Uncle Buffkin roared with laughter when she held her own — whether on the cottage law or the joys of being stranded at Scadbury.

The first time Tom tried to intervene, the old man waved him silent, chortling; the second, he harrumphed, "Be quiet, boy. Mistress Audrey wants no knight to tilt for her, eh?"

And it must be that even the most metaphorical mention of tilting raised thoughts of Frances and Essex — or why would Tom sit straighter and proclaim, "Mistress Audrey should have no need of one at my table — and much less to tilt for herself."

There was truly no blaming Uncle Buffkin when he exploded in a gale of cackling. "Too many books, Tomkin! Or else it's that chair giving you a stiff neck already… Though, I must say, neither Ned nor your father would have come up with that in a hundred years. Learnt it at Mr. Secretary's knee, have you?"

Could it be hoped that candlelight would mask the tide of heat rising up from Tom's neck to the roots of his hair? Whether it did or not, Audrey smiled and thanked him prettily, and Uncle Buffkin chortled to himself for the rest of the supper.

It wasn't until George excused himself, and said he'd go and sit with Edmund for a while, that Uncle Buffkin sobered. As the oldest kinsman, he announced, it was his duty to read a psalm in the rector's absence. Old imp! But while George huffed and muttered, Tom was enough Sir Francis's pupil to give a half bow with all the gravity in the world. "Most assuredly, Uncle. I was on the point of asking you, but I'm most grateful that you should think of it."

See how the old fellow huffed, wrong-footed — and see the glimmer in Audrey Shelton's carefully lowered eyes!

Deprived of the entertainment of an argument, Uncle Buffkin looked half irked as he read with a goat's grace and ear for poetry. Bent almost double to hold the book to the candle, he rumbled flatly the fine words of trust, faith, and awe to the counterpoint drum of the window that looked out over the herb garden, rattling in its hinges in the wind.

Standing at his uncle's elbow before the dais, Tom swallowed sigh after sigh, knees locked lest he shift his weight this way and that, as he'd done through countless sermons as a boy, in the family pew at St. Nicholas. Out of the corner of his eye, he watched George, leaning back on his heels, hands clasped behind his back in a manner that would have suggested the profoundest boredom, had his pale eyes not been fixed on Edmund's waxlike features. Across from him stood the women: Mistress Shelton foremost, her green velvet almost black in the gloom. Behind her was Old Kathryn, moist eyes glinting in the uncertain light, while Susan Foal fretted and glared at the guest's straight back, much like one deprived of her rightful place. Did she know of Edmund's short-lived courtship of Audrey? No doubt someone had found the time to whisper in her ear, since morning…

The placid Barker, perhaps — whom Tom was beginning to suspect was not so much a gossip, as a careful dispenser of truth and rumours, as judiciously seasoned as his fine dishes. With him were Skeres, Foal and Wollans, side by uneasy side after a wordless squabble for precedence. Last of all, back in the gloom, Will Everest tottered, half asleep on his feet — and yet not so forgotten that Foal shouldn't, now and then, turn to hiss at him. Unpleasant toad, Foal: grasping the chance to lord it over someone, like many who were made to feel they counted for little. And yet he was going to inherit... But no: it was Fair Susan inheriting through him, with a black apron over her kirtle.

Lord — but that window! Was there no way to secure it?

And in the midst of it lay Edmund. Was Edmund lingering — as Old Cicely had believed — a deeper shade in the shadows just outside the reach of candlelight, sneering at those he'd left behind, at their preoccupations, anger, and mistrust? Was he counting those who had been there the night of his ruinous fall, and those who hadn't? Even in death, he didn't look at peace — or was it the flickering light playing tricks, throwing shadows into the sunken sockets and beneath the jutting cheekbones? Stiffening his spine against a creeping chill, Tom let himself sigh.

When at last Uncle Buffkin reached the end, and begged the Lord to look well for wickedness in them all and lead them the way everlasting, Tom joined in the *Amen* with that fervour of relief that had earnt him many scoldings during his young years. He watched as the household dispersed — his household now, Lord help him — the uncles back towards the parlour, talking low among themselves, and the servants on their various ways. Skeres and the scullion headed kitchen-wards, hopefully for the warming pans to put in the beds.

Was it now Tom's duty to go and entertain his kinsmen? As he lingered, pondering duty against a great wish to seek his room, he observed Old Kathryn and Susan Foal hissing at each other at the foot of the dais. Oh, Jove — what now? Servants in Seething Lane weren't like this, nor in Barn Elms! Surely none would ever dare behave this fractiously under Lady Ursula's eye.

"Don't you like psalms, Mr. Walsingham?"

So startled he was by the murmur at his shoulder, that Tom swung around to scowl at the murmurer. But it was Audrey Shelton, quite unmoved by his scowl. Little vixen — surely *she* would never let her servants bicker like fishwives at Billingsgate! What had she asked, now? Yes: psalms.

"I like them very well, Mistress Shelton. I'd only wish to hear them read like the fine poetry they are."

She nodded, with the same pretty smile she'd had for his knightly interference at supper — then her eyes slid past him, to the dais, where Susan Foal was dragging a stool close to Edmund's head, the way she'd plant a banner on a battlefield. Old Kathryn was marching away to the kitchen, elbows wide and profile knitted — whether in defeat or satisfaction, it was hard to tell.

"Goodwife Wollans will be looking after me, I take it?" asked Audrey, one slender brow raised at Susan Foal.

And perhaps Tom shouldn't have sighed and told her, "Believe me, Mistress, it's just as well." He did it all the same.

"Oh, I don't know." She made a little moue. "I would have liked a quiet word with your housekeeper."

To put her in her place? A picture painted itself in Tom's mind of Audrey Shelton rattling Fair Susan well and truly — and only by a whisker did he bite down a huff of laughter. "You would?"

She nodded very seriously, her eyes fixed on the woman huddling beside the coffin. "Did you know that she spoke to your Constable Johnson?" she asked under her breath.

Now this! Tom gaped — most stupidly, he was sure. The constable? And Susan Foal? What had she told…? Of many questions, it was the most foolish that made its way to his lips: "How would you know that?"

Little wonder that Mistress Shelton gave a small, impatient sigh. With a last glance at the housekeeper, she drew Tom deeper into the shadows at the hall's far end, where Father and Grandfather's suits of armour stood by the wall on either side of the great door, distant candlelight playing dully on their sheen. And then, for good measure, she drew him a little further, into the dark passage.

Fingers tight on Tom's sleeve, she leaned close to whisper, "Goodman Wollans says that Johnson was here at about noon on Monday, when news of your brother reached the village."

"Constables do that, when there's a sudden death."

"Do they? Well, you'll know." A gleam of eyes. "The poor man just shuffled about a little with his hat in his hands, and couldn't wait to be gone. But..." A tightening of the fingers. "As he was going, he was stopped in the outer yard, and had a lively conversation with Mrs. Foal."

"One that Wollans didn't hear."

The shadow at Tom's elbow shifted. "He saw that the constable wasn't happy."

"For all we know..." He peered down the passage, towards the meagre light that filtered beneath the other door to the hall, where Susan Foal sat playing at widows. "For all we know, she was scolding him for dirtying the floors."

A click of the tongue, and the slender fingers left Tom's sleeve. "And surely two days later he sought a justice to denounce your housekeeper as a shrew!"

There was that, yes ... until one remembered that it was mostly Audrey's fanciful mind tying together the constable's visit at Annesley House and Scadbury. "Have you ever heard of *non causa pro causa*, Mistress? Just because one thing happens, and then another, it doesn't mean that the first caused the second. It's called a fallacy —"

"Nor does it mean it did not cause it." There was a light tapping — an impatient foot, Tom guessed. "And I know what a fallacy is, thank you."

All he lacked now: a philosophical vixen, of all things!

And then there came steps from the kitchen, and light, and Old Kathryn appeared, candle in one hand, warming pan in the other. The draught caught the flame and made it dance, ruddying the old servant's face.

"Lord love ye, Mistress — all in the dark…" She stopped short, eyes going round, and beamed. "And Mr. Thomas!"

There! Now this furnace of gossip he'd inherited would be alive with whispers of him and Mistress Shelton! Barely two days at home, and already hiding in dark corners with the woman his brother had courted once. What would Sir Francis… Oh, never mind Sir Francis: what would Frances think?

And while he stood dumb and flustered, Audrey sailed towards Kathryn, hand outstretched and smile bright. "Is that my warming pan, Goodwife? You are a marvel. I'll take the candle, before it's snuffed out. Do you always have such draughts? Good night, Mr. Walsingham," she greeted as they passed him, and they were gone.

After they disappeared up the Old Stairs, candlelight trailing after them fainter and fainter, he could hear Kathryn recounting the whims of draughts and airs, and Audrey Shelton laughing lightly.

Quite at home at Scadbury — far more so than Scadbury's own master.

Halfway up, he heard the two women sober, and exchange greetings with someone … and the muffled voice from above sounded like George.

Good — for Tom had a new question for his uncle.

He hastened up, as soon as the women's steps had faded, catching the man at the top of the stairs, half-bent over the banister to shine his own candle — a bare stub — down the well.

It's you, Tom!" he gasped, loud enough that the words stirred a small rippling echo.

Were you expecting ghosts? Tom bit down the retort, for the man was well in his cups. He looked like a ghost himself, stooping and colourless in the faint glow: eyes like glass and hair wild around his domed forehead, doublet undone at the neck and collar askew. The hand that held the candle shook. Jove… Before last Sunday Tom hadn't seen George in a long time; when had he gone to seed that badly? Perhaps it was half cruel to question him. A touch of pity battled briefly against the annoyance Audrey Shelton's words had raised, and annoyance won the day.

As Tom climbed up the last flight of steps, George forced a quivering smile.

"Seeking your bed, eh, lad?" he said, so cheerfully it was painful. "Good. Good. You've had long days, and longer still to come —"

"Has a constable from the village come to poke his head in here?" Tom asked, right through the inanities, and George's smile melted away. His wits were slowed enough by wine that the temptation to lie showed plainly in his mien, but then he looked away, shaking his head. "Who told you?"

What use was there in rousing more disquiet than already festered under Scadbury's roof? "Constables will pay a visit when there's a sudden death," Tom said with a shrug. "I wondered..."

George sighed so gustily that he nearly put out his candle, cheerful again of a sudden. "It slipped my mind, lad, truly — what with one thing and another. But, you know, he just... A bit of a dolt, isn't he? Didn't know what to do with his hat. He said he'd heard of Ned, and went away — just like that. A dolt, I tell you."

Too much, the mind of Walsingham's Wolfhound supplied. *Far too much of an explanation if it was so puny an event.* Tom quenched the thought — for this was his uncle, and sack-sopped at that — but still he asked, "Did he talk to anyone?"

"To me, I told you." George even pointed to his breast, and gave a high-pitched chuckle. "Said that he'd heard of Ned... If it was meant to be the parish's condolences, they need a man with better wits — ay, so they do."

And, plainly, if he'd seen Susan Foal accosting the constable, George wasn't saying. Not that Wollans had thought to mention it, either — at least not to Tom. Ah, well.

"Let's find our beds, Uncle," he said. "These days are long for all." And he let a chattering George see him to his room with what remained of the candle — glad that a sliver of light showed under the door: the Minotaur industrious.

He lingered on the threshold, listening to the rain that hissed and guttered outside, and watching George as he made his way to his own room, floorboards creaking under his unsteady steps after he'd disappeared in the gloom. Poor George — so fretful, so newly eager to please his nephew, so roundabout, so inclined to strange reliefs.

Oh, Jove rain on Audrey Shelton — for awaking Walsingham's Wolfhound, who now wouldn't go back to sleep!

And all the time, downstairs, the cursed window rattled.

CHAPTER 5

19th of November

Next morning, as soon as it was light enough for honest folk to call, the fabled constable appeared — as though conjured like a devil by much naming and a night of uneasy thoughts.

Faithful Wollans, Tom discovered, had refused to let the man past the gatehouse — although that must have been more to do with Susan Foal than the old tales.

Not that there was much witchlike to the man as he waited in the outer yard: a lumbering, brown-bearded, earnest-looking fellow in mud-spattered shoes, tugging at the collar of a too-tight doublet of mouse-coloured serge. He doffed his woollen cap when Tom walked out to meet him, turned it in his hands, and then donned it again.

"D'ye mind me, Mr. Walsingham? I'm Beveridge." He had a high, boyish voice that ill-matched an appearance of middle years, with a sun-burnt face and crinkles around the round eyes. "Dickon Beveridge, from Kemnal Farm. I'm Parish constable now."

"So I hear," Tom said, who did and didn't remember the fellow. There had been Beveridges around — but had he ever crossed paths with this one? "You came by the other day, didn't you?"

"Ay, Sir — and now, what with ye being here, I thought as I'd come back again."

So had he found his Justice of the Peace, or just his courage?

Ignoring Wollans's glare, and trying to also ignore the thought of Audrey Shelton looking smug, Tom led the way across the bridge and into the house. When they entered the hall, Beveridge took off his cap again. All across the long room, he held his eyes on Edmund's body laid out on the black-draped trestle — with a manner less of awe than scrutiny.

It was only once in the counting-room that Beveridge squared his shoulders, took a full breath, and said, "Ye're the last gentleman as needs to have the law explained, Mr. Walsingham, for my Aunt Turley used to call ye all but a lawyer. So ye won't be thinking as I'm out of my bounds here…"

That was who the man was, then: one of the late housekeeper's band of kinsfolk — and half chary of the welcome he'd have.

Well, the warmth of it would depend on several things. "Mrs. Turley was too kind," Tom said. "But I do know that constables looking into a sudden death is more by custom than by law. I thought you'd done that on Monday. Didn't my Uncle Guildford tell you of my brother's illness?"

Beveridge hummed, tilting his head this way and that. "He did, Sir, and he didn't. But, with all respect, Mr. Guildford ain't yerself."

"And that's a fact I won't dispute — but he has the advantage of having been here when my brother died. And the same goes for the servants. You talked with them, didn't you?"

One thing to say for Constable Beveridge: he wasn't the sort to rush into unconsidered speech. For a while he sucked his teeth, round eyes fixed on Tom, as though reckoning by sight what the new master of Scadbury was likely to know. It was three or four heartbeats before he came to a decision.

"Ay, well, Mr. Walsingham," he said. "There's the knot: Mr. Guildford told me one thing, and Mrs. Foal told me another — and I would like to hear the others, Sir. And ye yerself."

And, of course, if Uncle George had seemed cup-shot… Oh, Audrey Shelton was going to love this! "You have my blessing to hear the whole household, Goodman Beveridge. As for myself, I don't know what I could tell you, since, once again, I wasn't here." Unless… Tom narrowed his eyes at the constable. "And if Mrs. Foal told you otherwise, she's lying."

"'Tis not…" Beveridge rubbed at his full beard, brow creasing. "She didn't rightly tell as that you were here, Sir. 'Tis just…"

Yes — Tom would have been uneasy too, in the man's place — and a hit for Mistress Shelton. There being no point in beating about the bush, he straightened away from Wood's desk. "Let us be plain with each other, Constable: I can't see many reasons why my absence or presence that night would matter — and what anyone would say about that."

The man straightened too, as earnest as you please — more than earnest: stern. No longer Dickon Beveridge from Kemnal Farm, the housekeeper's nephew, but all the might of the Parish of Chislehurst. When one had never travelled much farther than Bromley, it had to seem like some might indeed. "I can't either, Mr. Walsingham," he said slowly. "Nor why folks should tell me one thing and another. Else I wouldn't be asking questions." Leaning forward with his chin jutting, Constable Beveridge was dreadfully earnest in the absurdity of his notion.

Still, he was not so far out of his right that he could be reasonably refused — and, in fact, why should he be? Hopefully, once he heard a few times the same unsuspicious story, he'd dismiss whatever Susan Foal had whispered in her spite. Tom would want a word with the woman later — but meanwhile…

"Very well then, Constable," he said. "Go ahead, question whom you like —"

And then there raised voices sounded outside, the door was thrown open, and a fuming Skeres strode in. And whom should he be tugging by the arm?

"Look who's eavesdroppin', Master!" the lad shouted, and gave Susan Foal's arm another yank fit to wrench her shoulder.

"You let me go, ye lurdane," cawed the housekeeper, black eyes flaming not a jot less when she turned them on Tom. "I don't eavesdrop on no one, Master! I was in the little room, a-working, and this great boar of yers…" Another savage tug.

As was to be expected, Skeres tugged back. "A-working, she calls it! With 'er ear right to the door!"

Unseemly as it was for Beveridge to witness such a tussle, Tom couldn't be too sorry: let the man gape, and see what sort Susan Foal was! Still, unseemly it was.

"Yes, Skeres, thank you. You can let go of Mrs. Foal now," Tom said, earning an unconvinced stare.

When she tried to wrench free, the woman found, like others before her, that one didn't wrench free easily from the Minotaur's grip. It took Tom's nod for Skeres to release his prey. *You'll know what you're about. Were it for me…* the lad's scowl said, but the obedience was prompt enough — and Susan was free to stomp away from him and rub at her arm.

On being sent to fetch Goodwife Wollans and her husband for the constable, Skeres went with no worse than a wordless mutter and a glare to be shared between Beveridge and the housekeeper.

"Unless you'd rather begin with Barker, Constable?" Tom offered. "Then there is young Everest, and Foal, too — my brother's *valet*." Out of the corner of his eye, Tom caught the housekeeper bristling at the emphasis on her husband's grand title.

Beveridge assured him that one or the other made no odds to him — and his gaze went to Susan Foal, who, instead of flouncing away as Tom had more than half expected, still stood by the door, making a great show of smoothing her sleeve and her black apron, and seething. Surely she couldn't be thinking to stay to hear the Wollanses questioned?

Just in case, though, Tom said, "You have much work to tend to, Mrs. Foal. I believe you already spoke to Goodman Beveridge the other day — unless he would hear you again?"

He turned to Beveridge — who never managed to answer, because Susan cut right in.

"Never mind what *he* wants, Master!" she hissed, and went to stand on her toes in the constable's face. "What I had to tell, I told ye, Dickon Beveridge — and look at ye, siding with the master, no matter who it is! Ye've a liver like a junket, all white and quivery, and I ha'an't naught to say to the likes of ye!"

Having delivered herself of this tirade, off she stormed — not to the little room, where she claimed to have been working, but to the Great Stairs — in great stomping strides. And devil pinch her and her sour temper!

"And just what did she have to tell you?" Tom tried, but truly, it was no great marvel when the constable frowned — uneasy but no less stubborn for it.

"Susan Foal, she calls me a pickthank, Sir — and if I told you what you ask, then she would have the right of it."

Devil pinch earnest-minded constables, too — but then, what could the fellow do, after Susan had challenged him? Not that she'd appreciate his silence if she knew. Ah, well: no point and less sense in making an enemy of him. "But she's wrong, isn't she? Very well, Constable Beveridge. You may use this room for your questionings. You'll want to hear me last?"

Poor Beveridge — cursed with a face that Sir Francis would call most transparent! Even as he crossed the fretful Wollanses on the door, even as he instructed them to answer the constable's questions, Tom caught quite clearly the flash of relief in the man's mien, darkening once again under a thundercloud of unease.

Why he should be surprised that both his uncles and Audrey Shelton were waiting in ambush at the foot of the Great Stairs, Tom didn't know.

"That's Constable Beveridge in there," he sourly announced. "He's questioning the household. Anything else you would know?"

While George had at least the good grace to look away, there were no words to describe Mistress Shelton's glance — or rather there were four: *I told you so*; as for Uncle Buffkin, the man didn't know the meaning of shame.

"Constables be damned!" he blustered, and struck the newel post's tiger-shaped finial. "What does he want again? Why did you let him in, Thomas? I wouldn't let the likes of him past the stables at Gore House."

Let him brag and boast, Sense counselled. *What does it matter?* Sense went unheeded. "Yes you would, Uncle," Tom bit back. "Constables do look into sudden deaths."

"Ay — and that he did the other day. What did Guildford tell him, that he's here to bother us again?"

It was a heartbeat before George found his breath. "Told him?" he cried, twitching like an indignant mouse. "That Ned was dead, I told him. That he'd been ill, that he'd fallen down the stairs —"

"Ha!" cried Uncle Buffkin with another flat-palmed slap at the carved tiger. "Your sister, rest her heart, always called you a lackwit. Why didn't you tell him that Ned had died in his bed?"

"With all the servants knowing that he hadn't?" scolded Tom in a whisper, mindful of Beveridge in the next room. "Truly, Uncle: lie to him, and then we'll never get rid of him. Besides, he won't bother you, since you weren't here."

"And neither were you, eh?"

Uncle Boarkin — that was what they'd called him as children, and the likeness was there, never more so than when his uncle twisted his thick mouth in amusement, and his small eyes sank in the creases of his cheeks. And what must amuse him at this moment, Heaven knew — but, with Leven Buffkin, wariness was always the more prudent course.

"And neither was I," Tom agreed, as though it were no matter at all. "He's a tad zealous, but we'll just let him do his asking. The sooner he's done, the sooner he'll go back where he came from. There's neither reason nor point in playing it high-handed."

Why couldn't Uncle Buffkin be like Uncle George, who just nodded and called it prudent? But no: Uncle Buffkin had to clap his hands in mocking applause.

"Prudent, ay!" he chortled. "You heard him, Mistress Shelton: spoken like Mr. Secretary's true boy, eh?"

"Prudency is a virtue, Mr. Buffkin," Audrey murmured, like the demure, insipid girl that she was not — and that, too, amused the old man greatly.

His great bark of laughter rang up the stairwell, and, when both Tom and George shushed him, he slapped a hand over his mouth. "Pardon me, Mistress Shelton — I'm an old lout," he rumbled. "Seeing as Thomas's zealous constable won't bother me, I'll get out of the way."

Bowing to Audrey, he waddled out without a word for either Tom or George — as a sign of how well he liked to be shushed.

Oh, Lord give patience…!

They all watched the old man go, with matching grimaces, and then George gave something halfway between a sigh and a chuckle.

"Good old Buffkin…" he said, smiling askew — and then brightened up. "Well, your constable won't want me, either — will he, Thomas? He heard what I had to say…"

Which was exactly why, in Beveridge's place, Tom would want to hear George again. "Ah, who knows? He may have other questions."

And see how George blinked. "But I —"

"Truly, it would be a kindness, Uncle, if you didn't stray too far."

There was no other word for it: George looked crestfallen. Under his reddened eyelids, his gaze slid to the parlour door. Was he hoping to renew his acquaintance with Ned's claret — Tom's claret now — and meet the constable sack-sopped?

"I believe…" Tom turned to Audrey. "You said, Mistress, that the tailor…?"

Never let it be said that she wasn't quick-witted. "Oh, yes," she smoothly answered. "He'll need to fit Mr. Guildford's gown again."

All the previous day, and today ever since dawn, the rabbit had been sewing away in an empty bedroom upstairs, overseen by Mistress Shelton. He would do to keep George from the bottle until the constable sought him.

With her foot already on the first step, though, Audrey stopped. "You told me once that there's a sundial at Scadbury."

A sundial — what on earth…? A memory stirred in Tom's mind, of a snow-covered graveyard in London, of a younger Audrey, and somehow there was the matter of a sundial… "My great-grandfather had one made, but I don't think —"

"I would greatly like to see it." This was said very pointedly.

"It was broken, Mistress. Why, I even think it was…" *Buried somewhere*, he didn't say, because at that moment he saw — and shame on him for not catching on at once. "Oh. But you'd still … yes."

Jove — what would Sir Francis think, to see a Service man of twelve years — never mind his own trusted kinsman — deal this clumsily with a matter of secrecy? Not that he had the slightest doubt of what the matter was — but any who saw them would suspect Heaven knew what conspiracy. Fates be thanked that George alone was there, halfway up the stairs, and too busy sulking to observe either Tom's awkwardness or Audrey's heavenward glance.

In truth, Tom had no notion of where the broken sundial was buried — but, since it was no matter at all, it was to the walled garden that he led Audrey. Foolish of him, perhaps, with the constable busy asking questions — and even more so if he didn't want his household to think that he had secrets with this woman.

He waited until they were in the garden to speak — and in a low voice at that. He caught the moment when she was taking in the autumn melancholy of the place, and answered the question before she asked it.

"Beveridge is here, and you told me so —"

At once she turned to him, garden forgotten. "What did he say of the letter?"

"Not a word."

"And you?"

"Neither did I, of course."

"Oh, Mr. Walsingham!" she exclaimed, sighing.

"I couldn't very well do it, could I, unless he mentioned it first? But he says he's here because my uncle and Susan Foal told him two different stories — and that's rather different than accusing me of murder, or even speaking of murder at all. He's just uneasy that someone must be lying." Tom didn't add that Sir Francis would rather approve of Constable Beveridge; plainly, Audrey did not.

"And you believe him?"

"I don't know — nor that some wicked penner of letters is out to see me hang…" This earned a scowl. "Oh, don't look daggers at me, Mistress Shelton. Tell me truly: who would do such a thing — and why?"

She nodded twice, very seriously. "I have been wondering myself, and this occurred to me: if you were proved a murderer, you'd lose your inheritance, wouldn't you?"

"Yes — but —"

"Who would profit from that?" she pressed. "Think: who stands to inherit after you?"

To inherit… Tom's jaw fell open. Lord, but this woman! "Why, you should write for the stage, Mistress!"

"I do wish you'd take this matter seriously! Who is your heir? You have one, surely?"

"My only Walsingham cousin, Sir Francis — the Queen's principal secretary."

And see if she didn't tilt her head, both brows raised, one palm raised questioningly, as if to say, *There you are!*

A cheerless laugh escaped Tom, louder than he'd meant in the damp air, making Audrey colour — and well she might, for truly…

And still she tried: "You can't know for certain —"

"Yes, I can," he said, most firmly. "Sir Francis took me under his wing when I was sixteen. Ever since he's been not just my master, but my mentor and my friend. He's never shown me anything but kindness. He trusts me, and knows that I would go through fire a hundred times for him..." He stopped short, half startled by his own vehemence — not that he didn't think every word from his heart.

Audrey took a breath to object — *none of this means he couldn't want Scadbury for himself*, was written plain in her mien — but whatever she saw in his face made her swallow it. She looked very young like this, with her dark brows drawn together and her mouth pressed thin, and Tom gentled his voice.

"I would trust Sir Francis with my life and my honour, Mistress," he explained. "He would never take away what is mine." *Not that he didn't take away Frances — twice now*, whispered the traitorous voice in his mind, which he hastily quenched, because of all the matters in this world, Frances was the one where his great cousin couldn't trust him, if only he knew. *And who can tell that he doesn't?* went the hateful little voice again — only now it sounded like Audrey Shelton, who wasn't yet surrendering.

"And after Mr. Secretary, who is in line?" She tapped a forefinger to her chin. "He has no sons, has he?"

"Only a daughter." Tom made himself not look away as he said so. "No male heirs — and this alone puts paid to these fantastical suspicions. Sir Francis would never want the family to lose Scadbury after his death." *Which may not be long in coming*, he didn't add, thinking of his great cousin's eyes burning with fever in his gaunt face.

Audrey Shelton clicked her tongue. "Then I don't know," she said, airy as you please. "But I stand firm about the letter: someone *must* have written it."

Just like a woman's logic! "That is supposing there *is* a letter, and of that I still have..." Oh, what was the use? She'd already wandered away along the gravel path to the thorny bushes, brushing a forefinger against the flame-coloured hips on the trellised roses. She picked one, rolled it between her fingers, and then called over her shoulder, "Where is the sundial?"

Oh, sink all the sundials in England! "I don't know — buried somewhere," Tom said — and see how she started and span around.

"Buried!" she cried, gaping — this girl who never batted an eyelash at the notion of murder, and blithely accused Mr. Secretary of conspiring out of greed! "You buried a sundial — and don't even remember where?"

"I didn't bury it myself! I told you, it was in my great-grandfather's day."

"You also told me," she said severely, "that there was a sundial at Scadbury — an old and small one."

"I never —"

"Yes, you did. Back when we met in London."

And that three years gone! Lord pity the fool who married this one. "Well, I don't know. The story goes that the sundial broke of a sudden, at the very moment when my great-grandfather's favourite son fell from his horse and broke his neck. So the bereaved parents had it buried..." And then, seeing how intently she listened, Tom just couldn't help himself, and lowered his voice to a grim whisper. "There were suspicions that a jealous brother had done the killing, but..."

It was less than a heartbeat, the intake of breath, the stare... Then Audrey Shelton narrowed her eyes at him. "That's never true!"

"No." He grinned, earning a sniff. "Our old nurse used to tell the tale — without the murderous brother, mind — but whether there ever was a sundial, I've never known."

"You horrid man!" she scolded — but he could tell that she wanted to laugh. It was short-lived, though, as she gathered her sternness around herself like a cloak. "But you *see*, don't you?" she asked. "Perhaps there never was a sundial at all, and yet here it is still, in stories — and stories are more stubborn than old ivy. Do you want a story of murder, false as it may be, twined around your name?"

That, for now, she was the only one speaking of murder, Tom forbore to point out — which was quite charitable of him, he thought, as they made their way back to the house.

Before the counting-room was a squarish, ill-lit space, with old chests and a press pushed against the walls. They called it the Little Room, and there Tom met Barker, looking ruffled.

"Mercy, but it's a fine life to be a constable!" the cook huffed. "Slothing about and harrying honest people!"

Tom raised a brow. Out of his new servants, he would have thought this one the least harriable of all. "Did he give you much grief, Barker?"

"'Tis just…" The scowl became a rueful smile. "I fear I told him that funeral dinners don't cook themselves. Oh, and he would see you, please you, Master — and Mr. Wood too, but he isn't here."

"Not that he ever is," Tom groused — but then… "What does Beveridge want with him? He wasn't even here when my brother died."

The cook's several chins tautened as he pursed his lips. "But he was, Master. The storm caught him here. Ever so bad it was, that Mr. Edmund had him stay, or he'd drown in the rain before he got home. He slept up in the green room right above here."

And this was the first Tom had heard of it! Why had nobody mentioned it in two days? How many more pieces of this story were still to be found out? Before he could ask Barker, the constable appeared at the door and Tom, dismissing Barker, followed him back to the counting-room.

Nobody had thought — or seen fit — to bring a candle for the constable, and the room looked very gloomy, the cupboards and doors black in the dim light. Leaning against the shelves so he'd have what light there was behind him, Tom crossed his arms and waited while Dickon Beveridge contemplated him, sucking his teeth. So long he was about it, that in the end Tom prodded, "Well?"

A hum. "Well, Mr. Walsingham. All tell it much the same, as that ye weren't here, the night Mr. Edmund fell down the stairs and died. I still have to hear Mr. Wood — but I reckon he'll say the same: Mr. Edmund was ill, he fell down the stairs, and ye weren't here."

"As I told you — and as my uncle told you, I believe."

"Ay, well." Beveridge tilted his head the other way. "What ye didn't say is as ye were here the same day."

Hadn't he? Tom went back to his first conversation with the constable, brusquely cut short by Skeres. Devil take it! Such an omission wouldn't look good — but then… "I was, yes," he said. "Is it of import?"

"Ye didn't tell me," Beveridge insisted, slow and mulish. "Mr. Guildford did — the other day and now — only, he didn't say as ye had words with Mr. Edmund."

A man, Thomas, is more easily ensnared with his omissions than with his lies.

Shoving aside this alarming maxim of Sir Francis's, Tom instead latched onto the Service wisdom of never looking alarmed.

"Do you have brothers, Constable?" he asked with the faintest smile, and earnt a sideways nod. "Then you know how it is. We had words, and then I went away, and that's all there was to it."

Constable Beveridge never took his searching gaze from Tom. "Ay but, Sir, ye still didn't tell me. So I came here because I had two stories — and now I have four."

Stories creeping like old ivy. Audrey's words echoed in Tom's mind. Creeping, strangling…

"Four?" he asked.

The debate showed plain on Beveridge's broad, leathery face: was this the same as telling? The same as picking thanks? And then a compromise was made, and the man nodded. "There's yerself, saying as ye weren't here; there's Mr. Guildford, saying as ye weren't, but had come by the same day; and there's others, saying as ye came by and made a row…"

"And that makes three," Tom pointed out when Beveridge dithered — and there was only one possible fourth. "And then there's Susan Foal, is there? What the devil did she say? But no!" He held up an impatient hand. "You won't tell me —"

And there Beveridge surprised him by cutting him short. "I'll tell ye this much, Sir, so ye can have your say if ye like: the fourth story is as ye came here wanting money from Mr. Edmund."

Devil pinch the woman! Uncrossing his arms, Tom pushed away from the shelves. "I didn't…" *My brother held back my annuity. He could have paid me instead of loaning out pounds by the hundreds.* He snapped his mouth shut on the angry retorts and counted in Latin. By *quattuor* he'd reined in his temper enough to smile, if a little sourly. "You make me sound like a roadside brigand, but I wasn't out to rob my brother, if that's what you've been told. I asked for nothing that wasn't owed me — and had been for a long time. I lost my temper, and he lost his."

The spell of silence, as Beveridge watched Tom and sucked his teeth, stretched long enough for them to hear half the noon bells from Chislehurst. *West wind, ill wind*, Wollans's voice echoed in Tom's mind from a long time ago — and then a door slammed somewhere upstairs, and Beveridge emerged from his musings and stirred like one coming awake.

"I reckon I'm about done, Mr. Walsingham. So, please ye, I'll be on my way." He cast about for his cap, found it on a chest, made his rustic bow, and was gone.

That he still had to talk to Wood, that the way things were couldn't satisfy whatever doubts had brought him back to Scadbury, that he'd been seeking a Justice of the Peace — all that was left hanging. Like a first sprout of ivy that, left to itself, would strangle trees and make walls crumble.

CHAPTER 6

"Should 'ave trounced 'im, that's what," the Minotaur muttered for the third time in a row. "Given 'im what for."

The first time, Tom had chided him — one didn't go about trouncing constables, even petty ones from measly little villages, as Skeres judged Chislehurst; the second time, he had grumbled; the third, he ignored his servant completely, and kept at his letter. He greatly wished for a writing table, because it was uncomfortable to write sitting on the bench under the smaller window of Edmund's room — his own room now, at last — with a hastily made fire at his side, and a draught whistling across his neck from under the casement. Then again, no table would have eased the discomfort of composing this particular letter.

As though Sir Francis had no other worries to trouble him — worries of the State and of his health… And still it seemed prudent that he should know, before some rumour reached him.

Quite what there was to know, though…

That the petty constable was nosing around Scadbury? That a strange lady had turned up with wild tales? That, absurd as it seemed, there was no telling whether some Justice of the Peace was likely to come charging in at some point?

The more he thought about it, the less likely it seemed that a magistrate would stir over a matter of contrasting stories — but there were always ambition, stupidity, plain zeal, and the Walsingham name to account for.

With a groan, Tom dropped the pen.

Skeres was making a pretence of tidying up, with singularly unconvincing effect, because Old Kathryn had aired and dusted the room to within an inch of its life, so that it was spotless — and cold as Tartarus. After spreading Tom's black suit and the clean shirts on the four-poster bed, Skeres was left with nothing to do, so he loitered around. Now he kneed a padded chair half a foot this way or that, now he tugged at the bed's green and yellow curtains, now he bent to poke at the fire — and all the time he mumbled to himself between one sigh and the next.

"Muster some good cheer, will you, Dolius?" Tom set aside for a moment the thought of the letter. "This, at least, should meet your approval."

This was the room that had belonged to half a dozen generations of Walsinghams — including a High Sheriff of Kent and a Lieutenant of the Tower. It showed: the bed alone, with its posts like slender twine columns, was as large as Tom's garret back in Seething Lane, while the oak mantel above the fireplace was finely carved with battle scenes. A soft-hued old tapestry covered most of the room's far end, and there were more clothes-presses, trunks and boards than Tom could fill with his belongings.

But did the Minotaur approve? At the question, he only raised a shoulder and mumbled some more — likely some unflattering comparison to His Lordship's place that were best ignored.

Moving to one of the chairs by the fire, Tom sank into the embroidered cushions that matched the bed-curtains, spreading his legs before him. "I thought I'd loathe this room…" he remarked in idle surprise. But then, the last time he'd visited, it had been a sickroom, glum and stifling with ill will and the smells of illness — while now… He took a breath of the clean air, of the scent of rain and beeswax, and half-smiled at the warm gleam of the wainscoting. "I'll need a writing table in here —"

"I should 'ave trounced 'im."

Oh, Jupiter — again! Tom opened his eyes to find Skeres at the great window, rubbing his cuff against the diamond-shaped panes to glare down at someone outside — Beveridge on his way, most surely — which brought back all of Tom's worries, and soured his humour.

"You must be going deaf," he snapped, sitting up straight. "What have I told you of trouncing Parish men?"

Never looking away from the window, the Minotaur hummed: "Ah, but let 'im show 'is face again…"

Like snapping at the bedpost! "You'll have no chance. You are for London — and will escort Mistress Shelton back to Lee on your way."

And now the letter. Tom recovered paper, pen and inkwell — no wiser to what he would write than he'd been earlier — and at once Skeres resumed his mumbling perambulations, the floorboards creaking under each heavy step.

"And while you wait," Tom called without looking up, "go and see about my table. A largish one — ask Mrs. Foal."

Which was likely to end in pitched battle but, hopefully, not before the letter was signed, sanded and sealed.

A forlorn hope. Skeres hadn't trudged away for a minute before, with a fierce knock at the door, the housekeeper barged inside, black-aproned and sullen. She curtsied with the grace of a cork bobbing on water.

"'Tis the table, Master," she announced. "There be no writing tables, just Mr. Wood's."

Lord give patience! "My father had one — old, with some carving on the legs and two or three drawers. What's become of it?"

Mrs. Foal didn't know. Mrs. Foal had never seen a table like that. It took an order to send up Goodwife Wollans in her stead, to jolt her memory.

"Mayhap at the gatehouse," she said, sniffing. "Mr. Edmund had some old things moved there."

This last was said with the kind of knowing, portentous gravity preachers used for the Commandments set in stone, so Tom wasn't truly surprised when an order to have the table fetched and brought upstairs was met most mulishly.

"Mr. Edmund had it taken there —"

"Yes, Mrs. Foal — and I'll have it brought back and to this room."

He held her bitter gaze until she looked away and did another of those graceless curtsies — this woman who, come Monday, would walk away with half the plate and half a fortune.

"Ay, Master," she grated. "'Tis yer table and yer house."

The gall of her! Flinging down the pen, Tom sprang to his feet. "Yes, it is. You'd do better to remember it," he snarled — and the funeral dinner be damned. "I've had enough of your insolence. Another ill word, another lie, another drop of venom, and you leave my house, together with your useless husband!"

An empty threat, for the most part, because Foal was still Edmund's executor — and one that Fair Susan didn't bother to acknowledge.

"So Dickon tattled!" She clicked her tongue in disgust. "Ever a quake-breech, he was — kissing yer shoe like all the others."

"Nobody's —"

"All tripping over their feet to please ye — and Beveridge is the worst, who isn't even yours to pay!"

Through the hot words crowding on his tongue, long habit made its way to Tom's mind, and the thought that some things were better not shouted for the whole house to hear. What would his father say to see him bickering with the housekeeper in this room? But then, Edmund had done worse things here with Fair Susan, hadn't he? Let their father's ghost decide which son was the greater fool! He strode close enough to lower his voice.

"Beveridge didn't let slip a word, if you must know," he said — which wasn't quite true. "But, I ask, would he be here at all unless someone whispered lies to him?"

Fowls went to war like this: standing on their toes, and craning their necks, and shaking in their anger.

"I didn't lie," she crowed, fisting her hands in her black apron. "I heard ye yell at Mr. Ned! Yell as that ye're broken deep, and he wanted ye ruined, and ye must have the money."

"Yes, and he yelled back at me. He called me all sort of names, and said that he'd see me in gaol still —"

"Ay, and now he's dead — and you be rich."

It took Tom a heartbeat to catch the woman's meaning, and when he did, it tore a gasp out of him. "You never dream…?"

"I don't dream naught, Master," she hissed. "I saw with me eyes the way he was after ye'd gone — all distempered and ill. He'd been sick, ay — but not sick to die. And then you arrived… Oh, I don't dream: I *know*, for he told me."

She threw up her chin with such a knowing sneer, it was hard work not to grab her and shake until her teeth rattled. Tom gritted his teeth instead, and snapped, "He told you what, devil take you?"

Her sneer slid askew; her eyes glimmered. "That ye didn't like it, to learn mayhap ye weren't no heir anymore, that's what he told me!" She splayed both hands over her bulging belly. So that was it. She was all fat, so it was hard to tell — but either way…

When Tom burst out laughing, her eyes went wide — but only for a heartbeat. "Laugh all you like!" she snarled. "I know the way it is."

"You stupid woman — you know nothing! Even if it were Edmund's bastard — and I wish you joy of proving it — there is no way that your child could inherit Scadbury."

Susan Foal's fingers curled, clawlike, crushing her black apron. "Ye say so because he isn't here!" she bit back.

"I say so because the law won't allow it, no matter what the father or anyone says."

"Not even the Queen? Mr. Ned said —"

"Mr. Ned led you around, Susan Foal!" Tom shouted. So much for discretion — but truly, this pig-headed shrew … and, worse still, Edmund! What had he been thinking, lying to her like this?

Perhaps she was wondering, too: see how doubt wrangled with fury in her black eyes.

Fury won, for the moment, and defiance. "That's the way ye tell it, Master," she spat. "But Mr. Ned said as ye'd gone white, when ye heard of the child."

"He was lying, for he never told me." Edmund, short-winded and sneering of worse surprises awaiting — but no, that had been about the money, surely…

Not that this confounded magpie would believe it, baring her teeth and cawing on as though she had reason: "Oh, ye threatened, and thundered…"

"What did I threaten?" Tom took another stride forward, vehement enough that she stepped back into an armchair, alarm flickering at last across her swarthy face. "What had I to fear from your bastard? I tell you: even if Ned had acknowledged it —"

"Well, he can't, now, can he?" she cut in. "And mind, I'll die before I let his murtherer step into his shoes!"

She whirled around so hurriedly that she lost her footing in the rushes. Without thinking, Tom reached out to steady her, and she flinched away from his touch, arms wrapping around her belly. Jove fulminate all vapourish women — what did she think he'd do?

With a last withering scowl, she ran off.

As her steps faded down the stairs, Tom was left staring, too stunned for anger. *His murtherer…* Small wonder that Beveridge should have come back!

And now that letter for Sir Francis had become more urgent yet — and far more awkward.

Mistress Shelton had her own notions on the matter. When Tom sought her — having finished his letter, and dispatched Skeres to the stables — she was to be found in the small kitchen, helping Old Kathryn make something that smelt like dried lavender.

Kathryn, it seemed, approved of her pupil.

"Ay, Mistress — you be good at it!" she exclaimed. "That's the way Old Cicely taught Her Ladyship when she was still a girl — Old Cicely as was Mr. Tom's nurse, back when the house was —" She stopped, catching sight of Tom on the threshold, and called, "There you be, Mr. Tom!" She rose, brushing her hands down her apron. "But I mustn't call you that no more, eh?" She grinned a little too brightly, and

Audrey, when she twisted around on the bench, studied him from under a furrowed brow.

What now — what else? Already informed of the housekeeper's outburst, no doubt. If he ignored their solicitude, would they drop the matter?

It was in that hope that he dragged up a smile. "As though I'd stand on ceremony, Kathryn. But I've come to fetch away your new helper. Mistress, my man will escort you to Annesley House now."

To see her, to hear the small "Oh!", one would have thought she'd forgotten that such a place existed. She smiled back — the tilt-headed, close-lipped smile that Tom was beginning to recognise as her steely manner. "With all the matters you have to preoccupy you, I wouldn't dream of adding another importunity. I can well stay until tomorrow — and be of some help meanwhile."

Ah, she would, wouldn't she? But this was a game that two could play — and he had learnt it at Mr. Secretary's knee. "It would never be an importunity to serve you, Mistress," he said, with the smallest bow. "But, if it will ease your conscience, my man is riding to London, so Lee is on his way. We've held you prisoner long enough, I think."

For the shortest moment she still hesitated, objections plain in the set of her mouth — objections that, Tom was ready to wager, had nothing to do with the making of lavender bags. Fates be thanked, she had the sense to not discuss them before Kathryn, who cooed and sighed at the leave-taking, as though Audrey had been a daughter of the house.

All the while it took to fetch her hat, gloves and horsewhip, Audrey Shelton held her objections in check; the moment they were alone on the bridge and away from prying ears, she stopped short, and gave them free rein.

"Truly, Mr. Walsingham, shouldn't I stay? I feel that I'm abandoning you."

Abandoning him! Thoughts of writing for the stage resurfaced — and Tom barely kept from voicing them.

"It seems to me that Lady Wildgoose is the one you've abandoned. Won't she be out of her wits with worry?" he asked instead — only for this vexing creature to wave and explain most airily:

"I told her that, if your sisters arrived, I might stay a day or two…"

As though Grace Wildgoose would believe that! She was bound to know that her god-sister had never met either Barbara or Mary. What would she be thinking? What was Tom himself thinking, for that matter? And, most of all, what was in Audrey's mind? And, because it was unseemly to ask her in as many words…

"Well, you've been a most generous friend — more so than I had any right to expect…" he tried, and waited for her to catch the unasked question — but no. She only smiled — the pretty, demure one — and turned away to watch the turbid water of the moat, until he was left with nothing to do but insist. "Without your help, I would have floundered in these confounded preparations —"

"Oh, the preparations!" Her grey eyes flew to his face, bright and sharp. "Black gowns and gloves are not the help you need in such a press, with a constable baying at your heels…"

"He hardly bays, poor Beveridge." Although that was mostly because he was more lyme-hound than terrier…

Utterly unsoothed, Audrey shook her head. "Goodwife Wollans and her husband are most worried — and now we know just what accusations that termagant is throwing…" She stopped short when he looked startled.

"Does the whole of Kent know?" he exclaimed.

And look: for a wonder, Mistress Audrey Shelton coloured and looked away, and the point of a riding shoe peeked out from the hem of her skirts to scuff at the dead leaves the rain had plastered to the bridge's boards.

"I'd gone upstairs to rest a little, and Mrs. Foal shouted so…"

Oh, yes — Father had always complained that voices carried through Scadbury like the wind in a valley! "Well then," Tom said, sighing. "Now you know Beveridge needed no unsigned letter to come haring at Scadbury, you can leave with a lighter heart…"

Not that she looked light-hearted in the least, or willing, as he escorted her through the stable yard, even more forlorn now the rain had turned it into a quagmire of mud and leaves from the bared honeysuckles.

"I'll need a cartload of gravel," he murmured — and why he was telling Audrey Shelton, he didn't know.

Having been busy lifting her hem away from the worst of the puddles, she agreed in full. "But," she said, looking up, "even if you think there was no letter…"

A terrier with a bone! "Mistress Shelton…" Tom took a deep breath. "We know who put the good constable to the scent — and not in writing."

"And then perhaps she sent him an unsigned letter, as if from someone else, to support her claim."

"Because, on seeing me, she became even more convinced that I'm a murderous scoundrel?" Tom huffed. "I can promise you: when I touched my brother's body, it didn't bleed."

Oh, the look of reproach! "Does this seem like a laughing matter to you, Mr. Walsingham?" Annoyance made her eyes glow. "Do think: Mrs. Foal feared that the constable wouldn't act on her word alone."

"And so she wrote a letter? I'm not even sure that she can."

"So she had someone else write it for her, or…" She tapped a gloved forefinger to her lips. "Or someone else entirely wrote it —"

"Someone else!" Tom stopped short at the stables' door. "Do you think there's a thicket of people believing me a murderer?" At once he wished he hadn't said it: look how she tilted her head, finger to her lips as she considered the notion — and liked it.

"Well, the constable does, for one," she mused. "Letter or no letter, he took her seriously enough that he sought a magistrate, and, whether he found one or not, he came back to ask questions…" Sparing a glance for Everest past the moat, she moved inside the warm, horse-scented dusk of the stables, lowering her voice when Tom followed her. "Did he ask where you were the other night?"

No — not quite, although the matter must have been on the constable's mind. But then… "It matters little, does it?" he asked slowly, as the thoughts moved inside his mind like bits of coloured glass. "Wherever I was, who's to say I didn't pay a servant to do it for me?" Had Audrey grown a little pale? "Which I did not," he hastened to say, only for her to toss her head in the way that made the feather dance on her hat.

"Of course you did not," she exclaimed. "But the fact that you didn't kill your brother, doesn't mean that nobody did. Can you be sure?"

Could he? The glass pieces were moving faster. The suddenness, the storm, the stairs, the strange omissions, the rich legacies… *He hadn't been ill to die*, Susan Foal had said — and Tom himself had wondered at first. But then… "A man can fall down the stairs alone, or he can be pushed," he murmured — and why he confided in this far too sharp, grave-eyed woman, he didn't know.

She clapped her hands together. "And now the murderer tries to throw the blame on you with that letter…"

Oh, the letter again! But, before Tom could protest, Skeres appeared, leading his own nag and Audrey's disconcertingly bright red mare.

"What murtherer?" he asked, with his most suspicious glower.

"I don't know that —" Tom tried, to no avail whatsoever, because Audrey cut right through him.

"Mr. Walsingham thinks that his brother was murdered," she informed the lad, as calmly as you please. "And I think there's an attempt to throw the blame on him. Regardless, the murderer is still at Scadbury."

The Minotaur's jaw fell open. He gaped at her for a moment, then at Tom. "Truly?" he asked.

"No," Tom said — to Audrey's glare. "I don't know, but I mean to make sure, as soon as you and Mistress Shelton leave."

The notion met with little approval. Skeres jutted out his lower lip, muttering like a displeased oracle, while Audrey Shelton asked, "And just how will you make sure — alone?"

Irksome vixen! "You know, Mistress," Tom groused, "I was dealing with murderers when you still learnt your French and your blackwork!"

And if he thought to discompose her, he was very much mistaken.

"I'm sure that you were," she said with a sigh, raising a brow. "And also that you had someone with you."

Which had Skeres grumbling under his breath.

What a helpless rye-straw did these two think him? "I'm hardly alone, am I? In my own house, together with two kinsmen and half a dozen servants." *One of them perhaps a murderer…* He held up a hand when Audrey made to speak. "Besides, Skeres will be back by tomorrow — that is, if you and he leave instead of arguing the day away."

Oh, she wasn't pleased, it showed plainly in the set of her mouth — and even plainer was the moment when she gave up the master of Scadbury as a lost cause.

"Very well then," she said, with that small toss of her head.

Before she changed her mind, Tom handed her into the saddle — and still, she bent down to peer closely at Tom.

"My conscience isn't easy," she said most severely. "If anything happens to you…"

Oh, Lord give patience! "Then you'll have the satisfaction of saying that you told me so." Tom patted the red mare's flank and nodded at a glowering Nick Skeres.

If you're still alive to be told, both pairs of eyes said with equal reproach.

And then they were gone, hooves splashing in the mud — and Tom, pushing aside that cheerful double valediction, turned towards the house, and the grim task he'd chosen for himself.

CHAPTER 7

Old Wollans didn't like what Tom had to say. He frowned at him, his filmy eye white and unblinking, two deep folds creasing his weatherbeaten cheeks. "'Tis an ill work, Master," he rumbled. "The dead should lie in peace."

Tom sighed deeply. "I wouldn't dream of it, unless I thought it must be done."

At her husband's side, Kathryn stood with both hands pressed to her bosom. She had crossed herself on hearing what Tom wanted.

"Is this what ye do for Mr. Secretary?" she asked, so softly Tom had to stoop to catch the words.

"Among many other things, yes." He waited. It was much to ask of them, unswathing Edmund's body so that he could observe it. "I'll do it alone, if I must. If you help me, it will be quicker and more respectful, for I wouldn't know how to swathe the body again." He watched the two exchange uneasy looks. "There's no one else I can trust under this roof — but I won't force you if you think it a sin."

With or without help, though, it had to be done at once, before the plumber arrived. Taking a great breath, Tom dragged a branch of candles closer to the trestle. Lord forgive him… He'd examined corpses before, more than his fair share of them — but none had been his brother's. Not that the slack, swollen face, with the dark lips slightly parted, looked like the man he remembered.

"You'd want me to find your murderer, wouldn't you, Ned?" he mouthed under his breath, and he drew back the black cloth, uncovering the linen sheet wrapped tight around the body. It showed white as bone in the grey light that rained aslant through the great window, making Edmund's face leaden by contrast — and the whole body, without its black drapings, seemed puny: so much smaller than the living Ned.

Death, Thomas, makes little of most men.

And Sir Francis had meant the remembrance, the legacy each leaves behind — or wishes to — but Death, it seemed, began its bleak work with the body first. Of a sudden, Tom's eyes stung — which was out of all reason, surely… Better set down to work. Linen strips bound cross-wise held the shroud in place: one knot at the feet, one at the hips, while a third strip waited to be tied over the face. Tom reached the middle one.

"Oh, Lord a' mercy…" Kathryn stormed up the dais and elbowed Tom aside. She looked him straight in the eye. "Master Tom, must ye do it?" she asked in a quivering whisper.

Poor, faithful Kathryn. Tom held her gaze. "I must know what killed him," he said. *Or who* — although that would only come in time, if he learnt enough.

The old servant's eyes reddened at the rim. With a great sigh, she began to undo the knots, only stopping to whisper sharply to her husband, "Will ye fasten the doors! No one needs to see him like this, poor lamb."

Something that Tom should have thought of, because truly he wanted no one to walk in on this. While Wollans drew the slide-bolts on the great door and the one to the passage room, he went himself to the door to the parlour, which had no bolt, and jammed a chair under the latch. Two more doors opened on the long passage — one towards the Old Stairs, the other kitchen-wards.

"Block one and hold the other," he ordered Wollans. And if anyone tried to enter and found the way barred… Ah, well, he'd better work fast.

Kathryn, he found, had unwound the shroud, uncovering what remained of Edmund Walsingham, clothed in his best shirt and nightcap. She was gathering the sprigs of rosemary that had been scattered around the body, and the pungent fragrance wafted up, not quite covering the still faint but unmistakable sour-sweetness of decay.

Well, he'd done this before.

First things first, he gently eased the cap off Edmund's head, all the time feeling Kathryn's reproachful gaze on him.

"He broke his head on a step, didn't he?" he asked softly.

"Two steps up from the bend." Kathryn's hand went to the back of her own head. "I scrubbed the blood away."

Edmund's mottled jaw was cold and clammy under Tom's fingers as he turned the head, heavy as a wet sandbag on the stiff neck. In spite of the greenish bruise spreading under the ear and into the jaw, no snap, no jerk of grinding bones called for a broken neck. The damage was all in the back of the skull, a little to the right — a jagged, puckered gash, a couple of inches in length.

When Tom held out a hand, nothing happened, and he looked up impatiently to find Kathryn bent over the body, fingers pressed to her mouth.

"A candle," he commanded, a little more harshly than he'd meant. The old servant hastened to take one from the branch and sidled up to light the wound.

It had been washed, but not sewn shut: the edges gaped stiffly, a dark grin among the thinning hair. Tom made himself ignore Kathryn's gasp as he touched it: the cold, leathery edges, scabbed all along, the slight, purplish swelling of the broken scalp.

Don't just trust your eyes, Tom had been taught by Ambrose Lopes, son and pupil to the Queen's own physician. *You'll learn more and better by your nose, your ears, your fingers.* Only, Lopes would know what to make of what he learnt. Tom pressed the swelling, and the bone grated and gave a little…

Devil take it! He snatched his hand away. What did he think he was doing? He gritted his teeth, rubbed his fingertips together — as though he could rub away the feel of his brother's skull yielding. Instead, blood flaked away, dark and dry.

"We washed him," whispered Kathryn. "But…"

We. She and Susan Foal vying for the right to do it, glaring at each other over Ned's dead body… The old woman who'd known him from a child, and the young one who'd shared his bed. Lord — but he was growing fanciful! "Was there much blood?" Tom asked.

She tilted her head, thinking. "A bit on the step, then under his head, enough of it as it ran down to the bend. It was curdled near black. And…" She paused, fingers going up to her right lobe. "Some from the ear, too. Not thick."

Which, Tom supposed, went with the bruise. The sort of injury that came from tumbling down the stairs, no matter how. A push would make no difference, would it? But on the rest of the body…?

Rather regretting Skeres's absence, he called to Wollans over his shoulder. The man started in the way of one who'd hoped to be forgotten — and see how Kathryn stared. Lord…!

"I need to turn him, and to lift the shirt," Tom explained with all the patience he could muster — which was little. "You go and hold the door, Kathryn."

Grim glances were exchanged as the two obeyed — the husband dragging his feet, the wife at a disapproving clip. She didn't linger by the door, though: after jamming another chair under the latch, she stomped back like a soldier going into battle.

"The two of ye lift him, Master," she whispered. "I'll see to the shirt."

And so they did. The body sagged, cold and heavy in their hands, the fine linen clinging to skin like damp parchment, yielding to the touch. When Kathryn gently peeled the shirt away, there lay Edmund Walsingham, like a wax doll with darkened nails and a swelling belly, and a map of black-green bruises curling around the right shoulder and hip.

"Let's turn him on his side."

Wollans caught Edmund's hip, jaws working as he muttered softly, while Tom lifted the shoulder, and Kathryn held the dead man's heavy head between both hands. A faint musk wafted up when they turned the body, like meat beginning to turn.

The bruises continued on the back, darker where the body had lain on the stairs' wood — unless…

"How did you find him?" asked Tom. "With his face down or up?"

Again the two servants sought each other's gaze, and it was Wollans who answered, blinking his filmy eye. "Staring up, he was," he rumbled. "Like one amazed. Like one irked."

And then someone had sewn the eyes shut. Tom was thankful to be spared his brother's last look of reproach.

I'm doing my best, Ned — not that his best was leading anywhere.

So the blood had pooled in the parts that lay lowest, obscuring any signs of hands or fingers on the back, the shoulders, the upper arms. Nothing showed on the front, nor on the neck. Nothing but the bruising of a hard fall. Nothing to suggest that Edmund had been grabbed or pushed. Nothing to disprove it.

But then, in truth, what had Tom hoped to find? Handprints showing the place where a murderer had shoved? "You can dress him again, Kathryn."

The old woman directed in quick whispers for her husband and Tom to move the body while she eased the shirt back in place. She was still tugging it over the bloated chest when someone angrily shook the door from the passage room.

"Who is in there?" called a sharp woman's voice from outside. "Open this door!"

Both servants froze as the bolted door rattled again.

"Quick, cover him," Tom ordered, because the owner of the sharp voice would find the great door bolted just as firmly, and then try the others.

"Is that you, Thomas?" she called from the passage. "Open the door this moment!"

Hastening to the stairs door, Tom unjammed the chair from under the latch, stepping back just enough to avoid the heavy leaf as it was thrown open, and his sister Barbara sailed inside like a Spanish galleon.

Barbara Walsingham, Mrs. Sherley these past fifteen years, sharp of face, of voice, of manner, brushed past her brother, and halted five steps away from the dais. For a heartbeat she gaped at the Wollanses — Kathryn stiffened in the act of folding the shroud over Edmund, her husband crushing an armful of black cloth — then she found her voice again.

"What do you think you're doing, disrespecting the dead?"

Tom stepped between his angry sister and the servants. "My bidding, Barbara," he said, as firmly as he knew how without raising his voice. "Not that they like it — but that's what they're doing."

And see how she whipped around, every inch as formidable as their mother had been, but with none of Lady Dorothie's weary tolerance for her menfolk in general. To be fair, Mother would have been sorely put out too, to find one of her sons tampering with another's dead body. Little wonder that Barbara, never patient with her youngest brother on the best of days, should seethe.

"Your bidding! Then I'll ask you: what do *you* think you're doing?"

A good question, if ever one was asked: right on the mark and bitter as gall. Still, because half a population crowded on the threshold — Foal, a strange fellow who must be a Sherley servant, and the returned John Wood, all round-eyed and speechless — this wasn't where Tom was going to answer. He ordered Wollans to close the door again, and let nobody through, and to help his wife set Mr. Edmund in order before the plumber arrived.

"The plumber has arrived already," Barbara cut in, voice lowered in turn. "And now he's all agog to run back home with tales that the new master of Scadbury is a lunatic."

And small blame to him! Tom pinched the bridge of his nose. "Well, he can wait a little longer. I'm sure someone will give him bread and small ale in the kitchen." Very much wishing that his sister might have found half an hour's delay along the road, Tom led her to the parlour, trying to pretend that the chair under the latch was nothing out of the ordinary.

On the threshold, Barbara stopped to glare once more at Old Kathryn, who, head lowered and shoulders hunched, was busying herself with the shroud.

"From my brother, nothing surprises me anymore, Kathryn," she said. "But of you, I expected better. What would my mother say of this?"

Poor Kathryn; Tom saw the hurt, thin-lipped glance she darted — not at Barbara, though, at himself.

Leave it to Barbara to storm into the parlour and begin to vent. Or rather, she simmered low in her throat — for Barbara was many things, but none of them a fool — and carried on at length.

She'd ever liked the sound of her own outrage, was Tom's least charitable thought as he waited, leaning against the mantel — and she thought her five years' seniority made him hers to scold. Not that he'd truly thought to keep much from his sisters once they arrived. Why, now that Beveridge had turned up, he'd be lucky to keep anything from the whole of Chislehurst — and he still knew so little of what had happened, in truth.

Meanwhile, it seemed, Barbara had spent her first wind, and had been expecting an answer.

"Heed me for once, Thomas!" She rapped her knuckles on the table, pale eyes a-glint. "Always lost inside your own head… But I'll know if I have to shake it out of you: what were you doing?"

Ah, well. Tom made himself not shift his weight. He was the head of the family now, and surely didn't answer to his sister. And if he chose to explain, he needn't be nervous.

Ned's pregnant doxy thinks to get rid of me on the gallows… "Someone, it seems, is whispering that Ned didn't die on his own."

"What on earth…" Barbara began, and then gasped as Tom's meaning sank in. For a heartbeat she stared, colour mounting up her neck, her cheeks. The moment it reached her brow, she snapped, "Fiddle-faddle!"

"Yes — except that the constable heard of it, and came here, and began to ask questions."

"You never believe…?" Barbara turned slowly to the door, and back to Tom, with her eyes narrowed. "Uncle George wrote that Ned died of an inflamed heart."

Poor, fretful George. "True enough — only, not the whole truth. Ned's heart was inflamed, *and* he fell down the stairs."

"And someone says…?" Barbara sank into the armchair, hands clenching in her lap. "And like the Wolfhound they call you, you thought you'd make sure? Lord a' mercy, Thomas — your own brother!"

Because it must be Tom's fault! Not the murderer's, not the maligner's, no — his own, for wanting to find out! He straightened away from the mantel. "And because it's my brother, must I let it lie? Don't you want to know if he was killed?"

"Well, was he?" she retorted like a whiplash. When there was no answer, she pressed on, sour and thin-lipped. "So you disturbed the dead for nothing! It may be everyday work to you in London, Thomas — but here, in your own house, on your own land, with your own brother —"

"Do you think that I liked it? That I wouldn't have rather —
"

A knock cut Tom short — which was just as well, for both he and Barbara were primed for a row of rows.

"Yes?" he called. "Come in." And who must obey, but John Wood? Of all who could have overheard the spat! "Yes, Mr. Wood — what is it?" Tom demanded, more sharply than he might have.

In any other, that blank, straight-backed manner would have looked like a pretence at not having heard, but the steward's cold censure couldn't be mistaken as he announced that the plumber was ready. "He would seal the coffin, if you please—"

"And who would you be, pray?" Barbara cut right through, head reared to look down her nose at the man.

If nothing else, it was good to see John Wood taken aback for once, as he bowed a tad awkwardly.

"Mr. Wood was Edmund's steward, Barbara," Tom explained — to a disapproving sniff from his sister.

"You should have told the plumber, Mr. Wood," she scolded, "that the coffin cannot be sealed until our sister arrives."

And with this, she swept out to the hall, as unstoppable as a ship in full sail.

How long had they spent bickering like children? When Tom followed his sister into the hall, the light had greyed a good deal. Candles flickered in the branches on the dais, and a coal brazier had been lit beside the empty fireplace. A couple of blackened iron pans sat in it, and the air smelt of damp wool and rosin, of beeswax, and the faint tang of heated metal.

And Edmund wasn't lying on the black-draped trestle anymore. Tom swallowed his surprise. Of course he wasn't. The heavy coffin lay on the floor, parallel to the dais, a dark, dull grey: surely the shrouded body had already been lowered into it.

Stopped in the act of lining up his irons, boxes, and earthen jars on a trestle table covered with canvas and straw, the plumber was being lectured by Barbara.

It should have fallen to the steward to deal with the man, but Wood stood sulking by the stairs door, with the manner of one much wronged. If Mrs. Sherley was so bent on meddling, then let her — and she was welcome to it, said his dark-browed face. For once, Tom rather agreed, or would have, but the plumber appealed to him, to plead fear of being on the roads in the dark, and he'd been set upon only last week near Foots Cray…

But what were the poor man's worries to Mrs. Sherley's will? "Mr. Walsingham will let you spend the night above the stables," she said, without a by-your-leave. "When my sister arrives, you'll do what you must."

"And what if Mary arrives late tomorrow, or the day after? Shall we keep these good folk prisoners? And then…" Tom looked down at his brother's waxy face. Even through the resin and the wool and the smoke and the drying rosemary, the smell of decay touched his nostrils. "It's been more than three days, Barbara…"

She exhaled sharply and looked away, at the coffin's lid that stood propped against the wall.

"Truly," Tom soothed, "Mary will understand." Or rather, Mary wouldn't care a straw — but this he wasn't going to say.

"Will she?" Barbara hissed. "And will she also understand that you begrudged Ned a new coffin?"

"I never…" Tom looked down at the coffin, stepping back to observe it better: dull, dusty grey, darker along the soldered seams. A sudden memory flashed in his mind of his father's coffin — the silvery, almost bluish sheen of new lead, the crisp seams glittering as they caught the light.

With a click of her tongue, Barbara threw up both hands. "Master Smith says your man was full of haste, and you wouldn't wait two days for a new coffin to be made, so they decided on this one." She pursed her lips around the two last words, like one chewing a sour quince.

Jove fulminate lazy plumbers and officious Minotaurs! But then… "Well, it's done now. Even if I send Smith back home at once, he can't make a new one and be here in time for the funeral…" Tom stopped short at the sight of Barbara's eyes reddening.

"And half of Kent will see Edmund go to his rest in a cast-off coffin!" she griped in a raw whisper, clutching her hands together. "What will people say?"

Let them say what they will — who cares a straw? Tom bit down the angry retort — because his sister was right, and his heart sank with the weight of it. Look at the wretched thing! Was that a poorly buffed scratch on the side? An indentation on the corner? There would be murmurs about it, about the miserly new master of Scadbury.

"Well, Smith can as well seal it," was what he said instead. "When Mary comes, it will be the last of my troubles." Because Mary would have her own cutting thoughts on the matter, and her husband too — Thomas Pelham, High Sheriff of Surrey, with that perennially raised brow, as though he couldn't quite fathom his wife's kin. And before them, Uncle Buffkin was sure to give him grief.

And all the time the plumber hovered hopefully by the table with his soldering irons.

Barbara sighed, a hand at her temple in the gesture Mother had used to make. "Oh, have it your way. You're master here at Scadbury now."

And whatever I do, it will be mine to live with. Tom nodded at Smith, and the man sketched a bow. He didn't look too pleased: the day was dimming fast, he and his apprentice would have to work by candlelight, and to sleep above the stables after all.

They went to work at once, stirred the coals in the brazier, put their irons to heat, and the solder to melt, greased their cloths with soft tallow. Patient and slow, they brushed the coffin's edges with rosin, dripped the molten solder in little blobs all around, the metal softly hissing as each tack was dripped. And then, with the help of Foal and young Will Everest, they lowered the lid over the coffin with a dull, hollow clang.

Tom found himself swallowing hard, and blinking as his eyes stung. At his side, Barbara bowed her head, her lips trembling: there had been no great love between either of them and their brother, and yet here they stood, moved if not deeply grieved that they had seen the last of Edmund until Judgement Day.

Smith, his bearded face lit like that of an intent Vulcan at his forge, began to pour molten lead in the joints to seal them, rubbing the seams into shape with a greased pad. Barbara's face had softened for a moment; now it hardened again as she watched the new lead gleam like silver against the older metal.

When the door to the parlour eased open, and George peered in, Tom shook himself from his contemplation. He nudged his sister, who looked up and in turn saw their uncle.

"He and Uncle Buffkin…" Tom murmured under his breath. "I haven't discussed much with them of what I told you. For now, the less they know, the better."

Barbara snorted. "Half your household is in it with you, Thomas — and the rest had a good eyeful of what you were doing when I arrived."

No doubt the Good Lord had created sisters to keep a man from over-reckoning his own cleverness. "Yes, and it wouldn't be half as bad if you hadn't made all the noise you did!" he retorted, which was petty and childish — because the whole of Scadbury had been abuzz with speculation ever since Beveridge's visit, and Barbara wasn't wrong in drawing up her chin and looking at him askance. Tom fetched a sigh. "Barbara, one thing is the servants' hearsay, and another would be my sister tattling of what I've told no one but her. Would you, as a favour to me, keep it between the two of us for now?"

For a heartbeat, he thought she'd pat his head, the way she'd done when they'd been small and he'd tried to mollify her. It seemed to work still, twenty years later.

"Oh, have it your way," Barbara said again, "as long as you are done disturbing Ned." And she went back to watch the poor plumber's work with gimlet eyes.

Later, when they'd had a dismal supper — a distempered Barbara dictating the men's humour — and more psalms around the offending coffin, Tom found that his steps carried him back to the hall. It was dark, but for a few candles, and deserted, but for Susan Foal. Watching all night again? Tom had the unpleasant notion that, if he sent her away now, she'd creep back the moment he was gone… Not that she was praying. Armed with a cloth, she was ferociously buffing the coffin's lid, grunting as she strained to reach the centre, never mind that she was too short for it. It must not have occurred to her to climb onto a stool — but then, even if she did, Tom rather doubted the old lead would polish.

It looked near black now, but for the glint of the newly made seams — and still, Fair Susan polished and polished.

Tom leant back against the doorjamb, tired of a sudden.

Was it truly just three days since he had been no more than Mr. Secretary's man, penniless, landless, and entrusted with the secrets of princes, risking his life at the drop of a hat? Oh, he'd yearned to own Scadbury now and then — as one yearned for things never to be had. Well, he was master of it now, and here he stood, with even the doubt of murder paling beside the worry of what the village would think of Ned's coffin.

CHAPTER 8

20th of November

Friday morning rose blustery and busy. The house was astir with much work; Barker and Kathryn argued in mutters about who'd burnt part of the new bread, and Wood's glover cousin came, bringing his wares damnably early and complaining that Foal had threatened him with the deeper side of the moat.

As he broke his fast alone in the small kitchen, Tom sniffed the tang of singed rye-bread, sipped at his small ale, and tried, as a diversion from darker thoughts, to picture Foal threatening anyone. All he could think of was the lap-spaniel one of his Guildford aunts had used to own, a fat, bandy-legged creature, bulge-eyed and cross-tempered, ever yapping and then running for shelter. And yet even the stupidest cur could be dangerous, given enough ill-will. Tom looked up as Kathryn bustled past with her head lowered, and disappeared to the old kitchen without a word. No honey with his bread, this morning; no kind word, no gap-toothed smile. He'd lost an ally there, thanks to Barbara's overbearing ways. And his own notions, in truth: back in Seething Lane, no servant would have batted an eyelid at being ordered to unwind a funeral shroud — but here it was different.

All was going to be different from now on. And why must the prospect of living in his own house put him in so bleak, so hollow, so lonely a humour, he didn't know, but he found himself wishing for the Minotaur's return and even, Lord have mercy on him, missing that strongheaded vixen, Mistress Shelton. Shaking his head at himself, he bit into a last piece of bread and butter. Even the manchets were much better in Seething Lane.

"Master?"

A lapdog — if ever there was one. It was all Tom could do not to burst out laughing at the sight of Foal on the threshold, squat and sullen, with that voice half snarl and half squeak.

"A man as asks to see ye, Master," he muttered, kneading his fingers as though he'd like to throttle this early visitor. "From London."

This had Tom springing up from the bench and out into the passage at once. From London — and not Skeres… "Didn't he say a name?" he asked over his shoulder, and Foal's pear-shaped form, black against the light from the kitchen, only lifted a pair of narrow shoulders and let them fall — the fool.

But no matter: the man from London was waiting in the guardhouse, pacing between the one window and the ladder that led upstairs, to Will Everest's room. The moment Tom entered, he swung around on his heel, with a fierce scowl that dissolved at once.

"God's nightgown, Mr. Thomas — but you've a household of nitwits!" exclaimed Kit Marley, with the grimace of the much put-upon.

Which was no doubt true of Foal — but never mind. "What are you doing here? Where's Skeres?"

It was plain how Marley swallowed a quip in the face of Tom's urgency. "I'm carrying letters. Didn't that hoddy-doddy tell you?" He dug out of his sleeve a square of folded paper, and then another. "And the Cyclops took a fall on the road. Broke his ankle. Couldn't ride…" *What will you have?* said the one-shouldered shrug — as though the Minotaur were a raw boy instead of a hardened rider of many missions. Marley held out the letters with a flourish. "So there was need of a messenger, and Lady Sidney thought: why not Marley?"

Frances... The flare of pain that always went with the thought of her had dulled to a pang over the three years of her widowhood. Now, Tom found, the looming shadow of Essex sharpened it again. The larger letter was superscribed in her elegant hand, addressed to Mr. Thomas Walsingham, Esquire, Scadbury Manor, and sealed with Sir Francis's private seal. That Mr. Secretary should use his daughter as an amanuensis... When Tom looked up, Marley must have read his thoughts, for he murmured, twist-mouthed, that His Honour wasn't well.

It was with a heavy heart that Tom broke the seal, unfolded the thick paper, and moved under the one window to read the half a dozen lines:

Thomas,

It is both extraordinary and most unwelcome that you, of all men, should find yourself so entangled the very moment you step into your own house. Though you make no word of it, your man Skeres tells of an unsigned letter that might have set these events in motion: such a letter could point to a more deliberate intention of putting you in harm's way. I have no need to state my complete trust in both your innocence and your ability to unravel this affair, but consider that scandal alone could harm you and the Walsingham name.

Sir Francis signed himself Tom's assured loving cousin — but neither that nor the assurance of trust concealed the great man's impatience, and even a measure of fretfulness. Could it truly be that someone was using Edmund's death to damage Mr. Secretary? It seemed like a long game, an unlikely one. It seemed far above not just the means, but also the wits of anyone he'd met at Scadbury so far. It stood on nothing but the existence of the unsigned letter — of which there was no proof yet, and pinch the Minotaur for bringing it up with Sir Francis. Oh, someone else should be pinched, surely, for Audrey Shelton must have filled Skeres's head with talk of the letter all the way from Scadbury to Lee.

"...and the other is from Her Ladyship."

Tom blinked out of his musings to find that Marley had run out of what patience he possessed.

"The one with the cord," he said, as though Tom could be mistaken.

This letter was bound rather than sealed, with a thin cord of grey silk, and one of those intricate knots that Frances so liked to tie — so perfect, so delicate and strong, and so peculiar, there was no mistaking them. *So you'll always know if I tied it or not.* Smiling a little in spite of himself, Tom sliced the cord with his knife and carefully put the untouched knot inside his sleeve. The letter bore no address on the outside; inside, it was closely written: *Tom, my very dear...*

Frances worried. She worried for Tom, that he should find himself exposed to these suspicions.

This is why, poor Skeres having injured himself — both in bones and pride — I talked Father into sending Master Marley in his place, who will show equal loyalty and ready wits, if perhaps no great sense.

And she worried for her father, who had suffered much through Accession Day and the festivities at Court.

Nothing angers me like seeing his foes and friends alike observe him askance, watch for a held breath, a falter — and wonder how much longer will Mr. Secretary Walsingham's hand steadily hold the reins of the State.

Like wolves. And now Tom himself was adding to these worries, those of Frances and those of her father — and not once had it occurred to him that the shaft might not be aimed at him!

"Lady Sidney says I'm to assist you as best I can," Marley said in an eager whisper. "Do they truly think you killed your brother? The heir suspected — isn't there a play…?"

Save us from poets! See if he wasn't all but bouncing on his toes… No great sense indeed!

"I'm sure you'll write it yourself," Tom groused. "See that you make the heir irreproachable and soon cleared."

Which had Marley laughing, high and clear. "Ah, but that's not how stories work: he must suffer greatly before he emerges in triumph! Danger and suspicion must gather thick around his head, as black a thundercloud as —"

He stopped short when the door was thrown open, and Uncle Buffkin strode in, booted for riding. The old man took in Kit Marley — the muddied boots, the dishevelled hair, the oxblood sleeves — and scowled.

"And why must half of Kent swarm us at first light, I will never know," he griped — and then, observing the letters in Tom's hand, he narrowed his eyes at the newcomer. "That's never *your man* back from London, is it? Either he's halved on the way, or you've a troop of them, Thomas…"

There were a good many things sure to put up Marley's back; mistaking him for a servant was one. The lad was already drawing as tall as he could, ready no doubt to proclaim himself a *Magister Artium*, or a poet, or both, but Tom had no particular wish to see what effect that would produce in Uncle Buffkin. "This is my friend, Uncle. Master Christopher Marley," he said. "Marley, my uncle, Mr. Leven Buffkin."

And while Marley bowed and Uncle Buffkin muttered under his breath, there came a knock on the door to the bridge.

"An important man, is my nephew. All these messages from London — and not a servant to answer the door…"

Where was Foal, devil pinch him, when he was needed? Ah, well… At the second knock, Tom went to open the door himself, to find on the bridge a stout gentleman in a dark cloak, brown of beard and moustache, with dark, hooded, studious eyes. Tom was sure he'd never seen him before — but then, who knew what acquaintances Edmund had made these past five years?

"My name is William Lambarde. I would speak to Mr. Thomas Walsingham," the gentleman said in a gravelly voice, so serious and blunt that it set Tom's teeth on edge.

He was spared the temptation to answer coldly, though, when Susan Foal barged in breathless, and at the same time Uncle Buffkin boomed:

"Lambarde! I didn't know you knew my nephew."

"I don't, Mr. Buffkin." The man called Lambarde gave a stiff little bow. "Nor did I know he is your relation."

"Are you here officially, then? Save and deliver us!" With a chortle, the old man came to lay a heavy hand on Tom's shoulder. "You must have done something bad, eh, Thomas, to earn a visit from the Justice of the Peace for Kent."

There — there! Tom felt cold of a sudden. Audrey Shelton was right, and so were Mr. Secretary and Frances: now he was in deep trouble.

It never rains but it pours, a part of Tom's mind kept repeating, as he sat with Lambarde by the fire in the withdrawing room. Once rid of Marley, and — with more difficulty — of Uncle Buffkin, Lambarde had shown himself eager to speak privately, and now sat with his fingertips brought together, contemplating his host the way the Sphinx must have studied Oedipus just outside of Thebes.

The man had an egg-shaped head, Tom observed as he waited, dark with close-cropped hair. And a thick nose. And a most unpleasant mole on his left cheekbone.

"I will say, Mr. Walsingham," he began at last, "that I wish Mr. Buffkin had made a less public announcement of my coming."

So did Tom, for that matter. "Well, you seem to know my uncle," he said, and Lambarde made a noise that could have been a chuckle or a clearing of the throat.

"Can it be hoped that your servants will be prudent?"

"Master Marley is no servant, and can be trusted to be discreet." Or so Tom hoped. "Mrs. Foal, though…"

"I see." Lambarde tapped his fingertips together. "The fact is, Mr. Walsingham, that I've no wish to make trouble. Despite what Mr. Buffkin thinks, I haven't come quite officially."

Did the man think himself reassuring, with all this roundabout hinting? Tom didn't bother to hide his growing impatience. "And may I ask why you are unofficially here?"

There was another of those gravelly hums, another hooded, searchful glance. Was the justice contemplating the fiery humours of youth? Not that Tom was a boy at eight-and-twenty, but Lambarde looked easily half as old again. Or was he sizing up Tom for a murderer? He squared himself in the padded chair, with a creaking of wood and old leather.

"Oh, it's very simple." He began to rummage in the pouch he wore at this girdle. "You understand, Mr. Walsingham, the natural death of a gentleman should not concern me — but…" He extracted a much folded paper — and Tom's heart sank.

He made himself not sigh as Lambarde unfolded what could only be one thing: Audrey Shelton's cursed letter.

"Someone, it seems, wrote this to your constable, the day after your brother's death." He handed it to Tom.

So here it was, not an object of myth, after all: a scrap of common paper no bigger that Tom's hand, folded in four, much dog-eared and grey at the edges and creases. It was easy to imagine a frowning Beveridge turning it in his hands, folding and unfolding it as he tried to decide what to do. It only bore two lines, scratched in brownish ink: *There was foule play at Scathbery with Mr. Ed. Walsyngam.*

"Unsigned," Tom murmured under his breath. A hit for Mistress Shelton — and yet no word of Tom himself, or murder, for that matter.

Lambarde raised his brows. "If it were signed, Mr. Walsingham, all would be much easier for me. Then again, letters of this sort never are. I do not like it, believe me, but tell me honestly: would you ignore it in my place?"

Jove, no! He'd study it with utmost care, draw every ounce of meaning out of the words, the manner, the aspect. Shaking his head for all answer, he rose to observe the scrap by the light of the candle-branch on the table.

All about it was coarse and common. The uneven hand, the watery ink, the rough-grained paper… Two sides were clean-cut, the other two torn carefully: a quarter of a foolscap. When he held it against the light, Tom observed the pale curve of a watermark, faint and uncertain. He squinted…

"You seek the mark? It's a plain pot."

Tom half whirled around. How hadn't he noticed when Lambarde had come to stand at his shoulder?

"I've asked my clerk," the justice said. "It's fairly common paper. There's a mill about Dartford, where they make paper like this." He took back the note and folded it carefully again. "It could come from anywhere."

"And from anyone. And it could be about anything. What sort of foul play do you suspect, Mr. Lambarde — and, while we are at it, why did Beveridge come to you with this?"

"Ah, yes." Lambarde rolled back on the balls of his feet. "Shall we sit down?"

It was the sort of invitation that never led to anything good. Tom gestured to the chair that the magistrate had just vacated, and, being in no mood to sit still, went to stand behind the other, leaning his crossed arms on the back. He was looming over Lambarde, if from a polite distance — and cared very little. Let the man make what he liked of it!

Not, much, it seemed: the magistrate made himself comfortable in the chair, smoothed his moustache, and nodded once or twice. "Well, then," he began. "First of all, imagine Constable Beveridge's quandary. I'm told you know something of this kind of work, so you will understand: he comes here with nothing on his mind but the customary visit, never expecting to hear rumours — but that he does."

"From Mrs. Foal, yes," Tom cut in. Should he explain why the woman was not to be taken at her word? Lambarde couldn't have failed to notice her in the gatehouse, eyes a-glimmer with smug triumph at the sight of a magistrate — and she was, no doubt, waiting to pour more of her venom in the right ear.

For a moment, Lambarde seemed mildly surprised. "You know that?" he asked.

"As you said, I know something of this work." Tom smiled thinly. "I drew it out of Beveridge — but I could have spared myself the trouble, for Mrs. Foal makes no mystery of what she thinks of me. I'm sure you'll hear all of it quite soon."

"And, when I do, I should pay no heed?"

Was this how this man worked — leading people along circuitous paths? Well, he wasn't leading Tom anywhere.

"Beveridge seems to think that you should."

"You misjudge him. He was half minded to dismiss your housekeeper's whispers — but then, the day you arrived…" Lambarde tapped the pouch at his side with two fingers. "Someone pushed this under his door. He did try to find out who, and when, but…" A shrug. "And that, in the poor fellow's own words, took away his sleep."

Until it dawned on him to go to Sir Brian Annesley… Tom bit down the words. Beveridge had never told him that, had he? Audrey had — and he didn't want her brought into this. "So he came to you?" he asked instead — and then a new thought occurred to him that should have come much sooner. "Why not to the coroner — whoever that is these days? That's the proper thing to do."

"Yes, if he wanted to spring an inquest on you — which he did not. Out of regard, I believe."

This, now! Tom snorted. "And he thought he'd do me a kindness by telling the Justice of the Peace for Kent instead?"

"Well…" Lambarde spread placating hands. "He sought counsel, you see, but he couldn't find Sir Brian Annesley, whom he knows and trusts, and to Mr. John Lennard he would not go, for he's related to you."

"My middle brother was married to his daughter — and if you think that Mr. Lennard would show me any consideration…"

"Beveridge does, so he sought Mr. Style in Beckenham — who would much rather not concern himself with one of your name. He suggested that Beveridge should come to me, though — and…"

"And here you are — not quite officially."

It seemed that Lambarde didn't much like Tom's tone, because, for the first time in this conversation, he frowned and sat forward.

"Mr. Walsingham, understand this," he said severely. "I am *not* shy of the Walsingham name — but neither am I eager to raise trouble around it with no good reason. And whether a bilious woman's words and an unsigned note make for good reason, I want to make sure for myself. So yes — here I am, not quite officially. And if I can ascertain that the whisper and the notes are nothing more than malice, I'll soon be satisfied — and you all the better for it."

The manner was so much like that of a put-upon tutor faced with a pupil's ingratitude, it might have been amusing, if only… Tom hesitated. Could he share his doubts — and, even more, Sir Francis's — with this unreadable fellow? For all his ramblings, Mr. Justice had given away precious little of his thoughts. Was it Julius Caesar who had written of uncertain fields and entrenching oneself? Tom didn't remember — but it seemed like sound advice at the moment, so he went to sit, said that he greatly appreciated the magistrate's caution, and waited.

It wasn't a long wait: Lambarde sat back, set his face in a frown, and began. He wanted to know, first of all, about Edmund's death.

Tom told him what he knew — leaving out for the moment his inspection of the body.

"But all this I've learnt from my Uncle Guildford and the servants — for, as I said, I only arrived the next day," he concluded. "You'll want to question them."

Again, Lambarde nodded and hummed. "I will, yes — but before that… If you weren't here when your brother died, surely you can prove your presence elsewhere?"

There it was — the question Audrey Shelton had asked, the question Tom had no good answer for. Audrey had believed him and worried; what would this Justice of the Peace do?

Oh, let him make of it what he must! "It happens, Mr. Lambarde, that at the time I was lost on Dartford Heath, sheltering in a ruined collier's hut, with a lamed horse for all company! Had I known I'd face a charge of murder, I might have stopped in Dartford."

Thus the Sphinx might have gaped at Oedipus, had he waxed sarcastic instead of answering the riddle. "This is not good, Mr. Walsingham," said the Sphinx, voice rising a notch — to which what could Oedipus do, but spread his hands?

"But after all, I don't know why. *Foul play at Scadbury* hardly points to me in particular."

It would have been more reassuring, had Lambarde not sat back, tapping his fingertips together and watching Tom from under hooded eyelids. "It doesn't, no," he admitted, "but your housekeeper certainly did."

Cursed woman… Tom rubbed at his brow. "Isn't it some sort of fallacy that you should corroborate Susan Foal's words with the note, and the note with her words?" he asked, tired of a sudden.

A mistake, for Lambarde was all severity again. "I'm sure you've learnt that Man's worst nature seldom conforms to philosophy."

Hardly the answer to Tom's question — not that it would matter if he raised the point. So, instead, he went for safer, firmer ground. "Well, then, here's an unphilosophical objection: how could I have entered the house again at night, and no one the wiser?"

"The storm…"

"The storm could have covered the noise of a broken window — but I'm ready to wager that no window was broken that night." Not that he'd thought to ask, but someone would have mentioned such a thing, surely?

Fingering his mole, Lambarde digested this. "Unless someone had let you in…" he began — and then the door opened, and Barbara marched in without a by-your-leave.

"You have visitors, Thomas," she announced, sparing the barest glare for Lambarde as he rose and bowed. "And the joiner's man has brought the bier."

"Perhaps…" Lambarde murmured to Tom. "I'd wait to have the coffin nailed, Mr. Walsingham —"

"It's lead, and sealed already, Sir — not that I see what business of yours it is," Barbara cut through — who had the sharpest ear, and no patience for that kind of tactful murmuring, much less when it was meant to exclude her.

"Barbara," Tom tried, "this is Mr. Lambarde, the Justice of—"

"I know." She frowned at the magistrate. "Our uncle told me."

"And this, Mr. Lambarde, is my sister, Mrs. Sherley."

Lambarde bowed again, utterly unperturbed when Barbara's displeasure didn't abate a whit. Then again, Heaven knew how many disapproving gentlewomen he had faced in his capacity.

"I have no wish to disturb your mourning, Mrs. Sherley," he said, with an all but paternal manner. "I hope it won't become necessary to open the coffin again. I'm sure your brother agrees with me."

But the man had never had to deal with Barbara Walsingham — who, instead of deferring to the men, coldly surveyed her brother, mouth turned downward.

"I dare say he does," she said. "And one of these days he'll make a fine Justice of the Peace. But our brother died of an inflamed heart, so I would hear what a magistrate wants with us."

She glided inside — and on her heels came swaggering Uncle Buffkin and then a more reluctant Uncle George. Behind him, Tom caught a glimpse of Marley, in whose face the door was pushed shut. The family closing ranks!

Time to take the reins. Tom went to stand by the chair at the table's head. "Since we are all here," he said firmly, "you may as well know that doubts have been raised about Edmund's death. Mr. Lambarde —"

"Ha!" barked Uncle Buffkin.

"And who raised these doubts, pray?" Barbara wanted to know.

Uncle George gasped and swallowed hard.

"Mr. Lambarde," Tom repeated a little more forcefully, "does us the courtesy of looking into the matter quietly — which we all appreciate, I'm sure."

See Uncle Buffkin's piggish eyes glitter — one who wasn't closing ranks, after all. "I'll wager you're the prime suspect, eh, Thomas?" He roared with laughter. "In debt up to your ears, and now you inherit…"

"Truly, Uncle!" Barbara protested — thinking perhaps of those visitors she'd mentioned, waiting in the hall.

It was Lambarde's turn to draw straight and stern. "There are no suspects yet, Mr. Buffkin," he said. "There is no certainty of a crime — yet. Rumours reached me, and I'm here to see that they are either dispelled or acted upon."

"And I ask again: who started those rumours?" This from Barbara at her most matronly.

"An unsigned letter," said Lambarde — a wisely vague, if truthful, answer, had not George chosen that moment to find his voice again.

"And Mrs. Foal," he stammered. "But she…"

Barbara turned an incredulous glare from her uncle to Tom. "*Susan Foal?*" she exclaimed. "That creature who calls herself a housekeeper? And she presumes…?"

Well, Lambarde was going to find out soon enough — but still, must Uncle Buffkin chortle and pat Barbara's hand as though she were an upset child?

"There, there, Barbara lass — never look this agazed," he mocked. "It was Ned who taught the hussy to presume a good deal."

One would have thought she'd never heard of such a thing, judging by the way she gasped. But at least, bless her, she shared the notion that family matters were best not discussed before a magistrate.

"You have visitors, Thomas," she repeated, with a most unsubtle tilt of her head. "I am sure Mr. Lambarde will spare you while you greet them."

There was no blaming Lambarde for looking a little amused as he bowed again, and said that he wouldn't want to impose more than was needed. Still, as they all filed out, with George lingering last, the magistrate stopped Tom.

"But I'll have a word again with you later, Mr. Walsingham," he whispered. "Are you truly so deep in debt as Mr. Buffkin says?"

Not truly. Not as things go in London… Oh, what was the use? This keen-minded fellow was going to find out all too soon — perhaps he'd found out already, if he'd spoken to Beveridge — and lying wouldn't help. "My uncle has a taste for exaggeration," he said with a sigh. "But about this he doesn't exaggerate much."

"Then inheriting will spare you a good deal of unpleasantness."

So evenly it was said that, had it not been for the keen gaze that went with the words, they wouldn't have seemed what they were: an accusation.

On the threshold where he still dithered, George gaped and then scurried away.

"You frighten my uncle, Mr. Lambarde!" Once more, Tom's attempt at levity raised the magistrate's hackles.

"I would rather frighten you," he replied, bristling. "Or not frighten, but… Can you deny, in good conscience, that you stood to gain from this death more than anyone else?"

And wasn't that a jest? Well then, let the man have the truth, since he must meddle. "In the best conscience, yes: I can." Tom heard his own peevishness — and didn't care a straw. "My father left Scadbury so encumbered with debt, that it will be a marvel if I don't sink under the weight. And besides, what ready money there is won't go to me. If you seek those who stood to gain, you should look to my brother's steward and valet —"

There was some satisfaction in seeing Lambarde rear his head in surprise — but the surprise was not over what Tom thought, and the satisfaction was short-lived.

"You were present when your brother made his will?" the magistrate asked.

Curse it! "No…"

Lambarde hummed. "Then you heard from someone who was. Was this before or after your brother's death?"

A chill crept down Tom's spine. Too many times he'd played this same game of suspicion not to see his mistake. Sir Francis had taught him early on: *Pick answers out of men piecemeal, Thomas.* And now here he was, being questioned for lies, omissions, contradictions. One thing he'd learnt: hesitation never helped; lies that could be disproved helped even less.

"Afterwards," he said slowly. "I was told the gist of it when I arrived — but..." But, of course, Beveridge would have told the tale of the row between the brothers, as he'd heard it from Susan Foal?

"But?" Lambarde pressed — the Sphinx, awaiting for the wrong answer, for the wrong silence, for the mistake.

But Oedipus knew the game, too. "I'm sure you heard that I visited my brother on the day he died, and that we argued over money. Well, among other things, he told me that I wouldn't find his will to my liking."

See how the Sphinx exhaled through that thick nose, and, as it were, stood back. He harrumphed and pulled at his moustache — irked, no doubt, that he had been seen through.

"It still means very little, Mr. Walsingham. You still might have thought to get your hands on enough money..."

"I might — and would have been wrong — but about the estate itself I had no illusions."

For a few heartbeats, Lambarde chewed his lip. "It is an irregular request, I know," he said then, with the brusqueness of one disappointed. "And you would be justified in refusing if I were to ask to see the estate books — but...?"

If this was another snare, it was a pointless one: whatever was in the books, it was nothing Tom would want to hide, so he nodded most courteously. "If it will convince you that this inheritance was never going to save me, then you have my blessing. You'll have to ask my brother's steward, though — for I have yet to see the books myself."

And still Lambarde narrowed his eyes, suspicious fellow that he was — until something else occurred to him. "The steward, you say? The one who inherits?"

"Indeed. You can ask him at once."

And how the magistrate would have taken a demurral or, Heaven forfend, a downright refusal, Tom would have liked to know — for ready acquiescence only made him glower more darkly.

CHAPTER 9

Wood wasn't in the hall. Half a dozen visitors were — villagers and gentlefolk alike, and Marley among them — gathered in loose knots around the dais, some talking to Uncle Buffkin, some whispering among themselves. Now that the body was sealed in its coffin, the fireplace had been lit again. Barbara stood by it, occupied with old Mrs. Carmarden, who had been Mother's friend until they'd quarrelled — while Uncle George… Where was he, now? Ah — there was George by the passage door, in close conversation with Susan Foal. It was to them that Tom made his way, pausing to exchange nods and greetings with the visitors — half of whom he wasn't sure he knew — wondering at how things had changed in five years; either he misremembered the endless stream of visitors pouring to Scadbury after Father's death, or Ned had let things grow sour between manor house and land.

How many will come to see me lie here when my day comes…?

Jove, what a thing to wonder! Shaking himself out of his melancholy, Tom reached his uncle, who startled, and the housekeeper, who glowered.

"Find Mr. Wood, Mrs. Foal," he ordered. "Tell him I would see him at once."

One thing to say for this woman: she possessed a certain rough skill in shaping wordless obedience into an insult. The glare, the brisk curtsey, the prompt turning on her heel and waddling away…

"And this is the housekeeper?" asked Lambarde, as he followed her with his eyes.

Not for long, Tom didn't say. "You'll want to question her."

The notion made George stiffen. "That spiteful, dishonest hag?" he ground out. "That devil's limb —"

What had Fair Susan done now to put the man so out of sorts? Before Tom could ask, the passage door opened, with Wollans holding it for Everest and Jack Fuller carrying the bier. It was unfortunate that young Will, walking backwards, should stumble in the rushes: the bier rocked, and Fuller dropped his side with a curse.

Oh, Lord — see how Mrs. Carmarden leant forward in her chair, better to enjoy the sight of Scadbury's clumsy servants bickering with the joiner's man, of Wollans scolding, of Everest calling names, and of Fuller shoving the scullion, because he couldn't shove Wollans. Rising like a thundercloud, Barbara made ready to bear down on the unruly little group, but Tom was closer. Twice in three days he'd met Jack Fuller, and was already heartily sick of the man.

"Enough!" he hissed, and grabbed him by the shoulder, just as Marley trotted up to do the same on the other side. And didn't Fuller shake free, and draw back a fist, ready to strike at the nearest captor? Only, when Marley stepped aside, the joiner tripped and crashed down onto his hands and knees. Growling, he pushed his straw-like hair from his flushed face and tried to scramble up, grabbing wildly at the cupboard and hitting one of the goblets, which clanged to the floor — and just then Wood strode out of the counting-room, with Susan Foal on his heels.

The steward went to grip Fuller by both shoulders, whispering forcefully in his ear.

"Send him on his way, Mr. Wood," Tom ordered. "And, Fuller, tell your master I want someone else tomorrow for the funeral. Someone who won't be drunk."

Muttering though gritted teeth, Fuller let Wood drag him none to gently too his feet, and lead him away towards the kitchen. All around people stared — and little blame to them: Barbara white with anger, Mrs. Carmarden by the fire with her withered face scrunched in disapproval, several others struck speechless, and Susan Foal thoughtfully watching Wood and the limping Fuller go.

"I am very sorry." Tom pitched his voice for the whole hall. "Please, do not be alarmed."

The low whispering hum of a funeral visit resumed, if a little awkwardly, while Wollans and Everest recovered the bier and carried it close to the dais. It would take a pair of farmhands later to move the coffin on it.

At Tom's elbow, Kit Marley picked up the fallen goblet and straightened with a grin, as pleased as though he'd thrown out Fuller with his own hands. "Witless churl — too ale-sopped to keep his feet…"

"Yes, and lame from a child."

This earned a grimace. Was the poet sorry for the man, or chagrined to have his imaginary fight still reduced in valour? By the time Tom had finished the story of Fuller trampled in the stables, Wood was returning, and Tom beckoned him over.

"Mr. Lambarde has my permission to see your books, Mr. Wood." Tom looked around, seeking the magistrate, only to find him disappeared — together with both uncles. Had the man begun his questioning already? "Ah, well — when he finds you, show him the estate accounts. And, Mr. Wood —" he dropped his voice to a cold whisper — "Jack Fuller claims to have your protection, for some reason — but understand well, you and he both: that gives him no licence to brabble under my roof."

See how the steward squared already stiff shoulders. "I would never —" he began, and paused, lips compressed and nostrils flaring as he took his temper in hand. "Ill as you think of me, Mr. Walsingham, I'd never encourage this disorderly behaviour."

Which Tom rather believed, in spite of his dislike of the man — but still… "He says that, when my brother threw him out, you found him work with Burten."

John Wood gave a long sigh. "He came to me in despair — and… In all honesty, Mr. Walsingham, when your brother dismissed Jack Fuller, it wasn't over his drinking. He'd always been a braggart, and a great liar — but no worse a drunkard than most."

"Fuller says the Wollanses made him up as one."

"It wasn't the Wollanses who had him dismissed." The steward looked pointedly over his shoulder at the counting-room door, where Susan Foal had stood and wasn't anymore.

You weren't this skittish once, Fuller had sneered at the woman. The more he learnt of her, the less Tom found to like — but had Fuller been blameless? "And you found it an injustice."

This seemed to prickle the steward's Puritan-like conscience. He shook his head, one palm raised as if to call Heaven to witness: what could a good man do, in the face of obdurate unfairness? Or, at least, that was what Tom would have supposed the gesture to mean. Wood's words, though, were different.

"I was minded to plead for the lad with your brother, but…" He pursed his lips. "The household was in turmoil enough, and I thought, Lord forgive me, that Jack Fuller out of the way would be one burden less on Mr. Edmund's mind."

Well, he still painted himself as acting in Edmund's best interests — and yet was he confessing to imperfect judgement?

"Which still didn't make it fair?" Marley asked, all mock innocence — which had the steward drawing tall again.

Truly, a full beard was all the man lacked to make his fine, burning-eyed face the mien of a prophet. Even his whisper sounded noble. "Whether for presuming or meddling, I was punished with great disappointment. Fuller got with child Burten's sister… He married her, yes — but, from what I hear, he isn't a good husband to her, and he's become the drunkard he was called. Yes — I was punished."

Oh, Jupiter — *he* was punished? What of Fuller himself? Even more, what of Burten and his sister? "It seems to me," Tom said, bristling, "that the punishment fell on others."

As if there was any discussion to be had with this sanctimonious sort! The steward coloured a little, but lost none of his prophetical manner. "The Lord in his wisdom knows where to rain his ire, Mr. Walsingham, and each man's conscience will speak to him. Mine, I assure you, is heavy."

What did one say to this? Nothing that was good, surely — so Tom dismissed the steward and took a deep breath, not quite sure whether he wanted to laugh or count in Latin.

For his part, Marley had no such doubts, reckoning by his snort of laughter. "Never say there's a lack of hypocritical asses among Protestants!" he chuckled, not half as softly as would have been prudent.

With a wince, Tom observed the visitors: when had they grown in number to be half a score? And was the old fellow by the passage door Robert Mace? But then, all day people had been coming and going. Fates send no one had heard Marley's sally — least of all Barbara and Mrs. Carmarden.

"Go and find Goodwife Wollans," he instructed. "She'll find you a bed. And, Kit, this is not London, and it isn't Cambridge. Keep your irreverence to yourself, will you?"

It wasn't half reassuring, the poet's bright-eyed grin — nor was the cheerful, "Never fear, Mr. Thomas," as he sauntered away.

Mrs. Carmarden was full of chatter about the spat she'd witnessed (never any good, those Fullers were), and gleefully curious about the man who wasn't Tom's servant. So was Barbara, in truth, but Tom eluded both women with vague lies of Marley being from Sir Francis's household, and fled to greet the rest of the visitors — a varied company of tenants and acquaintances, and little Mr. Hearsdon, the one who spoke of Ned with true warmth and regret. It took a few tales of rides and hunts before Tom could extricate himself and pass on to a wiry, ruddy man with large, deep-set eyes.

"I'm William Richbell," this fellow said in answer to Tom's greeting, and waited with his head tilted, as one unsure of his welcome. "Richbell from Bromley, Mr. Walsingham. I was indebted to yer brother…" He waved vaguely towards the dais.

Oh, Jove — another one. Another come to beg for leniency from the wrong man — and this time Tom wasn't going to divulge more than was wise. Could this Richbell be led away before he gave Mrs. Carmarden more to tattle about? Why couldn't Barbara get rid of the woman? She was never thinking to have her for dinner?

And yet Richbell made no sign of waxing pitiful. He stood there, hat in his hands, soulful eyes fixed on the coffin that, in daylight, looked still more mottled and uneven. Was he, too, reckoning the cheap indignity of it?

Bold as brass on the part of a supplicant, for all that there was nothing pleading in the man's manner. He just sighed at times, and shook his head as if marvelling at God's inscrutable ways, and looked respectable and thoughtful.

So much so that, after an interval of this, Tom felt compelled to prod this most placid of debtors. "You farm land, don't you, Master Richbell?" he tried, not that he knew for certain, but the man's whole aspect said *yeoman* — and indeed, the fellow nodded.

"Ay, Sir — ay, so I do. Me own farm just out of Bromley. And 'tis more than a year now as I've bought another bit of land, Chislehurst way."

Which was where Ned's money had gone, as likely as not. "That was bold of you, with the bad harvests and all."

"Ay, well." Richbell gave a mournful half-shrug. "Thank the good Lord, we held our own."

It was more than Tom could help, to blink at this prodigy of prodigies: a debtor given the chance to blame a bad harvest and plead for time — and not taking it? Surely, this was contrary to the very nature of Mankind? The wind itself seemed to mark its astonishment by rising of a sudden, with a great rustle and whisper all around the house. Tom smiled in spite of himself — for the wind always made much of itself at Scadbury, whistling in the passages, howling around the chimneys, raising swarms of sparks in the fireplaces, rippling the placid water of the moat, filling the fire-less rooms with that sweet, damp scent. He'd always liked it as a boy.

Richbell, too, was staring at the leaded window but without any liking in his sad eyes. He would be going before it got to pouring, he said — and took his half-solemn leave with the air of one who had no great weight on his soul besides the natural fear of God's judgement.

"Scuttling away, is he?" Uncle Buffkin chortled, coming to stand at Tom's shoulder. He didn't chortle it half as softly as he could have — but, if Richbell heard, he made no sign.

"Why should he be scuttling?" Tom asked in his best careless manner. At worst, it would show no nervousness; at best, it might draw something out of his uncle, if he knew about Richbell debt. After all, it would have been just like the old man to goad Edmund about those outlandish provisions.

But no: all the question earnt was a curl of the mouth.

"Who wouldn't scuttle from a house with a magistrate ferreting about?" Uncle Buffkin smoothed his bristly moustache and glanced askance at Tom. "Why, Thomas — you wouldn't do ill to scuttle yourself…"

"Well, *I* have done nothing that I should flee from a magistrate. Has Richbell?"

The old man's fleshy face creased. "Richbell?"

"The scuttling one." Tom nodded at the passage door, through which the man had disappeared. "One of Ned's debtors, it turns out."

"That one? Now you mention the name…" Uncle Buffkin squinted at the window, as though through it he could still see the farmer. "Do you think he made lard of your brother because he can't pay?"

That placid, sad-eyed man, a murderer? Besides… "To hear him, he can."

This seemed to greatly disappoint Uncle Buffkin. "Ay, well. Still, I'd tell Lambarde. God willing, he'll go after Richbell and leave us all alone."

"Even if Richbell's innocent? Even if there's no culprit because Ned wasn't murdered at all?"

The look this earnt, the snort — they were nothing less than pitying. "Truly, boy — have you learnt nothing from that cousin of yours? As though it were a matter of innocent and guilty! I'll grant you, Lambarde isn't of the worst, for he has a conscience — but he's eager. In your place, I'd keep well out of his way."

"Do you know him well?"

A harrumph. "Oh, things one hears. Draper's son and ambitious, writes books and dedicates them to the Earl of Essex… Things one hears, living in Kent. You'll have to learn a lot, Thomas — if you don't end up on the gallows first."

Should the notion of his nephew hanging have the old man in such a rolling, shaking fit of chuckles? The two women by the fireplace turned to him with matching frowns, while Hearsdon and another, less gentlemanly visitor, hovering close to take their leave, looked awkward — and small blame to them.

And all the time he exchanged parting words with the two men, one thought kept buzzing in Tom's mind: of all the patrons in the realm, must Lambarde dedicate his books to Essex?

It was only a little later, as he fled upstairs, away from his uncle, Barbara, Mrs. Carmarden, Wood at his ledgers, Lambarde and everyone else, that Tom wondered if Richbell knew that his debt was not to the new Mr. Walsingham. Then either Foal or Wood must have told him, promised easier terms, perhaps. Why Richbell and not Mace, though?

He halted at the top of the Great Stairs, hand curled around the tiger finial, and wondered at his room's door, just across the landing. Instead, Ned had gone all the way to the Old Stairs… And right across from his room, half ensconced in shadow, a narrow flight of steps led up to the garrets. Unlike its twin, atop the Old Stairs, this one must be used rarely, now that the household had so shrunk. Tom climbed up. It was quite steep and narrow, little more than a ladder…

And there was a notion: was this why Richbell and not Mace had been told of the will? Because old, gnarled Mace would have trouble climbing up and down here? Had either Wood or Foal promised Richbell easier terms if Edmund died — or even partial remission?

The steps creaked a little, but the sound was nothing that wouldn't be lost among the noises of the storm. At the top, a low door opened into a cramped attic, with a shuttered window at the far end. Tom went to throw the shutter open, letting in the dim afternoon light and the wind. Years upon years of dampness had stained the whitewash yellow at the corners, and a couple of stripped cots and a chest were pushed against the walls. Perhaps Kathryn would have to put the place back in use now, if Mary brought servants with her — but meanwhile… Tom tried to imagine Richbell smuggled up here by his accomplice, waiting for his chance. But how had they known that Ned would wander about alone and unattended? Was it a common occurrence? Or had the plan been for Richbell to enter his room? And all the time Foal would have been in bed with his wife, while Wood should have been sleeping in his own bed in Chislehurst, had it not been for Ned's insistence.

Tom shook his head. It was too fantastical, too far-fetched, and besides, the dust lay thick on both floor and furniture — undisturbed but for his own footsteps.

Surely, neither William Richbell nor anyone else had absconded up here, waiting to ambush Edmund. With a sigh, Tom secured the shutter and sauntered back downstairs, thinking as he went, tapping his knuckles on the smooth banister to mark the points of his inner argument.

Item: *Non causa pro causa*: even if Richbell knew about the will, it didn't mean that he or anyone else had murdered Edmund.

Item: The observation of the body gave no indication that he had — or had not — been. But…

Item: The surgeon had found nothing in Edmund's death that didn't match his illness.

Therefore…

Quæstio: Had there been a murder at all?

There was little to support such a suspicion — why, but for Susan Foal's witless prattle, and the cursed note, there would be no suspicion at all. A pity that Lambarde, Jove rain on him… But no: to be fair, in the man's place Tom might have disregarded one angry servant's whispers, but never the whispers *and* the note.

Which, again, begged another *quæstio*: who had written the note?

Was Lambarde wondering about that too? Was it safe to share Sir Francis's doubts with him? Would he listen to the man he seemed so minded to suspect? Which seemed greatly unfair on the magistrate's part, considering the will…

Fates send that the man came to see the logic of it: who would have wanted Edmund dead *after* he'd made his last will and testament? Those who knew they stood to gain by it or the heir who lost by it, and could still hope to change his brother's mind? Ned had hinted that Tom wouldn't like his will, and Susan Foal was ready to swear to that. It would give her a calenture to know her vapours might, in the end, clear Tom.

He descended the last flight of steps in a hurry. Now let Lambarde see this. The man might be prejudiced, but he was no fool, and once that was cleared, let him chase the murderer if he liked; Tom himself would go after the nameless writer of notes.

All the visitors had departed from the hall — surely, like Richbell, in the hope of avoiding the worst of the weather. Could it be hoped that the absent Barbara was seeing Mrs. Carmarden on her way? Lord forfend they should put up the old tattle-monger for the night, for a storm was brewing: the wind had stiffened, making the wretched casement rattle harder than ever, and the flames hiss and smoke in the untended fireplace. Several candles on the dais had guttered out, while the others burnt fitfully, and the black drapery billowed under the coffin. When a sudden gust flung the rain a-spatter against the leaded glass, the casement slammed on its hinges, and the draught lifted one heavy damask fold so high it hit a candle-branch.

Tom lunged to catch it as it tottered, one candle rolling to the floor and breaking.

"All I lack now!" he muttered, as he blew out the remaining flames. "What a lark, Ned — if now Scadbury burnt down around my ears!"

"Mr. Thomas!" a breathless voice called, and Tom, caught being sour to his dead brother, whirled around to find a wind-blown Kit Marley beside the door to the Old Stairs. "I've looked for you high and low…"

When asked about Lambarde's whereabouts, the poet waved the matter away.

"He's talking to your sister, I think — but listen!"

"Oh, Jove!" What would the man be putting in Barbara's head — or Barbara in his? Before Tom could make for the parlour, though, Marley came to catch him by the sleeve.

"Heed me, Mr. Thomas!" he insisted, eyes aglow, voice lowered to a player's whisper. "Did you know there was a groom sacked on Martinmas?"

So Skeres had said — a Kickly, wasn't it? "So what of him?"

"What of him!" Marley laughed a little wildly, throwing up both palms. "What of the fellow thrown out of roof and work, and branded as a thief? And mind, perhaps he was, perhaps he wasn't — but no matter: he wants revenge! The first stormy night he comes back. They called him a thief? Then a thief he'll be, by God. He breaks in, looks around for something to filch — but … your brother catches him." A look of angry surprise, a pointed finger. "*What are you doing here, you filthy prigger? I'll have you in gaol for this…* But Kickly won't have it. He goes to silence his old master. He's younger. He has the strength of fear, of anger. He grabs him…" Marley mocked gripping Tom by the front and shaking. "*Curse you and your name for ruining a honest man!*"

"Why, you should write for the stage!" Tom looked pointedly down at his crushed front, and Marley released him with a shrug and a grin. "Why on a stormy night?"

"Because of the noise. He knew the house, knew that whatever racket he made would be lost in the din."

"He was a horse-groom, Marley, he lived above the stable. If he ever entered the house, it must have been the day my brother sacked him."

Back at Cambridge, Christopher Marley must have been the sort that fellow disputants wished to strangle. All but bouncing on his toes, he held up a triumphant forefinger. "Ah, but he must have, if he stole a silver spoon," he exclaimed. "And even if he didn't, wouldn't he have heard about the storms from the others? I have — before I was here half a day…"

"He may well have — and still it wouldn't make him a murderer. And, thief or not, there was no sign that anyone broke in the night my brother died."

His argument well punctured, Marley blew out his cheeks and shrugged a shoulder. "He could…" he began, and stopped with a click of the tongue, Geve Kickly forgotten as he scratched at a stain on his sleeve, just above his cuff. His oxblood sleeve.

Jupiter — and now the rabbit-tailor had fled home… When Tom groaned softly, Marley looked up and made it plain that he hadn't forgotten the groom at all: "He'd only need an open window, after all, or an ill-closed door."

"Ay — and you'll need funeral clothes." Marley was small and slight. Nothing of Ned's would fit him, and it would take three of him to fill the Minotaur's black doublet. "Off with you, back to Goodwife Wollans. Tell her to find you something." He held up a hand when the lad would have protested. "You're part of my household, right now."

Any other man would have taken this for the vexed dismissal that it was, surely? But not Kit Marley, who instead stood there, head tilted most birdlike — trying to decide, Tom would have wagered, if the notion pleased or offended him.

He was still at it when the door from the passage room opened, and a smallish young lady stepped in, attired from head to toe in the deepest, costliest black velvet.

"Tom!" she called, and he hastened to meet his younger sister.

The moment he reached her, Mary batted his outstretched hands away.

"They say you've killed Ned!" she cried — and whether the burning outrage was for him or *them*, Tom couldn't tell.

"Well, I did not!" he protested — and Lord smite all tattlers — but Mary was unappeased.

"They say you threw him down the stairs," she wailed, tears welling. "And that the justice has come here to throw you in gaol… Oh, Tom!" Flinging her arms around his neck, she began sobbing, and he held her, as he'd done when they were children, and he'd consoled her of some girlish grief when no one else would.

"They'll hang you!" she gasped between sobs, arms tighter and tighter around him.

Over her shoulder, Tom met her husband's glower. By the sight of him, Pelham was thinking of the gallows, too.

Tom had only met the man two times — one being the day he'd wedded Mary. Still, this third time at once confirmed the old impression: when it came to his wife's family, Pelham was mostly wary. Now, with this talk of murder, see how he curled his thin lips and scowled down his Roman nose…

Perhaps there was no blaming him — but must he take Mary by both shoulders and detach her from the embrace?

"Mary, my dear," he rumbled, leading her to the chair by the fire. "You'd better not…"

Just shy of fifty years and nearly twice her age, solemn and large of frame, his manner towards his wife was that of a tutor towards a pupil — one that wasn't docile in the least.

She shook free when he would have made her sit. "Oh, for goodness' sake! Whatever he's done, are you afraid I'll catch it?" she griped.

Good old Mary. "Not that I've done anything, mind," Tom said. "In truth, I don't even know that Ned was murdered."

"Then…" Mary stopped in the act of unpinning her hat from her hair. "Then why have they come here to arrest you?"

"Nobody's come —"

"Is that him — the magistrate?" Her gaze travelled past Tom's shoulder, and he turned to see Marley hovering a dozen steps away.

"No," Tom said flatly. What did the lad think — to protect him from his own sister and brother-in-law? "Thank you, Master Marley." He nodded at the door — and see how reluctantly the poet went away.

"Is that your servant?" asked Mary, with such suspicion that Tom couldn't help himself.

"Believe it or not, that is a poet," he said.

If Mary was perplexed, her husband plainly had no liking for verse-makers.

"And what could you possibly want with a poet, Walsingham?" he asked, mouth turned down. He said *poet* the way another could have said *rat*.

"Oh, that's the way my brother is. It used to be only dead Latin poets — but now..." With a little sigh, Mary abandoned her gloves and hat on the sideboard, and put both hands against the small of her back.

Again, Pelham took her elbow to steer her towards the chair. "In your state, Mary..."

"I'm with child, not ill," she grumbled, but let herself be led and seated this time — only to bounce up again when Barbara emerged from the parlour.

"You are with child?" Tom asked. Nobody answered him, but as soon as the sisters embraced, Barbara stepped back to take Mary's hands and keep her at arm's length, and smiled — rather a wonder in itself. "Ah, Marykin — well done!" she exclaimed.

Mary laughed and cried at once, and Barbara stroked her hair, and Pelham watched his wife with great satisfaction. Had Edmund looked like this at Susan Foal? Well, she could give him no heir… Idle thoughts — and meanwhile, having followed Barbara, Lambarde stood on the threshold, hooded gaze travelling from Edmund's worn casket to Edmund's siblings — one carrying new life in her womb, another, for all he knew, a murderer.

Not liking that gaze at all, Tom rushed the introductions.

"This is Mr. Lambarde, the Justice of the Peace for Kent — and my sister Mrs. Pelham, and…" He let it trail, seeing how Pelham and Lambarde bowed to each other with every mark of mutual acquaintance, if no great warmth.

"We've met often enough, haven't we, Mr. Pelham?" Lambarde said, with the bland smile of one for whom the High Sheriff of Surrey and Sussex held no terrors.

Not that Pelham looked minded to inspire any such feeling — at least not on his brother-in-law's behalf. Did he think himself subtle in the way he straightened just a little away from Tom? But perhaps not; perhaps he meant it to be plain. *I will not be embroiled in this dubious matter*, his whole manner said, so plainly that Mary, God bless her, glared at her husband. Even Barbara looked faintly offended — although, just what had she and Mary expected? Then again, they had little knowledge of Sir Francis's declining health and of what it meant, while Pelham was one of those watching and waiting.

And trust Lambarde to read it all like a hornbook! In the sudden icy silence, broken only by the wind soughing down the chimney, he even turned to Tom with a raised brow — and truly, Tom had to look away before he huffed with laughter. What could the magistrate be thinking of the Walsinghams? Perhaps he would have had cause to think even worse — for Mary, a hand on her still unswollen belly, looked braced for battle — but the Heavens took pity, though in a strange fashion. Of a sudden, the sash of the great window flew open with a bang, and the wind entered like a wild thing, stirring the black draperies, blowing out the remaining candles, making the open parlour door slam shut.

With a strangled shriek, Mary scrambled away from the sparks exploding out of the fireplace and batted at her skirts.

"Do something, Thomas!" Barbara cried, and hurried to the passage door to call for Kathryn.

There was a chest pushed to the wall under the window. Tom leapt onto it, caught the swinging sash, and pushed it back into place, fumbling with the latch — nothing more than a rust-black hook-and-eye. It clicked a little, but didn't feel fast under Tom's fingers.

"Oh, mercy — again!" Kathryn's voice came together with a flicker of candlelight reflecting in the rain-flecked glass panes. "The hook won't hold when the wind's up in earnest."

The old woman, Everest, and even Wood had all come running at Barbara's calls. Snatching up Kathryn's rushlight, Tom took a better look at the latch. The hook's curve gleamed dully in the greenish glow — worn smooth with years of use, its tip dulled, the eye stretched to an oval…

"The hinge has a wobble," Kathryn said. "With a wind strong enough, the sash will shift and rattle. My husband's told Mr. Wood again and again, but…"

There was no answer from the steward.

Stomach clenching, Tom felt the lower strap-hinge. It bit deep into the grey wood — but the pin felt loose. Not much — just enough that…

"And when did that happen last, Goodwife?" Lambarde's even, deep voice asked.

Kathryn shook her head. "I wouldn't rightly know…"

"The night Mr. Edmund died," Wood said. "He heard it bang from his bed, and sent Foal down to close it again."

And see how all the colour drained from Will Everest's face — Everest, who had been keeping watch later, and been chased away. See how he swallowed hard, eyes sliding from Foal to Tom, and from Tom to Barbara when she huffed in impatience.

"So, what does it matter?" she asked.

Ah, but it mattered very much — in ways that didn't escape Lambarde.

"When was that?" he asked and, on hearing that it had been just after dark, when Foal brought up Mr. Edmund's posset, he nodded thoughtfully. "But the hook won't hold when the wind is up in earnest, will it? How was the window in the morning?"

"Closed, Yer Honour," said Kathryn. "Closed tight, and still showed the mischief: all the chest wet agin' the wall, and a right puddle, all the way there." She pointed halfway to the dais — an exaggeration, likely, but still…

"A right puddle … as if the window had stayed open for hours while it rained?" asked Lambarde — just the question Tom would have asked in his place. "Are you sure it was closed in the morning, Goodwife?"

Also, just the question to make Kathryn bristle. "I'm old, Yer Honour," she bit back. "But I can still tell open from closed."

"I must say I don't understand, Lambarde," Pelham rumbled in a most high-sheriff-like voice. "What does a puddle matter?"

If Pelham had decided to side with the family, he'd chosen a bad time to make his stand. Tom turned to the scullion — because he had a fair notion of what had happened, and better that he tease it out, rather than Lambarde.

"Will Everest, heed me." He grabbed the lad's arm when he tried to cringe away. "When my brother sent you away, was it to close the window?" A nod. "Then you took refuge in the kitchen: would you have heard if the latch had come loose again?"

A shake of the head, a thick sniff.

"And how was it in the morning?" prodded Lambarde, coming to loom over the lad's other side.

"Open!" Mary slapped a hand to her mouth. "That's what it was. And Ned heard it, and…" Her voice wobbled, and Barbara and Kathryn rushed to her, each with her own brand of consolation.

While the old woman cooed and caressed, Barbara chided, "Tush, Mary. Don't be silly," and then asked, "Is that why Ned went a-wander instead of staying in bed?"

She asked it of Tom, and he answered, ignoring Lambarde's displeased humph.

"He heard it bang again, and had nobody to send down, for he had chased away young Will. Perhaps he called — and no one answered, so he took it into his head to go and do it himself. And then, who knows? Dizziness, a stumble…"

"Poor Ned!" Mary's eyes welled up again, and Kathryn cooed and stroked some more.

"But this good woman found the window closed in the morning," Pelham objected, to Kathryn's vigorous nod.

Tom nodded. "Oh yes, didn't she, Will?"

For a heartbeat the boy just stared, mouth quivering at the corners — and then he broke down. "The morning," he sobbed, "when they found Master, Mrs. Foal wanted the candles, and I went to the hall, and the window was open, and I…" He stopped, swallowing hard, and drew a sleeve over his mottled face.

"You thought you'd be blamed," Tom finished for him.

A forlorn nod, and when Will spoke again, it was in a low rasp. "Mrs. Foal was a-screaming as I'd left him alone. She'd call the window me fault, too..."

"And so you closed it again." Tom turned to his audience, palm raised in the gesture of a disputator closing his argument — not that he'd helped himself by it.

"Yes — yes." Pelham's relief was plain as daylight. He nodded and even moved to stand at Tom's side. "So, Lambarde, you see..."

Lambarde didn't look pleased in the least, and yet, when he raised his objection, it wasn't the one Tom had expected. "What I see is that Mr. Walsingham asks his own questions, draws his own conclusions..."

And this time it was Mary who jumped into the fray. "Well, it's what he does for Mr. Secretary."

Which Tom had never told his family — so how did his sister know? But here was a conversation he'd rather not hold before his sisters, Pelham, and half the household.

"We'll discuss this, Mr. Lambarde." Tom had had a dozen years to observe in Sir Francis this manner of smooth authority that left no room for objection. To observe and to learn it. "You're tired, Mary, and Kathryn has your room ready, with a good fire in it."

No room for objection — unless one was Mary Walsingham. "I'm not tired —"

"Yes, you are. It's a long way from Laughton — and in your state."

This sent Kathryn and Barbara clucking, and made Pelham tutorish again — just as Tom had hoped — and even Mary couldn't resist as she was swept away. She paused just long enough to throw a baleful glare Tom's way — *this was low and you'll pay for it*, the glare said — and then they all disappeared.

"When you expect your second, and your third, Mary — then you'll do as you please..." Barbara, four times a mother, could be heard lecturing in the passage.

Oh, Jupiter. Resisting the urge to pinch the bridge of his nose, Tom dismissed Everest with orders to find a way to secure the cursed window for now, charged the steward with summoning the smith, and led the bristling Lambarde to the parlour.

Here, too, the windows rattled in their frames, and the fire had been neglected. Tom poked it alive, adding a piece of wood, and all the time he felt Lambarde's glare on him. When he straightened, he found the magistrate standing by the leathern chair he'd occupied earlier, one hand on the back.

"Mr. Walsingham," he began slowly, "you asked earlier how you could have entered the house. I thought someone could have let you in — but now I have a better answer."

Ah, well, the moment he'd felt the loose hinge, Tom had known what conclusion the magistrate would draw — not that it made the conclusion right.

"No, you don't!" he bit back. "Do you truly imagine that I'd pretend to leave and turn back, on the odd chance of finding a window open? Who would count on such a happenstance? A loose window means little enough."

Displays of impatience weren't going to win Lambarde's sympathy: here was the Sphinx again, narrowing severe eyes at Oedipus. "It means that you could have entered the house."

"Then anyone could have!" Tom retorted. "Including several who had more cause than I. Jack Fuller and Geve Kickly were both grooms here, and my brother sacked them both for no great reason. And then there are two farmers who must repay large debts next Lady Day..."

"The contents of the will, the names of those who might have wanted rid of your brother… You know many things, Mr. Walsingham." *Too many, if you ask me*, hung unsaid.

"Will you believe that most of this I was told without asking?"

Lambarde gave a thin, vinegary smile. "I'm sure you were trained in the art of being told things — but no matter. Will you leave the questioning to me?"

It was a demand Tom would have made in the magistrate's place — or so his conscience whispered. The whisper was ignored.

"You entertain these suspicions over my brother's death, you aim them at me — and I should sit quietly while you do your best to prove me guilty?"

"What would you do, in my place, with a suspect wanting to unravel a crime that might be of his own doing?"

"For one thing, I wouldn't ignore all chances in favour of just one!" Patience wearing thin, Tom stepped in front of the magistrate. "Will you at least consider those other men I named? Any of them could have climbed up from the bridge and over the wall into the herb garden. Well, not Mace, perhaps, who is old and half-crippled…"

"Climbed the bridge…" Lambarde ran a hand down his beard. "And how many of them would know to do that, instead of jumping the causeway's gate and trying for the back of the house?"

"Good Lord — Fuller for one, and Kickly for another." *First stormy night*, Marley had said. "Both lived here for a time: they'd know of the bridge, of the loose window…"

"And so would you."

"And always you'll circle back to me alone — and still you expect me to trust you?" Tom caught himself, cursing inwardly. Was his vexation beginning to sound a tad desperate — in words and in manner? It certainly had given Lambarde pause.

For a few heartbeats, the magistrate considered, tapping his fingertips together. In a lull of the wind, the fire clicked softly in the grate, and the rain whispered on the diamond-shaped glass panes.

"As a justice, I'd expect it, yes," said the man who dedicated his books to Essex.

And what else did he do for his patron? Might Essex think to direct Scadbury into Sir Francis's hands, as a show of friendship — even if it came burdened with the little matter of a kinsman on the gallows? Oh, Jove! Inside his mind, Tom gave his fanciful self a good shake. Not even Essex would be this foolhardy — and besides, when would Lambarde have had the time to consult with the earl? That said, when it came to trust… Ah, well: the pause had been too long to leave the man in any doubt.

"Don't you allow those you mean to indict to defend themselves?" Tom asked instead.

"You're not indicted, that I know…"

"Let us speak plainly, Mr. Lambarde: are you not considering it?"

The wind picked up again, slanting the rain against the window — and again Lambarde hummed to himself, fingering his mole.

"Very well, Mr. Walsingham," he said at last. "I'll say that, if your brother was killed, you strike me as the most likely suspect. You had little to gain, you say — but did you know this, back then? I'll also admit, though, that so far I can't be certain that a murder occurred at all. Until I can be, go ahead, ask your questions: unless you are the murderer, you'll want the truth exposed. But..." He held up a warning forefinger. "Let me not find you interfering with my own investigations. Let me not discover that you tamper with the truth —"

"Sir!" Tom took an angry step forward. What was the man thinking? "I'm not in the habit —"

And then raised voices sounded from the hall, the door was thrown open, and Uncle George all but fell across the threshold, wild-eyed and breathless. "Tom, your man — he says..." He ran an unsteady hand through his hair. "There's a dead body in the moat!"

CHAPTER 10

Kit Marley stood by the fireplace in the hall — drenched, shivering hard, white to the lips.

"Mr. Thomas!" he cried at the sight of Tom. "I was… She…" He swallowed hard and straightened, mouth pressed in a thin line. "There's a woman in the moat. It's the housekeeper."

Lord have mercy… Tom fought down a shudder — and, out of the hundred questions that surged and whirled in his mind, he asked, "Where?"

"Ah…" Marley looked about, eyes rolling a little, as though the body could be tucked somewhere inside the hall. "By the causeway…"

Waiting for no more, Tom ran off, not caring who followed. *Wait*, commanded Reason. *People fall. People drown of their own accord…* Yes, people fell to their death by accident — into the moat, down the stairs — but twice in five days?

It was raining hard as he crossed the kitchen yard at a run, raising great splashes in the puddles, with Marley and George on his heels. There were men milling across the causeway: Barker, all geniality lost for once, and Wood, and Barbara's coachman. Everest crouched with one foot down on the low outer wall, holding on to the causeway's edge, trying to reach down towards something light-coloured afloat in the rain-pocked water. Stepping closer, Tom made out the human shape, buttocks up. Bent over the inner wall, Foal hunched low over the water, kneading his hands together. "Susan!" he wailed. "Susan! Susan!"

Wollans came from the pantry, carrying a pole with a hook on one end — the one that was used to fish out what laundry the wind happened to throw into the moat — and by the kitchen well stood Barbara and Old Kathryn, clinging together. Barbara called something that was lost in the hissing rain. *Is it true?* most likely. *Is she dead?* Tom sent George to get the women back inside, and took the pole from Wollans.

"You and Barker, go and fetch a board," he ordered. Then he stepped onto the causeway and knelt to reach down with the hook.

It was Susan Foal, skirts billowing around her, long black hair spread wide in the murky water. Her white coif floated alone, a couple of feet away. Tom reached further — and nearly tumbled down headfirst. Hell and Tartarus! He hurriedly sat back on his haunches, swallowing memories of nearly drowning in the moat at ten.

"Here!" Grim but glint-eyed — Lord save us all from poets! — Marley reached down a hand. Tom grasped it, and, so braced, leant lower until he managed to hook the woman's kirtle.

Foal surged to his feet. "Don't hurt her!" he howled.

"She's past hurting, you fool!" Tom bit back through gritted teeth as he pushed to steer the body towards the bank. Hopefully, the rain had covered the unkind words. At last, Everest caught hold of a handful of sodden skirts. Marley dragged Tom to his feet, and they reached the others.

Susan Foal had been no slight woman in life. Dead weight that she was now, and in her waterlogged clothes, it took the efforts of five men to haul her out of the water and onto the muddy grass, where the body sprawled face-down, wet skirts tangled around the legs. The body of this woman who for a scant few days had been his servant and, without knowing him, had done her best to brand him a Cain. *I'll die before I let his murtherer step into his shoes*, she'd snarled at him — and now she was dead.

"Your pardon, Mr. Walsingham."

A hand to the shoulder startled Tom as Lambarde made his way towards the body and, with the scullion's help, turned it onto its back. Crouching, he pushed aside the heavy black strands of hair and weed, revealing half-lidded eyes and a slack face. When the head lolled to one side, a good deal of water gushed out from between the parted lips — but not enough to wash away the whitish froth around the mouth and nostrils.

"Drowned," Tom murmured, bending over Lambarde's shoulder to better watch. He pointed, and the magistrate nodded grimly.

"But how did she fall into the moat in the first place?" he wondered — and, with a sideways glance at Tom, he added under his breath, "You understand that now there must be a coroner's inquest?"

"Now that you have two deaths in the same household, and each makes the other dubious — yes," Tom answered sourly — but in truth, what else could Lambarde do?

To his credit, the magistrate didn't seem very happy. He pushed himself to his feet, rubbing his hands together, and stepped aside as Wollans and Barker laid a door on the grass, and the men clumsily busied themselves shifting the body onto it.

"Besides..." Clearing his throat, Lambarde inched close enough to whisper to Tom alone. "Constable Beveridge tells me that this poor woman and your brother..."

Rather more than that, in truth... Hadn't Susan boasted of being with child to Beveridge? Ah, well — no matter: even if she hadn't, it was bound to come out sooner rather than later. Better that the magistrate heard it from Tom himself.

"She claimed to be carrying my brother's child," he murmured — and couldn't quite read Lambarde's frown. Was he surprised? Disapproving?

"And is it true?" the magistrate asked, as even as a man could be with rain droplets running down his nose and moustache.

Was what true? That Susan was with child, or that the child was Edmund's? Either way… "How would I know?" Tom answered wearily, and then turned to beckon to Wood.

All this time the steward had scowled at the proceedings, displeased and aloof. On being told to find a suitable place where the body could be decently laid, he was at once full of sombre, deferent advice. The great cellar would be best, he said. And he would send for the midwife, because Mrs. Wollans couldn't see to the body alone…?

Mrs. Wollans? Now, here was a quick taking of sides — raising Kathryn to housekeeper-hood, at least in name! The cellar was a good idea, though, and so was the midwife — although…

As the men raised the body and carried it towards the house, with Foal trudging after them with hanging arms and head, Wood hastened away to direct them, and Tom called him back.

"Mr. Wood, have the midwife fetched, but she must not touch the body yet — nor must anyone else."

The steward looked as though he'd object, but didn't. With a frown for both his master and the justice — who looked halfway between vexed and approving — he nodded deeply enough for a bow, and hurried away. Tom didn't envy him having to deal with Foal.

"I pity that poor husband," Lambarde said, echoing Tom's own thoughts, if in a more charitable vein. He then moved towards the house, picking his way through the puddles, with the air of one with much on his mind.

"This is an ugly affair, Walsingham. An *ugly* affair!" Pelham repeated for the dozenth time, scowling at the withdrawing room in general, and at his brother-in-law in particular — as though it were Tom's fault. And for the dozenth time, Uncle Buffkin added his own gleeful prediction that they'd never get rid of Lambarde now.

Barbara, sitting at the old virginals with Mary, turned to glare at the men. "Oh, enough, Uncle! Why should the magistrate bother? We've had drownings before, and there was never a fuss made."

Which was true and wasn't, for a young stable groom had died years back, jumping into one of the fishing ponds and never coming up — in full view of a score of people. Barbara didn't see the difference, plainly, but everyone else did — Uncle Buffkin first, who rolled back on his heels and chortled.

"But this time this magistrate will think that Thomas did her in."

Both girls cried out, Pelham glowered, and George, at the room's other end, dropped the lute-book he'd been thumbing through.

"And thank you, Uncle," Tom griped from the fireplace, where he was trying to warm himself. "A most seasonable jest!" Not that he expected the old man to be chastened, and indeed, look at the sneer that creased the fat cheeks askew, look at the tilted head. *And am I wrong?* Leven Buffkin's whole manner asked — and, as if to answer him, right then William Lambarde walked in with back straight and countenance severe: no longer the awkward half-guest, but the Law of Kent itself.

"Now, Lambarde," Pelham began, squaring his shoulders in turn. "What is all this about?"

Surrey and Kent facing in battle — but, if Surrey held rank, Kent was on his own ground.

"This, Mr. Pelham, is about the Queen's justice on behalf of a woman," Kent answered. "A poor servant, dead in sudden and uncertain circumstances. You of all men, as High Sheriff, would never want me to disregard her death."

Oh, he was good — Jove rain on him. Speaking as though that shrewish hussy, in her death, stood for every humble subject in the Realm expecting justice! And didn't she, in a way? How could anyone counter such an argument and not appear either petty or ill-minded?

Swallowing a sigh, Tom spoke through both Pelham's wrong-footed hum and Uncle Buffkin's contemptuous sniff.

"None of us would dream of it, Mr. Lambarde," he said, mostly in firm warning to his kinsmen — and, if Barbara raised a hand to her temple with a half sigh, Lambarde accepted the words with a small, stiff bow.

Mary alone seemed touched by the dead woman's fate. "Was she truly with child?" she asked, eyes large and voice trembling a little. Now, knowing Mary, it was her own impending motherhood speaking, and even then she would have been less tender, had she known just whom Fair Susan had claimed as her child's sire — but, bless her, her question made them all look a little less heartless.

Or it would have, hadn't Uncle Buffkin snorted, "That one was no more with child than the town bull!"

Which made Mary tear up, and Barbara exclaim, and Pelham rumble, and George startle…

What a marvellous thing, a family! Tom checked a bitter laugh as Lambarde turned pointedly to him alone.

"I'd have a word with you, Mr. Walsingham," he said, turning his back on everyone else. He must have a family too, after all. "And with your man, the one who found the body."

All being so disordered, there was no one around to fetch Marley — and Tom went seeking himself, Lambarde following across the dark hall and empty passages. All wariness had gone from the justice, and all uncertainty. Even his step had become a forward-leaning, bull-like charging.

"You assume that Susan Foal didn't fall into the moat by her own clumsiness, I take it?" Tom probed when he'd had enough of the solemn silence.

The answering nod was nothing less than grim. "I can't assume anything else. And don't mistake me, Mr. Walsingham. I speak to you more than I should — but, more than ever now, you are under suspicion."

Little wonder, perhaps — and yet Tom stopped in his tracks. "Is there a killing you won't blame on me?" he griped. "I argued with her, yes: I told her there was no way her bastard child could inherit in my place — even if it was Ned's, which I take leave to doubt. But even if it was…"

"Oh, I know the law — but there is the matter of your brother: what if Mrs. Foal could prove that you killed him? Holding you under her thumb might have been fruitful…"

Why, no: she said she'd die before she let me succeed… Tom snapped his mouth shut on the imprudent words. "This is all conjecture — and thin as air!" he protested instead. "You can't know what that confounded woman had in mind."

"I know that she called you a murderer — and now she's dead."

It took counting to *tres* before Tom's logical mind mustered an objection. "And if she meant to keep me under her thumb, as you say, why go and babble to the constable? Either cleared or hanged, I'd be no use to her!"

Perhaps he should have counted for longer.

A small frown rippled across the magistrate's mien and then cleared. "Well, then perhaps she meant to expose you instead," he said. "Perhaps she wanted your brother's murderer brought to justice. Or she'd been made to believe that her child could inherit. I'm sure you've learnt that people can very well act on blind or false premises."

Or else, people let themselves be swept away by their own philosophical bent, and led their foes to conclusions that would have been best left unreached.

They found Marley hunching on a stool by the fire in the small kitchen. His doublet hung on a chair's back, while he peered into the flames and ate bread and cheese. He sprang up, wary as a hare on hearing that the Justice of the Peace for Kent wanted to question him.

Lambarde had an air of expecting to be left alone with the poet — but when Tom went to perch himself on the chest under the window, he heaved a sigh and set to work.

"You are Mr. Walsingham's servant," he said — not in the manner of a question — and frowned when the answer was a shake of the head.

"I am Christopher Marley, of London." The usual little pause — for Kit spent much time with the players. "*Magister Artium*, Cambridge."

Well, if nothing else, Lambarde was taken aback.

"Like myself, Master Marley is in Mr. Secretary's service," Tom explained. "But he also has another mistress in the Muse."

Marley looked pleased, and Lambarde blinked — perhaps at finding himself saddled with a poet, or another of Sir Francis's men — but recovered quickly.

"Well, I suppose a Master of the Arts can find a dead body just as any other man — and perhaps will be more eloquent in telling how it happened?"

It was plain the justice neither missed nor liked the way Marley sought Tom's nod before shrugging and saying, "It was floating face-down in the moat, right by the causeway."

Not much, as poetical eloquence went — nor as a witness. Even not knowing, as Tom did, how unusual a terse Marley was, Lambarde pricked up his metaphorical ears.

"You didn't see Mrs. Foal fall in the water?" he prodded.

Marley shook his head. "It… She was already there when I…"

"There by the causeway, you say — but where? Near the island or away from it?"

"Halfway, I'd say. I…" Marley frowned a little, looking at nothing. "I doubt I'd even have seen it, otherwise, for it rained hard, and I was running, looking at the house."

Too much! Tom made himself not scowl. Had no one taught the lad to answer to the point when questioned? But then, the poet often overran the service man in Marley.

What Lambarde made of it was hard to tell, as his hooded gaze never strayed. "You didn't move it?"

"You were there, Sir: you saw it was out of reach until Mr. Walsingham pushed it with that pole."

"You didn't think to save that poor woman?"

No, he hadn't. See the blank-eyed gape: it hadn't even occurred to him — and now he thought that it should have. "But, short of jumping into the moat…" he stammered — and then a reasonable answer dawned on him. "I only thought of fetching help from the house."

Lambarde hummed. "You'd come running to the causeway, you say. Where were you running from?"

So this was the man's method: asking a question, then a different one, and then going back to the first — a clever way of wrong-footing a man.

It worked on Marley, who floundered for a moment, and thought to cover it by going to feel his damp doublet. "I'd been knocking at the bridge door. When nobody opened it, I thought of the causeway, and the kitchen door."

"Weren't the stables closer?"

"Were they?" The lad looked up, frowning. "I didn't think of it. What did I want with the stables?"

"Oh, nothing. You wanted inside the house — back from… Where did you say?"

And there went Marley's patience — never great to begin with. "Does it matter, Sir?" he snapped. "The rain caught me halfway to the village, and I came back running, and if I hadn't, that poor woman would still be there in the moat!"

Having learnt this particular Sphinx's dislike for a snappish Oedipus, Tom pushed himself off the chest. "Truly, Mr. Lambarde, what's the aim of this?"

Also, the Sphinx didn't like to have Oedipus rescued. "The aim, Mr. Walsingham…" he began — and then stopped. "Do you know when Mrs. Foal was last seen alive?"

Did he? Tom thought back through the harrowing day. "You remember when I sent her to fetch the steward for you? She and Wood both came back when the joiner's man raised that din. That's when *I* last saw her."

"So did I." The magistrate nodded. "The same goes for Mrs. Sherley, Mr. Buffkin, Mr. Wood, and Goodman Wollans. The scullion doesn't know for certain, and the cook didn't see her all day. I'll have to hear Foal and Goodwife Wollans — but let's say for now that she died between the raising of that din, as you say, and the raising of the alarm. An hour, perhaps? My aim was to ascertain that there was a time in that hour when we only have Master Marley's word for where he was."

There was a loud, half-laughing gasp from Marley, just as Tom protested:

"Mr. Lambarde, thoroughness is a virtue, but you must consider that Master Marley never set foot in Scadbury until this morning. I doubt he even crossed paths with Susan Foal."

Not that the Sphinx regarded this as an objection. "He works for Mr. Secretary," he said — as though that explained everything.

This time there was no stopping Marley, as he leaned back on his heels with one brow raised and sneered. "A great man who, as everybody knows, thrives on the assassination of housekeepers —"

"Marley!" Tom scolded, but Lambarde ignored the sally, or at least the foolishness of throwing sallies at the Justice of the Peace for Kent.

"A great man who perhaps wants to protect his cousin," he corrected. "And you, Master Marley, have been described to me by one and all as Mr. Thomas's man."

"Well, he's not! And you're much mistaken, if you think that I ordered him —" The rest Tom swallowed, as a rain-spattered Kathryn appeared in the doorway and paused, startled perhaps to be met by the glares of three arguing men.

"Please ye, Master," she murmured. "'Tis the knives…"

So they were all having a belated dinner — while Tom tried to deal with death and suspicion, shivering in his damp clothes and famished. Not that Kathryn was at fault, so he curbed his impatience and bid her come in.

She did, with head lowered, and not another word was passed while she counted a handful of silver knives from the cupboard, the silence only broken by the rain outside and the small clinks of metal as Kathryn worked in haste. See how intently Lambarde watched her buff each knife with her apron, how he observed in which drawer they were kept… Just in case another death occurred — a stabbing?

Never had Old Kathryn so rushed a task. She locked the cupboard — and see, she had the keys already! — and curtsied herself out in a low-gazed hurry.

The moment the door closed behind her, Marley drew breath to protest, but Lambarde held up a restraining hand. "I'm not saying that you have done murder, Mr. Marley — only that you could have. And you are not alone in this." He turned to Tom. "What about you, Mr. Walsingham? Do you have someone to vouch for you in that hour?"

"Yourself, for a good part of it. My sisters, my uncles, my brother Pelham, and then…" Tom stopped short. And then he'd wandered upstairs alone, following the rather fantastical notion of Richbell in the attic. How long had he been there? Long enough that Lambarde would easily ascertain his absence, surely. "And then, for a while, I was upstairs —"

"In my company," Kit Marley jumped in — so earnest, so round-eyed…

Jove rain on the lad! Did he think Lambarde would miss the falsehood?

He did not — how could he? "Truly, Master Marley?" he demanded most severely. "Won't I, by questioning the servants, find that you've been with them for most of that time?"

Which meant he'd done so already — and still Marley ignored Tom shaking his head, and insisted that he'd talked with Mr. Thomas in the hall.

Had they never made him read Cicero in Cambridge — that lying was the best way to be disbelieved, even in truth?

It was no wonder that Lambarde's frown grew blacker with each word, and that he should turn to Tom. "You should advise your man against lying to a magistrate, Mr. Walsingham," he said harshly. "Lies won't change the fact that you had a chance to drown the housekeeper, and reason to do it — unlike those other men you propose as suspects for your brother's death. You could have killed Mr. Edmund Walsingham to inherit, and Susan Foal to silence her accusations."

"But…" How many times had a hesitation, an uncertain answer, a moment's floundering sharpened Tom's suspicion? Never again, his heart vowed, while his mind whirled like a handful of glass bits thrown in a cup. It seemed a long time — and so it must have seemed to the waiting Lambarde — before a notion formed. "Unlike them, you say — but why? Why wouldn't your reasoning apply to each of them?"

"Wherever they were when your brother died, they weren't here today."

"Ah, but Fuller was, and also Richbell — one of the debtors — and in truth there's no saying who may have been here, what with all the coming and going. And…" A new thought struck Tom, a bit of glass catching the light. "And here's another that I hadn't considered: what of Foal?"

Startled, Lambarde reared his head. "The husband?"

"Why not?" Tom's clenched shoulders loosened at the familiar sense of an argument unfolding as he spoke. "Perhaps he was eager to inherit, or he'd had enough of his wife in Edmund's bed, or both — and Susan knew and had to be silenced…"

"She didn't blame her husband, though. She blamed you."

"Oh, I can think of all sorts of reasons. She blamed me at first, and then began to see something different. Or throwing the blame on me was the plan, but Susan lost her nerve when you began to ask questions. Why, Foal might even have meant it all from the beginning: kill the master, have his wife blame the master's brother, kill his wife to cinch the brother's guilt — and there he is, rich, unsuspected, free of a cuckolding wife and bastard child." Not that Foal struck Tom as possessed of enough wit for such an intrigue — but he wasn't going to say so. "And besides, unlike me, he was indisputably here when my brother died. Can you, in good conscience, discard him as a suspect?"

No, he could not. And perhaps it irked him that he hadn't thought of it himself. Surely, he didn't like it when Marley clapped his hands.

"*Ut erat disputandum*!" the lad gloated. "Well argued, Mr. Thomas."

Unhelpful imp! Tom swallowed a smile — but, in Lambarde's place, he would have turned the same sour glare on Kit Marley.

"If you would fetch the man Foal, Master Marley," the magistrate ground out, and see with what promptness the lad obeyed.

Once they were alone, Lambarde paced to the window that faced the kitchen yard, and stood looking at nothing for a time, then turned and crossed his arms.

"You'll say that the Foals also wrote the letter, then?" he asked.

Ah, yes — the cursed letter. And for this Tom had no true answer. "Well, not Susan." He tapped the scarred wood of the table as he thought. "I doubt she could write — but her husband might have, thinking that Beveridge disbelieved his wife." It still sat ill with him to imagine Foal as a country Machiavelli, deviously bolstering his wife's accusations, and all the while looking to get rid of her. And it seemed harder still to believe when the man shuffled into the kitchen, all but shoved by Marley, whose grim manner was belied by the glint in his eyes. Most soldierly, he placed himself by the door, with arms crossed and face a-scowl — never mind that the room also opened onto the yard, and never mind that Foal was twice as big, had he been inclined to fight.

Not that he looked to be. He hunched sideways, twisting his pudgy hands and wheezing. Now and then he would dart up a red-rimmed glance — every time inching and shuffling a little farther away from Tom and the justice, and away from Marley.

"You are Robert Foal," Lambarde said after a while.

The answer was delivered to the floor. "Ay, Yer Honour."

"Did you know that Mr. Edmund Walsingham had made you his executor?"

"Mr. Edmund was good to me."

Which hardly answered the question, but Lambarde forged ahead. "Had you been his manservant for long?"

Tom leant against the mantel, thankful for the warmth on his chilled back, and set about learning Lambarde's ways: a question, then another or two, then back to the first. He'd try it the next time he questioned a suspect … *if* he ever came to pursue a murderer again.

A shiver ran dawn his spine. He was the suspect now. He had been questioned in this same manner, and would be again. He risked the gallows … not if there was no better than Dobbin Foal behind the intrigue — but what if Sir Francis was right? What if the letter was the work of a subtler mind, bent on wreaking havoc near the throne? Could Lambarde unravel that sort of tangle? Would he want to?

"Do you know what your wife claimed?" The magistrate had either lost his patience or come to a further stage of his method — one that Foal liked even less, judging by the way his wheezing breath hitched. "She claimed to be with child," the magistrate insisted.

"She was."

"And she claimed that the child was your master's."

For a heartbeat Dobbin Foal worked his jaw under his dark beard and scowled up at Lambarde like a hog about to charge.

Behind him, by the door, Marley watched with fascination.

"Cuckolded husbands have sought blood before, Foal," Lambarde said. "You never came when Mrs. Sherley called to have the hall window closed."

See how the man blinked, mouth slowly falling open. "I…" he squeaked. "In the old kitchen — there I was."

"Will Barker say the same?" Tom asked, and the servant's wheeze hitched.

"Ye reckon as I killed her?" he gasped, turning on Tom. "I knew of the babe, so I did! I was agreed with her. The moment Mr. Edmund set sight on her, she said it was our fortune made. She said I mustn't touch her…"

"Bawd to his wife or cuckold?" asked Marley airily — and see how Foal stomped his feet.

"I was agreed!" he bawled.

"Let's say you were," Tom cut in. "It still doesn't mean she agreed that my brother should be murdered. And when she found out, she wouldn't let it go unpunished."

Even in his fury, Dobbin Foal cowered and cringed. "Ay — but not me!" he cried, spittle flecking his beard. "'Tis ye as she blamed, not me!"

"At first, yes." Tom took a step forward, and the servant one backwards. "Perhaps she'd been told so. But then something made her think…"

Another half-step, and Foal bumped backwards into the cupboard. He held out pleading hands to Lambarde. "Don't listen, Yer Honour! Blaming me when all under this roof hated Susan — him, most of all!" He pointed at Tom. "For she had his brother's child in her belly!" Having raised his voice to a scream, the servant choked on the last word and fell quiet, panting hard and rolling his eyes.

After a short while, Lambarde spoke evenly. "That's as may be, Foal, but you never answered the question: where were you, other than in the kitchen?"

A little start, some shuffling, and then: "The well," Foal mumbled. "Ask Mr. Barker — it's him as sent me out for water, for all that it poured."

"The well?" Lambarde raised both brows at Tom.

"Out by the dairy — and in full sight of the causeway."

With a low, ragged moan, Foal pressed his short fingers to his temples.

"I'll ask Mr. Barker — and I'll ask him how long it took you to fetch that water. Now you may go, Robert Foal." Lambarde huffed with impatience when Marley waited for Tom's nod before stepping away from the door — and all but growled when, in throwing the door open to flee, Foal revealed an open-mouthed Everest.

Stumbling out of the way, the lad gaped after the scurrying Foal until he remembered he was carrying a message.

"Please ye, Masters, there's Constable Beveridge as would see the justice," he blurted out in one breath, and then ran for the safety of the scullery.

This was a bedlam, not a household. And now Beveridge, too…

"I sent for the constable," Lambarde announced, drawing himself up to his full height. "And if you don't mind, Mr. Walsingham, I'll see him without your presence."

A protest rose to Tom's lips — and he didn't voice it. Hardly worth the trouble and, besides, there were advantages to having Lambarde otherwise engaged for a while. "By all means, Sir," he said — a little sourly for appearance's sake. "You're welcome to use the steward's room. Throw out Wood, if you must."

It was almost diverting, the way any show of acquiescence on Tom's part brought a suspicious frown to Lambarde's brow. Still, with the constable waiting and — no doubt — some plan in mind, what could the magistrate do but go?

The moment his steps faded in the passage, Tom blew out his cheeks. "The devil!" he murmured — and, because there was no knowing how long Beveridge would keep Lambarde busy, he shook himself into action. Marley was still at the door, peering down the passage, and Tom sent him to make sure that dinner was still in progress.

"What if I were to eavesdrop on the law?" he asked. A somewhat tempting prospect — but…

"No, I have another task for you. Now find out if they are at dinner, and come back at once. And when we're done —" Tom glared at the poet — "then you'll tell me what you were thinking, lying to Lambarde like that. Now off with you."

Protest plain in his eyes, Marley hurried to obey, for a wonder.

Now for a candle… There was a dusty beeswax stump in an earthen holder among the odds and ends on the mantel. It would do better than a rushlight. By the time he'd lit it from the fire, Marley was back, skidding around the doorjamb like a boy.

"You sisters, your uncles and your brother-in-law — all at dinner in the parlour. The Wollanses are serving the baked lamprey. The boy's in the scullery. Of Wood and Foal, there's neither hide nor hair to see, and the law is camped in the hall."

In the hall? Beveridge must have told of Susan eavesdropping from the pantry… "Good," said Tom. "Now come with me." And, having made sure that nobody was in the passage, he led the way to the Old Stairs — under which a flight of stone steps led to the biggest of Scadbury's three cellars.

"You wait here," he instructed Marley. "If anyone tries to come downstairs, stop them."

"And just how do I do that, pray? Cudgel them on the head?"

The question was fair enough. A stranger barring the way to the cellar… "Well, I'll wager you none of my kinsfolk will come near. If it's Old Kathryn, Wollans or the cook, just tell them that I'm there." Kathryn wouldn't like it, perhaps — but she wouldn't object other than with pursed lips and half-burnt manchets in the morning. "The scullion you shoo away. If it's

Wood or Foal… Why, you write plays: if you can't make up something, then who can?"

He was halfway down when Marley called to him, leaning through the half opened door. "And if it's Mr. Justice?"

What then? Tom shrugged. "Oh, let him through — and welcome! He can't think worse of me than he does already."

The boyish laugh faded away as Marley pushed the door to, and Tom descended to the great cellar — and to Susan Foal's body.

CHAPTER 11

The air smelt of damp brick and sour ale, and the light flickered on the walls, fingering its way over casks, barrels, and shelves of earthen crocks, dancing with Tom's shadow on the vaulted ceiling. A narrow doorway led to a second, smaller chamber: at its far end the barrels had been pushed up to the wall to make room for a trestle, and on it lay the body, covered with a sheet.

Shivering in his still damp doublet, Tom lifted the cloth and folded it away from the slack face and the shoulders.

They had not undressed her. Tom had ordered that they shouldn't, but the urge to settle the dead properly was strong. Then again, nobody had much liked Susan Foal…

All the more need to do it quickly, a voice from long ago echoed in Tom's mind. *Ye want a ghost with a grudge at yer bedside?* Who had said it? And who had been the unloved dead? Idle thoughts, and the candle-stump wouldn't last long — not to mention that, no matter what Tom had told Marley, he'd rather not be caught down there by Lambarde.

Better to observe the body, while he could. The soggy skin, the glassy eyes under the lowered eyelids, the parted lips gone a dark grey. Even in death, Susan Foal looked sullen. A ghost with a grudge. The all-important froth around her mouth and nostrils had grown harder to see. There had been tiny bubbles in it; now it had dried to something like a trace of beaten egg-white. Lambarde had observed it past doubt, but would the inquest jurors notice it? Hopefully, the coroner would — but then, what did it matter, beyond the fact that the woman had still been alive when she'd fallen into the water?

The justice plainly thought she'd been pushed. Still, would a shove — or a fall — have been enough to kill her? Even if Susan couldn't swim, even if she'd been hampered by her skirts, or seized by a cramp…

The crack of thin ice, the sudden shock of cold, the water burning up mouth and nostrils, the muddy blackness, the seizing lungs, the slowed limbs, the blind, unthinking terror…

With another shudder, Tom shook himself out of the memory. He'd been only a small boy, then, and the water freezing — but yes, he could have died of it, if his brothers hadn't fished him out. How much harder, or easier, would it have been for a grown woman? Had she tried to scramble up, or even to just hold on and keep herself afloat?

Folding the cloth back further, Tom uncovered a rough, short-fingered hand and set the candle close to observe it. And see: the palm was covered in cuts and scratches. Some looked old, some fresh, for all that the water had washed the edges white, and left mud inside. One fingertip was torn, three of the nails broken. The other hand was much the same, the only difference being that something dark had caked under the fingernails — either mud or moss.

Susan Foal had fought for her life, whatever noise she'd made lost in the rain. And, as she'd fought, she'd been close enough to the bank to claw at the dirt — but if someone had shoved her in, and held her down until she'd died…

The face showed no injuries, nor, when Tom hitched aside the too-fine collar, did the throat. How did one hold a fellow creature in the water?

Everest crouching on the bank, a foot braced, one hand holding on to the causeway, the other reaching down… Tom mimed the gesture: pushing down, hand clawed — but not around the throat.

Ignoring the unpleasant clamminess of the skin — like wax that had gone cold but not hardened — he turned Susan's head aside and lifted away the wet hair plastered to the neck. And there it was: darker against the marbled duskiness of pooling blood, a bruise — small in size, a little elongated in shape. When he checked the other side, he found another mark, a little smaller: a forefinger to go with the thumb. When he parted the hair, he saw three more little bruises on the scalp: the fingers of man's hand.

With a sigh, Tom drew up the sheet to cover the body. He wasn't quite sure what he'd thought, what he'd hoped for, but now he knew past question: Susan Foal had been murdered.

Emerging from the cellar, with his candle guttering and mind a-whirl, Tom found his sentry gone.

Tartarus pinch the man! "Marley!" he called under his breath. "Kit Marley!"

No answer. Oh, for Skeres who, for all his Minotaurish ways, would never wander off when given an order. Why, likely even Audrey Shelton wouldn't just blithely walk away of her own unannounced counsel. Fuming, Tom strode into the passage — and ran straight into the errant poet, hurrying from the kitchen on tiptoe and peering back over his shoulder.

Before he could open his mouth, Tom found himself shushed, steered back past the stairs, pushed into the empty little room and past that, to the pantry.

"Have you gone mad?" Tom tried again. "Where the devil did you disappear to?"

But Marley had the tight-lipped smile Tom remembered from Rheims, from London, the smile of discoveries to impart. "I was keeping watch," he whispered, "to no earthly use, for not a soul came by — when … what do I hear? Voices from the hall. Oh, they were trying to be quiet, but that constable of yours isn't very good at whispering. He pipes, rather — and, by the time I'd slipped close to the door, he piped this: 'Mr. Fremlyn wouldn't hear no word of it…'"

"Fremlyn? Is that the coroner?" Tom asked, earning a shrug. "But why wouldn't the coroner hear of it? What did Lambarde say?"

"He called the constable a thundering babbler, and hauled him away to that passage room."

Small blame to him, considering… "But you never let that stop you, I take it?"

A pleased chuckle. "I go to the door, put my ear to the crack — and… 'You'll have to ride to Rochester,' says His Justiceship. 'I'll give you a note, and you ride at once. You can take my horse.'"

"A coroner from Rochester…" There was a squat, honey-brown glazed jar on the table. Tom picked it up and turned it in his hands as he considered. "It's not for a servant's death that the local coroner won't do, is it?" He looked up to find that Marley had turned grim.

"The constable said they'll never be back before tomorrow, and Lambarde grumbled that at least the surgeon and the plumber will arrive in time."

"The plumber…" Lord! Tom thumped the jar back on the table. "The coroner is not for Susan Foal. It's my brother…"

"And will you let him?"

"If he wants an inquest called, I can't refuse. But even if he doesn't, even if he only wants to make sure, what would it look like if I stopped him?"

"Ay — there's that." And Marley looked so very crestfallen…

"You never think I had a hand in it, do you?" Tom asked — more sharply than he'd meant.

"A hand… No!" Marley's protest was so shocked and so loud that Tom had to hush him — and then the lad looked away. "Did you know that Watson killed a man?"

Well, this now! Watson: half poet and half lawyer, one of many tame Catholics in the Service, until he'd betrayed Tom's trust — and, much worse, that of Sir Francis. Overbold, and thoughtless at times — but, truly… "How?"

A shrug. "Back in September. There was this fellow who had a grudge against him, and thought he'd take it out on me. Watson defended me, and he never meant it, but… We ended up in Newgate both. A sennight I was there, before my bail could be arranged."

"I didn't know. I would have…" Done what, exactly? And with what money? "What of Watson?"

A shake of the head. "Still there. He did kill the man — though they say he'll be pardoned. But…" Marley looked up, turmoil in his eyes. "In that sennight, there were two men brought away to the gallows. For murder, Mr. Thomas — and one of them was innocent, I'd swear."

Loyal idiot. Tom sighed. "And so you thought you'd lie for me to the justice?"

"For all the good it did…" Marley looked down and nudged a small barrel of apples with his toe — feeling foolish, for once and for a wonder?

"No good at all, and some ill, likely," Tom scolded. "You shouldn't have put your truthfulness in question — not with Lambarde already leery of you."

Marley kicked harder at the barrel. "Pompous ass! Besides, for all he knows, the housekeeper could have drowned all by herself!"

"She didn't, though." Tom recounted his finds, and Marley frowned down at the floor, as though he could see through it, down to the cellar.

"Are you going to tell Lambarde?"

Was he now? Humming, Tom picked up the jar again, with its tightly tied string, the parchment cover stained with dark red. Would the pooling blood conceal the finger-marks by the time the surgeon and the coroner arrived on the morrow? Then again…

"I'll wager you, he'll find out for himself before night — but he's already convinced it was murder."

Marley kicked the barrel again. "Pompous ass!"

"Leave that alone, will you?" Tom snapped, thinking of Kathryn. "And what must Lambarde think, with two deaths under the same roof in five days?" He raised a palm to stop Marley's objection. "A fallacy, I know — but he's told me that he won't ignore facts because they aren't philosophical enough."

"And must you help him in his bad methods?"

"We'll see." Slicing away the string with his knife, Tom raised the parchment cover, and a syrupy childhood scent wafted up. He smiled in spite of himself. "Cherry conserve!" He looked up to find Marley twisting his face in disgust. "You heathen!" He laughed and grabbed a horn spoon from a jug on the shelf. "My old nurse used to give me a spoonful when I found trouble for myself." And today qualified, didn't it? Smile fading, he spooned up a whole cherry, deep-red, glistening with syrup — and at once he was nine again, savouring the sugar, the burst of fresh sourness. *Good for a scraped knee or a scraped soul*, Old Cicely murmured at the back of his mind. And then she'd scold him for a glutton as he took a second spoonful. *Ah, well, I'm in more trouble than you'd ever imagine, Cicely, with an irked justice breathing down my neck...* "But I'd truly like to know why Coroner Fremlyn won't do. Did you hear anything else?"

"Ah! I'd forgotten!" Marley hit a palm to his brow. "They went out then, and I didn't hear another word — but there is something that I saw."

"Another letter under the door, saying that Mr. Walsingham is a lamb of innocence?" Tom groused, around a third mouthful of cherries and syrup. He'd gone without dinner, after all.

"You'll rot your teeth like that!" Marley said. "But it's like Paul's yard in London, that hall of yours. I'm still with my ear to the crack, when I hear someone come from the parlour. Off I run through the great door, out to the porch — and who must be there? Your uncle — the thin one — scampering away from the door to the passage room, making pretend he'd not been eavesdropping!"

"My Uncle Guildford?" Tom stared. Of all the people in Scadbury, of all his family present and absent, meek and nervous George was the last person he'd have expected to listen in on a magistrate. Had he just passed by, and heard voices? Why hadn't he been at dinner with the others? Then again, George had been uncommonly twitchy these past days. Could there be worse than too much sack to it...?

And then Kathryn bustled in, catching Tom at his third spoonful of conserve. "Mr. Thomas!" she scolded. "That was for dinner..." Then perhaps she remembered a small boy consoled with a treat — and her thin-lipped scowl softened. "Master Marley, be a good lad: tell Mr. Barker to have an eel-pie and some ale for Mr. Thomas in the small kitchen, will ye? And for yerself."

A servant's errand, and yet — *mirabile visu*! — Kit Marley complied without so much as a scoff. He must be cutting, Tom thought, a truly wretched figure.

The moment the door closed, Kathryn fetched a great sigh. "I'll have to sponge those clothes of yers," she said. "Now go and sit by the fire a little, while ye eat."

She waved him away and took the jar to scoop the rest of the cherries into a bowl — and Tom knew himself forgiven for the matter of Edmund's body, if nothing else.

Dusk was beginning to close in by the time the midwife arrived from Chislehurst — a strong, neat woman of middle years, with no eyebrows over sharp brown eyes. She'd been delivering a babe when Everest had gone to fetch her. "And Susan Foal won't be in no hurry ever again," she said with the serene briskness of one who saw birth and death entwine all too often. If anything, Bridget Platt seemed a little put out that this new Mr. Walsingham shouldn't know her by name.

And how would I have learnt that from London? Tom bit down the flare of irritation. London, Barn Elms, the Royal court, the rest of England, Scotland, France … all of that must seem as far off as the moon, when seen from Chislehurst, and just as inscrutable in its fixed remoteness. In this narrow world of village and manor house and farms, though, the master of Scadbury just knew certain things — and Tom did not.

"Well then, Mistress Platt, this way." As stiffly courteous as you please in reparation for his shortcomings, he led the midwife and Lambarde to the Old Stairs. They had a sort of procession following: Uncle Buffkin repeating his sally about the town bull in spite of Barbara's reproaching hiss, and Kathryn, and Foal, cringing and wheezing, quite the grieving widower — or the frightened culprit. At the cellar's door,

Lambarde stopped and announced that he alone would go down with the midwife. "And Mr. Walsingham," he added before Tom could protest. No doubt he would rather have had Beveridge or Pelham, for officialness's sake — but the constable was on his way to Rochester, and Pelham had ensconced himself in the parlour with the general manner of one who would not take sides.

So they climbed down, the three of them, followed by a chuntering in which the words "town bull" could be heard.

Earlier, when he'd stolen down alone, the quiet had been dull and commonplace; now the whispers and the hushed steps of three people gave the cellar a chapel-like gloom. It dispelled only a little once four candles were lit in the smaller chamber. Tom and the magistrate stood back while Bridget Platt, intent of eye and spare of gesture, removed the sheet, folded it, put it aside on the top of a barrel, and then lifted Susan Foal's skirt and petticoats to the waist. When she slipped a hand under the sodden, crumpled shift, Tom found himself looking away, studying the packed dirt floor and a cobweb between two casks. Out of the corner of his eye, he caught Lambarde doing the same, and for a while the silence thickened, until the midwife huffed softly. Moving at the body's side, she began to undo the laces of the brown wool kirtle. The wet knots must have tightened, and she picked at them with patient, methodical fingertips.

"There be signs, Sirs," the midwife called after a while. She had unlaced the front and drawn down the shift, baring the big breasts. "She always had big bosoms, Susan had — but ye can tell from the nipples, and from the veins, ye see'"

They did not, because they were looking away — or at least Tom was. Lord, but it was unchristian, surely, to watch this woman half-naked in death, all the worse because Edmund…

"And how sure are these signs?" he hastily asked.

Bridget Platt never hesitated. "Sure enough," she said. "But please ye, Sirs, I would feel the womb."

Hadn't she already…? Tom swallowed the question. The womb, not the belly.

"Go ahead then, Mistress Platt," said Lambarde, untroubled when the midwife went to part Susan Foal's short, stout legs.

Easy enough for him — no worse than an unpleasant duty! The woman hadn't drowned in his moat. She hadn't brought suspicion on his head, both in life and in death. She hadn't shared his brother's bed in adultery. She wasn't bearing, perhaps… From that last thought, Tom would have gladly shied away — but right then Bridget Platt straightened and announced that Susan had been with child.

So Uncle Buffkin had been wrong after all, was the first inane thought that formed in Tom's mind. Not that it meant the child had been Edmund's — only that it could have been.

"Are you sure, Mistress Platt?" Lambarde asked. Did he harbour some doubt? It was hard to tell from the pursed lips, the hooded eyes. "You will have to bear witness at the coroner's inquest."

The midwife nodded twice, prompt and assured, as though she'd done little but testify on murdered women all her life. "As sure as can be, Sir. My oath on it," she said, and began to put Susan Foal back in order. Susan Foal who, had she lived, would have borne a child fated to carry resentment and trouble, ever wondering and wondered at.

"Well, she wasn't lying on this," Lambarde murmured, barely louder than the swish and rustle of cloth as the midwife worked.

And yet it struck Tom that this discovery was of no great relevance after all. "It changes little, doesn't it?" Oh, it had to be ascertained — but what did the certainty change, when truth, lie or suspicion would have made no difference to a murderer? He made to say so, and stopped short: the magistrate wasn't listening. He was frowning at the body, at the heavy head that the midwife's ministrations had made loll to the side.

"Stop, Mistress," he called. Stepping close, he moved the candle to observe the back of Susan Foal's neck, just like Tom had. "Let us turn her."

More muddy water trickled out of the mouth when they pushed the body onto its side. Once the black hair was lifted, the marks showed, black in the candle's light.

There was a gasp from the midwife. "Lord save us — poor girl!" she breathed. The first word of pity Tom had heard for Susan Foal.

"Of this, Mistress Platt, you'll say no word to anyone," Lambarde ordered, and then slowly turned his gaze on Tom. "And, Mr. Walsingham," he said, voice hard and cold. "*She wasn't lying.*"

Cicero again, his argument reversed: not having lied about this, perhaps Susan Foal had been truthful about other matters too? Lambarde had all the air of thinking so — Tartarus take his narrow mind.

When the midwife shook out the sheet to let it billow and descend on the body, the draught that sent the flames a-quiver could have been the ghost of Susan Foal — making trouble even in death.

It seemed to suit Lambarde's notion of propriety, and the dignity of his office, to gather the whole family in the parlour, and announce most solemnly the housekeeper's condition and the manner of her death.

"Therefore, you all see why a coroner must be brought in," he concluded — and at that, the first stunned silence broke into confusion, and all spoke at once.

"It still doesn't mean that Edmund knocked her!" shouted Uncle Buffkin, just as Barbara angrily drew up her chin.

"You're never suggesting, Sir, that one of us would drown a servant?" she demanded — a perfectly witless protestation that was seconded by her husband, newly arrived and still in his mud-spattered riding clothes.

"That stupid woman!" Mary blustered, for all that her eyes were welling again, while Pelham, a hand on his wife's shoulder, droned on about the impropriety of it all.

"Not before my brother Walsingham's funeral," he kept repeating.

To hear them all, one would have thought that Susan Foal had had herself murdered to spite them… Which Tom wasn't far from feeling himself — petty and unchristian as it was.

From the window, where he stood with arms crossed, he counted only two silent heads: George, dull-eyed and gaping from one person to the other, and Lambarde, braving the storm in his sternest manner. Surely at any moment he would bring up his renewed suspicion of the master of the house — and announce his intention to have Ned's body observed, too?

But he did not. He glared coldly at them all — and if he waited for them to see reason, or even just the unseemliness of it all, Tom wished him joy of it. Or perhaps what Lambarde waited for was some telling outburst, a sign of guilt, of fear?

Tom stepped forward, one hand raised. "Come, come, it must be done," he called, voice pitched above the chattering. "Or would you rather ignore that a Walsingham servant was wilfully killed?" This earnt a measure of quiet and some muttering. "But the inquest won't be held before the funeral."

It could not be, since the coroner must arrive, and the jury must be summoned, and the justice could have pointed this out — but, again, he did not.

Instead, he nodded deeply, and said, "Indeed, Mr. Walsingham, it will not."

So stiffly formal, so acquiescent on the face of it... Tom found that he liked this compliance very little.

Barbara, mistaking it for victory, thought to pursue it. "Why she can't be brought to some more fitting place, I'm sure I don't know," she said, tapping impatient fingers. "The church, perhaps..."

And leave it to Uncle Buffkin to chortle unamiably: "Ay, Barbara lass — so she can share the nave with Edmund for his funeral!"

Not that he was wrong, but ... Jove! "The inquest must be done as close as possible to the place of finding," Tom interrupted sternly. "Must it not, Pelham?"

No High Sheriff could ignore an appeal to uphold the law, and the rest could only fall in line.

See Sherley nod his fine grey head, long face arranged in all solemnity. "You're master here, Walsingham," he conceded — bless him. "If you call it fair, then fair it must be to us all."

Not that the girls agreed, one sniffing, the other pouting, nor Uncle Buffkin, nor, Jove rain on all ingrates, did Lambarde. Hadn't Tom just sanctioned his inquest?

"The law calls it fair, Mr. Sherley," the magistrate retorted, head drawn high and only lacking the scales to make a figure of Justice itself.

And after that, Fates be thanked, the arrival of Guil's widow was announced, with her two daughters, and Barbara and Mary charged out to the hall to welcome and berate their sister-in-law, and otherwise overwhelm her. The husbands followed, and the uncles, and in a moment Tom was left behind on the parlour's threshold, alone with the justice.

"I sent for my own coroner, from Rochester," the magistrate said. "A man who enjoys my trust."

And for the plumber, Tom didn't say. "I can't decide whether you warn or threaten," he said instead — a most unseemly bit of levity, after all. See how Lambarde glared.

"Before coming to me, Constable Beveridge also tried Coroner Fremlyn in Kemsing. I don't suppose you know him any more than you do Justice Styles?"

And how did they all expect him to know these things, these people? "Truly, Mr. Lambarde, as I keep saying to you and everybody else, I've lived in London and in France for a dozen years. Kent is mostly a boyhood memory to me."

Not quite true, perhaps, and the wrong thing to say. To the magistrate it must have sounded like *Kent is beneath me*, judging by the testiness of his retort: "Well, I don't think Fremlyn knows you, either — but your name made a great impression on him. His health worsened at once, and his certainty set itself in stone that no mischief could be attached to Mr. Secretary's nephew."

Cousin. Tom swallowed the correction he'd been making half his life, as well as a bitter laugh. Whatever the wolves thought at Court, Kent still continued in awe of Sir Francis's very name. "You seem to think that I make unfair use of the name I bear. I'm kinsman and servant to a very powerful man, yes — but I've never believed myself above the law for it."

In the gloomy hall, when they pushed her before the dais and the black coffin, Guil's younger daughter burst into tears, to her mother's dismay and her aunts' chiding.

Unbothered by little Tibby's sobs, Lambarde hummed. "There are, it seems, those who think you might," he said. "Or at least, they cannot tell which nephew's interests Mr. Secretary would have at heart. I'm sure you understand why I sent for Coroner Coates, whom I trust to suffer no such qualms." The man's mouth quivered in the smallest of smiles. "I'll pay Mr. Secretary the compliment of assuming that he wants truth and justice."

What did one say to that? "A fair assumption, and a compliment that Mr. Secretary would appreciate." Tom gave a most courtly nod — for all that in his mind Doubt wondered: *and what does Essex want instead?* If he wanted anything at all…

Because he couldn't ignore his brother's widow, Tom excused himself and went to join his sisters and kinsmen. All the time, the question kept repeating in his mind — clacking like pieces of glass that didn't make a pattern.

Even when Lambarde departed for the Tiger's Head Inn where a room awaited him, and Uncle Buffkin called it good riddance, the relief was scant. It could hardly be otherwise, with the two dead bodies, and the suspicion that hung in the air as heavy and cold as the smell and the rain — and then, to complete the day's bleakness, Rector Harvey made his appearance, bulge-eyed and breathless with the news of a second death in Scadbury, and offended that no one had thought to advise him.

"I had to learn of the mischance from my own servant, Sir," the man complained, dripping rainwater from the hem of his black scholar's gown — collar askew and yellow curls plastered to his head. "And he heard of it at the Tiger's Head!"

Well, it had been too much to hope that Everest's fetching of the midwife could have gone unobserved — but at least the lad had had sense enough to not babble of murders. Tom pretended to pay heed to a third repetition of how Mr. Harvey had lost his hat to a gust of wind along the way — a wind so awful and tremendous it could only portend…

Having had the day he'd had, and having been torn from his supper, Tom was in no mind to humour the man.

"Yes, Sir — yes: a message would have spared you a pointless journey," he said — sharp enough that nobody would have mistaken the words for courtesy or apology.

Glaring most stonily, Harvey drew as tall as he could — which wasn't much. "Even if it weren't for that poor woman, Mr. Walsingham, it is the eve of your brother's funeral." He pronounced each word like a bell tolling. "I promised to hold a prayer tonight, for the comfort of you and yours. You may have forgotten, but I have not."

The prayer — yes, and nothing that resembled preparation had been made. With a sudden pang of guilt, Tom looked around to find that — bless Old Kathryn! — at least the candles still burnt on the dais. Not that he cared a straw for the rector's bruised importance — but Edmund was another matter. Poor Ned, with his solemnities pushed aside by the housekeeper's drowning…

"I've…" *I've been accused of murdering my brother and, now that the servant who accused me has been killed, the magistrate is minded to blame me for both…* "We've all had a trying day, Mr. Harvey. I'm sorry."

It is sometimes easier, Thomas, to appease than to convince, Sir Francis was fond of saying — and sometimes, when out of charity, would gloss this piece of wisdom by adding, *especially with fools*. Whether Richard Harvey was a fool or not (and Tom had his own notion on the matter), the apology disarmed his displeasure at once into condescension.

"I'm sure you have much on your mind, Mr. Walsingham," he conceded. "Better men have faltered under the weight of adversity."

Oh, Lord give patience, because Tom had none of his own left. After an inward count to *quattuor*, he ushered the rector into the parlour — and let his sisters make what they liked of him! — and fled in search of a servant. Having the misfortune of being at hand, Wollans received rather brisk orders to arrange things for the prayer. At least the man was too old at the game — or too used to Edmund's ways — to be discomposed.

"Ay, Master — ye worry none: it won't take a wink," he assured, and placidly set to work at once, stooping-gaited but efficient.

A pity that Wollans lacked the education to match his housekeeper wife as Scadbury's next steward. In the midst of this consideration, Tom caught a flash of movement at the hall's far end — an indistinct shape, barely visible between the two suits of armour.

What now, what else…? Tom stalked that way, ready to rain his ill-humour on a gossip-seeking servant… And instead he found Marley, eyes bright with mischief even in the gloom.

"What now, Kit?" Tom began, and stopped short at a gurgle of suppressed laughter. Oh, Jove… "You're not in your cups, are you?"

"I'd never — but… Is that Dick Harvey? Dick Harvey is your parson?"

And what was so amusing about it? "For my sins, yes. You know him?"

"He was down at Cambridge when I was. He's a babbler only fit for the Iron Age. Does he still fancy himself a great astrologer?"

"We haven't progressed far enough in mutual acquaintance to discuss astrology..." Tom stopped. What had it been, though, about the portentous wind? "We never have a Dr. Dee in Chislehurst, have we?"

A ruddy flare as Wollans revived the flames in the grate, throwing Marley's face into relief for a moment, and showing the glee in his eyes.

"Doesn't he wish!" The poet's voice quivered with laughter, even after Tom hushed him. "Unless that's just why he's here."

"I am, also, in no spirit for riddles..."

"Your rector published a prediction, back in Cambridge, of fierce winds to come on a certain Sunday. It was to be a great disaster, a half apocalypse, a harbinger of whatnot — because his calculations said so. When the Sunday came and nothing happened, did all Cambridge laugh, town and gown both! Rhymed to death, Dick was — like the ass he is. I wouldn't have thought him the sort to learn a lesson, mind, but perhaps even he saw the wisdom of burying himself in some paltry village..."

An urge to defend the village stirred, and died the early death of moot points. The paltriness of Chislehurst might be an impression born of too many years in London and Paris — and, paltry or not, it was where Tom was burying himself to play the country squire.

Oblivious to the dolefulness he had stirred, Marley was still happily digging at Harvey. "Even Lord Essex wasn't overjoyed when the dummel dedicated his next book to him —"

"Essex!"

"Some Ramist babble or other — in execrable Latin, if you ask me. But then, the Harveys — there are three of them — are all windy-headed ignoramuses."

Essex again! Tom was beginning to feel besieged. "Must all the world address a book to that one?"

Had no one ever taught Kit Marley not to laugh around a funeral vigil? "Ah, as Harvey himself might say, no planet has so many moons as the rising one..." He let it trail, a frown plain in the changed tone. "Why, who else does?"

"Lambarde," Tom ground out — and waited, watching as Wollans moved chairs and lit candles. It was no more than a heartbeat as the poet put two and two together.

"Oh," he murmured — only to brighten at once: "Well, do you want some Virgil? Bees swarm to the new hive — but, say I, it doesn't mean the hive either deserves or likes it. Do you think...? I'd understand Lambarde, but Harvey? What could he do?"

A thin draught slithered like a chill finger down Tom's neck and he shivered. "Push unsigned letters under the constable's door?"

"It seems a long game, too subtle for Dick Harvey. Unless..." Marley threw a glance towards the parlour door. "Did your brother put him where he is?"

Put him...? Oh. "We don't *put* rectors in St. Nicholas. Rochester Cathedral does, I think."

"And are they Essex men, in Rochester Cathedral?"

That now, was worth finding out — for all that the game seemed quite long, even for some Essex-minded canon.

The parlour door opened, and the meagre shape of Rector Harvey was thrown into relief against the golden light inside. Wollans stopped his work.

"If you would find your master, my good man?" the rector called in that whitish voice of his. He sounded displeased: what had the girls — or Uncle Buffkin — done to irk him?

The question mostly answered itself as a glint-eyed Barbara emerged behind the rector and nodded at the servant. "Find Mr. Thomas, Wollans, and tell him that Mr. Harvey is ready, will you?" she said, as though the man hadn't spoken.

And see how the rector snatched his rolled tippet from his pocket, shook it loose, and swung it across his shoulders.

"Dick Harvey isn't pleased," Marley snorted — which made all turn their way and notice them.

Oh, Jove — did Tom lack trouble, that he should have Cambridge grudges firing up under his roof? He glared sideways at Marley. "Can you bring yourself to behave through a few psalms and a prayer?" he hissed, and raised his voice to be heard across the hall. "I am ready also, Mr. Harvey," he called — and then, with a somewhat chastened poet at his side, he walked into the circle of light around the coffin, towards the glowering rector and his glum-faced relations.

It surely was a minor kind of Cain-ness that, as Rector Harvey droned out psalm after psalm, Tom's mind must wander round and round — and not about Ned's death, nor the murder of Susan Foal.

Or at least…

Marley must be right, surely: it could be no more than chance that both Lambarde and the rector had ties to Essex — if they had ties in truth. The good Lord knew how many men across the whole of Kent, across the whole of England for that matter, were penning hopeful flattery for the young rising star. And yet, Tom found it difficult to forget that Essex had grown up as the ward of Lord Burleigh, that old, shrewd half-enemy of Sir Francis.

A harder rattle of the great window recalled Tom to the hall: to the droning Harvey, to the girls with their husbands —

Sherley piously nodding at the notion of having been searched and known by the Lord; to Uncle George hitching a little away from the others, his lank hair falling across his eyes; to Marley at his elbow, the very picture of Meek Loyalty; to round-eyed Poll, always sitting a little sideways like a plump mouse ready to bolt; to the servants standing at the back in a depleted row now that Susan Foal was lying instead in the great cellar and her husband was nowhere to be seen.

Poor Ned — nobody would watch over him on his last night at Scadbury…

His last night, that was, unless the surgeon in the morning found reason to hold an inquest into his death too.

Except, the Rochester coroner wouldn't arrive before the funeral. Would Lambarde go to the lengths of ordering a postponement out of no more than a suspicion and an unsigned note? Did he have the authority to do so? Not unless the surgeon found solid evidence of foul play, surely?

Lambarde had denied any wish to make trouble, and he was said to have a conscience — but…

"Tom!" came Mary's sharp whisper, together with a jab of her elbow, just too late to let him join in with the scattered, ragged chorus of *Amen.*

He nodded ruefully at his sister, who rolled her eyes as Harvey cleared his throat, opened his bible, and started the Lesson.

"*For the trumpe shall blowe, and the dead shall ryse incorruptible, and we shall be chaunged. Death, where is thy sting? The styng of death is sinne,*" Harvey grimly bleated, and, as if in answer, a log toppled on the hearth with a dull thump, blowing out a billow of smoke. At Kathryn's nudge, Everest scurried to mind the fire, while the rector glowered at them all, and the acrid tang jolted Tom's mind awake.

Why, the last thing Essex would want was to harm the man whose power he meant to inherit by marrying his daughter. Sir Francis had enemies aplenty — but none of them was patron to Harvey and Lambarde. And, most of all, would any of them, or Essex for that matter, condone murder for the slender chance of harming Mr. Secretary through his kinsman?

"*Lord have mercy upon us...*" intoned Harvey — and indeed, have mercy on fools who let their thoughts tangle together.

It was most absently, and with his lips alone that Tom joined in the Lord's prayer — his restless mind busy with questions.

If Ned hadn't been murdered, why kill Susan Foal?

If the unsigned note was no threat to Sir Francis, what was it then?

Or was it, and Susan Foal had stumbled upon some larger secret?

What made Lambarde so keen to prove Tom guilty?

Though he'd have no watcher, this night Ned was going to have the distant, sleepless company of his brother.

CHAPTER 12

21st of November

Lambarde's arrival caught them at breakfast, an assembly of black-clad, taciturn ghosts, eyeing each other's funeral garb with either sourness or displeasure — Tom's old Court velvet earning the most vinegary appraisals.

"The man suffers no qualms, does he?" groused Uncle Buffkin, as Tom rose to follow the steward to the hall. "Hardly past dawn, and he's here to bother us!"

And that started a torrent of complaints around the table, on which Tom was glad to close the door — but truly, how much black bile must a man be harbouring, to find relief in a magistrate's arrival?

"I thought, Mr. Walsingham, that you'd rather have it all done well before the funeral," was Lambarde's salutation. And surely now he was going to announce that he also meant to have Edmund's body investigated, perhaps an inquest called? But no. Instead he introduced his companion, a long-faced, narrow-mouthed man in a long coat and with a satchel on his shoulder: Longe, the surgeon out of Greenwich.

Longe didn't look happy to have been summoned to Scadbury again, and by a magistrate's order no less. *The man's an ass*, Ned had said. *Told him to his face.* So perhaps now, as he eyed the new master, he was wondering just how alike the Walsingham brothers were — and small blame to him. It was with all his courtesy that Tom offered to escort the surgeon to the cellar, so he could examine Mrs. Foal's body. As good a time as the magistrate could wish for, to declare his intentions, surely?

But no, he didn't — and it was the outside of enough.

"Unless you'd rather wait for the plumber, Mr. Lambarde?" Tom asked, in his most innocent manner.

See how Lambarde's face darkened, and how the surgeon halted mid-step.

"The plumber?" exclaimed Longe — no complete fool, whatever his failings as a surgeon — looking from man to man as Tom and Lambarde glowered at each other.

"I'm sure that Mr. Wood can show Mr. Longe to the cellar," Lambarde ground out at last. "I, Mr. Walsingham, would have a word with you."

What protestation the surgeon would have made died at the sight of Lambarde's forbidding manner — and, if Wood had perplexities of his own, he masked them with unperturbed primness, and off they went.

So they were left facing each other, questioner and suspect. For all the times he'd played this game, Tom had always been the questioner, and it was mightily uncomfortable not being the Sphinx.

On the other hand, Lambarde was fuming, flushed to his ears, lips tight and eyes narrowed. "How?" he seethed. "How did you come to know?"

"Not from Beveridge, if it eases your mind. And, for a question of my own, when did you intend to tell me of the inquest you want done into my brother's death?"

"It's just…" Lambarde turned away, breathing sharply through his nose. It was debatable how well he'd reined in his temper when he turned back to speak in a grating whisper. "An inquest is just what I've been trying to avoid, if only you would see it. But now, the woman who accused you is dead —

murdered. In conscience, what am I to do? Why, what would you do in my place?"

And that was the crux of the matter, wasn't it? It made Tom uneasy that, in the man's place, he'd likely have done much the same. Except... "I wouldn't act in this slippery manner of yours."

"Why, you just..." Lambarde flung up a hand. "My slippery manner, you call it? You ask your own questions, try to influence me, have your people spy on me — and then it's *my* slippery manner! In all my years of being a justice, I've only found one sort of people trying so hard to stay ahead of me, Mr. Walsingham: those who are guilty."

"Then the serpent is rather biting its own tail, don't you think? The more you think me a murderer, the more I want to find the truth; and the harder I try to clear myself, the guiltier you think me. And if that's all you have against me..."

"And here you philosophise again! What I have against you, is that I see only one reason to drown that poor woman: to close her mouth, because she knew who the murderer was."

"And must I be the murderer?"

"You forget it's you that she accused."

Always that... If the old crones were right, and the dead lingered while the body awaited burial, the spirit of Susan Foal must be laughing to see what she'd done with her charges ... and then a thought stirred inside Tom's mind, like a bit of glass catching the light. Her charges, yes! "No, Sir — it's you who forget: she had accused me indeed, she'd shouted it to the four winds already. For me it was late to silence her — just as it was late to kill my brother once the will was made..." A mistake! Tom halted, seeing Lambarde's mien clear.

"Ah, but you didn't know what was in the will —"

"Susan Foal swore otherwise —"

"You would have me disbelieve her on everything but this?"

"And you would take her word on everything but this?"

"But no matter. Say that you did know." The magistrate raised a triumphant forefinger. "It was not to kill your brother that you came back that night — only to persuade him."

Tom laughed in disbelief. "And, with persuasion on my mind, I stole into the house through a window in the middle of the night?"

"But," Lambarde forged on, ignoring the interruption, "as they had already done that day, tempers grew hot, and you did in rage what reason would have forbidden —"

"Good Lord — and Susan Foal? Did I kill her in rage too, after she'd already done me all the harm she could?"

"Ah, but had she?" Lambarde stroked his beard, frowning like one trying out a new thought. "Say that at first she just voiced a suspicion that Beveridge could have disregarded. But later … perhaps she learnt more. Perhaps you said or did something to firm her suspicion —"

"So I'm a fool, as well as a tartar!" Tom flung up both hands. "And what of the letter?"

Another might have faltered, conceived a doubt; William Lambarde only scowled most mulishly. "Say what you will, Mr. Walsingham: none of this clears you."

Lord smite all blind, narrow-minded ram-heads! "And you wonder why I strive to clear myself?" Tom strode away — three angry steps, and then came back. "You've made up your mind on circumstance and slander, and —"

And it was a good thing that, before worse words were exchanged, Barbara marched in through one door, followed by the Sherley coachman, just as Wollans hurried in from another.

"Thomas!" Mother had always said Barbara had a clarion's voice. "What's the plumber doing here again?"

Having come to announce the same arrival, Wollans stopped in his tracks, his one good eye travelling from Barbara to Tom and back again, not quite knowing to whom he spoke: "Smith says as the magistrate sent for him, please ye Master. Mistress."

How much it pleased Barbara was plain at once. "And here I thought you had seen reason, Tom, and sent for a new coffin…" she said, and as she spoke, she slowly turned to glare at Lambarde.

And with that, the cat was out of the basket. Pelham, Mary, Sherley and the uncles were pouring out of the parlour, so Tom pitched his voice for the whole company. "Oh, it's all Mr. Lambarde's doing. He called in Ned's surgeon, too — he's downstairs, having a look at Susan Foal, but I rather think that he's meant to observe Ned's body."

But for Mary's gasp, a heartbeat of silence met the announcement, until Pelham asked slowly, "Did you know of this, Walsingham?"

"Mr. Lambarde didn't see fit to let me know." Only half the truth, but Tom wasn't minded to tell the High Sheriff of Surrey how Marley had eavesdropped on the law. For a moment he thought that Lambarde would… But no: the man squared himself, blank-faced before the hostile gazes — the Sphinx inscrutable.

"You all understand, I'm sure — as Mr. Walsingham does — that, under the circumstances, the body must be examined."

Inscrutable and shrewd, Jove rain on him! If Tom did object now, what would it look like?

Not that his family saw that: Pelham had reservations, Sherley had doubtful hums, Mary had no intention of allowing such an unchristian act, Uncle Buffkin had to point out that Edmund had kicked out Longe for a dunce — and George… Wonder of wonders: stung out of his torpor, Uncle George called it a shame and the most brazen piece of meddling he'd ever seen. "Have you no respect, Sir?" he blustered. "My nephew will never allow this paltering with his dead brother!"

What a marvellous time to shed the moping drunkenness... Tom put a hand on his quivering arm. "I'm sure that paltering is the last thing on Mr. Lambarde's mind, Uncle," he soothed, only to have George turn on him, wild-eyed and gasping.

"Tom, for shame!"

And see how betrayed he looked — no matter how Lambarde assured that all would be done most respectfully.

"And what's respectful in it, I'd like to know!" huffed Barbara. "And also what's the need. My brother did it already, didn't you, Tom?"

Well, that shook Lambarde out of his stoniness. "You did?" He glared at Tom, and on Barbara forged, with all the misplaced complacence in this world.

"And it was bad enough without strangers violating Edmund's very coffin on his funeral day!"

All earnest reason, Sherley came to stand at his wife's side. "After all, Sir, what can your surgeon see that Walsingham didn't?"

And, being Anthony Sherley, he'd meant it to be placating, no doubt about that — but truly, it was no wonder that Lambarde was struck speechless. For a moment he gaped, before he found his voice again.

"Can it be that not one of you understands...?" When words deserted him, he shook his head and began again. "An inquest must be made, unless it can be ascertained that Mr. Edmund Walsingham died of nothing but his illness. And you understand, Mr. Sherley, that such certainty cannot come from your brother-in-law, who is under suspicion —"

"Oh, baggage!" Mary cried, moving to stand between Tom and the startled magistrate — bless her silly heart. "You've come here with ill will towards the Walsinghams —"

"Mary," Tom warned — and, if she kept seething, at least she bit down whatever other unwise thoughts she'd meant to voice.

Lambarde, though, was truly shaken now. Had he never, in his years as Justice of the Peace, come nose to nose with gentry pride? "Mr. Pelham, I appeal to you…" he called, only to meet a new vexation — for Pelham had drawn a little apart from the commotion. Apart from his wife's kin. What retribution would the scowling Mary dole out later, Tom would have liked to know. "It is all most unusual, Mr. Justice," this Pilate of Surrey said, shaking his head, and then, to signify that no more would be had of him, he went back to pick up a prayer book someone had forgotten on the chest, deaf to Uncle Buffkin's snort and George's breathless protestations…

And all under the eyes of Wood and the surgeon.

Lord knew when the two men had appeared in the doorway, what part of this squabble they had witnessed!

"Enough!" Tom snapped, sharply enough to earn silence. "Mr. Wood, if you'd show Mr. Longe and Mr. Lambarde to the counting-room." See how uncles and sisters drew together into the tightest knot. Lambarde would have protested, perhaps, but Tom spoke right through him. "A bare moment, Mr. Lambarde, and I'll join you."

He'd seen arrested traitors go less grimly than the justice did, as he followed Wood and the disgruntled surgeon. The moment the door closed on the three men, the family knot came undone again in a storm of hisses.

"He must not…"

"You can't allow…"

"It is unchristian..."

"Enough, for God's sake!" Tom hit a palm on the back of a chair. "It will seem like we have something to hide. Like *I* have something to hide, because you all forget that this is mine to decide."

"*His to decide*!" Barbara scoffed. "And what of Edmund?"

Mary and George both nodded belligerently, but it was Uncle Buffkin who gave an unpleasant chortle.

"Ah, never you mind Edmund. Who cares, as long as the new master's cleared of all suspicions — eh, Tom?"

Nasty old fool, ever needling and taunting for the hell of it! Tom bit his underlip. *Unus ... duo ... tres...* "It's a good deal worse than suspicion, now — as near to charges as makes no odds, and for something that I didn't do. And even if you don't care that I'm innocent, what do you think will happen to Scadbury, if I go to the gallows? It goes to Sir Francis first, and after him to the Crown, because we're the last Walsinghams, he and I. Is that what you want — not that it matters much? Is that what you think Ned would have wanted? Or Father? And that matters little, too — because they're dead, and I am here, and I'll say it again: the decision is mine to make!"

At last, this shut their blathering mouths! Or most of them, at least, for while uncertain glances were exchanged, Pelham emerged from his book to ask, "Yours to make — and made already, I take it? Wise of you, yes."

Pilate, offering support when there was no more need of it! "Not that I have many other courses, have I?" Tom bit back, more than a little sourly.

Sherley was next in finding his voice again. "But, my dear lad, since — thank the good Lord — you're innocent..."

"I am, and I'm not even sure that Edmund was killed at all. Someone did drown Susan Foal, though, and I'm not beginning my days at Scadbury with murder unpunished, and doubt hanging over my head."

"And you'll trust that man to find the truth!" Mary cried, stamping a foot the way she had as a child, but for the touch of anguish in her manner. "What if he decides his findings prove you guilty?"

"Ah, but I don't trust Justice Lambarde a whit," Tom said, with the thinnest of smiles. "I'm just not letting him decide I'm guilty for lack of findings."

Lambarde had dismissed Wood and was trying to smooth the surgeon's ruffled feathers — with such success, apparently, that Longe leapt up from the steward's stool to salute the arrival of a Walsingham like a besieged town its relief.

"The woman was held underwater, Sir," was his salutation. "No question of it. She had marks —"

"Oh, Mr. Walsingham saw the marks. Well before I did, I'll wager." Lambarde gave a vinegary smile. "There's little that escapes him."

Oh, Jupiter… Ignoring the dig, Tom prodded the surgeon instead. "Yes, Mr. Longe?"

It was enough to win the surgeon over to his side. Perhaps the man had a conscience to go with his calling. Had Lambarde made little of his observations? See how pointedly Longe only addressed Tom.

"I'll bear witness to the drowning and the marks before the coroner's jury, Sir — as is my duty. But now I find that's not why I was called here, and the true reason offends me, as it must offend you, Sir. " Grey-shot brows drawn together, he delivered each word as though he were before the coroner already, marking each with a finger's tap on the table. "I saw Mr. Edmund Walsingham shortly after his death, which was caused by an inflamed heart and a disorder of the humours. I'd been treating him for these — although the patient wasn't exact in following my prescriptions."

The eternal excuse of the *medicus*: the patient's fault — but, in fairness, Edmund had not been meek. How exact Longe himself had been, though... "What of the crack on the head?" Tom asked. "You must have seen that, surely?"

A nod that was nothing short of solemn. "I did, Sir. A wound procured while falling down the stairs — and no question of it."

When Lambarde cleared his throat, and asked whether the wound had been bad enough to kill, the surgeon's manner stiffened at once — but still he spoke to Tom alone.

"Perhaps, Sir — and perhaps not. Men have been known to survive such injuries, but Mr. Walsingham was ill. Whether he fell because his heart gave out, or his heart gave out because he fell, that's something the whole College of Physicians couldn't tell you." Having delivered himself of this speech all at once, he had to take a breath before adding, "And there is nothing more that I could say on the matter — not if I examined the poor gentleman a hundred times."

A few hours more in the magistrate's company, and Longe would have learnt the futility of arguing. So convinced he was that he had scored a hit, that he gaped at finding Lambarde quite unmoved and suggesting that one more examination would be enough to search for marks of violence. "You had no cause to seek them the first time, after all."

No one leaps at the chance to have himself proved wrong — or even careless, and Longe was no exception. "But, Mr. Walsingham," he appealed, "surely..."

And, alas, Tom could only shrug both shoulders, shattering the fellow's newfound trust in Scadbury.

"I'm sure you were as thorough as could be, Mr. Longe," he said, "But, since nothing else will satisfy Mr. Lambarde, let's have this second examination — and, if you please, let's have it quickly. I have no wish for the funeral guests to arrive and catch us with our hands in my brother's coffin."

Poor Ned, fated to find no rest!

Like the first time, there was a sense of wrongdoing to it. Worse, perhaps, because back then (not even two full days ago, truly?) it had been Tom alone, with the Wollanses faithful and dismayed. Now, once the plumber had undone the seals, the offended surgeon set to work under Lambarde's scrutiny, while Barbara and Mary had taken up a grim guard duty in the passage room, lest some early mourner should make an appearance. Uncle George just hovered around the hall, pasty-faced, uneasy and unhelpful. Even Kit Marley, having found his way to Tom's side unasked, stood still and quiet, for a wonder.

Inside the coffin, decay was wreaking havoc, and the sickly odour wafted up when the winding sheet was folded back.

"What you expect me to find now, Mr. Justice, I don't know," the surgeon muttered, moving the blackened rosemary sprigs out of the way.

Two days had bloated the face past recognition, spread a yellow, mottled greyness over the cheeks and jowls, drawn back the blackened lips, and sunken the eyes deep in the sockets.

Hissing through his teeth, lip lifted in fascinated disgust, Marley took a step back, and Tom had to fight an urge to do the same. He'd already seen what he'd been able to see, after all…

But then, no matter what he'd said, Tom didn't trust Longe to have been thorough the first time. A sick man, a ruinous fall, no reason to suspect foul play: why look too hard into it? Now, though, under the magistrate's impassive stare, what would he do — hastily confirm his first findings? Or admit he had misjudged the case at first, even make up some discovery to appease Lambarde?

The head rolled limply aside under the surgeon's touch, showing the wound that had grown dark and flat. Tom clenched his jaw at the sight of the Longe's knobby fingers probing it, at the memory of bone yielding under his hand. From across the open coffin, Lambarde was watching him, perhaps taking his unease for that of a murderer facing his guilt.

Shall I touch the body to see whether it bleeds? Tom had the sense to force back the flippancy — barely — but held the hawkish, hooded gaze, until Lambarde walked close and bent over the wound, with a frown creasing his face.

"You say this blow could have killed or it could have not, Mr. Longe," he said. "But what if someone had struck it, causing Mr. Walsingham to fall?"

Oh, Jove! "Nobody did. He struck his head on the lowest step but one as he fell…" Tom hit a palm against his hip when both men glared at him. "Oh, come now, Mr. Longe. I was only told that, but you must have seen the blood!"

It was now the surgeon's turn to bear the weight of two glares, and he shook his head. "They had washed it away by the time I arrived," he explained, "but each and every servant was eager to describe it — even the steward: a smear of it, with some hair, on the step's edge, and a puddle on the landing, under Mr. Walsingham's head."

Terriers with bones sprang to mind when Lambarde asked, "All the servants? The housekeeper, too?"

"Mrs. Foal? Yes. The most eager of them all, she was." Even Longe mustn't have much liked Susan Foal. "But in the end, what does it prove, Sir? Whether the heart gave out because of its own inflammation, or because someone pushed the poor gentleman, the Queen's own physician couldn't tell you."

Longe named the Queen's own physician as he might have that healer centaur of legend, Chiron. Knowing Doctor Lopes well, and counting the doctor's son Ambrose among his friends and helpers, Tom very much wished for either man's keen, knowledgeable eye to observe the manner of Edmund's death, and perhaps to see what a provincial surgeon might well miss. Why hadn't he sent for Ambrose?

And perhaps Lambarde shared those misgivings. "And there is nothing else, Mr. Longe?" he prodded. "Nothing else that you see now?"

"There is much less to see now than I could see five days ago, Sir. But, now or then, I find nothing to say that Mr. Walsingham was pushed."

Or that he wasn't, whispered the unpleasant voice at the back of Tom's mind, as if prompted by Lambarde's grim, jaw-working silence — but, a lame victory being better than none, he asked, "Now, Mr. Justice, can we lay my brother to rest?"

What could Lambarde do but concede? He could hardly have the funeral postponed now, but happy he was not.

"Yes, Mr. Walsingham. You can lay his body to rest," he said, and stalked away.

"Now there's a bullish one!" Marley's whisper quivered — either with contempt or amusement. "I'd be wary of him, you know."

"I'm very much minded to be," Tom answered, while beckoning to the plumber.

Smith and the apprentice set to work at once, reviving the flames in their brazier while Kathryn, who had come to the hall unnoticed at some point, bustled around with an armful of fresh rosemary sprigs. Some she threw on the fireplace to sweeten the air; the rest she put in the coffin while she tidied the disturbed sheet. And all the time, she half murmured of unchristian doings, and half told Tom of those early mourners Mary and Barbara were keeping prisoners in the drawing room.

Tom fetched a great breath of rosemary and decay and molten lead and rosin. "Well, Kathryn," he soothed, "the good Lord willing, this is one thing settled."

With one last tug at the winding sheet, Kathryn gathered the rotted sprigs and stepped back from the coffin. "Ay, Mr. Thomas, one thing," she murmured, and frowned up at his face. "And what of all the rest?"

For one so chary of all vain ornament of speech, Rector Harvey managed to stretch the funeral service quite long. It was near on two hours before, with Edmund Walsingham properly buried in the family chapel, they left the church and stepped out into the wind. As Mary, on her last brother's arm, lifted her veil to squint at the greying sky, Kit Marley appeared at Tom's other side.

"What did I tell you?" he whispered. "The Iron Age!"

Oh, Jove! The laugh quivered low in Tom's throat — because the darkest suspicions hung over him, and the rector was a windbag, and they'd just buried Ned, and…

"Don't you dare!" Mary hissed, digging her elbow in his ribs.

And right she was — but Marley leant close to whisper, "Crave pardon, Mrs. Pelham — it's all my fault: passing on

Cambridge commentary on Rector Harvey's ferrous rhetorics…"

Mary opened her mouth to scold — but the corner of her lips quivered, and even the veil she lowered in haste couldn't hide the dancing of her eyes. "Master Marley, you are an imp!" she muttered — and there they were, the three of them, fighting laughter in the middle of the village graveyard, while half of Chislehurst crowded around to offer bows and condolences, and the parish poor crowded at the lychgate, waiting for the doles.

"Let's get you home, before the High Sheriff's wife makes a scandal." Tom looked around for the Pelham carriage that should have been brought over to convey the ladies back to Scadbury. "Now, where on earth has your coachman wandered?"

In one of those fits of willingness he displayed at times, Marley ran away to find out.

"Oh, must I go?" Mary protested. "I've had enough of Cousin Maria already. Would you credit, all the while they buried Ned, she murmured about you bringing here a Spaniard — and a handsome one, too!"

Devil tie Maria Guildford's busy tongue in knots! "Yes, you must — and do quench that notion. John Cardenas is as English as we are — and Sir Francis's man through and through."

"Because you're head of the family and say so?" Mary groused, but off she went to join Barbara at the door of the recovered carriage — glad, no doubt, for a chance to quench Cousin Maria in any way.

As if Mary's departure had been a signal, the crowd closed around Tom — farmers and tenants, villagers and gentry — and among them, the only unaccompanied woman; who must it be but Audrey Shelton? Black didn't suit her, Tom observed, as she repeated her condolences, and those of her father, for the third time in as many days. Black made her sallow and colourless, and washed her eyes a pale hazel. He much preferred the look of green on her…

Fool that he was! Tom jolted out of his contemplation at Mistress Shelton's sudden tilt-headed silence. Now she'd think him a wool-gathering dolt — and small blame to her.

"If you would ride in the carriage with my sisters," he proposed, which was even worse, because, even if there were room for her, all he lacked was for his sisters, Mrs. Carmarden, and — Heaven forfend! — Cousin Maria to wonder why Mistress Shelton must ride with them. Fates be thanked, she waved the offer away.

"I would rather walk — but *have* you?" she enquired.

Had he what? What had she asked while he'd considered her choice of colours? He turned away for a moment to greet an old man from one of the farms. When he went back to Audrey, she was observing him with one raised brow.

"You haven't listened to a word I spoke," she said, with a little sigh. "Mr. Walsingham, I understand that you have much on your mind — and truly, I should have stayed the other day! — but have you formed some notion of who murdered your housekeeper?"

To think how sternly Tom had lectured his family and household to keep the matter quiet! Well, it had always been a forlorn hope, what with half the village knowing…

Or did they? Last night Harvey had known of Susan Foal's death, but not of the manner of it — but then, Audrey hadn't heard of it in Chislehurst.

"Old Kathryn told you," he said, eyes narrowed — and didn't she have the gall to glare back?

"And you won't scold her for it. She worries so!"

"As well she might, I'll say — but..." *Why do you?* Before Tom could voice that particular thought, a distraction intervened in the shape of a man raising his voice across the graveyard.

"Enough, Mace!" the voice commanded — so sharp it took Tom a heartbeat to recognise it as that of John Wood. So the fellow could shout, after all.

"Ay, Mr. Wood, enough — and outside of it, I say!" old Robert Mace bit back, bristling as he faced the steward. "And I know what to think, I know..."

Others were moving towards the commotion or away from it — each to their humour — while Dickon Beveridge and St. Nicholas's ancient sexton hurried to restore order. The constable got there first, and took Mace by the arm, rumbling earnestly to him, until the farmer shook free and limped away, muttering to himself.

"Now what was that?" Audrey wondered aloud.

A very good question indeed. "I'm minded to find out," Tom said — and Fates be thanked for Grace Wildgoose unhurriedly coming to join them.

"What an interesting village Chislehurst is!" she said, placidly smiling. "Shall we go, Audrey? My poor coachman has found the place, after all. We have a seat for Mr. Walsingham, if he would join us..."

No, you would not — and I would walk with you, said the little dance of Audrey Shelton's dark brows; Tom ignored it completely.

"Thank you, Lady Wildgoose — I still have a matter to attend to here. I'll see you ladies at Scadbury." And, equally ignoring Mistress Shelton's small gasp, he hastened away to catch Wood.

As it happened, John Wood was in an ill humour — of which the fled farmer was not the sole recipient. Taking leave of a spare fellow in dark grey, he squared himself, arms crossed, to meet Tom like Leonidas the Persians. A thin-lipped Leonidas in the simplest black and falling bands.

"Was that Old Mace?" Tom asked, by way of greeting. He could have asked a tad less Persianly — in fact, it would have been wise, since the man was still the steward of Scadbury and Ned's executor — but, for once, cursed be wisdom! "He looked rather out of charity with you."

The steward had looked ready for battle; now his scowl deepened to grimness.

"Old Mace indeed, Mr. Walsingham — and very much out of charity. It seems that *someone* has been discussing his debts with him."

There was no mistaking the man's intention. "If by *someone* you mean me, Mr. Wood, all I said is that I don't even know if I'm the one to pester. Why should he think to come to you, I wonder?" And if Tom had spoken for no better reason than to irk the man, the shot perhaps had been less wide than he thought.

See how a wave of colour rose to darken the man's cheeks. See how he hesitated before answering, "He just thought that, as Mr. Edmund's steward, I should know who it was."

"And was he right?"

Whatever uncertainty had tied Wood's tongue, it was gone in a moment, replaced by that purse-mouthed primness that seemed to be the man's habitual manner. "Mr. Walsingham, your brother placed his confidence in me, and I won't break it," he proclaimed. "You will know soon enough — whatever you haven't learnt already from looser mouths than mine." With that, he stalked away to the lych-gate for the giving of the doles, chin held so high it was a marvel he didn't walk into any of the gravestones — and if this truly was the way of prophets, one couldn't much fault the kings of old for throwing one to the lions now and then.

Well, a day or two, and Scadbury — and Tom — would be well rid of John Wood. Now to forge through the funeral dinner, without even the consoling prospect of a quiet, empty house on the morrow — not with the shadow of the coroner's inquest looming.

The carriages had all gone, Marley and Cardenas had disappeared, and a few stragglers could be seen hurrying along the lane, Scadbury-wards. Taking a great breath of damp air, and wishing he'd thought to have his horse brought to the church, Tom slipped off his gown, threw it over his arm, and took off towards home at a good clip.

CHAPTER 13

There was a large yew tree at the end of the graveyard's wall, an ancient thing with a cordlike bole as wide as a man's waist. Under its branches, so green in the muddy light, George Guildford hunched, crushing one by one the blood-red berries scattered underfoot.

"Uncle!" Tom called — and George looked up, wild-eyed and dishevelled, wispy hair falling around his brow at sixes and sevens.

"Tom," he answered and, when he tried to smile, his lips hardly quivered up enough to show teeth.

Who would have thought that George would be so affected? "Come, Uncle. Mary says that Barker's marchpane is worth a good deal of bother."

Again that sickly smile, and the man fell in step. For a short while they walked side by side — George with his head low, and Tom unsure of what consolation he might offer.

They'd gone perhaps halfway when George, never looking up, murmured, "It was good of you, Tom, to make me a pall-bearer. Ned wouldn't have done it."

It would have been cruel to point out that there had been little choice, given the dearth of male relatives. "Yes, he would have," Tom protested, as heartily as he knew how. "You are Mother's brother, and ever a favourite with all of us. You'd have borne my pall, had things gone otherwise."

"Your…" George stumbled to a halt, bloodshot eyes bulging. "Dear lad, I never…"

And just for whose funeral might Ned have had to choose pall-bearers? Tom patted the man's arm. "I know, Uncle. Never look so stricken."

They resumed their way in silence, and Tom's thoughts had strayed back to Wood and Old Mace arguing in the graveyard, when George began again.

"What I mean, Tom…" He cleared his throat. "Ned wasn't always good to me. You're not like him, Tom. You call me a favourite with you all, but it's for yourself that you speak." He nodded earnestly when Tom made an unconvinced murmur. "Yes, yes! I was never a favourite with Ned — and of late he'd grown downright spiteful."

What a thing to discuss, back from the man's own funeral… "I wouldn't take it to heart, Uncle. Ned was unwell, and besides, he was snappish with everyone."

"And you should know, eh? Here I am, complaining, as though you hadn't burnt yourself at that fire." George shook his head most mournfully. "Ned would be singeing my ears by now — but you're nothing like him. Out of all of Dorothie's children, you always were the kindest."

Which wasn't saying much, in truth, even if it were true. It didn't seem to Tom that he'd been especially kind to George, and all the praise was making him uneasy — and suspicious.

"Ned called you to Scadbury to be his witness, after all."

With a bitter laugh, George bent to tear a branch from the hazel hedge. "He knew I wouldn't refuse a few days at Scadbury. That much generosity he could afford." A snort. "A dole! Even the Parish poor he used better."

So there was nothing for Uncle George in the will — or even worse…

"Did you ask him for money, Uncle?" Tom asked with a wince. "It was like asking the doorjamb —"

"Don't I know!" Cheeks crimsoning, George flung his stick to the ground. "He laughed at me. Had I no brothers of my own to fleece? Did I think he had trunks of gold sunk in the moat?"

"Oh, the trunks in the moat! I wish I had a groat for every time I heard that one." Tom's huff of laughter wasn't very cheerful, and his suspicions deepened when George, after some low-headed nodding, kicked at the stick and darted a sideways glance that didn't reach Tom's face.

"But you're nothing like him, lad," he repeated. "You know how it is, eh?" He looked up with a skewed twitch of his lips, like a winning smile dead in its infancy. "You won't refuse to help me…?"

There it went. Tom's stomach sank. "Uncle…" He fetched a breath. "I'll help if I can, but —"

"Or course you can!" George stopped, grabbing Tom's sleeve.

"I'm so deep in debt myself, it's a marvel I'm not in gaol."

"But you have Scadbury now! Lands…"

"Yes, and all of it encumbered. What I have is a roof over my head, and debts so large I have no hope of repaying them while I live!"

Letting go of Tom's sleeve, George stepped away as though from a rotting fish. "Just like your brother," he snarled. "The very words. And all the time, he was loaning off small fortunes…"

"And you say that now those small fortunes will go to Wood and Foal!"

Deaf to this piece of reason, George snarled on: "You knew of all these debts, and still kept wanting money, and were angry that Ned wouldn't give it!"

"And I got next to nothing, for all that I was the heir, and only asked for the annuity Father had willed me..." But what was the use? There George stood, shoulders hitched to his ears, jaw working and lip jutting, his whole face a web of lines and purple veins. Tom sighed. "I'm not refusing you on a whim. Let me read the will; let me see the books. If I can —"

"Ay, and while the grass groweth, the horse starveth!" George cut through, face twisted. "Just like your brother, that's what you are!" And, spinning on his heel, he stomped away, plashing in the mud, not caring that he soiled his mourning gown. He all but ran into a man who came around the bend from the direction of Scadbury: Kit Marley.

Fastidious as a cat, the poet drew away from the peril of mud stains, and joined Tom.

"Mrs. Pelham was growing worried that you'd lost your way," he announced, and glanced over his shoulder at the angrily departing George. "What have you done to him?"

What, indeed... "I explained to him that land and gold are not one and the same."

"Ah, the eternal curse of the wealthy: leeches all over you."

Such a world-weary air as an earl's son might show. Tom had to smile — though he sobered at once. "Still he must be desperate, poor Uncle. Asking my brother for money was never pleasant, and seldom fruitful at all — even when asking for your dues." And, as he said it, a new, most unpleasant pattern formed in his mind.

"So..." For a few steps Marley frowned at the hedges. "He tried to fleece your brother, and was sent on his way. When was that?"

Had George said at all? These past days, surely... Tom very much disliked the direction of Marley's thoughts — all the more because they echoed his own new misgivings. But Long Affection balked in disbelief: "Come now, Uncle George?"

Marley nodded towards the lane, where George had disappeared around the bend. "You just sent him on his way, too — and by the looks of him, you can be thankful there were no stairs nearby."

Affection still fought — and Pity. "Haven't you seen him? He's sack-sopped more often than not!" *As though that must absolve him...*

A shadow dulled Marley's gaze. "Killing a man isn't as difficult as they'd have it, Mr. Thomas," he said, voice too hollow for flippancy.

Which Tom ought to know better than most, having seen men and women kill for all sorts of reasons. "But still... Uncle George? And what of Susan Foal, then?"

"Who knows?" Marley's sudden melancholy was gone as soon as it had come. "Perhaps she'd seen him do it —"

"And then waited until morning to raise the alarm?"

"Well, no..."

"And when she did, she accused me instead?"

"Then that sour husband of hers saw it, and only told her yesterday, and she wanted to expose him — your uncle, not her husband... Oh, I don't know. I make plays, not..." He waved a brusque hand that dismissed at once the lane, grey sky and meadows, Chislehurst and Scadbury, and the whole bleak, unyielding world that no poet's skill could shape aright.

And yet... "You know, it's true that Fair Susan might have learnt better after having accused me..." Tom let it trail. For all that he'd used the argument with Lambarde, it was hard to imagine an enlightened Susan Foal eager to undo the ill she'd caused. At first he thought it was that same unlikelihood making Marley snort — but no:

"Not all that fair, was she?" he teased, all glumness gone. "And if your brother thought so, it's just proof that Scadbury is better off with a new master."

It was Tom's turn to snort. "My sister has it right, Kit Marley: you are an imp! Come now, before my kin and neighbours throw poor Cardenas in the moat for a Spanish spy…" He stopped short. Would the day come when they would jest about the moat again?

The wind was picking up, sharper than it had been; Tom donned his gown again and, all levity gone, they took off at a good pace.

Seen from a distance, black tails flapping behind him, Tom was sure he must have looked like a crow bound for Scadbury.

Wasn't it wrong that they should gather to feast on fine meats, ale, hippocras, and cider in the same gloomy hall where Edmund had been lying a few scant hours earlier? A foolish thought — one that had earned a chiding on the day of Guil's funeral — and it was true that all wore black and partook in solemn quiet.

Or quietly enough, at least. As for solemnity…

There surely was none to see in Cousin Maria — violet-eyed, dimple-cheeked Maria, with the soul of a ferret, and a tongue like scissors — who had claimed a seat near Tom as soon as the sweetmeats where served and the seating order loosened, and kept gazing at John Cardenas in delighted horror.

"He's no Spaniard, Maria — how many times must I tell you?" Tom didn't bother to keep the weariness from his voice. "He's here on Mr. Secretary's behalf." And carrying letters: one from Sir Francis, half formal condolences and half cousinly warmth, and one from Frances that sat still unopened inside Tom's doublet.

"He looks like one, though," Maria insisted, in such shameless tilt-headed appraisal that, across and down the table, Cardenas was pretending utmost absorption as Rector Harvey held forth. "So dark, such fine eyes…"

"As though you know what a Spaniard looks like!" Mary sneered from their cousin's other side.

Maria ignored her entirely to move her attention to Kit Marley, who, after dining somewhat below the salt, had been captured in conversation by Sherley, who nursed poetical ambitions of his own. "And that other one, he's not truly a poet, you know? Mr. Wildgoose calls him a playmaker."

Oh, Jove… "He *is* a poet, and a fine one. A very learned Cambridge man who also writes plays."

"The unusual people you find, Thomas!" Maria shook her head like one commiserating over an illness. "But I thought you only liked the poets of old Rome — all of them dead?" And what she found so amusing in it that she had to stifle a giggle, Tom truly didn't know.

Half-a-dozen seats away, where she sat with the Wildgooses, Audrey Shelton looked up from a plate of comfits and gave him a small grimace of sympathy. What storm of rumours would it raise if he went to speak to her, instead of wasting time on moulded jellies and inanities while a murdered woman lay below? Not much, perhaps, if he reached her while doing his rounds as the host and chief mourner. Little as he fancied the rounds themselves, it was a relief to rise and escape his cousin's clutches.

But, as Maria latched onto a sullen, glaze-eyed Uncle George, the limits of Tom's plan became apparent at once when Poll's father, Mr. Lennard, having caught hold of his late son-in-law's brother, began to expound in a reedy voice on the need for a new Justice of the Peace at Scadbury.

"Your brother Edmund never cared for the position." He waved a thin, liver-spotted hand. "And in truth I doubt he had the ability — but you… If nothing else, I'm sure your uncle could pull a string for you —"

"Cousin," Tom corrected — pettily enough, but truly! "My father was first cousin to Mr. Secretary, who will pull no such strings. And poor Ned had every ability it takes to be a country Justice of the Peace." *And that's not much, Jupiter knows — but to belittle a man at his own funeral table, with the crumbs of his funeral marchpane still in your beard…*

"*Poor Ned*, you call him?"

Fortunate as the interruption was, Tom could have wished it hadn't come in the shape of Uncle George rising unsteadily and shouting, "Poor Ned, rest him as he deserves, refused his uncle a loan!"

A dropped spoon tinkled in the sudden silence, and for a heartbeat all sat frozen, a black-clad tableful — like one of those Flemish paintings, had they not all stared agape at the panting, dishevelled drunk.

Barbara thawed first. "Uncle, for goodness' sake!" she hissed, reaching for George's sleeve. He shook her away and slammed both palms on the table, bloodshot eyes ablaze.

"Never a groat to spare for his own uncle, had poor Ned," he growled. "And yet he left a hundred pounds to that sly, purse-mouthed scoundrel of a steward — and let me not even begin on the fair Susan —"

Devil pinch all drunkards… "Uncle!" Tom hastened around the table, reaching his kinsman in three strides and grasping him by the elbow — and now what? Tussle with the man?

Even a sack-sopped fool can profit from hesitation. "And you!" George whirled on Tom, spittle flying. "Look at the new master in fine velvet!" He sneered and bent in a mocking bow that would have toppled him over the table, hadn't Tom caught him. "Beggared you as much as he could — that's what poor Ned did —"

"Uncle, enough!" Tom shook the man a little, and then Kit Marley was there, and Kathryn.

"Come, Mr. George — come ye now and have a good rest," the old woman cooed, while they half steered and half hauled George away.

"Velvet days are over, Tomkin!" the sot hiccoughed, digging in his heels at the threshold. "Poor Ned saw to it — and that wretched woman…"

And then he was gone.

Oh, Lord…

Slowly, Tom turned back to his guests. Sherley, Cardenas and Poyntell had risen, but all others still sat in their places — some agape, some full of scandal, some glint-eyed and savouring the rumours they would spread. Audrey Shelton and Cardenas alone — bless them! — looked worried. Mary squirmed halfway between fury and tears, while Foal and the Pelham servant, who had been waiting at table under Kathryn's prickly guidance, stood like fence-posts by the sideboard — Foal scowling blackly, and the other wondering, no doubt, what sort of home his mistress hailed from.

Tom made himself not clear his throat. "I crave the pardon of you all," he said, as firmly as he could manage. "My Uncle Guildford is unwell."

And trust Uncle Buffkin to find a chortle: "Ay, drinking away his grief — the old tosspot!"

Would ignoring the rudeness make the others disregard it too? In that vague hope, Tom forged on. "Please, do not let it distress you. Shall we drink to the memory of my brother?"

This jolted Pelham's man to life again, and Foal too, if rather more sluggishly. More wine was poured and drunk — but was it a great marvel that nobody's heart was in it? Soon afterwards the guests began to disperse and, by Tom's reckoning, not a moment too soon.

The Wildgooses were among the last to take their leave — Grace claiming, after all, a measure of friendship with Barbara. Enough of it, in fact, that Tom's sisters walked these particular guests out to the courtyard, and the moment the door closed behind the chatting group of women, Tom sank onto the long bench in the passage room, elbows on his knees and head between his hands.

Jove on his Olympus — what a day!

Let him never have another funeral to arrange… But then, who was left to him? He wasn't even sure who would arrange his own burial if he died tomorrow, if he went to the scaffold as a murderer…

How he startled when, of a sudden, the door to the guardhouse opened, and a woman's voice exclaimed: "Mr. Walsingham!"

Of course, it must be Audrey Shelton frowning at him. "Are you ill?" she asked, briskly moving close.

It would be just like her to take it into her head to feel his forehead and call for a posset. Before she could, Tom rose in haste. "Only feeling sorry for myself," he hurried to say. "I thought you'd gone." She'd never managed to stay behind again, had she?

"I forgot my gloves," she said — and never mind that she had them in her hand. "And feeling sorry for oneself is time wasted. Tell me of the housekeeper."

And at that, the laugh that all day had itched at the back of Tom's throat tore free — not half as bitter or mad as he'd expected. "Oh, Mistress Audrey," he gasped, "one cannot be sorry at all with you around!"

Did all her hats have a small feather curved to dance when she tossed her head? "What you find so amusing I don't know. Tell me of Mrs. Foal before Grace comes to find me!"

Why he should do so, Tom couldn't think — and yet tell her he did. As succinctly as he could, he told her of the drowning, of the marks, of the inquest — and, while he was at it, of Lambarde and the examination of Edmund's body.

She clapped her hands once. "So at least he's convinced that there was no murder there?"

"He's convinced that a jury would believe so. On the other hand, now he suspects me of drowning Susan Foal."

"Then he's a halfwit!" she scoffed. "Why would you kill her, since you had no murder to cover?"

And wasn't she past belief! "So it's not that I wouldn't do murder — just that I lacked a good reason for doing it?"

Save and deliver — she considered her answer, with a tilted head and a little frown, as though for a bona fide question, until Marley burst in from the guardhouse.

"There you are, Mr. Thomas. There's a note —" He stopped short at the sight of Audrey, clamping his mouth shut and studying her distrustfully. She, it must be said, returned the gaze in kind.

"This is Master Christopher Marley, Mistress Shelton," Tom explained. "*Magister Artium.*"

Not that she was impressed. She returned Marley's perfect — if stiff — bow with the barest nod, and when she commented, "Mr. Walsingham's poet," it lacked even the smallest tinge of warmth.

Mr. Wildgoose calls him a playmaker, Maria had said. A playmaker and what else? The lad's reputation in London wasn't what one would call immaculate. The dislike was mutual, in any event: Marley stood still, plainly waiting for Audrey to go away, while Audrey made no sign of leaving — and both looked at Tom expectantly.

"So, what is it, Marley?" he prodded, and gave Audrey a half-bow. "If you will excuse me, Mistress Shelton?"

But did she curtsey and go on her way like a good girl bound for Lee? Not at all! "By all means," she said — and retreated no farther than the window that looked upon the herb garden, where she made an unconvincing pretence of peering at the sky.

Where was Grace Wildgoose when she was needed?

For his part, Marley drew Tom to the farthest corner and handed him a foolscap folded in four, sealed with ochre-coloured wax, and addressed in a strange hand to *Mr. Thomas Walsingham, Esq.*

"Lambarde's man just brought it," he murmured under his breath — and Audrey Shelton must truly have vixen's ears: Tom had barely slid his thumb under the seal, when she reappeared at his elbow.

"Lambarde — that's the justice, isn't it?" She whispered too, making herself a member of the conspiracy. "*Has* he seen reason?"

As though he would! Tom quickly read the half-dozen lines. "He has seen his coroner arrive, rather," he said — to whom, he didn't know, since Marley and Audrey were both peering over his shoulders on either side. "Constable Beveridge is summoning the jurors already: Susan Foal's inquest is to be held here at Scadbury, tomorrow after church. Wonder of wonders, Rector Harvey has agreed to keep Morning Prayer short."

"Your magistrate deserves Heaven just for that!" Marley laughed. "But I'll wager he and that constable of his had the jurors list all drawn up last night!"

Which was, all things considered, not unlikely, and wasn't further discussed only because the sound of voices came from the guardhouse, much to Audrey's annoyance.

"Here they come, searching for me!" she huffed. "I must go — I'll be here tomorrow for the inquest."

"You will?" Tom wondered — quite foolishly.

She stopped with her hand on the latch. "I did see your housekeeper the day before she died," she threw over her shoulder, one brow raised. "The coroner might want to question me."

The day before… Oh, what was the use? "Don't forget your gloves!" Tom said for all answer. This she ignored — and then she was gone.

"Jupiter!" With a sigh, Tom lowered himself onto the bench again, leaning back against the cold wall, and then wincing away from it at the thought of his black velvet.

"The gall of her!" Marley exclaimed — which moved Tom to a fleeting grin. "What will you do?"

What could he do, really? Tom shrugged. "Have the hall ready for the coroner tomorrow." About which he'd better instruct the Wollanses…

With a sigh, Marley went to sit by Tom's side. "Isn't it strange," he asked, "to hold an inquest on a Sunday?"

Just what experience of coroners had he gathered, besides his recent misadventure? A thought best put aside, most likely.

"A whit unusual, yes, but not unheard of." Tom perused the note again. "Perhaps our good Lambarde is eager to go home … not that I'm holding him back, mind." The short, brisk sentences, the angular hand — the magistrate's own, surely, for that of a clerk would be more regular … and what was that? Just off the middle of the blank half of the sheet, he made out the pale curve of a watermark, faint and uncertain. Just like…

He turned around to the window, holding up the sheet against the dull afternoon light, duller still through the thickness of the glass. "Look, Kit. What do you see?"

"The watermark?" The poet squinted. "A … pot, is it?"

"A plain pot, yes. The same as the unsigned note. The same sort of paper."

Grabbing the note to better see, Marley whistled low. "Then…"

"Then nothing much. It seems it's quite common paper." *It could come from anywhere*, Lambarde had said. Tom tapped a finger against the sheet's edge. "Did Lambarde's man say from where he carried it?"

"The inn — the something's head."

"Tiger."

"The Tiger's Head, yes. They're all holed up there: Lambarde, the coroner and the constable. Do you think…" There it was again, the bright-eyed eagerness. The lad turned around, one knee on the bench. "Then the little poet comes from the inn?"

"There are not very many places around Chislehurst where he could have found this sort of paper. The inn, the shops, perhaps the rectory…"

Marley gave a gleeful chuckle. "And wouldn't Dick Harvey make the finest sycophant! What of gentle houses, though? Anyone who sat at your table today knows how to hold a pen … but no, you said it was a chicken's scrawl."

"That means little enough — hands can be counterfeited. But you'll find finer paper in gentle houses."

"Will I?" Mouth skewed, the poet rubbed Lambarde's note between thumb and forefinger. "Fine foreign paper doesn't come cheap. It's good for letters, and fine copies of poems — but I'll wager you, even here in Scadbury the accounts are kept on cheaper stuff."

Back in Seething Lane, there had been no extravagance — but good beeswax candles and good paper had been ready at hand for all of Sir Francis's men, from secretary to scrivener. Scadbury, though… Tom couldn't imagine Edmund squandering money on quires of costly Italian paper for the kitchen accounts, nor any of his dinner guests. "And you'd win," he sighed, deflated.

Marley, on the other hand, rallied at once, springing to his feet. "Still! It's worthwhile knowing where in the village they use this." He flicked a finger at the note. "I think I have a sudden thirst. What ale do they brew at your Tiger's Head?"

"It's not ale that you'll have, if you ask the wrong question…"

This earned the blithest laugh. "Have some faith in me, Mr. Thomas. I'm a Service man. You've shops here, haven't you? And wouldn't it be a lark, if I also paid a little visit to Dick Harvey?"

"Kit…" Tom began to warn, and the lad waved a hand.

"I jest, I jest. Never you fear, Mr. Thomas." He folded Lambarde's note and thrust it into his sleeve. "I'll be canny as a water-snake!" And he ran away — a snake who sang, "Heigh-ho, Red Rose," as he went.

Fates send he didn't find trouble, because Tom had had all that he could stomach already.

All through their childhood, there had been no place where Mary couldn't find Tom, no matter how he hid — so it was little marvel when both sisters found him in the withdrawing room, where he'd ensconced himself at last with Frances's letter. Such a read it had been, that he welcomed the invasion, even when Barbara chided him for missing supper, and Mary complained that Ned had never let her bring Mother's virginals with her.

"Can I now, Tom?" she asked, tracing a forefinger along the dancing muses on the old painted case.

She was welcome to it, Tom assured. Utterly unmusical as he was, even he knew that Mary's playing was dismal — but if it made her happy…

Tucking the painful letter into his sleeve, he threw a leg over the chair's arm and sat back, taking in the fire's warmth, the whisper of the rain outside, and the women's chatter as Mary stroked the untuned keys…

Until of a sudden Barbara was griping, "…and because once Ned was half minded to marry her, now she thinks to play the widow?"

"Oh, not the widow," snorted Mary. "It's the affianced bride that she thinks to play! Isn't it, Tom?"

And here he'd been thinking these magpies had come to seek and offer comfort… Tom sat up and glared. "You two should thank Heaven that Mistress Shelton thought to do the offices of a friend — or God knows what muddle I'd have made of the funeral —"

"Thomas Walsingham!" Barbara shot to her feet. "You're never thinking…?"

Oh, Lord… Was he? Wrong-footed, Tom gaped up at his sister — not that he could have answered if he'd known, for Mary jumped into the fray.

One never knew which way Mary would jump; this time it was on the side of Audrey Shelton. "Why not, Barbara? He needs an heir."

"And must he marry the first shrew who comes to order him about?"

"Oh, enough, you geese!" Tom snapped, rising to his feet. "Ned isn't cold in his grave, and here we are, bickering about my wedding and my heir!"

And if he'd thought to quail his sisters, he was much mistaken.

"You never cared for Ned," Mary exclaimed, to a gasp from Barbara — but the worst of it was that Mary was right.

"Oh, let her, Barbara: I never cared a whit for my brother — the nice Christian fellow that I am!" Tom ground out.

And off he stalked, slamming the door behind him.

Marley returned late, flushed and half cup-shot, but full of tidings — which he related sitting cross-legged on the truckle bed that had been Skeres's and now was his in Tom's room.

The paper with the pot mark, he said, was to be found at the Tiger's Head, at the blacksmith's, and at the rectory — where he had not, he swore, provoked the rector beyond the request for a list of possible dates for Susan Foal's burial. The paper bore the pot mark, and Marley was gleefully proud of his work, even when Tom pointed out that this hardly singled out Harvey.

"What you proved is how common that paper is," he said, sighing. "Which is no help at all."

"Oh, but it is!" Marley had charmed out of the Tiger's Head's maid the titbit that, like Jack Fuller, Kickly was an assiduous, if impecunious, customer — but… "Unlike Fuller, nobody has seen Kickly this past week or so…" he announced most portentously. "Even his mother doesn't know where he is — and here's the best bit: Geve Kickly's father was a respectable farrier. He died youngish, leaving wife and children destitute — but before that, young Geve had a little schooling."

This, now… Tom sat up in his bed. "Enough to scrawl a line or two?"

Across the fireplace, the poet's eyes glinted in the dim light from the banked embers. "*And* he could find the paper anywhere. Now, imagine you are Kickly, and Susan Foal has you sacked. Soon after, the master dies, and you try to make mischief for the woman…"

"But the mischief falls on some other head."

"As if all who can write were clever!" huffed Marley. "He's the sort who sneaks back to Scadbury, to see how his little revenge misfires. Once here, he spies Susan Foal — or she him — and push comes to shove…"

"And then he drowns her?" For the marks on Susan's neck spoke of cruel purpose — and from what Skeres had heard… "My people here call him a sneaksby."

Not that this discomfited Marley in the least — in fact, he rose onto one knee, propping an elbow on the newly brought writing table. "Yes — yes!" he cried. "Because, even as she holds onto the bank for dear life, even as he reaches down to help her, she still calls threats. Marrowless nithing, she'll have him whipped for this, thief and murtherer to boot! They'll crop his ears, and then who'll ever hire him…"

"Until fear does the work of courage." Tom waved for quiet. "Just don't go writing a play, will you?"

"Well, now you say it, a craven taunted into violence…" And there went a poet launched on the wings of a notion.

Tom lay back against the pillow and tried to sort through his more earthly thoughts. This was, he had to admit, as good an explanation as any that had presented itself, encompassing both the unsigned note and the housekeeper's death. If only they had Kickly to go with it…

"We'll try it on Lambarde tomorrow," he promised a much pleased Marley. "If he can be induced to consider it."

He blew out the candle after that, and soon discovered that there was no sleeping, with so many thoughts moving inside his mind.

There was Frances's letter, for one thing — each word a stab of pain. *I wish I could be at your side tomorrow*, she'd written, *and, more with every day that passes, I fear I can never be at your side again…*

There was Lambarde, still unconvinced of Edmund's death, still so stubborn in his suspicions.

And there was Marley's notion, which seemed sensible one moment, and slippery the next.

For the dozenth time, Tom turned to lie on his side, and a long-suffering sigh came from the truckle bed, where Marley must be lying equally awake. Tom squirmed against the unfamiliar pillows.

How many times had he lain like this, sleeplessly casting about for answers? And how many men and women, innocent and guilty alike, had stayed awake in fear of what answers Walsingham's Hound would find?

Lord — but it was galling, to fret on the wrong side of the game!

Observe the joints and flexures of affairs, Thomas.

With the echo of Sir Francis's instruction in his mind, Tom tossed on his back and started over again.

Item: On Martinmas, Susan Foal had had Edmund dismiss Geve Kickly as a thief.

Item: Geve Kickly had disappeared.

Quæstio: when, exactly — *a week or so* being unhelpfully vague?

Item: five days later Constable Beveridge had received the note that, if Marley was right, should denounce the Foals' foul play, but…

Item: the plan had misfired, and the blame had fallen elsewhere.

Item: three more days, and Susan Foal had been drowned in the moat.

Quæstio: could it all be Kickly's puny revenge, waxed into murder? And would the waxing take eight days…?

Oh, this kept tying itself in knots!

When Tom turned again, the truckle creaked, and Marley's voice came through the darkness.

"God's nightgown — do you ever sleep, Mr. Thomas?" he groused.

Ah, well… "Awake, are you? Then answer this: if Kickly wrote the letter to get back at Susan, why not name names while he was at it?"

A small groan, and a yawn. "Because he's a sneaksby and a fool? If he named names, the Foals could see through it…"

"And if he didn't, someone else could suffer for it."

"You think it ever occurred to him? Why…" Of a sudden, Marley's voice sounded more alert. "Perhaps that's why he went into hiding — when he saw that his little net had caught the new master by mischance."

"But how would he know?"

A snort. "You think you're keeping secrets from the village? The Tiger's Head is all astir with the inquest, and the drowning, and Scadbury's black doings."

"My black doings, you mean…" And little marvel, with the coroner staying there and Beveridge summoning jurors — but then, they'd known of Susan's death almost at once. "So he heard, and ran. But if he was so afraid, why come back yesterday?"

"Ah, that…" The truckle creaked, there were steps and a pale shape approaching, and then the bed sagged under an added weight. "Because his conscience bit him until he came to clear you?"

"The conscience of a thieving, craven sycophant?"

"Ay, well…" A bounce. "You never know, and something must have brought him back."

Or must it? "If he ever did come back. If he truly killed Susan Foal." Tom exhaled loudly and rubbed at his tired eyes. At once the notion seemed like so much smoke. "If it wasn't Foal, because her vapours over my brother's death were muddling the succession…"

"Ah, now what is more powerful? Greed or Fear? And there is Jealousy — no matter what Foal says — and Revenge firing Kickly's faint liver… Why, you've a whole morality play, Mr. Thomas!"

Hear the voice of one who was already making up lines in his head! "Shut up, Marley," Tom ordered through a huff of laughter. "Tomorrow, after the inquest, we'll find Kickly. Now go to bed."

With a sigh and a mutter of who'd been keeping them awake, the weight slipped off the bed.

CHAPTER 14

22nd of November

The coroner's inquest started off as unpleasant and as useless as Tom had expected, with a small crowd of curious observers from the village, fresh from church, and twelve good men and true trampling with muddy shoes and solemn miens between the hall and the cellar. They must have been made of stern stuff, these yeomen and craftsmen who, for the most part, only cringed a little under the weight of Barbara, Mary, and Old Kathryn's displeasure.

The coroner, of course, was impervious to the glaring of gentlewomen and formidable old servants alike, and neither he nor his very young clerk batted an eyelid to find that his table had been set upon Edmund's funerary dais. Even the black draperies, lugubrious and dusty in the light of the November sun, failed to disconcert Mr. Coates of Rochester. A solid, square-faced, almost bald fellow, he wasted no time, and questioned the witnesses with the weary briskness of one who had done it a hundred times before.

Christopher Marley, of London, (*Magister Artium*) described finding the body in the moat.

The surgeon Longe confirmed that Susan Foal was drowned, and that she bore marks of a struggle, from being held underwater, most likely.

Then Robert Foal was called, whose low-headed manner could be that of either a distraught widower or of a frightened culprit. He'd seen his wife around the house all day, he said, but not for a while before she died, and he didn't know who'd seen her last. And then he looked up, scowling fiercely. "But she was with child," he cried, currish babbler that he was. "Mr. Edmund's child, and all here were jealous and envious!"

Oh, did this rouse them all — jurors and watchers! Devil pinch Foal with a fork — for no matter how sternly the coroner reprimanded him and called his words irrelevant, there went the whole hundred abuzz with rumours.

Thundering for quiet, Coroner Coates called for the next witness. Jack Fuller limped askew to the dais. Lambarde's hand was plain in the arranging of the inquest, the magistrate having been there to see the joiner's man and Wood go out together, and Susan Foal about the same time…

Fuller, only half sober, said that yes, he'd seen Susan Foal — well and alive in the kitchen yard when he'd gone away, after bringing the bier. "And Mr. Wood can vouch for it," he said, raising his voice and scanning the room for the steward. "Can't you, Mr. Wood? He walked me back for a bit…"

Most of which no one had asked him, and there was no blaming Coates for looking thoroughly fed up with the denizens of Chislehurst. He dismissed Fuller with another reprimand, and when Wood was called next, the steward was met with a cold glare that warned against any more intemperant talk. Coates could have spared himself the trouble: John Wood confirmed that he, too, had last seen Susan Foal in the kitchen yard, just as Fuller had said — with all the appearance of good health.

Last called was Bridget Platt, the midwife who, having been fetched from Shott's Farm by Mr. Justice's order to visit the body, could bear witness before God himself that Susan Foal had been with child.

On this solemn note, Coroner Coates deemed the inquest concluded and addressed the jury.

"You have heard the finding of the body," he said, "and the testimony of Master Longe, surgeon, who affirms upon his oath that the woman Susan Foal came to her death by force and violence, being cast into the water, seized by the neck, and forcibly held down, whereby she was drowned. You shall therefore give your verdict that she died by wilful murder, at the hands of some person or persons unknown. So say you all?"

A chorus of "Ay!" followed, and Coates's clerk busied himself with the closing formalities.

"Well," Mary murmured, watching as jurors and observers departed, "you'd think it was all done to advertise our business to the whole parish!"

When Uncle Buffkin snorted that she could well say to the whole lathe, Barbara followed the old man's gaze, and caught her breath sharply.

"Don't turn, Thomas. Don't look," she said, bristling. "She's here again…"

And Tom turned and looked, not surprised at all to see Audrey Shelton by the suits of armour, deep in conversation with Sherley and a thin, sallow-faced fellow… Now *this* was a surprise: Audrey must have made a vow to meddle — but what was Richbell doing at Scadbury again?

Off to join the little group Tom went, ignoring his sisters' hissed calls and Uncle Buffkin's chortles.

"Mistress Shelton had never attended a coroner's inquest before," Sherley announced at Tom's approach, as the lady in question bowed her head in greeting. She wore no feather in her hat, today.

So this was the vixen's explanation — idle curiosity? Tom bowed in return. "Hadn't you, Mistress?" he asked, smiling just enough to convey his disbelief to her. He then turned to Richbell. "Nor had you, I take it, Master Richbell?"

The farmer turned his hat in his hands. Nor had he ever wished to, he said — but, after coming from Bromley for the funeral, he'd stayed with his cousins in Frognal. "And when I heard of the mischief with Mrs. Foal, begging yer pardon, Mr. Walsingham, I thought as maybe the crowner would want to ask questions of me."

This, now... Tom caught Audrey's raised brows and tilted head. "And why on earth would he?"

Richbell shrugged a shoulder. "'Tis that Mrs. Foal, Lord rest her soul..."

"It seems, Thomas," Sherley leant close to murmur, "that Master Richbell saw your housekeeper the day she died."

"That he *spoke* to her," Audrey put in.

With a little bow, Sherley stood corrected. "He spoke to her, yes — and Mistress Shelton and I were persuading him that it is his Christian duty to tell you, Thomas."

To tell the Justice of the Peace, rather — but Tom was very thankful for these two's disregard of legal propriety. "And what did you tell my housekeeper, Master Richbell?"

The hat made another turn in Richbell's hands. "'Tis more as she spoke to me, Master," he said. "I knew Mrs Foal by sight, from coming here before, but she'd never talked to me. The other day, though, she sought me out as I was leaving, and asked about me debt."

The brazenness of her — grieving for Ned, clamouring for justice, and still making certain of her husband's inheritance! "Whether you'd repay it?"

"Well, no..." Richbell rubbed at his chin. "Mayhap she was minded to. She asked was I owing money to Mr. Walsingham — and what it was to her, I didn't know. I said so, and, 'Come,

come, I know as ye do,' says she. 'Then you've your own answer,' say I, and give her the good day, for I had no mind to discuss my business with her."

"Certainly not," Tom said, mind suddenly a-whirl. Wood leading out Fuller, and them both seeing the housekeeper in the kitchen yard, and Wood returning to the hall — and only after that had Richbell left, when the weather had taken a turn for the worse. "Which way did you leave, Master Richbell? Through the bridge or the causeway?"

"The causeway, ay. I'd left me old nag hitched behind the kitchen, and Mrs. Foal followed me there, with her apron over her head, as it was starting to rain."

"Did she follow you off the island, too?"

A shrug. "If she did, I never saw her. Once in the saddle, I turned me collar up to me ears, and off I trotted, with never a look back."

"And did you see anyone else in the yard?" Audrey asked — and, if until then Richbell had answered readily and placidly enough, now wariness crept into his mournful eyes.

"The murtherer, you mean, Mistress?" he asked. "Must I speak to the crowner? Ye never think…?"

"No, Mistress Shelton does not." Tom darted a sideways glare at her, and she pouted. "But *did* you see anyone else as you left — or along the road?"

"No, Master, I didn't see no one." The farmer shook his head. "If I had…"

If he had, Tom assured him, it wouldn't have saved Mrs. Foal — and, since he hadn't, he was free to go, with no need to talk to the coroner. Nor to the justice, Tom didn't add.

The farmer, full of gratitude, had barely scuttled away when Audrey Shelton held up a slender forefinger.

"He saw Susan Foal last!" she whispered. "Not the steward, not the joiner: Master Richbell did!"

"And what does that mean?" Sherley asked, more puzzled than not.

"That there's a shorter time for the murder to have been done," Tom explained. "And that most likely Wood didn't kill her, for he was back inside by then."

"But…" Sherley stopped short. All had gone or retreated, and the three of them were alone in the hall, but for Wollans and Everest, busy taking down the trestle table the coroner had used. With a look at the servants, Sherley drew Tom aside by the passage door — and, looking a tad put out when Audrey followed, he asked under his breath, "You suspect your own steward?"

It struck Tom that he had little reason to do so, and yet he did — less than he suspected Foal or Kickly, but not by much. "Ned's steward, truly," he corrected. "And I have no great cause to trust him."

"An even greater sin!" Sherley exclaimed and, catching himself, he lowered his voice. "That he should have killed his master…"

A pious and trusting soul, Barbara called her husband — and not always in praise.

"Oh, not that. I'm more and more convinced that Edmund wasn't killed at all — but there's the matter of Susan Foal. Several who were in Scadbury the other day could have drowned her." He had to smile at the perplexity that twisted Sherley's face. "Not you, Sherley," he reassured — but must have fallen short of the mark, for almost at once Sherley made his excuses and left in search, he said, of his wife.

The moment he was gone, Audrey Shelton rose on tiptoe in her eagerness. "You shouldn't discount the steward, Mr. Walsingham —"

"But I don't," Tom replied.

As though he'd never spoken, Audrey forged on in a galloping whisper. "I didn't like to bring it up before Mr. Sherley, but that Marley of yours says you were alone at the time of the drowning — and if you were, then Mr. Wood..." She stopped short and frowned at Tom. "You don't? Oh, good. Then you keep Wood among your suspects."

"I would — I will, if I find a reason why he should want Susan Foal dead."

"Well, if he..." She halted mid-breath. "But no, you say your brother wasn't killed. Then... Now, you'll scoff at me, but there's the unsigned letter."

Tom sighed. "I'm not scoffing at all. You were right from the beginning — or half right, at least: if Edmund wasn't killed, then it's a matter of this other foul play."

He'd already begun to tell her of Geve Kickly before it occurred to him to wonder: was it wise to discuss the matter with this woman who was, after all, a stranger? He was almost glad when voices rose of a sudden beyond the door that stood ajar.

Men's voices were raised — squabbling in the passage...

Jove fulminate all unruly servants! Now they were going to have a piece of the new Mr. Walsingham's mind! Fuming, Tom made for the door, only for Audrey to lay a hand on his arm. She shook her head, a forefinger across her lips. "Listen!" she mouthed.

It was Barker's voice at first, for once waspish and cutting: "...ever playing the tyrant where she could, doing nasty tricks with silver spoons — I'll wager..."

“Ye cur — and she not dead a day!” The protesting squeak was unmistakably Foal’s, soon cut through by Barker again.

“You ought to know the way she was, Dobbin Foal. Singeing your ears for you up to the hour she died!”

And then came what must be Jack Fuller’s voice, sneering and slurring: “She had an adder’s tongue, me Sukie had —”

When Fuller’s words broke off in a huff, drowned out by Foal’s wordless snarl and a thump, it was the outside of enough. Tom strode into the passage to find Fuller on the floor with Foal on top of him, wheezing and squirming, and Barker calling both men names. It was a short-lived arrangement: the cook stepped back at the sight of his master, and not even the advantages of surprise and Fuller’s lameness were enough to keep Foal where he was. With a mighty grunt, Fuller shook free, and rolled over the servant’s round form just in time for Tom to grab him by the scruff of his neck. He hauled the man up — or would have, but a flailing arm caught him right across the mouth. He stumbled back, catching himself against the wall and tasting blood in his mouth.

“Master!” cried Barker.

“Mr. Walsingham!” cried Mistress Shelton, as Foal lay on his back, flapping his limbs like an upended tortoise.

Fuller, down on his knees and sobered of a sudden, stared with bulging eyes. “Please ye, Mr. Tom, I…” he stammered. “Don’t ye tell Frank Burten —”

“Not another word out of you!” Tom growled around a split and swelling lip. “I’m sick of having you thrown out of Scadbury — three times in three days you’ve made trouble. My brother was right to get rid of you!”

Fuller was scrambling upright clumsily. “Master, don’t you—”

"Tell Burten? You can wager I will, devil pinch you! If he wants to work for Scadbury again, he'll need another man to send."

"But the crowner —"

He whirled around — they all did when Marley hurtled in, coming from the kitchen, and stumbled into the prone Foal.

"Just in time, Master Marley," Tom greeted, at his most quelling. "See that this fellow leaves Scadbury once and for all."

At once the poet turned soldierly, with jaw set and shoulders squared. "Off with you, Fuller," he ordered, and all but hauled the man away, sullen and unresisting.

"Good riddance," Foal whined, who had managed to drag himself onto his hands and knees. He clearly wasn't expecting to be turned upon — but truly…

"And you!" Tom loomed over the dunce where he crouched, braced against a chest. "Brawling in my house! You're my brother's executor — but mind: the moment the will arrives from London, I'll have it read before the whole family, and then you'll leave Scadbury at once." Which was impractical in many ways, for there might be work to do for the executors, and one less servant would be trouble — but Tom was in no mood to hear objections. As Foal made to protest, he took another step forward. "Meanwhile, stay out of my sight — and of my hearing!"

He stalked away as Foal fell back on his backside. Barker and Mistress Shelton followed, both nattering — the cook that it had been unchristian to pick on a dead woman, and he shouldn't have, but that Foal blurting what he had before the coroner had vexed him greatly; Audrey that he should have that lip tended to — until Tom stopped short in the middle of the hall, brusquely enough that Barker ran into him.

"Enough, Barker," he said severely. "I much disliked Foal's babbling too, but I expect you to be an example to younger servants, not to stir trouble among them." He turned to Audrey. "And thank you, Mistress Shelton. You'll be impatient, I'm sure, to ride back to Lee."

It worked on Barker, but Audrey summoned Kathryn, and between them they dragged Tom to the stillroom, across from the small kitchen.

He couldn't even protest properly, with two women fussing over him, talking over his head, washing his split lip with a cloth dipped in vinegar that stung like the devil…

"Oh, do keep still!" Audrey snapped, dabbing away at his lip. "I'll set you a-bleeding again, if you don't… Here, sit down."

She tugged him towards the bench, and Kathryn pushed him to sit.

Oh, Jove! "I wasn't hurt in battle, you know," Tom groused, to no avail whatsoever.

He'd never known, as a boy, whether he liked Mother's stillroom, with its shelves full of gleaming jars, the bitter brews, and the sharp smell of ointments mixing with the scents of dried rose petals and lavender. It had been forbidden to children, and because of that, infinitely tempting. He hadn't entered the place for years, now, and the half-forgotten odour, the bunches of dried herbs hanging from the ceiling — it all brought back childhood accidents, falls from trees, ferret bites, and scoldings. Nothing pleasant had ever come out of those jars that Audrey and Kathryn were rustling through.

"Ah, here it is!" the old woman exclaimed at last, and, when she took off the lid, a rank, greasy, musty stench was released. "The comfrey salve."

"Not on your soul or mine, Mrs. Wollans!" Tom rose abruptly, swatting away from his face a hanging bunch of rosemary. "It's just a scratch, and I'm not going around smelling of turned fat."

He should have known better than to try and quell Kathryn with a reminder of her new rank. She clicked her tongue and frowned. "But scratches fester, Master Tom," she cooed, just as she had used to do long ago. Before he could make a sound, Audrey took the jar from Kathryn and dipped her cloth in it.

"One'd think that grown men…" She reached up to dab the offending salve on Tom's lip.

It, too, stung on the raw cut — and just as he flinched away, hissing through his teeth, a voice came from the doorway, quivering with laughter: "My mam used a smear of honey."

How long had Marley stood there, leaning against the doorjamb with arms crossed, eyes dancing at Tom's discomfiture? Honey — a children's remedy! Out of the corner of his eye, he caught Audrey raising her eyes to Heaven in a manner of tried patience, while Kathryn smiled her gap-toothed smile.

"Honey, Master! Just a tip of a spoonful. Honey makes no stench." She bustled away, smiling wider still when Marley half-bowed her out, and called her a Kentish Panacea.

"Thank your Fates she doesn't know you called her a heathen goddess," Tom groused, much to Marley's amusement.

"Oh, who knows with these wise old women, with their salves of herbs picked under the full moon?" The cheer was short-lived. Careful to push the door to, the poet went to perch on the nearest stool, serious of a sudden. "Are we after Kickly?" he asked. "That unknowing mother of his, I'd swear she lies through her teeth."

"Then you'll ask her again, to begin with," Tom said, and turned to Audrey. "Mistress, you heard what Barker said about silver spoons?"

She tapped her lips. "That Mrs. Foal played nasty tricks with them? I wondered…"

"Well, here's your answer: that groom I was telling you about, was sacked for stealing a silver spoon. But if that was Fair Susan's nasty trick…"

"Wronged, even Fear hungers for retribution!" Marley flung up a hand, back to last night's playmaking — and little wonder that Audrey should spare him a frown before asking of Tom:

"But why would she?"

And of course, Marley must wave a hand and say that women were full of whims, so Audrey asked tartly whether men, instead, always acted out of perfect reason…

"It seems," Tom cut through the bickering, "that my brother got rid of Fuller not because of drunkenness, but over Susan Foal."

"So, if she did it with the one, why not the other?" There was a row of small glass bottles on the table. Marley picked up one and turned it in his fingers, squinting at the spidery hand on the label. "Was Fair Susan on a crusade against all grooms?"

There came a dainty sniff from Audrey, as she paced along the shelves of jars. "Why, Master Marley, you know the way women are," she threw over her shoulder. "So full of whims…"

Jupiter, these two! "But why indeed, Mistress Shelton?" Tom stood with his best air of command. "Mrs. Foal wanted Kickly out of Scadbury — and we're going to find out why. You'll flush out young Geve, Marley — beginning with his mother's cottage, and Mistress Shelton will tease out of Barker and Kathryn the matter of the spoon, before she leaves for Lee."

"Now —" she began — but Tom shook his head.

"I might have made Barker a little shy of me for the moment," he said, "and you have a way with my people, Mistress. Meanwhile, I'm off to Foots Cray, to prove another notion."

"Another?" If Marley was disappointed that Tom still hadn't quite espoused his theory of Kickly, he forgot it on hearing of William Richbell, waylaid by Susan Foal to talk of his debt…

"To little use, as it turns out — but couldn't she have done the same with Old Mace, and, who knows, to more success? She might have found out something of import about those cursed debts."

Marley whistled low. "A busy woman, Fair Susan was!"

"Busy as the devil himself: either she was behind the foul play, or she stumbled into it."

"And if we find the foul play, we find the murderer?" Audrey mused.

"Yes, my Lady Reason — so we do." It warmed Tom's heart, the way these two invested themselves in his troubles.

He bowed to Audrey, clapped Marley's shoulder, and they all moved at once — Audrey still unconvinced, and Marley mistranslating Ovid *extempore* as he went: "See us all, driven abroad as the winds be scatter'd to the four corners of the world — from orient Persia to the setting sun, and from parch'd Libya to Scythia's frost-chained shores…"

Or at least to Chislehurst and Foots Cray, hunting for cooks, and grooms, and farmers — which wasn't half as heroic, but… Ah, well — Fates send they all came back with answers.

It was half an hour at a good trot from Scadbury to Foots Cray, with bare alders and willows for all company, and the chuckling river. The November sun made the shallow waters gleam, and threw the shadows of the trees in thin bars across the narrow, rutted lane.

Tom had no mind for the pale sky or yesterday's raindrops bejewelling the stripped bushes. He kept thinking how all morning Lambarde had made himself scarce. Silently present at the inquest, he had left Scadbury with no more than a stiff exchange of bows. Sulking in disappointment at his failure to prove Edmund's murder, or mustering the troops of his arguments to blame Susan Foal's death on Tom?

What a bleak game this was — with the scaffold if he failed to checkmate the murderer of a woman who had wanted him dead, and if he won, a prize of endless Novembers in the dark, draughty, disordered house that now belonged to him the way a millstone would. And his old life all but lost, slipping out of his hands, with Mr. Secretary declining, and Frances…

"Mr. Walsingham!" A call from behind him startled him out of his moping — and look! A green-clad horsewoman and a groom emerged from the alder-fringed curve, at a trot that was daring for one riding side-saddle.

Lord give patience… "Mistress Shelton," Tom greeted as soon as she was close enough, keeping from his manner anything that could be read as a welcome. "I thought you were off to Annesley House."

Not that she cared a whit. "And so I am," she said, airily as you please while she drew her horse to pace abreast with Tom's. "It's fortunate that we meet again, though. I can better tell you of my mission to the kitchen."

"Very kind of you."

"Goodwife Wollans was sorry to see me go, and Barker would not speak ill of the dead…"

"I'm sure."

"But, on the other hand, conscience bid them both tell the truth: Geve Kickly is a fidgety, sour-tempered lad, hard-working but slovenly. Mrs. Wollans, though, wouldn't have called him dishonest."

"And what of the spoon?"

"Ah, you see…" Audrey frowned in the sun-dappled distance, recollecting. "Mrs. Foal had been buffing silver and found a spoon was missing. But, Barker says, she waited two days before crying thief, right after Wollans sent Kickly to the kitchen for some reason or other. Mercy me — but the more I hear of her, the less I like her!"

"So now the spoon will be at the bottom of the moat, or buried somewhere… Yes: Susan Foal had no mawkishness on the score of hurting people, and a sour-tempered lad might well seek revenge for it."

"One more suspect for Justice Lambarde, isn't it?" she said, with the cheer of one picking yet another strawberry, and then she set her horse trotting again.

Tom followed suit, and in a thrice they were in Foots Cray. When Audrey turned with him into the lane to Mace's farm, he didn't even try to protest.

Old Robert Mace's farm, and the house on it, must have been of some substance at some time. These days the fields were tilled sloppily, and the house, with its sagging thatch, and the weeds growing on either side of the door, looked battered.

So, to Tom's surprise, did the old man himself.

They found him sitting by the fireplace in a smoky little parlour. At the sight of the visitors, he tried to climb to his feet, showing a bruised face and a swollen hand wrapped in bandages.

"Don't, Master Mace," Tom urged. "What on earth happened to you?"

With a pained hiss, the old farmer lowered himself back into the chair, while a timid young woman fussed about seating down the strange lady and gentleman.

"I was set upon, Yer Honour…" Mace began — and then stopped long enough to send the young woman for perry. "Wife of me nephew, as works the land with me," he explained. "A good girl enough, but afeared of her own shadow, she is. Less as she knows, the better."

Not that the tale was overly gruesome: a big man, cap low over his eyes and cudgel in hand, had jumped poor Mace as he walked back home from Edmund's funeral, along that same willow-edged lane along the Cray. The same encounter the plumber had suffered last week, surely… And something to bring to Constable Beveridge's attention.

"Like an ape he pounced — *like an ape*!" Mace, it seemed, had seen an ape once, and was keen to impress this knowledge on them. "He dragged me from me nag, lay into me, snatched me purse… Then two lads from the mill came a-running, Lord bless them — else I'd not be here to tell it."

And he would have gone on, if Tom hadn't firmly steered him towards the matter of Susan Foal instead. Here was another who had disliked the woman — not that it came as a great marvel.

"After I came to see ye at Scadbury, Master, I sought Mr. Wood. I asked Mrs. Foal where he was."

So nothing like Susan's own tale… "You didn't ask to speak to me again?"

"Why, no! 'Twas Mr. Wood as I wanted, and had me nose bitten off for it — and what did I want with Mr. Wood, pestering me betters? 'Twas for the money I owed, said I, as was no business of hers, but I was out of heart with worry — and did she ever so change her manner!"

"She questioned you about the debt?"

Had Tom sprouted a second head, the old man's wonder couldn't have been greater. "Ay, Yer Honour, so she did — long-nosed shrew!" he exclaimed. "So I said I'd come back another day — and even that irked her."

"And come back you did, on Friday, didn't you?" For it had been him in the hall, and no mistake...

The farmer nodded, sucking his teeth. To see him, one wouldn't think that second trudge to Scadbury a great pleasure.

"Ay, so I did, and much good it did me! Shame on me, said Mr. Wood, for troubling young Mr. Walsingham by his brother's dead body! Not as I meant to, Yer Honour, not after what you'd said of the will. Good for Mr. Wood, said I, if thirty-four pounds are a piddling matter to him, but they ain't to me!"

"And what did he say to that?" Audrey asked before Tom could.

"What did he say, Mistress?" Mace hummed. "Naught, he said, for then they came to say as Mr. Wood was wanted, and he bundled me out like I was the village beggar — *and never ye dream of bothering Mr. Walsingham, Robert Mace*!"

This last was said in an imitation of Wood's haughty primness, down to the pursed mouth, so perfect that Tom bit his lip to fight a grin — tasting honey and blood where the cut still stung, and earning Mistress Shelton's sideways scowl.

"And so you tried again the next day, at the funeral," she said to Mace.

"Ay, Mistress, for it is me land as is at stake." A shake of the grizzled head. "And all I gained from it was a cudgelling."

"But you had words with Wood," Tom pointed out.

A grunt. "Ay, words: that I must wait for the will be read, and not trouble ye, and what's in the will is no business of mine. Yer Mr. Wood can thank that Beveridge lad that words were all we had."

"And you can thank him too, Master Mace — for a brawl wouldn't have helped your cause." Perhaps Tom's severity would have been more convincing without his own split lip. He stood and gathered his gloves. "I'll have more to tell you when the will comes back from the Probate Court."

The old man, bruised face creased and injured hand resting in his lap, didn't look very reassured.

As they went to leave, the timid niece was waiting at the gate, still in her grey-blue church best.

"Yer Honour, please ye…" she murmured. "Did Uncle Mace tell of the quittances?"

On hearing that he hadn't, she glanced over her shoulder. The door was closed, and no one stood at the window, and still she lowered her voice. "He had the quittances with him when he came to Scadbury…"

She stopped, and Audrey finished it for her: "And the purse was filched by that man like an ape."

The niece nodded, looking away.

Hardly a good thing, but at least this was one fear Tom could allay. "I'm sure the steward will have marked the payments in his books, Goodwife," he soothed — although the untidy scraps of paper in Wood's drawer came to mind. Had Mace's payments been made before the steward and Susan Foal began their games of sun-and-moon?

Her face cleared in relief, and then clouded again. Afraid of her shadow she might be — but never the dullard her uncle thought her.

*

It wasn't until they were in the saddle again, and the path to the village broadened enough that they could ride abreast with the groom behind them, that Audrey asked, "But in truth you're sure about the will, aren't you?"

Sharp-witted vixen! "I've only had hints, but enough to know…" Tom hesitated for the barest heartbeat, frowning at the squat tower of Foots Cray's church across the tilled fields, dotted with cawing crows. Ah well, she knew so much already, he could well tell her of Edmund willing all that he could to Foal and Wood.

"Wood and Foal…" Audrey murmured. "The steward and a servant?"

"Who also happen to be his executors…" Catching his breath, Tom smiled at the well loved feeling of pieces falling into place. "And both Wood and Foal's wife were eager to keep poor old Mace away from me…"

"Or else, Wood was, and Susan Foal wanted to know why…" Never let it be said that Audrey Shelton was slow of wit. "Either more foul play, or another who could want the woman dead — or even both…" she went on, with a gleam in her eye. They'd entered the scatter of timber-framed cottages that was Foots Cray, and across the green the lane crossed the road to London, where they were to part ways — he to Scadbury, and she to Lee. Suddenly, Audrey exclaimed and drew the reins.

"I lost a glove, Jenkin!" she called to the groom. "Do go back, and see if you can find it!"

Obedient lad that he was, Jenkin touched his hat and wheeled his mare about, plodding back up the lane in search of the glove. Would he find it? Tom wondered, thinking of yesterday — but perhaps they were used to Mistress Shelton's ways, at Annesley House.

"Gloves get lost a good deal," Tom said with a smile, that fell — together with his stomach — at the sight of her thin-lipped resolve. What had she taken into her head now?

"I will not," she dictated, "argue with you before Grace's groom — so it's better that we agree now: I'm riding back to Scadbury with you."

And why he even tried to object, Tom didn't know. "Mistress Shelton —"

"Things are coming to a head. You'll need someone to rely on, someone who knows the matter, and will be clear-sighted about it."

As his own family could not be, most likely. "Kit Marley is a Service man and far from a fool."

"Oh, Marley!" She clicked her tongue. "Poets are flighty and fanciful. He may be of assistance with a dagger, but you need someone with a level head, Mr. Walsingham. Someone guilty of foul play, and likely also a murderer, is waiting back at Scadbury."

"All the more reason why you should stay well away."

"Oh, I won't put myself in danger." She gave an impatient shrug of the sort that, had she not sat on horseback, would have been a stamp of the foot. "What you need is Justice Lambarde on your side — and he still has to be convinced."

"And you would do that for me?" Tom asked — and, seeing the frown gather on her brow, he shook his head. "I don't doubt that you could, Mistress — why, I'm beginning to believe you could convince the devil himself. It's just that not many would throw themselves…" How to say this, now, and not call her a meddler?

No need for it, for she was quick to read him, and a sliver of a smile softened her sharp manner. "Into what doesn't concern them? Father says my meddling ways will be the ruin of me. But I'll tell you two things, Mr. Walsingham. One is that I can't abide stillborn justice — and that's what it would be, to have a murderer not caught, and an innocent man not cleared. The other…" She nudged her horse a step closer. "I don't forget that we were to be sister and brother…"

"And to dislike each other heartily," Tom put in — and, for a wonder, see Audrey Shelton wince!

"For several reasons I never could make myself like your brother. One is that in me he saw first the means of keeping Scadbury from you."

Ah, Ned… "It would have been in the way of things that his sons should inherit."

"But all this…" She waved her whip at the cottages around them, as though they stood for Tom's whole tangle. "All this is still born of Edmund's ill will towards you, wed to circumstance. Because I escaped being part of it, we can be friends instead of disliking each other — and…" She reached out to rest a hand on Tom's arm. "Here is a third thing: I will not abandon a friend in need."

So earnestly she looked up at him, eyes bright in the autumn sunlight, hand firm on his arm, this woman who could not abide stillborn justice — both in spilt blood and blood ties, it seemed… It was something Frances might have said, and hard to either dismiss or reject.

Lord deliver him, for he was going to regret it, most likely… "I think your horse has a limp, Mistress Shelton. Hadn't you better ride back to Scadbury with me, where Wollans can have a look at it?"

This time the smile was fuller, as Jenkin trotted back without the glove.

"I have it, Jenkin," Audrey lied blithely. "Mr. Walsingham found it."

And off they went to Scadbury — together.

CHAPTER 15

That flighty and fanciful creature, Kit Marley, was waiting in the stable yard for Tom's return. He scowled at the sight of Mistress Shelton just as she scowled at the sight of him, but whatever ill will they bore towards each other was lost in the exchange of tidings.

"Good," was Marley's grim comment on what they'd learnt from Mace. "For Kickly's as resentful as can be, but also half dead with the flux at his cousin's cottage. He's been like that for four days, the cousin says — and I doubt he could have drowned a kitten the other day, let alone Fair Susan. Not that he wouldn't have liked to do it."

"He took no spoon, I take it?" Tom asked, earning a snort.

"To hear him, what he took was a good look at the Foals being..." Marley darted a glance at Audrey. "Quite amorous."

"And so much for the babe being my brother's!" Tom exclaimed, with unchristian triumph — but truly!

Whether Audrey's disgusted sniff was for Fair Susan's questionable virtue, or for the surfeit of foul play, it was hard to tell. "So Kickly did write the note?" she asked — and again Marley shook his head.

"Wishes he'd thought of it, he says — but no. They bribed him to be quiet at first — a pittance, he says. And when he asked for more, lo! The spoon went missing."

"And after that, who would believe a thief? She wasn't a complete fool," Tom sighed — for Dobbin surely lacked the wit for it. "Perhaps that's what my brother liked in her." Not the most elegant subject to discuss before a young lady — but he could have spared himself the trouble, for Audrey's frown had another cause.

"And we're back to the door," she said, tapping her lips. "If Geve Kickly didn't write the note, who did? Not that there was a lack of foul play around Edmund. I almost begin to pity him."

It was a matter that would have to wait, though, for Wollans entered the stables then, and exclaimed at the sight of Tom.

"Bless ye, Master!" cried the old man. "What are ye doing here? There's the messenger from London come: he's brought the will!"

The wretched will, at last… "Well, if nothing else, I will have answers," Tom ground out — and, dispatching Kit to Chislehurst to fetch Lambarde, he hastened to the house.

A gathering of thirteen filled the parlour. An ill number, Uncle Buffkin made sure to point out, as he took wide-kneed possession of one of the armchairs by the fire. The other remained empty, the women sitting stiffly at the table with their husbands. Uncle George pushed his chair as far from the table as he could, and poor Poll hovered, until Barbara lost her patience and hissed at her to not be a goose and sit down, for Heaven's sake. As Poll obeyed in flustered haste, Barker and Wollans filed in quietly to stand by the door, while Wood and Foal took their place as the executors, standing at the table's head together with the messenger from London, a spare, much-whiskered fellow.

Tom went to stand by the fireplace, so he could see them all — a cheerless group painted pale gold and grey by the afternoon light, quiet but for Foal's wheezing, and Sherley, who leant to murmur to the unheeding George. Quiet, that was, until the door opened to reveal Lambarde, coming last either by chance or Marley's play-craft.

The whole room stirred.

"Why…" George began, eyes bulging, and there was no mistaking the sourness in Barbara's murmur. Wood scowled, and Mary threw up a hand…

"I've asked Mr. Lambarde to be present," Tom said very firmly, before more could happen. "I'm sure I don't have to explain why. Please, come in, Sir."

"Thank you, Mr. Walsingham." With a dry look at Tom, the justice went to stand by the empty armchair, ignoring the stares and frowns, and Mary twisting in her chair to ask in an angry whisper why the man must be there at all.

"Make an effort and trust my judgement, will you?" Tom whispered back.

A glare was exchanged between brother and sister, and Pelham's raised brows said that he shared his wife's dislike — but there was that to being the head of one's house under one's own roof: at least in public, it restrained objections.

At Tom's nod, the court's messenger held up the will for all to see — a folded sheet of parchment, with a largish brown-red seal dangling from a tag.

"Witness you all that this is the seal of the Prerogative Court of Canterbury," he said, loud and imperious, and lay the will on the table.

Without a look for Foal, Wood moved to take it — and stopped short when Tom spoke.

"Mr. Lambarde, will you do us the service?"

More astonishment — as was to be expected — with Pelham muttering how unusual it all was, and Uncle Buffkin wondering half-aloud if this was how things were done around Mr. Secretary. Wood paled with anger, snatched away the hand he'd reached out, and stepped back most pointedly — Rightful Resentment itself.

Observing it all from under his heavy eyelids, Lambarde walked to the table, unfolded the large parchment and began to read.

"*In the name of God amen. The twelfth day of November 1589 and in the thirty-first year of the reign of our sovereign Lady Queen Elizabeth,*" he relayed, in that same dry, flat voice he used whenever he donned the mantle of his office, "*I, Edmond Walsingham of Scadbury in the parish of Chislehurst in the county of Kent esquire, being sick in body but of whole and sound mind —*"

Here came a snort from Uncle Buffkin, which Lambarde ignored.

"*— thanks be to God do make this my last will and testament.*"

There was the usual bequeathing of the soul into the hands of almighty God, with a lengthy formula. Had Ned copied it from Father's will? But perhaps not, for Wood was the pious sort, well able to come up with it. Then came the generous doles, already given out to the Parish poor. Then the family: brothers-in-law, uncles, cousins (Maria among them), a couple of friends, each receiving a piece of gold of thirty shillings. Poll let out a tiny gasp at the mention of hers, and whether she deemed it generous or paltry there was no saying, for she checked and looked down at once. Barbara and Mary, knowing no such qualms, both scoffed in turn.

"And wait…" George grumbled. "Just you wait!"

"May I continue, Mr. Guildford?" Lambarde asked with iron mildness, and George, spreading both hands with a huff, threw himself back into his chair.

But he'd been right, for now came the surprise Edmund had promised. It began with *all the plate, household stuff, and implements now being at Scadbury*, being given to Foal and Wood for the special trust they'd enjoyed.

Even having more than half known from Uncle George, it stung — and see the girls exclaiming to each other in outrage.

And then from worse to worst. The lease of Dartford Manor, for fourteen years to come, went to Foal — or rather through Foal to the babe Ned had thought his, had Susan lived. And then the debts: one hundred and eight pounds due by Richbell, and forty-four pounds due by Mace…

Forty-four… Tom watched the gathering — and found that all were watching him in turn. And well they might, because truly…!

Foal looked as though he'd have gladly hidden under a floorboard, while Wood stared ahead like an offended Seneca — and what he had to call offence, Tom didn't know, since, out of the debt money, a hundred pounds went to him, and twenty to Foal. Last were ten pounds for Barker, and nine for Wollans, and what remained went to settle some debts — and those Tom resented less, but that it all made one tune: *all that is in my power*, Edmund was singing from the grave, *I give away to the servants I trust better than my own blood.*

And if George felt ill-used, what was Tom to think, never mentioned once? The brother and heir might never have existed, judging by the will… And no, not even that: never mentioned and, by omission, spitefully left with an all but bare house, for all that was not bequeathed went still to Wood and Foal — Lord smite them both!

Even Guil's daughters each received, as an afterthought, five pounds' worth out of the plate that didn't have the tiger's head.

"Oh, Poll!" Mary laughed — just a tad too shrill. "I want to see your girls squabbling with the steward and the valet over the plate!" She held up a finger. "But nothing with the family tiger on it, mind! That goes to servants and strangers."

And with that, she at once crushed whatever satisfaction poor Poll might have felt, and made an epitaph for Ned's last will and testament…

But no, by Jove! Not to these men who had played foul with Edmund — because so they had, and the will showed it. Tom stepped forward, drawing as tall as he knew.

"No, it doesn't Mary," he snapped. "You said it: it has the family tiger, and it belongs to the house. I'll be damned before I see it scattered away."

There was a satisfied "Ha!" from Mary, and Foal stared, round-eyed and round-mouthed, and Wood began to protest:

"Mr. Walsingham, the law —"

"The law indeed!" Tom glared at the steward. "By law I can and will have inventories made, for one thing, of what belonged to my brother and what to the house. For another, I would question whether my brother was in his right mind when he made that." He gestured to the parchment, to much nodding from his sisters and their husbands, and to a wordless squawk from Foal.

Pelham lifted his chin to look down his long nose at the two men. "Executors have been known to steer a will in their favour, haven't they?"

This sent Wood a-bristle. "Your own kinsmen were there, Mr. Walsingham. Ask them who it was who tried to sway your brother…"

Who would have guessed the day would come when they'd see Leven Buffkin squirming in unease? "We asked had he lost his wits," he muttered. "All that money, and stripping the house bare… We called it unseemly to his face, didn't we, Guildford?"

George was past anything but a bitter laugh and a shake of the head, and see how Wood drew back his shoulders and reared his head.

"And meanwhile," he cried, "I and Foal only obeyed our master's will."

"Oh, I'm sure the foul play had been done already." Tom watched each face for a reaction to his words. Lambarde, he observed, was doing the same — not that there was much to see, or rather there was too much, for all exclaimed, and stared, and glowered…

Wood most of all, and Foal too, made sanguine by the steward's manner, and yelping how good Mr. Edmund had been to him.

It was on him that Tom turned, sudden enough to make the man flinch. "Good to you and your wife, wasn't he? Had he known that you weren't as chaste with her as you made out, though…" So Geve Kickly hadn't lied: Foal's face empurpled, eyes a-bulge like those of one choking. "And you, Wood. What of my brother's trust, had he known how you fattened your own purse?"

"I never —" John Wood snapped his mouth shut on the rest. Was it uncertainty flickering in his eyes?

"Never?" Tom pursued. "Then you'll explain why my brother died believing that Robert Mace still owed him four-and-forty pounds, when near a fourth of it had been paid back."

Twelve voices exclaimed, and all gazes fixed on Wood.

It was like seeing the cogs and wheels turning behind the steward's dark eyes, grinding falsehood and truth together. What could he deny? What must he admit?

"Old Mace can show you the quittances I signed," was what he said. "I never meant to deny the payments."

That the quittances were gone was for another time. Now… "You just didn't mention them to my brother," Tom said.

"Mr. Wood," Lambarde began, speaking for the first time since reading the will, "when I inspect your ledgers, will I find those payments recorded?"

All held their breath for the answer — and Tom expected a confident lie. Instead, Wood shook his head and ran a hand down his square jaw.

"In all truth, Sir, I don't remember," he replied, sighing — to more exclamations and Uncle Buffkin's snort. He looked from Lambarde to Tom, and lifted an upturned hand in a helpless gesture. "Your brother, Mr. Walsingham, had lost interest in Scadbury. He'd come to rely on me very much, these past years — and I … I didn't deserve his trust. I was remiss and slothful, and the Lord's punishment awaits me for this —"

"Oh!" Mary half-rose, clapping a hand to her mouth. "And when Ned found out, he murdered him!" she cried — and for all that Barbara, for once the voice of reason, declared her sister a goose, that set the whole room astir.

For once and for a wonder, John Wood was shaken. "I was the last to want Mr. Edmund dead!" he shouted, over the sudden storm of exclamations. "You see that, Mr. Walsingham, don't you? The heir was sure to look into the books, to find them ill-kept. Why, I even slipped a note under the door of Constable Beveridge —"

"You did!" Tom's voice pitched high of its own accord. "You would have sent me to the gallows?" In speechless anger, he turned to Lambarde, who held up a placating hand.

"I don't think Mr. Wood meant any particular harm to anyone," he said, to a chorus of derisive snorts from Tom, his sisters and Uncle Buffkin.

To all of them Wood pleaded, his noble air a good deal tarnished: "I didn't know there would be accusations! I only wanted to delay a review of the accounts, to gain a little time so I could cover my mistakes..."

"Time until Lady Day," Tom cut in. "When at least Richbell's hundred pounds would come in — and since you'd led my brother to make you both legatary and executor..."

And that was as far as he went before havoc exploded, with the sisters blazing, and Uncle Buffkin cursing, and Poll sobbing God alone knew why, and Sherley calling the Lord to witness, and Pelham barking that surely, surely then the will could never be valid...

Through it all Tom stood back, sourly observing how the chance of subtracted money inflamed them all far more than the certainty of false accusations had, until Lambarde called for silence — and had to do it twice.

He had already asked for Scadbury's accounts, he said severely, and now meant to have them.

As though Tom would raise objections! "You already have my blessing, Mr. Lambarde. I'm sure Mr. Wood will show them to you — at once."

And what could the steward do? He half bowed to Lambarde as he motioned towards the door. To see him go, head thrown back and face set, one would think him Daniel, on the way to the lion's den.

As they went, the magistrate stopped to murmur to Tom, "It seems that you unearthed the foul play, Mr. Walsingham. Next time, perhaps, you'll be so good as to warn me that digging is afoot, and I'm to dig."

Which might or might not be unfair, depending on just what Kit Marley had explained, but Tom found that he had no stomach for more bickering. The moment the door closed behind Lambarde and Wood — with Foal in tow as the other executor — and all began to exclaim over Ned's insane will that would have the whole lathe murmuring, Tom made his escape.

In the hall, Barker still hovered, making a pretence of tending the half-dead fire. Tom didn't bother fighting the tug of a smile. "I didn't see you flee, Barker," he said, and the cook's wary frown dissolved into angelic ruefulness.

"Mrs. Sherley made sign that we should go — and very right she was, ay, very right…"

Trust Barbara to keep her head throughout the mischief. "Don't fret. You're not to blame. Besides, you heard nothing you wouldn't have learnt soon."

And if a tinge of sourness crept into Tom's voice, Barker had the wits to ignore it. He bowed a little, all meekness. "But I would say, Master, I'm past thankful."

Was he? Ten pounds was a goodly sum — but little enough when one thought of Wood and of Foal. For better and for worse, though… "It's my brother you must thank."

The cook looked away, chins folding on each other as he nodded at the rush-mats. "'Tis just… Well, with all that's happened…"

Of course. Tom nearly laughed at his own sluggishness. "Never fear, Barker. Whatever happens with the will, you and the Wollanses will have what Mr. Edmund left you. I'll see to it."

At once the man's mien cleared. "I never doubted it, Master — and I promise, you'll have the most faithful servants in us all."

And here was more innocent-eyed angling. Had the three of them drawn lots to see who'd go ahead and sound out the new master? Or the four of them, rather…

“It’s good to know,” Tom said, and added that Everest, too, would have his twenty shillings, and be kept. “Unless he’s too much of a dullard?” he asked, for what he’d seen of the lad hadn’t been overly promising.

“No, poor Will — just much trodden. I wouldn’t speak ill of the dead, Master — but Susan Foal liked to lord it over grooms and scullions. I’d tell him sometimes, it was just the way she was, tigerish even to her betters, but…” A shake of the head.

As Tom had cause to know — and why he should defend the woman, he didn’t know, but… “In fairness, she’d taken it into her head that I’d harmed my brother.”

With a scowling, rumbling harrumph Barker signified what he thought of the notion. “It would have earnt her a box on the ear, in Her Ladyship’s days. Ranting at you and Mr. Guildford!”

“Mr. Guildford…” Tom murmured, stomach clenching. He’d seen it too: Uncle George and Susan talking in a corner of the hall, he sullen and she…

“Ay, Mr. Guildford.” Barker nodded fiercely, chins a-quiver. “And what *he* must have done, poor gentleman, I don’t know.”

What, indeed! The bits of glass inside Tom’s mind shifted into a new pattern — one that he thoroughly disliked.

The island had no wall to the east, climbing down gently to the moat’s sluggish current. A few trees stood in the corner behind the kitchen: a couple of pear trees and a medlar — now bare — a holly bush, a willow that trailed its branches in the water. The willow had had twin trunks once, when little Tom and Mary had fled to this spot to play, secluded enough to imagine adventurous woods and great rivers, and still within easy view from the kitchen’s back door. Now only one trunk remained, the other cut to a low stump right by the water, and there George sat, hunched with his elbows on his knees. Was this where he hid most of the time?

"Uncle…" Tom called from a dozen steps away, and George hardly stirred, barely glancing over his shoulder and then going back to peruse the muddy water, made green by the cloudless sky.

"You mind that old carp, lad?" he asked, when Tom walked close. "The one you children liked to feed? I'd bring you and Mary here, with the breadcrumbs in a kerchief… A big beast, he was. You mind him?"

To hear him, one would have imagined George bringing them here all the time. It must have happened once or twice. "Yes, poor fellow," Tom said. "Dead these six or seven years now — but, Uncle… I've something on my mind. Would you walk with me?"

George's shoulders fell, and he hunched lower still with a great sigh. Had he been waiting for this? He made no move to rise. "Here will do, Tomkin," he murmured and, bending to pick up a handful of pebbles, he tossed one in the water. It made sluggish circles, and a fish swam up, only to turn away again.

Tom hooked an arm around the surviving trunk. "Susan Foal…" he began slowly, and George's back grew stiff.

"What of her?" he asked, with that wary blankness that marked bad liars. It was the sort best dealt with bluntly.

"She was quite blustery to you, wasn't she? And you think little of her honesty."

The rest of the gravel went flying into the moat, hard enough to splash. "Because she was a devil's limb —"

"What did she know, Uncle? What did she want from you?"

Any other man, Tom would have hammered with questions as he crumpled, as he took his head in his hands and pulled at his thin hair — but this was George, the uncle who had always tried so hard to be a favourite.

Tom softened his voice. "What did she have to hold over your head?"

The answer came unsteady and muffled through splayed fingers. "The night Ned died…"

Oh, Lord! Tom turned so sharply that George stammered to a gawping halt. Lord save them all — had Ned been murdered, after all? Heart sinking, he prodded, "The night he died…?"

"I couldn't sleep, Tom, couldn't lie abed — what with the storm, and my bad thoughts, and too much claret. Then I heard a noise and went out — and there was Ned, atop the Old Stairs with a candle. He called to me, I don't know what. Oh, I'd have run, if my legs could have carried me — for I'd had enough of him at supper — and he kept crowing — and then…"

"And then?" Not that Tom truly wanted to know…

With a groan, George lowered his head again. "Then he clutched his chest and dropped the candle, and there was…" A gesture of both hands, as if of something tumbling.

Good Lord! It must be a relief, surely? But… "You didn't try to help him?"

A jerk of the head. "When the candle went out, it was as if the devil had released me, and I ran."

"And you didn't think to call for help?"

"I was dead drunk, Tom…" George winced at his choice of words. "I … I ran back to my bed."

And poor Ned had been left like a rag thrown down the stairs, with a burst heart and a broken head. Tom shuddered. God send it had been quick. "And in the morning, all called it a mishap…" he said with a bitterness that melted a little before George's ashen, tearful countenance.

"What would it seem," the man wailed, "that I hadn't even tried to help my poor nephew?"

"Nothing good," Tom agreed. "But when they began to talk of murder…?"

The wail turned into a strangled yelp. "Worse and worse, don't you see?"

Heaven give patience, because what Tom had was fraying quickly. "What I see, is that I'm suspected, and you've known all the time it was no murder at all, and still said nothing to clear me!"

"I wanted to, lad, I swear! But that Susan Foal… I don't know how she knew…"

Had she heard Ned move? But no, she wouldn't have waited until morning. "She likely didn't. She angled, she pretended to know more than she did. I'm sure you told her most of what she held against you."

"She said they'd suspect me, if I made a clean breast of it. I'd argued with Ned, hadn't I? And I was so drunk I couldn't truly tell what happened…" George raised pitiful eyes to meet Tom's gaze. "And she was right, in a manner of speaking: whether I ever laid a hand on him or not, I've killed Ned."

Had he? If the surgeon was right, between the fall and the burst heart, there was no saying which had caused the other. But what was the use in burdening George's conscience?

"It was an accident, Uncle — and then that cursed woman kept you from clearing me…" At least here was confirmation that Ned hadn't been murdered, and Susan Foal had been lying out of ill will. "Now you can tell Mr. Lambarde —"

"No!" George stumbled to his feet, one hand braced against the rough-barked tree, the other gripping Tom's arm. "He'll think I killed them both — Ned in a drunken rage, and the woman because she knew… I'll end up on the scaffold!"

He shook like a leaf, poor George, and rolled his yellowed eyes in terror — Uncle George, who had fed the carp with little Tom and Mary, and laughed with them, and kept their childish secrets, who had begged for money from two nephews and been refused…

With a sigh, Tom nodded. Surely there must be some way to clear himself without betraying George?

Hope seized the wasted face, as wild as the fear it fought and chased. Speechless and wet-eyed, Uncle George gripped Tom's arm hard, then released it, and threw himself down onto the stump again, panting and holding his head. Whether he was sobbing or laughing, Tom didn't want to know.

CHAPTER 16

Was there truly another way? Tom wondered as he fled around the kitchen's corner — and ran straight into Justice Lambarde, of all men. It was no blind chance.

"Were you thinking to tell me, Mr. Walsingham?" the man asked, with arms crossed and that hooded glare.

The gall of him! But glaring was a game that two could play. "Eavesdropping, Mr. Justice?"

"Not as a habit, I assure you. But…" Utterly unperturbed, Lambarde tilted his head towards the invisible George. "It's a good thing that I did this time."

That he was right only made it sting worse.

"He's my mother's brother…" Tom tried.

"And he was bitter towards Mr. Edmund. Do you truly believe him?"

It should have come as no surprise that Lambarde had heard of George's outburst at the funeral dinner, nor that he'd hidden among the trees to listen — for all his Catonian airs. Tom bit down the flare of vexation, and considered: did he believe George in truth, or only out of relief that Ned hadn't been murdered?

After all… "I think that my uncle is honest in his fear," he began slowly, "that he saw what he says he saw — befuddled with sack or not — and that nobody killed my brother at all, unless you call murder giving him a fright."

For a wonder, Lambarde nodded, fingering his mole. "There is still Susan Foal, though," he said. "Mr. Guildford believed she could send him to the scaffold, murderer or not. And I'm sure you've seen the way fear and wine beget the worst sort of courage."

It was only too common — but … George? Tom shook his head. "I won't believe that of my uncle."

Could it be a shadow of regret flickering in Lambarde's eyes? Displeasure, surely. "In your place, I'd be eager to believe it — because … make no mistake, Mr. Walsingham: what is true of your uncle, goes for you too."

Again! Jove fulminate all stubborn fools. "I never drink to excess, Mr. Lambarde," Tom ground out.

"But you said it yourself: you are an agent or Mr. Secretary's *Service*." Oh, the subtle disgust he put into the word! "It wouldn't be befuddled anger, with a man of your ilk."

His ilk! So that was it — a Service man must be a heartless murderer on principle? "Devil take it!" Tom snapped — and never mind counting in Latin. "You heard my uncle! And even the cursed letter was just Wood's stratagem!"

"None of it clears you any more than it clears Mr. Guildford — not when it comes to Susan Foal: why, if we believe your uncle, it's you that she wanted to see hang."

I'll die before I let his murtherer step in his shoes, she'd said — and even dead she might have her wish yet.

"The dratted shrew is laughing at me from the grave!" Tom ran a hand down his face — and, when he looked up, Lambarde was studying him with the intent, narrow gaze of one seeking signs of guilt. "And you!" he snapped. "Have you ever truly considered that Foal, that my uncle, or Wood, or Geve Kickly, or anyone else in Scadbury or Chislehurst could have drowned her?"

"Wood?" The magistrate reared his head.

"Yes, Wood — if Susan Foal knew he'd been dishonest…" But what was the use? Lambarde listened in the most disbelieving manner. Tom threw up a hand. "Why should you bother, when there's Mr. Secretary's dangerous man to blame? For one who makes so much of not being swayed by the Walsingham name, you're mightily set on holding it against me!"

"I never…" Lambarde began heatedly — only to check himself and turn away. There was a sort of petty satisfaction in discomposing this fellow. He was quick in mastering his temper, though. When he turned back, his dark eyes were amused. "I think I see, Mr. Walsingham, how some might find you vexing," he said, "but perhaps you are not wrong: that you'd make a good murderer doesn't mean that you are one." He held up a finger when Tom half choked at that. "I'll grant you: the assumption has bent my thinking. In my defence, a suspect doing his own investigation — and keeping it mostly to himself — elicits little trust."

So does a magistrate purblinded by assumptions… By a whisker Tom swallowed the retort. Having sown a seed of doubt in the man's mind, why ruin it for the sake of having the last word? But the urge must have shown, for Lambarde's frown returned, and he took his leave stiffly.

But then, why should the magistrate be well disposed towards Tom, when his own uncle wouldn't lift a finger to clear him? When Tom looked back, George had slunk away — for all his talk of favourite nephews … but that had been before Tom had dithered about the money, hadn't it? At least Lambarde had heard the man's admission — but would he be of a mind to consider it?

With a great sigh, Tom sank to sit on the stump George had so hastily vacated, and leant back against the trunk, wondering if he should be relieved.

At least, observed Reason, now it was certain that Ned hadn't been murdered, and that the unsigned note was no intrigue against Sir Francis.

On the other hand, the murderer was still at large, and Lord knew what havoc he'd find in that scoundrel Wood's accounts.

And this was another thing, Reason insisted. If Pelham was right, Wood's dishonesty was grounds for challenging the will, and could keep those two thieves from stripping Scadbury bare as Ned had intended.

Scadbury, where he was stranded for good, alone, bogged in debt, only a dozen miles from London — and yet he could have been lost on the moon, so cut away he'd be from every friend he had, from Sir Francis, from the Service, forever from Frances…

"You'll catch your death of the damp," a woman's voice called.

Startled, Tom jumped to his feet. So caught up in his thoughts he'd been, that Audrey Shelton had come upon him all unobserved.

"Mistress Shelton," he greeted, and fetched what smile he could. "If the damp killed, England would be a damp desert."

A very poor quip, it was — and she dismissed it with a tilt of the head, utterly unfooled. And yet there was a gentleness to her way that was almost alarming.

"You're feeling sorry for yourself again — but I will say that you have cause. What your brother did…" She shook her head. "I call it spiteful and disloyal."

Was there anything, O Jove, anything in Scadbury that she didn't know? Tom's mouth wanted to fall open; he checked the urge, and hoped it hadn't showed. He hadn't spared a thought for what Audrey would do, once she'd come back with him on her errand of friendship — but truly… "The tidings have been quick to find you," he said, sighing, and she shook her head.

"Now, before you blame your servants, I heard it all from the withdrawing room," she said.

So blithely she said it, this time, Tom's jaw did fall open. "You've no compunctions!"

Most young women Tom knew would have blushed at that… Or would they? Well, Audrey did not. She tossed her head instead. "Your Master Marley was there too."

Better and better… "And I'll scold him, too — but, like me, he's a Service man. You are a well born lady —"

"And this should make me worry less than he does?" she bit back. "Would it please you better if I'd asked him after he had eavesdropped? Not that I ever would — but worry I do, and so…" She shrugged her slender shoulders. "I listened!"

"Oh, Lord!" How did one respond to this, but with a laugh? "How is it that Marley eavesdrops and you listen?" This she didn't deign to answer, so he motioned for her to sit on the stump. "Well, now you know what sort of family we are: all fiercer in defending the plate with the tiger's head than in resenting Wood's false accusations."

"Oh." She frowned. "Master Marley said so, too. He had many names for them all."

"Did you think him wrong?"

"I hoped that you could think otherwise," she said, her face scrunched up, one hand raised to shield her eyes against the glare of the slanting sun on the moat's south arm. At that moment, it struck Tom that he had two friends: this keen-witted vixen who could not abide stillborn justice, and mercurial Kit Marley, ready to lie and go to war for him. Misguided both, most of the time, and yet both loyal…

And in a day or two, both would be gone — Marley back to London and his players, and Audrey Shelton to whatever northern county she called home, unless her father still haunted the Court.

And he would be stranded here alone, to become a penny-pinching miser like Ned.

Must he truly let them — let *her* go?

Of course he must, and any other notion was most fantastical and mad.

He needs an heir, Mary's voice said in his mind. And to beget an heir, he needed a wife. *Frances*, his witless heart cried. Mrs. Frances Walsingham, sitting with him in the book-filled writing room, discussing cherry conserves with Kathryn, and smiling as she watched their children and little Bess play in this very spot on a June day of green and gold…

But it was November now, the days were short, and never in this life could he have Frances.

So why not this clever, wilful woman, whom he didn't want to see go away?

He must be mad, no doubt — touched in the head, because otherwise there was no explanation for the way he blurted out, "You wouldn't have let Wood go all but unchallenged."

She opened her mouth to retort, and then closed it, to study him with narrowing eyes. "I wasn't there — Heaven forfend, for your sisters think me a meddler as it is."

Not that *listening* behind a door would change their minds — but they'd never told her to her face, had they? *They* being more than just Barbara and Mary, it occurred to him, for there would be no lack of whisperers to call her ways forward these past few days. It was that thought, and an absurd urge to shield her that swept him on. "It wouldn't matter what they think, if you were to be my wife."

Lo and behold: Audrey Shelton struck speechless — and, it must be said, she coloured prettily.

Well, there was no unsaying it. More than a little astounded at himself, he rushed on before she could find her voice again. "If you would, I mean — and if your father..." Babbling, that's what he was. He took a breath, and with it, Reason, which must have fled for a while, entered him again. "I'm no great prize, Mistress Audrey. A country gentleman who doesn't even know yet just how penniless he is..." A fortune-hunter to her father's eyes, a spy, one who would always love another woman...

While he blackened himself in his mind, she had recovered her composure, and was frowning up at him.

"Well, you're honest enough," she said. "And you're loyal to a fault, and you're clever enough — though not all the time — and good-hearted, I think, not that it's always a strength. It's more than can be told of many men I know."

It took him a moment to sift through her words — and still he wasn't sure. "Then you'd marry me?" he asked, like the dunce he was.

It was no marvel that she sighed a little. "Oh, Mr. Walsingham, you'll ask again, won't you? You will go to my father when you are in your right mind, when you are not in mourning and under suspicion of being a murderer?"

"You think that I...?"

"Now you're being foolish. That's why I want you to ask again when your wits are not addled."

Surely few men had ever had their offer doubted so in its soundness? But then, in fair truth, not many women must have been asked for their hand in marriage in this manner.

It was, on the whole, a great relief that right then a voice could be heard calling for Mr. Thomas, and a flash of oxblood sleeves showed among the trees.

"Marley!" Tom called. "Kit Marley — here!"

What Marley thought, when he hastened by, of finding Tom and Audrey alone, he didn't say — but surely, the small bow he had for Mistress Shelton was of the coldest, and when he spoke, it was to Tom alone.

"God's nightgown — that was something!" he huffed. "The messenger has left — thinking that the air at Scadbury is pernicious, I wouldn't wonder — and Foal has tried to sack the cupboards. He whines that half of what's in them is his."

"Does he now? The fellow is a pest. Can I kick out one of the executors?"

"No need. Goody Wollans, bless her heart, has beaten him away with the fire-poker, and promised more if he tries again."

"Now this I would have liked to see," Audrey said with a merry little laugh — and Tom felt the colour rise to his face. Good Lord, he'd just offered to make her mistress of a house where servants brawled and stole, a house of which, by the letter of Edmund's will, he only possessed the empty walls.

Both Audrey and Marley must have observed his glumness, for there was a beat of silence before the poet exclaimed with a gaiety that was near painful: "At least, Mr. Thomas, the justice has decided that your brother wasn't murdered."

"Has he?" Audrey asked, all interest again, to which Marley answered that so Lambarde had told Mr. Pelham.

"Which you just happened to hear," Tom groused — and he told his own two intelligencers of George's confession. "There remains the matter of Susan Foal, though, for which Lambarde still suspects me."

"Rubbish!" Marley kicked at a gnarl of willow roots. "Why, half the household had reason to get rid of her. Your uncle to shut her mouth, Foal out of shame and jealousy or greed, Wood if she knew what he was up to, Wollans to have his own wife housekeeper, the cook —"

But to this Audrey scoffed. "Come, you never think that Barker would do murder — or Wollans!"

"You never know, Mistress. You can mean no worse than defending yourself, and then..." Marley shook his head like one ridding himself of cobwebs. "And then you never know. Even that poor scullion could have done it, after one scolding too many. Tread a worm on the tail..."

"But this particular worm you may strike off your list, Kit — and Wollans too. They've always known that I'd get rid of the Foals..." Tom stopped short. "Jove — I didn't mean..."

Audrey reached out to pat his arm with a small smile. "We won't tell Mr. Lambarde — and yet... I'm sure Wollans knew to bide his time, but the scullion? He's only a boy, and Grace's groom says he's not very sharp. If Susan Foal taunted him..."

Will Everest in the passage room, sullen and afraid. *You be sacking me, Master?* "Oh, she did worse," Tom remembered. "She promised to have him sacked."

"And how could he know you wouldn't do her bidding like your brother? So..." Marley held up a hand and counted off his fingers. "We're left with Mr. Guildford, Foal, Wood, and the scullion. I'm almost sorry that sot Fuller is cleared: revenge is potent in stirring the humours." And see if he didn't tilt his head, frowning at nothing as he repeated the words under his breath — scanning them in his head to make them into a line, Tom could have sworn.

"It's in plays that people kill in revenge!" Audrey exclaimed — who had never been at risk of dying on a revenger's blade.

"And besides, the steward is cleared as well, isn't he? As cleared as Fuller is, and afterwards he was in the house at the time of the drowning."

"Yes, he…" Tom stopped short as the glass bits in his mind rose and fell in a whirl.

Susan Foal playing sun-and-moon with the ledgers…

Susan questioning Richbell and Mace…

Mace and Wood interrupted in the counting-room…

Mace set upon on his way home — by a man moving like an ape.

Richbell seeing Susan Foal in the yard, the assiduous customers at the Tiger's Head, and…

"And Shott's farm is out Sidcup-way!" he exclaimed, and two pairs of eyes stared at him. "Greed is just as potent as revenge — and Rector Harvey's servant learnt of the murder at the Tiger's Head, didn't he? Where's Will Everest?"

He found the boy in the scullery, rinsing the plate from dinner in a basin. He cringed away when Tom strode in, with Audrey and Marley on his heels.

"Where did you fetch Bridget Platt from, the other day?" Tom asked.

Poor Will gaped and pointed vaguely with a wet hand. "Shott's farm. Her sister said as she'd gone there."

"Did you tell the sister why you wanted the midwife?"

A shake of the head.

"Did you go near the Tiger's Head, then or when you walked her back?"

Another shake. "They live this side of the village, the Platts."

There it was — all the pieces falling into place! "Quick, Marley, my arms and yours," Tom ordered. "You come with me, Will: I need two horses. And you, Mistress, find the justice: tell him to keep everyone here."

Marley sprinted away to the house, and Tom made for the courtyard, with Everest in tow.

"But wait…" Audrey called after him. "Where are you going?"

"Chislehurst," Tom answered over his shoulder. "Tell Mr. Lambarde of the midwife!"

And off he ran.

By the time they thundered into Chislehurst, most villagers were at Evensong, and Tom sent Marley to find the constable in church.

Marley wouldn't have it. "You're not going against a murderer by yourself!" he said — as if Tom hadn't done just that for a dozen years…

"The sooner you fetch Beveridge, the sooner I'll have two men with me!" Tom retorted and, waiting for no answer, spurred his horse to a gallop.

Jack Fuller's cottage lay off the lane to Frognal, amidst an unkempt patch of garden, where two geese squawked at the newcomer. Just as Tom leapt out of the saddle, a woman's scream joined the racket.

"Fuller!" Tom called, pushing past the wicker gate and swatting away the geese. The door yielded to the smallest push, and let him into a low, dark kitchen. In what little light came through the ivy-smothered window, he stumbled into an overturned stool. "Fuller!"

The woman screamed again, and Tom made for the back door that gaped open. Behind the cottage, a strip of coarse grass sloped down to the pond, which gleamed like bronze in the sunset, fringed with bare bushes on the far side. A shed stood at right angles with the house, and from there came a wail. Unsheathing his rapier, Tom reached the door and threw it open. There stood John Wood — dishevelled and panting, blood staining his falling bands and ashen face. He stumbled back a step, catching himself against the warped planks stacked in the corner.

"Mr. Walsingham..." he gasped, eyes sliding to Tom's rapier.

"Where's Fuller?" Tom squinted past the steward's shoulder, inside the shed, where the woman was keening softly.

"He wanted to kill me... I had to..." Wood took a hitching breath. When he spoke again, his voice was steadier. "He drowned Susan Foal."

"I'm sure he did," Tom said.

Wood's shoulders fell, and he raised a bloodied hand to his brow — only to stop short and narrow his eyes. "You're sure..." he repeated under his breath. He took a step back when Tom crossed the threshold.

"Give me your knife, Wood," Tom ordered and still the steward retreated, swallowing hard.

Stacks of broken rafters encumbered the place, the floor strewn with dirty straw and sawdust. On a bench, the blade of an axe gleamed dully in the scant light. As he stepped inside, Tom saw out of the corner of his eye a foot shod in a mud-caked shoe, toe pointing upwards, and then a leg... *Here lieth Jack Fuller.*

With a cut throat and bulging eyes he lay — and by the body, not touching it, a woman knelt in bewildered terror. The air was thick with the smell of old sawdust and blood, and moths of dust danced in the finger of westering sunlight that slanted through a gap in the wall.

"Your knife," Tom repeated, pointing the rapier at the steward's chest — and the man's right arm stiffened, denouncing the knife concealed behind his back.

"He was a murderer!" Wood tried. "He would have killed me if —"

"I'm sure — for you never quite lie, do you?" Tom took another step forward, part of his mind cursing at the cramped space that would make a rapier more hindrance than help. "You carve out enough of the truth that it may seem like something else. I've seen Jesuits do it like this." A blood-curdling insult, judging by the flash of the black eyes, and the ugly rush of colour.

Another step, and Tom had Wood backed into a corner. "Didn't he want to run as you told him? Did he have regrets, that you made him drown Susan Foal?"

John Wood seemed to sway, heedless of the point that tore his sleeve at the shoulder — until he could haul Fuller's wife to her feet, and press a bloodied knife to her throat.

With a curse, Tom stepped back.

"I won't go to the gallows." Wood tightened his hold on the woman. "Drop that sword. And step away from the door."

Even his voice had changed to one breathless, hard-edged burst after another, and the flicker in his dark eyes didn't bode well for young Goodwife Fuller. Or rather the Widow Fuller now, with blood on her apron and a bruise swelling purple across her cheek. She slumped in Wood's hold, stupefied by fear, whimpering softly as the blade grazed her throat.

What help was there? Slowly, Tom lowered his rapier.

"Drop it!" Wood ordered, tightening the arm around the woman's waist.

Holding the hilt by the pommel, Tom lowered the rapier to the floor, and Wood moved close enough to kick it away.

"You'll kill me too, Wood?" Tom asked. "You have two lives on your conscience already."

"Oh, why didn't you stay away?" Wood groaned — and could it be true torment that creased his face? "If only Mr. Edmund hadn't died…"

"So you could go on fleecing him, and he'd never care enough to notice? For all your talk of trust … a strange conscience you have!"

"He never cared!" Wood snarled. "Scadbury and all the lands could rot, for all it mattered to him. And the Lord knows I tried. The loans, the lease — all my work. I've kept Scadbury afloat these years."

"You've kept your pockets well lined — and Susan Foal knew that."

"That Jezebel! After Mr. Edmund died, she began to ask questions. Her halfwit husband, Richbell, Old Mace…"

"And then she happened on you and Mace in the counting-room, and she heard enough to make certain. She followed you outside when you led Fuller away, and … what? Did she threaten you?"

"She'd seen the quittances. Not that she could read them, but she'd heard what they were. And she knew enough of the will from Foal to understand."

"So you left Fuller to deal with her."

A groan. "All saw him leave, all saw me come back — and Richbell had met her in between… It was perfect."

"But Fuller had had a fondness for her. He went straight to the Tiger's Head, and toasted poor dead Susan — before news of her death was out of Scadbury."

"Always a want-wit, he was!" Wood kicked the dead body again. "Even with Mace…"

A want-wit with an ape's gait… "It was his notion to steal the quittances, wasn't it?"

"As though that should help. And now I come to pay him, to send him running — and he tries to kill me!" Wood choked out a laugh, bitter as gall. "He only had to run! You'd all have thought him guilty. All I needed was a little time so I could have my money and flee…" His face turned noble of a sudden — the prophet again. "My money, ay — for I never forced your brother. He thought I deserved more from him than you did, and I won't go to the gallows for it. Come, Mr. Walsingham: away from the door."

He pressed the blade a little harder, and the sting awoke the woman from her terror. She keened, and squirmed hard enough to make Wood shift… In one motion Tom snatched up the closest stool, swung it at Wood's legs, and sprang to his feet. He lunged to grab the screeching woman, shoving her out of harm's way. Out of the door too, hopefully, but there was no time to make sure, for Wood had fallen across the bench and, when he twisted around, he held Fuller's axe.

"*I will smite them, that they shall not be able to stand*!" he bellowed, and swung in a vicious arc.

They'll fall under my feet, Tom's mind supplied as he leapt out of the way, stumbling backwards into the planks — and Fates be thanked that he lost his footing: with a spray of shards, the heavy blade buried itself in the rotting wood just above his head.

"Flattering yourself, Wood," Tom taunted — if rather breathlessly. "The Lord shall not throw down your enemies…"

With a grunt, Wood dove for the door — or would have, but Tom shoved a broken plank between his feet, sending him down on his stomach, earning a kick as Wood scrambled past the threshold on his hands and knees, then gained his feet in an awkward run. Tom threw himself after him, grappling him from behind.

"*And your footsteps shall slip*!" he growled.

Untimely triumph: the man writhed like an eel, and freed himself enough to bury an elbow in Tom's stomach. It wasn't hard: even winded, Tom held fast as they went rolling down the slope in a snarl of legs and arms, until they splashed in the pond. It was no more than a couple of feet of murk — just enough to drown a man.

Wood had landed on top of Tom, a dark shape pushing him down into the water, a pair of hands around his neck. Like Susan Foal in the moat…

But this wasn't the moat. Braced against the sloping, muddy bottom, Tom pushed himself out of the water to swing a punch at Wood's face.

Unfooted, Wood flailed and fell backwards in a great, glittering splash. Tom lurched to his feet after him — and Lord, how heavy were his limbs … heavier than those of his quarry, who pushed away, paddling for the other side… But there were men on the other side, running and shouting, their long shadows falling across the gilt water, and Wood changed course, making for a big hawthorn bush still sprinkled with clumps of red haws. Tom followed clumsily, stumbling to his knees when the bottom sloped up suddenly under him. Wood reached the bush, grabbed for the lowest branches, hauled himself up — and of a sudden Audrey sprang out from behind the bush, swinging a large stick two-handed.

"Stay where you are!" she shouted — madwoman that she was — and, when Wood lunged to tear the stick from her, she hit him on the shoulder.

Snarling, Wood fell back into Tom, and they grappled again, just as more men came running to the bank: Beveridge — Fates be thanked — and Kit Marley.

"But be done!" Tom gasped — untimely again: Wood tore free and, as Beveridge reached down to grip him, he dragged the constable into the water.

To a yelp from Beveridge, and a curse from Marley, Wood tried to scramble up the pond's bank, steep on this side — but Tom was upon him, grabbing him by the collar, thrusting him towards the splashing constable and the bank, where, behind Marley and the stick-wielding Audrey, others arrived at a run. Lambarde, his servant, the groom Jenkin, Chislehurst's blacksmith, and a puffing Uncle Buffkin.

A dozen hands reached down to catch Wood who, all the fight having gone out of him, let himself be dragged up none too gently, while Marley helped Tom out of the water.

"God's nightgown, Mr. Thomas," the poet stammered, white to the lips and eyes agleam, a hand tight on Tom's shoulder where he knelt in the muddy grass. Tom grabbed Marley's arm and pulled himself to his unsteady feet. Audrey was there, wrinkling her nose at his bedraggled state.

"Are you mad?" Tom asked through chattering teeth, and she shrugged.

"He didn't run, did he?" she had the gall to say, and she turned towards Lambarde, who had taken charge. Even as Beveridge and the blacksmith led him away, Wood stared at Tom with burning eyes — the thieving, murderous steward Edmund had trusted so well.

"It's not for the gold my brother gave you!" Tom called, making his voice firm. "You go to the gallows for Susan Foal's blood."

EPILOGUE

No matter how many times he called it ridiculous, Tom wasn't suffered to leave the chair by the cottage's hearth, where he sat with a blanket around his shoulders, and a pot of cider in his hands.

The cider was indifferent but warm, which was pleasant, for the water had been cold, and dusk had brought a stiff breeze — but truly…

"I've been drenched worse, more times than I can count," he protested for the hundredth time. "And it's high time we rid Goodwife Fuller of this invasion."

"We will go," Audrey said with the bland firmness she would have used with a fractious boy, "when you have warmed a little." She sat at the little table, head tilted and face severe in the greenish glow of a rushlight — and, Lord save and deliver, Kit Marley stood at her side and nodded in agreement.

"Besides," she resumed, "Goody Fuller does not mind us — do you, Nan, child?"

And how she'd already learnt the woman's name, Heaven knew — but Nan Fuller shook her head with lip-quivering fervency. "Not a whit, Yer Honour," she blurted in a small, childlike voice.

Well, he'd saved her life, Tom supposed. For the first time, he observed her: too thin, ill-used and, once they rode away, alone in the house where her husband had been killed. *Fuller is not good to her*, Wood had said. Perhaps she was better off without him — but what would become of her now? Both in the future and tonight, for it was too late to fetch her mother from Bromley.

"Is there a neighbour, Goodwife? Someone we can fetch to keep you company?" he asked.

For a couple of heartbeats she twisted her hands in her bloodstained apron and then, eyes filling with tears, she named Bridget Platt, who lived nearby.

Not that Marley was overly happy to be sent away, but still he went promptly enough to fetch the midwife, and poor Nan Fuller, with an awkward curtsey, set about tidying up her ill-treated kitchen. For a heartbeat, Tom watched her work. Married in the wrong sort of haste, the widow of a drunkard and a murderer — and all because Edmund's mistress had wanted rid of Fuller, and Edmund's steward had wanted a hundred pounds. There were far unhappier victims than himself of the foul play at Scadbury.

"There will be need of a new maid at Scadbury," he murmured, and turned to find Audrey observing him — serious, but with a smile in her eyes, which glowed golden by candlelight.

"You'll make a good lord of the manor, Mr. Walsingham," she said — which she meant as praise, no doubt, and yet it sounded like a judge ruling on the rest of his life.

"Why?" he asked bitterly. "Because I want to give this poor child some compensation for the ills she's suffered out of my house?"

With an impatient sigh, Audrey leant across the table, a hand flat on the scarred top. "Because," she corrected, "you have uncovered intrigue and murder, cleared your name and that of your uncle, seen a measure of justice done, discovered the means to undo your brother's unfair will — and still find it in your heart to shoulder what you can of poor Nan's ills." Could it be hoped that, in the flickering gloom, she missed the heat rising to Tom's cheeks? Whether she did or not, she wasn't done. "They'll like you better for it," she said — this vixen of twenty who'd spent half her life at Court. "And for having justice done."

Looking away, Tom gave a small huff of laughter. "As long as they can forget what I was before. Lambarde thought me a murderer because of the life that was mine. The life I can't have anymore and, I very much fear, won't let me ever fit in here…" He shook his head and she moved to sit on the stool at his side. Aside from the rustling of her skirts, and the rising wind outside, all was silent. Where had Nan Fuller gone?

"There are worse things to be than Mr. Secretary's man," she said, with the smallest smile. "We'll convince all of Kent that you are fearsome but fair." Tom watched her long and well, her sharp, delicate features limned red-gold by the fire, an escaped fair lock curling against her temple. How he had resented Philip Sidney, for marrying Frances and loving another woman — and here he was, doing the same: the Fates at work, no doubt, and laughing. Unless Sir Ralph Shelton had too many objections in store…

"I can't imagine that your father will be overjoyed with a penniless spy for a son-in-law…" Tom murmured — and see: when Audrey smiled in earnest, it made a dimple on her cheek.

"The day I turned five," she whispered, "I told Father that I would choose my own husband. He more than half expects me to do it — and it will be his own fault: he suggested a Walsingham first."

The laugh bubbled up of its own accord. "I'll have the finest sundial in the realm made for you, Audrey Shelton," Tom said — and reached down to take her hand.

HISTORICAL NOTES

In the name of god amen the 12th day of November 1589 and in the 31st year of the reign of our sovereign Lady Queen Elizabeth I Edmond Walsingham of Scadbury in the parish of Chislehurst in the county of Kent esquire being sick in body but of whole and sound mind thanks be to god do make this my last will and testament…

Edmund Walsingham, Tom's unmarried and childless older brother, died at Scadbury on the 16th of November 1589, having made his will only four days earlier. It was, by Elizabethan gentry standard, a peculiar will in several ways.

Edmund's witnesses were two uncles and a brother-in-law, so there was no lack of male relatives around; and yet, he chose two servants as his executors. What is truly unusual is that these same two men received the bulk of the money and, basically, everything that was inside Scadbury Manor. To each of his living sisters and their husbands, to his widowed brother- and sister-in-law, to a number of uncles, cousins and/or friends (the difference between the two wasn't always clear with the Elizabethans), he left a gold coin apiece and, in one case, a horse. To the daughters of his dead brother he left — definitely as an afterthought — some plate. Once a few debts were settled, and an uncommonly substantial sum was doled out to "the poor people of Chislehurst", everything else — more than £150, the lease of a manor, all of "the plate household stuff and implements [at the time] being at Scadbury" and Edmund's "goods and chattels" — went to the servants, most of it to the two executors, John Wood and Robert Foal.

Tom, the only living brother and heir, is never once mentioned: by reading his brother's will, one would never guess he ever existed. This, together with the highly uncommon way in which Edmund disposed of everything that was not entailed, makes it hard to imagine that there was much affection between the brothers. It must have been the kind of will that made the whole lathe whisper for weeks — and, of course, it was bound to make novelists run with it, centuries later.

This novelist ran.

Let me begin by saying that almost everyone in Scadbury is taken from Edmund's will: Uncle George, Uncle Buffkin, Barbara and Mary with their husbands, Cousin Maria, Guildford's widow, Edmund's friend John Hearsdon, the servants — John Wood, Barker, the Foals, the Wollanses, and poor, ill-used Everest — and the debtors Mace and Richbell, are all named in this peculiar document. For the rest, William Lambarde was the Justice of the Peace for Kent, and Martin Coates was a Kentish coroner who worked more than once with Lambarde at the time, while Richard Harvey, brother of the more famous Gabriel, was rector of Chislehurst in 1589 (after making an astrological fool of himself at Cambridge and coming nose to nose with Thomas Nashe, among others). Many other "speaking parts" (including Constable Beveridge, the Poyntells, Percival Eliot, Bridget Platt, and Longe the surgeon) were named using Jean Fox's Index of West Kent Wills. This meticulous, invaluable resource allowed me to cross-check most of the people in Edmund's will, and find actual residents of Chislehurst and other places at the time, so that I made up almost no one in *Death At Home.*

What I did make up are the roles I gave to some of these people (alas, there remains no list of Chislehurst constables for the time), the murders and the resulting investigation, the presence of Skeres and Marlowe at Scadbury at the time of Edmund's death and, most of all, the presence of Audrey Shelton. There is no evidence that Audrey was ever even supposed to be betrothed to Edmund, or that she ever visited Scadbury before marrying Tom. As for her being Lady Annesley's goddaughter, I based the idea on the less than common first name the two shared, and some coincidence in the times at which Audrey and the Annesley daughters were at Court. It is highly likely that the two families knew each other — which may or may not have weighed, a dozen years later, in the appointment of Tom in a minor role in the lawsuit about Sir Brian's apparent "lunacy" — a case that is said to have partially inspired Shakespeare's *King Lear*.

Having said all that, it is perhaps a bit of a paradox that I didn't even use all the people in Edmund's will: there would have been several more uncles, cousins, brothers-in-law and friends — but that of the historical novelist is a strange job: sometimes we add to history through invention and guesswork; sometimes we prune history's abundance so we can fit it into the shape of a story.

A NOTE TO THE READER

Dear Reader,

Thank you for reading *Death At Home*. I hope you enjoyed it.

While working on this book, I spent a long time with Edmund Walsingham's will. You could say that I spun my whole plot and moulded most of my characters from the words an ill Edmund dictated 436 years ago. Back then, as now, wills were written to distribute property, not to explain feeling — and yet, this one, with its choices, insistences, afterthoughts, and omissions, repeatedly suggested a strain that no clause ever names. Reading it, I found it impossible not to feel that Edmund was making a statement: all that he could take away from Tom he did, to the almost exclusive benefit of two servants he deemed trustworthy, honest and faithful. This was one of those moments when fiction felt less like invention than like listening, and what I heard was a man who went as close to disinheriting his brother as he possibly could, and had little trust in the rest of his family. I wonder what Edmund would make of my view of his will — beyond being most likely horrified at the murders I threw in… But then, *Death At Home* is, in some ways, also a book about what survives us — and how little control we have over the meanings others draw from what we leave behind.

And one last thing: word of mouth — both literal and digital — is all-important to an author. I would truly appreciate it if you'd drop by **Amazon** and **Goodreads** to post a review and let other readers know that you enjoyed this novel. I'd also love to hear from you, if you like, through my **website** or **via Twitter**, where I tweet under the handle **@laClarina**.

Thank you, and we'll meet again in the pages of Tom Walsingham's next adventure!

C. P. Giuliani

www.ingramcontent.com/pod-product-compliance
Ingram Content Group UK Ltd.
Pitfield, Milton Keynes, MK11 3LW, UK
UKHW041332110326
11205UKWH00018B/1413

9 780854 958580